THE WATCHERS

THE WATCHERS

Shall only the righteous survive?

Douglas C. Atkins

iUniverse, Inc.
Bloomington

The Watchers
Shall only the righteous survive?

iUniverse books may be ordered through booksellers or by contacting:

iUniverse
1663 Liberty Drive
Bloomington, IN 47403
www.iuniverse.com
1-800-Authors (1-800-288-4677)

ISBN: 978-1-4759-1549-5 (sc)
ISBN: 978-1-4759-1550-1 (hc)
ISBN: 978-1-4759-1551-8 (e)

Library of Congress Control Number: 2012907261

Printed in the United States of America

iUniverse rev. date: 4/17/2012

Chapter One

5. And all shall be smitten with fear
And the Watchers shall quake,
And great fear and trembling shall seize them unto the ends of the earth.

6. And the high mountains shall be shaken,
And the high hills shall be made low,
And shall melt like wax before the flame.

7. And the earth shall be wholly rent in sunder,
And all that is upon the earth shall perish,
And there shall be a judgement upon all (men).

8. But with the righteous He will make peace,
And will protect the Elect,
And mercy shall be upon them.
And they shall all belong to God …

Chapter Five

4. With your impure mouths against His greatness.
Oh, ye hard-hearted, ye shall find no peace …

Chapter Ten

8. Watchers have disclosed and have taught their sons. And the whole earth has been corrupted through the works that were taught by Azazel: to him ascribe all sin.

—Enoch 1:5–8, 5:4, and 10:8

Prologue

1956

The table in front of Dr. Raleb Eitan contained a priceless array of ancient scrolls, but all he could see was the book of Enoch.

"This right here is the greatest discovery in the history of mankind," he said. He had read the book of Enoch hundreds of times over the years. He fully believed in its prophecy and knew one day it would come true.

"Not at all," said Father Józef Milik. "The most important are the books of the Hebrew Bible. Those texts we found at Qumran are centuries older than anything we had before 1947."

Raleb bent over the table in the scrollery in the Palestine Archeological Museum and thought for a moment. Of course finding the book of Enoch was the most important discovery. Milik didn't know what he was talking about.

"Don't be foolish, Father. The Jews used the book of Enoch for nearly six hundred years. Beta Israel Jews and some small Christian groups even use it today. And the find was written not in Ethiopic, but in Aramaic, which shows its use was more widespread than previously thought. As an Enochian scholar I can tell you there are almost sixty Biblical references, so it follows that a large part of the Bible is based on the Book of Enoch. And you also have to consider that what Enoch said is true."

"Yes, other groups indeed use it. But as for its truth … a prophesied judgment day will happen according to Revelations, not some poppycock trash. Scholarly reputations, including yours, will be built and destroyed on decoding these Dead Sea Scrolls. People will think you've lost your mind if you go telling them there's truth here. Demon angels taking human form … what a crock. Anyone who believes that is a lunatic."

"But it is truth," Raleb said. "Explain that."

"Look, Doctor, we didn't invite you to the scrollery to discuss religious beliefs. We want to know if you'll come on board to help us piece together the many pieces of the scrolls."

"I thought I'd find some open-mindedness here, but—"

"We're all Catholic priests. We might not even ever tell the world what has been found among the scrolls. If you believe that bologna, maybe you don't belong here after all."

"But the world needs to know. That's why it's important to tell everyone."

"Well, no one will ever hear any of those lies from us," Milik said. "If you think the masses need to know, spread the word yourself. That ought to do well to make you look like an idiot."

"Maybe I will, Father," Raleb said. "Maybe I will."

Chapter 1

The Future

His mouth was very dry—for the moment, anyway. Water was so expensive that he often felt guilty spending so much of the church's money to satisfy his thirst. But soon enough he would succumb to his passion for lemonade and mix yet another one. Shaul Eitan sat at his desk looking out of the window down on the campus. He didn't like the location. He would have preferred the woods of Montana, or the snow of Lake Tahoe. He hadn't chosen the location, however, and neither had his father or grandfather. The headquarters of the Church of the Elect had always been in the hot, dry, boring environment of Pecos, Texas. The reason for the location was that the surrounding desert rivaled that of the Middle East, where the scrolls had been written. Also because it was very secluded—over two hundred miles from the nearest town and a long distance from the nearest cell tower so there was no coverage; the only phone was by landline. This was just as Shaul wanted, as his subjects were never interrupted by calls on their cell phones.

"Excuse me, Brother Shaul," his assistant said from the door, "the two elders from Turkey are here to see you."

"Please show them in," he said and then stood up to greet them as they entered the room. The two elders were both dressed in Saudi disha dasha robes and wrapped white turbans as was traditional for elders from the Middle East. "Brothers, please come in. Sit down."

"I am Brother Dabir," said the shorter one, "and this is Brother Ali." Before the two sat down, they exchanged the traditional brotherhood handshake.

"Could I offer you something to eat or a drink, perhaps?" Shaul asked as they sat. They both accepted the drink, and Shaul poured them lemonade over ice.

"Now," Shaul Eitan said, "I've heard about your work in the Middle East. You run the region very well. And your efforts and connections in China are well known. Let's discuss business. As you have been told, for some time, the church has been planning the apocalypse. "

"We are very familiar with it, Elect One." said Dabir. "We feel that through our international connections, we could bring a lot to the project."

"Yes, go on."

"We work in Muslim countries, while at the same time we do diplomatic work in China. We are well connected with governments in the Middle and Far East."

"Continue," Shaul said.

"We believe that if we were to use these connections, we could obtain the destructive power that you will need to make the project a success."

"Interesting," Shaul said. "You realize the implications for us and the church members?"

"This project is nothing to be taken lightly," Ali said. "It would mean the end of civilization as we know it. But … the apocalypse will finally bring freedom from the Watchers and peace to the righteous of our church."

"Yes," Shaul said. "This will bring on the day of judgment. The

Watchers will suffer for eternity. Once the Lord of Spirits re-creates everything, the Elect will live on His beautiful earth forever."

"If we didn't realize the implications," Dabir said, "we wouldn't be here to offer our help. We have come a long way to talk with you about this, Brother Shaul. We are connected enough to make this happen."

"All right then. How will you make it happen?"

"We are very close with many members of both of the Chinese and Iranian governments. Both of those have the military strength to provide the firepower to allow the church to complete the project."

"That may well be true," Shaul said, "but if they suspect that we will bring on the apocalypse, they will never make a sale to us."

"Of course," Dabir said. "That is why we have told them we need all this firepower to attack US military and business interests around the globe. With your permission, we will ask them both for prices for the shoulder-fired launchers."

"They would have to be very powerful," Shaul said.

"We obviously know the desired effect. There is a whole new generation of high explosives that can achieve what we want."

"I could act alone; however, I would like to talk to the rest of the elders about this. I am convinced that we must go through with it, but we need to know if our finances will allow this purchase. Do you have any rough figures?"

"We haven't talked with the Iranians yet, but the Chinese gave us a price range of four to nine thousand each, depending on what we want."

Shaul leaned back in his chair and smiled. "It has potential," he said. "But nine thousand is way over budget. Do you have any further information that we could look over?"

"Oh, yes, Elect One," said Ali. "We have brought detailed plans both from China and Iran." He produced a folder from under his coat and handed it to Shaul.

"Thank you. I'll talk it over with the other elders. Do you anticipate being here on campus for a few days?"

"We will stay as long as it takes to get our plan approved," Ali said.

"Good. We'll look over the plan and play with our figures. Check back with me tomorrow."

Shaul stood up and extended his hand, signaling that the conversation had ended. Again they exchanged the brotherhood handshake, and the men left.

Shaul thought about the proposal. He wondered if a day would come when he could go to the Middle East. Like the other three major religions, the Church of the Elect had been started there by his ancestor, Raleb Eitan. And, of course, Enoch would have wandered there around 200–300 BC. Shaul went over to the window just in time to see Ali and Dabir walking across the campus. They were walking very slowly, and Shaul knew this was because there was a lot less oxygen outside. Shaul understood very well the reason for their slow pace.

He savored another sip of his cold lemonade and noticed that his guests had left some of theirs. *What a shame,* he thought. Water was so expensive and rare. The earth had suffered such abuse. Now all the water was controlled by a megacompany called Aquasuperior. There was no naturally fresh water left in the world. It all came from desalination plants. Not only that, but Aquasuperior also had dibs on much of the oxygen used inside buildings. Historically, oxygen had once made up 20.9 percent of the atmosphere, but now it was only 18.4 percent—perilously close to the slightly less than 17 percent needed for human respiration.

Everything was synthetic, including the trees on campus and the grass under Ali and Dabir's feet. The earth must have been grand in Raleb's time, before resources ran out. Real live grass. He'd heard that they had some of the real stuff in northern California, though that could be just a rumor. He remembered reading about rain forests and that once they had supplied a great deal of oxygen to the atmosphere.

Their day would come. *The Watchers.* The day of judgment would come soon. The archangels would make them pay. They would suffer unimaginable agony beyond the end of the earth.

Chapter 2

Aquasuperior Corporation occupied the top twenty floors of one of the most prestigious addresses in Boston, above the banks, law firms, and financial institutions. Erebos Meyer's office was on the corner of the top floor. The building was over a hundred years old yet had all the latest technologies. When it had been built, a wide variety of woods had been available for construction. His office was paneled in mahogany on the bottom half of the walls. On the upper portions, Meyer had hired one of Boston's best artists to paint murals. On one wall were luscious parks filled with people and their dogs. On another wall was a jungle scene with animals he had never seen that were long extinct. His office overlooked points north and the harbor. He thought about the harbor and the sea. People had been talking about global warming for many decades. Even today there were heated arguments among scientists and the public. Didn't people know that if global warming were real, the seas would have risen? He looked down at all of the berths, wharfs, and distant beaches. He was thinking that some of these would have disappeared if the oceans had gotten higher. No … there was no global warming. There was a lack of oxygen, a dependence on hydrogen for energy, and a world in need of Aquasuperior's fresh water, but at least no global warming.

Meyer pushed on his intercom's button. "Is Ping out there yet, Linda?"

"Not yet, Mr. Meyer," she replied.

"Send him right in when he arrives, please." Ping Sabino wasn't late yet, but he made a habit of always arriving early for meetings, and Meyer wondered what had happened. Soon enough, though, Linda opened the door. She was very beautiful, just like all the other women Meyer hired.

"Mr. Sabino is here," she said. Ping came through the door. He was right on time. Roberto Sabino was nicknamed Ping because of his computer hacking abilities. He was famous for his inventive use of an attack hackers called a *ping flood.* In a ping flood, a hacker builds a network of hundreds or even thousands of computers by hacking into them and taking them over. The infected computers are called zombies. The hacker then taps into his network of zombies and uses them to send thousands of ping requests a second to a particular target—say, the computer network of a company the hacker has a grudge against. If the volume of ping requests is more than the victim's computer network can handle, it shuts down.

"Ping," Meyer said, a little excited. "I was beginning to wonder why you weren't here early."

"Oh, I just got tied up at network admin. Kamryn was having trouble."

"Are you ready for this?"

"I'm ready and willing. But I'm not sure if I'm able."

"Of course you are," Meyer said. "I have a great deal of confidence in you, Ping. I wouldn't have asked you to be VP if I didn't. Now let's look at what I've got."

He went over to the large, elaborate conference table he had placed under the jungle picture. He kept the table in his office so that he could roll out papers for large projects like the one before them. Meyer flattened out the big roll of construction plans. On the top sheet was an architect's drawing of the plant.

"Here it is," Meyer said proudly. "Our new standard desalination plant design. They can be built fast and easy. Relatively inexpensive compared to our other models. With these, we will provide the entire world with the water everyone needs. We dominate the world's water distribution as it is. With these new plants, we will control 100 percent. Then we can charge as much as we want. We're still waiting for bids to come in."

By the end of the twentieth century, there had been a billion people who did not have access to safe water. By the time Meyer had founded his company, the world population had outpaced demand even further.

"But I still don't know why you put me as executive vice-president," Sabino said. "I'm a hacker and a network administrator, not a construction expert."

"I have faith in you," Meyer said. "You always seem to be able to kind of, shall we say, *extract* business intelligence from anyone who tries to enter the market. That shows me you can think things through. You're very resourceful and show no fear. I want to see you grow to even greater heights at Aquasuperior. We've hung out for years. We partied until we were sick in B-school. Even when you were working on your CS dissertation, you were always able to schedule plenty of time for us to party together."

"Yeah, the good old days."

"You're a manager, Ping. Your actions speak louder than anything I would ever see on your résumé."

When Meyer got his venture capital to start Aquasuperior, Sabino had been the first person he called. Today, Sabino owned a large stake in the company. Now Meyer's company had grown exponentially. Meyer had been able to buy out his venture capital partners less than two years after getting funding. With the earth's fresh water supply completely dried up, Aquasuperior had more desalinization plants than anyone else in the world—over eight thousand.

Then, after the company had accumulated enough cash reserves, they had begun splitting water for hydrogen fuel and oxygen for breathing. They practically controlled the world's fresh water supply, and they could charge whatever they wanted. They had a lot of competition for oxygen. For the hydrogen, they had a distribution deal with Nexton. When it came to fresh water, Meyer and Sabino crushed anyone trying to enter the market, including plants built by municipalities. Meyer had political connections around the globe, and he knew how to use them. Both in their forties, they still trained together—both were experts in Muay Thai.

"Kamryn's doing really good," Ping said. "What can we do to advance her? She still has a lot to learn, but she's unbelievably smart and—"

"Not to mention hot," Meyer said, interrupting with a smile.

"—in a month or so, she should be able to take over as network administrator. If that happens, I'll be able to dive right in as VP."

"That sounds fair. You can do it. I have confidence," Meyer said. "We build several hundred plants a year, but we need to increase that to wipe out our competition. We have a timeline and need to stick to it. You're the man to make it happen."

Chapter 3

Shaul was sitting in his office enjoying another lemonade. It was his life's only indulgence, so he drank them often throughout the day, though sometimes his conscience pained him as a result. This part of Texas was especially hot and dry, so he needed to drink a lot so he could talk with people without a dry mouth. He didn't know if it was his age, sixty-three, or just the dry air, but he was always thirsty. He made sure he had a freezer full of ice. It was the only frivolous indulgence his office had. The walls were plain desert brown with two small windows, a shabby old desk, and a few metal chairs. Part of the philosophy of the church was living simply. And so he did. No one on campus was allowed to wear fancy clothes. Plain and simple: that was how the righteous lived.

Nearly three thousand people lived on campus. Shaul tried to make it a point to meet everyone new and to have an open-door policy for anyone who wanted to talk. That often made his schedule rather crazy, but his father had been the same way, and Shaul felt he should emulate him as much as possible. Today there was a group of four potential members arriving to check out the church. They were coming to his office to meet him in just a few minutes. He thought it was important to know who your parishioners were.

Then you could draw on their strengths. Would they be good financial supporters? Would they make good evangelists? Could they be trusted to tell the truth about the apocalypse? Would they be tough enough to be disciples? Would they be loving and good with kids?

Again Shaul thought how much he admired his father's style. During Shaul's childhood on the church campus, his dad always had introduced him to the new people. Dad had always drawn on people's strong points and had spent a great deal of time teaching Shaul how to find the best in people. Shaul remembered lots of times playing with the other kids as he was growing up. His father always had been there with him having a game of tag, wrestling, or playing catch with the kids. Shaul always tried to be the same way with his own kids and all the other kids on campus. Funny thing, though—his father had hated lemonade. Maybe Shaul wasn't a true Eitan after all, he often thought with humor.

Brother Gabriel, Shaul's assistant, came to the door. "Brother Shaul," he said. Big and powerful, Brother Gabriel would be able to inflict suffering on any sinner when the day of judgment came to pass.

"Are they here? Show them in." The four of them entered, and Shaul gestured for them to sit down. "Anyone for a lemonade?" he asked. Two men already had bottled water. The other man and the woman accepted.

"My name is Brother Shaul," he started. "Many people call me *Elect One,* because I run the Church of the Elect. Feel free to call me either. Now, who am I talking with?"

"I'm Michael Poirier," he said. Poirier was dressed in a fine, three-piece Italian suit. Poirier came from the east. Gabriel had had them all thoroughly investigated long before they even left New York.

"We're all brothers here," Shaul said, thinking the fancy clothes had to go. "No need for last names. Glad to meet you, Brother Michael."

Poirier continued, gesturing to the others. "This is Brother Parker and Brother Byron. And this is my wife, Sister Maria."

Well, he picked that up quick, thought Shaul. On top of that, Shaul was impressed that the two were married. "Why have you come to the Church of the Elect?" he asked.

"We were Catholics," Michael said, leading again. "You know how things are. Even after the Vatican allowed priests to get married, there are, of course, still sex scandals in the church. We got sick of it. We're looking for an alternative."

"You won't find any scandals here at the Church of the Elect," Shaul said. "One of the church's main beliefs is fidelity. The minute someone is caught cheating on their spouse, they are banished from the church for life. We don't recognize divorce in the church. Myself, I have been married for forty-one years. My wife complains about all the hours I put in here, but other than that, we get along okay. I have two kids and, so far, four grandkids. Tell me, what do you know about our church?"

"Only what information has been transferred to us online. We have lots of questions about angels and the day of reckoning."

"For starters, we are the fastest growing church in the world, with six million members. We believe that fallen angels take human form and live among us. We call fallen angels the Watchers. They are the rich and powerful who rule the world—presidents, prime ministers, CEOs of big companies, military leaders, and rulers. They fool the world by pretending to be concerned about other people, the environment, and society in general. The population of the world has destroyed the environment. They've ravaged the atmosphere and used up all our water. What the Watchers and those they rule have done is to bring the earth to the brink of extinction, and the church will rectify that for our followers. Fortunately, you will be safe from that as long as you live among us. Pure and simple, the Watchers are making the Elect suffer.

"As far as the day of reckoning is concerned," Shaul continued, "it's not too far off. When that day comes, the fallen angels and all those who have followed their ways will suffer in agony until the end of the earth. However, we righteous will live forever in a world of peace and bliss.

"Finally, while we are here on earth, we believe in family life. Some people think that's old fashioned. I'm a grandfather and proud of it. I love my grandchildren very much. My father ran the church, as did my grandfather and his father before him, and so on."

"How does the church get its money?" asked Byron.

"Same as any other church: donations and endowments. Many people who chose to live among us even sell their homes, donating that money to the church and making home a church facility someplace in the world. We have some very large donors. We are very conservative spenders," Shaul continued. "That's why you won't find any air conditioning on any of our campuses."

"That's why it's so hot in here," Poirier said.

"Yes, and that's why I drink so much lemonade," Shaul said with a smile. There was a moment of silence. "Well, if there are no more questions, I can send you on your way. You'll find some brothers in the reception area who will show you where you will sleep, should you choose to stay. They will get to know you and help you find where you might fit in here. We even have a special handshake they will teach you. A little quirky fun. It's been a pleasure meeting you."

Everyone stood and shook hands. After they left, Shaul sat down and thought about them for a moment. As usual, he hoped they would make the church their home and that they would bring something good to the table. Then his mind drifted to the proposal from the two Turks. He picked up a copy of the Chinese rocket blueprints. It all looked pretty good. The elders had approved fifty million dollars right away. Although the idea of bringing the apocalypse upon the Watchers came from the elders, Shaul alone was the voice of the church, and his subjects would listen only to him. The elders were a bunch of old men everyone called brothers. All of the men were called brothers, and in fact even Shaul allowed himself to be called brother, as he felt it fostered equality among the ranks. The two Turks had some major Asian and Middle Eastern connections. The Arabic middlemen would be useful in smuggling the rockets between countries there and other places with Muslim populations. The Chinese obviously had a good product, but they asked a high price. It might cost a bit more or less, but these estimates made the day of judgment look possible.

Chapter 4

Sabino sat at his desk reviewing internet activity by company employees. Boring, but part of the job. He was particularly interested to find that two different people had posted encrypted messages through instant messaging with links to a darknet – invitation only websites designed totally for nefarious purposes with passwords virtually impossible to crack. The only reason someone would do that, he figured, was to send classified information to someone at another company. Posting on an encrypted IM allowed anyone to read the message if they had the private key to decrypt it. There would be no way to know who was decoding the messages. The destination of the message was untraceable, unlike an e-mail. There were two posted by someone named Cindy Cobb in marketing and one by Timothy Lacombet in facilities. The only ones who had the authority to use encryption software were the higher-ups. He looked at their names and where their desks were located. Cobb's was in one of the dozens of cubicles in the sales and marketing area, and Lacombet's was also in a cubicle, just a smaller area.

He got up from his desk and went out the door. Kamryn Rodgers sat there at her desk. She was such a beautiful woman, and so very smart. She was also very athletic, like everyone at Aquasuperior world headquarters.

Kamryn was an excellent choice to take over his position. He thought of how they had met. Human resources had hired her to oversee network security. He had fallen for her the moment their eyes met. Brown, highlighted hair. Curvy body. About five feet, five inches—just the right height to cuddle. A face that simply made him melt with desire. And a real fine southern drawl. Perfect. He hadn't been able to help flirting with her, she was so funny. They had gone out for drinks and dinner just a few days after she was hired. She liked to snuggle, but it had taken her a long time to be ready to make love, unlike many of the other women in the office. Most of them went to Erebos's sex parties. Kamryn wouldn't think of it. She said she first had to be convinced he was the right person to build a serious relationship with. He, on the other hand, was convinced she would be the mother of his next child. He already had two children of his own, and more would build his gene pool. His kids were both pretty small, though. For a flash, he thought of Meyer's kids. They were giants: fifteen and seventeen, both well over six feet and two hundred pounds. Perfect for reproduction, unlike his two. Perhaps he and Kamryn would do better.

"Hi," Sabino said.

"How're you doing, Ping," she said. "What's up?"

"We have a situation. A couple of people have been sending encrypted instant messages. I thought we should check them out together."

"Sure. Do we want to go talk to them?"

"No, they might not be at their desks," he said. "I thought we could call them from my office." They both went in, and he clicked on the speakerphone and thought Cobb's number that he got from the readout.

"Cindy Cobb," a voice announced.

"Hi, Cindy," Sabino started. "My name is Ping. I'm from Network Administration. We've noticed something a bit irregular up here and I wanted to talk to you about it."

"Sure, what's the problem?"

"I noticed you sent encrypted messages on an IM chat, and I was wondering why?" There was a pause.

"I'm afraid that wasn't me, Ping. I wouldn't know how to encrypt anything if my life depended on it," she said. "I'm not even sure that I know what encrypted is."

"That's very interesting, because it seems that you must have installed some software in order to do that."

"Is this a joke?"

"I assure you that it is not," Ping said.

"It must be a joke, because I can't even turn on my computer without help. Ask my supervisor, or anyone up here. Ask the help desk about me. Everyone there knows me … really well!"

"Hold on a second," he said and put her on hold. He turned to Kamryn. "What do you think?"

"Let's check with the help desk," Kamryn said.

"It'll only take a second. The help desk is 3296." Kamryn thought about the numbers, and in one ring someone answered. Over the last several decades telecommunications had made tremendous advances. Although they were only in the experimental stage, there were some models of phones that were actually implanted into the brain, and communication could be accomplished telepathically. The implants were called *telepathic phones* because everything happened in the mind. Typically, one thought the numbers to reach a party and then talked out loud if one wished others to hear.

"Help desk. This is Lenny," answered a familiar voice.

"Yes. Say, I've got a question. Have you ever heard of Cindy Cobb?"

"Ditzy Cindy? I sure have."

"Would she know how to install encryption software?" Sabino heard a laugh.

"She can barely type her name. Who are you kidding?"

"That's all I needed to know. Thanks, Lenny," Sabino said and hung up.

"Someone must have done it when she wasn't at her desk," Kamryn said.

"That has to be it. Unless she's playing dumb. I don't think so, though." Ping pushed the hold button. "Cindy, you still there?"

"Yeah, I'm here."

"I guess you're off the hook," he said. "Sorry."

"That's okay. Is there anything else?"

"Yeah, I guess. Have you recently spent any time away from your desk? Out on business, perhaps?"

"Well, yes. I was at a marketing conference for the last two days."

"Thanks," he said and hung up. "Interesting. It seems someone else must have posted those messages. That leaves us with Timothy Lacombet. Shall we try him?"

"May as well. Let me try," Kamryn said. She looked at the screen and again thought about the numbers next to Lacombet's name. The phone rang through, and it was picked up on the first ring.

"Hello. This is Tim Lacombet." It was a recording. "I will be out of the office between March 3 and March 10. If this is an emergency, please call my supervisor, Irving Bloom, at 3387. Thank you."

"Where does that leave us?" asked Kamryn. They both looked at each other for a second.

"I'm not sure. Like you said, perhaps someone's posting from other people's desks when they're not there. It could also be that someone hacked into their computers and used them as hosts." Sabino thought about his early days as a hacker. Host computers were basically launch pads for attacks on other computers. He used to hack into people's computers and find their passwords. Then he could remotely use their computers to send out e-mails with viruses. That way, if the authorities traced the virus back to the original computer, the person who owned the host would be blamed. "I know one thing though. We'd better find out."

Chapter 5

At home, Shaul sat in his favorite chair thinking about his day. He and his wife lived in a small house supplied by the church. His parents had had a much larger house. Shaul had had plenty of room to run around when he was a boy, but once Shaul grew up and got married, he realized that it would be cheaper for the church to fill a smaller house with oxygen than the larger house he had lived in during his childhood. This house had been just the right size to raise two kids. But when family came to visit, it seemed tiny for both of his kids, their spouses, and the four grandchildren. In fact, it was like a madhouse.

He and his wife lived simply. No air conditioning, only ceiling fans. Plain furniture, except the recliner, his favorite chair. Of course, he had his glass of lemonade. He placed it on the floor. He thought he would have a little nap before supper. The late day sun shined in his face. It was hot. A peaceful, warm feeling overcame him.

He tried to think of what part of the book of Enoch would be fitting for a moment like this. Warm. Comfortable. He could always dream about chapters if he thought about them as he was about to drift off. The first journey of Enoch—that was a good one. He thought about it, and soon he drifted off to sleep.

He had been brought to a strange land where there were creatures of fire. They changed from fire to human form at will. They appeared as men and then as fire. These beings brought him to a very dark place. The clouds were stormy, near black. In front of him was the biggest mountain he had ever seen, its summit reaching to heaven. Upon the mountain there were caves. In some were the treasures of the universe, gold and diamonds and other jewels never before seen on earth. From other caves came bellowing thunder as if coming from massive trumpets. Then there were some caves whose depths went to the core of the earth.

Out from one of these caves came a beast bearing a bow and quiver. It held a sword made of lightning. This beast led Enoch to living waters where massive waves erupted and formed figures of wild animals and monsters and men with battle-axes and spears. The water led to the west where the sun was setting, splashing an evil blood red among the turbulent clouds. Across the land he saw a river of lava flowing into the water, creating turbulent clouds of steam that erupted into the heavens.

Suddenly the darkness came, and they walked over a barren land where no man had ever walked. Mountains frozen as if in deep winter surrounded them. In a moment, the skies lightened and Enoch saw how beautifully he had furnished the earth with the riches of nature, and in the firmaments of heaven blew winds from the north, west, south, and east. The clouds swirled like cyclones with paths between them where angels were walking. The landscape changed to a place where fire burned day and night. In that land he saw seven mountains made of magnificent stone: one of colored rock, one of pearl, one of jacinth, and the rest of red boulders. The mountain reached to heaven, and on its sapphire summit stood the alabaster throne of God.

Beyond these mountains was the end of the earth. He saw a deep abyss with columns of fire worthy of heaven. The burning pillars rose and fell and rose and fell again and again. Beyond the abyss, the land was unearthly and not firmly founded to walk upon. There was no water, no birds, and no animals. The great mountains melted, and it became a deathly land—a prison. The Lord bound the fallen ones who were consumed by their guilt for ten thousand years.

The angel Uriel said to Enoch, "Here shall stand the angels who have defiled the daughters of man. Their spirits have taken many forms, making sacrifices to demons and gods. Until the day of judgment they will be put to death, and also death to the women who were led astray. When this day of judgment comes—"

"Shaul."

"—it shall be the end of all things."

"Shaul, wake up," intruded a voice. "It's time for dinner."

He slowly came back to reality. *Yes, that is how it will happen … at the end of the earth, the Watchers will pay.* He stood up and went for dinner.

~ ~ ~

Like everything else on campus, the conference room was very plain. The only pictures on the wall were of four of his ancestors who had run the church. On the west wall were his father, grandfather, and great-grandfather. Shaul didn't want his picture up there, because he knew the apocalypse was near, and painting a portrait would be a frivolous waste of money for the church. The chairs were nothing extraordinary, though they were padded. The table was rather extravagant. It had been bought by his great-grandfather, and from what Shaul had gathered, he had been a flamboyant sort of man with the habit of freely spending the church's money.

Finally, by itself, right in the center of the east wall, there was a painting of his truly magnificent ancestor, Raleb Eitan, the great founder of the Church of the Elect. It was on the east wall because

Raleb came from Israel, and so did the church. Israel was east of Texas. Raleb had had the opportunity to work on the Dead Sea Scrolls once in Jerusalem back in 1956. That was when he was inspired to start his own church based on the book of Enoch, who was Noah's great-grandfather, as it says in Genesis.

There were four people in the conference room with Shaul. This was the first meeting of its kind. They were all elders working on the apocalypse. They were all exchanging stories, and it was rather loud. The acoustics in the room were very poor.

One of the elders stood and tried to bring the meeting to order, but there was too much jabber, so Shaul stood and took over. He knew he had power over them all. "Let's get down to business, Brothers," Shaul said in his booming voice. Everything went quiet. "I want status reports on what you field personnel have been up to. Brother Henrique, what about you?"

"My brother has been at Nextron for about six months, as some of you know," he started. "Their CEO is definitely one of them, and so are many others there. He pays himself millions of dollars each month. Yeah, each month! He has lots of properties around the globe. Many righteous people he pays as servants. He runs his company like a dictator, though everyone who works directly under him seems to admire him, for some reason. He is a great speaker and motivates just about anyone he comes in contact with. No question about it, he is a Watcher."

"What about security at their hydrogen plants?" Shaul asked.

"Not much of a problem in industrialized countries, but more so in less developed countries. Their security guards are armed, but we could eliminate them when the day comes without any problem. They are easy targets."

"Who does their security, or is it in-house?"

"Integrated Security Services, Limited, out of London," Henrique said. "They are very large, but they don't spend a lot of time training their employees in the art of defense."

"Yes, we know them. Brother Charlie, isn't Integrated your assignment?" Shaul asked.

"Yes, Elect One," said Charlie. "They are one of the largest international security companies. They do test on procedure, but there's no physical field training, though a lot of their personnel are former mercenaries. In countries like the US, they need permits to carry firearms. So some of their people, actually, Brother Henrique, are very tough. Nextron is their largest account."

"I stand corrected," Henrique said. Then he continued. "We'll need to neutralize their distribution infrastructure. They work with Aquasuperior to obtain hydrogen for distribution to filling stations and homes. Nextron also makes a lot of their own hydrogen and sells the oxygen to consumers. Of course, we all know they are the largest producer of auto and heating hydrogen in the world. But if we destroy Aquasuperior, we eliminate much of Nextron."

"Brother Emerico, tell us, how is Aquasuperior shaping up?"

"I have just started receiving messages from our person there. It is a company founded and led by Erebos Meyer. He must be a Watcher. The name *Erebos* means "darkness" or "the underworld," and his last name means "leader." I would be surprised if he were not Azazel himself. He has a great following. He sits on the boards of many environmental organizations. He is a consultant for the EPA and other government agencies. He speaks at many environmental conferences, and Aquasuperior has its own foundation that funds green housing organizations. They've grown phenomenally fast and are quite large. Of the twelve thousand desalinization plants around the globe, Aquasuperior owns about eight thousand of them. They control roughly 80 percent of the fresh water in God's creation, and about 20 percent of the hydrogen, as well as a significant amount of oxygen."

"What do their processing plants have for security?" asked Shaul.

"They use in-house security. Meyer requires that all of his employees are extremely physically fit and able to defend themselves. If it comes down to hand-to-hand combat, it will be tough, as their guards are especially well trained. Their processing stations in civilized countries rarely use armed guards, but like Nextron, in poorer regions it's a necessity to use small arms and tight security around the plants. Of course, fresh water is so expensive, tribal warlords, terrorist groups, and rogue governments are always trying to take over their plants, and everyone needs hydrogen and oxygen if they can afford it. So those are very heavily armed and generally successfully defended. Nonetheless, I feel our approach will easily fix that problem."

"Yes, of course it will," Shaul said, but he had a nagging feeling that his plan wasn't quite comprehensive enough. "Sounds like we're coming along quite well," he said after a brief pause. "How are we making out with our conferences to find the righteous, Brother David?" Shaul liked him because he held the same name as David in the Bible. Brother David was always prepared to take on giant projects like organizing a large-scale effort to find out who was worthy of living on earth after the apocalypse.

"We have twenty-two simultaneous evangelism conferences going on in the US and around the world," he stated. "They are well attended. More and more people are being convinced that the world is run by the Watchers. Catholics, Protestants, Jews, and Muslims ... they're all coming our way. We have found many large contributors this way and can easily fund the apocalypse with many millions left over. We should think about an actual date."

"We have told our men in the Middle East to start making the deal. Okay, Brothers. Let's set a date." The other men nodded and muttered. There was a loud rumble of approval. "How about in three months—July 4, Independence Day. The day of death for the Watchers and all those they have corrupted, but liberation for us."

Everyone laughed and shook hands. Jubilation filled the air.

Chapter 6

There were three women and three men, including Meyer, in the back of his limousine. Everyone was from the office. One woman was five months pregnant. The father of her child was also in the car. They were drinking champagne. Foolishly, the pregnant one drank too, but Meyer noticed she hadn't finished her first glass yet.

They were all heading to Meyer's mansion to have a party. Once the fun started they would exchange partners. Meyer considered himself a sexual athlete, as he could have many partners in one night. He was kind of attracted to Linda Tobin, the pregnant one. There was something erotic about a woman with child. All of a sudden, his whole body tingled. He really wished they were home so he could desecrate her body.

"Anyone for more champagne?" he asked. A few glasses were extended toward him, and he started to pour. The car hit a bump and some spilled on his lap. "I guess someone will have to take my pants off when we get home."

Everyone laughed. He was feeling a bit drunk; they all were, except Tobin. He didn't remember how many glasses he had drunk. The limo pulled through the gates of the estate. The house couldn't be seen from the road. An eight-foot cement wall surrounded the property. There were Electronic gates and a road that wound through the wooded grounds on the way to the house—an English Tudor. It had three stories and the half-timbered façade typical of the style. The parking area in front of the house always amazed Meyer as well as his guests. The lot was made of thousands of cobblestones. The center of the lot was a large circle. From the middle, the stones were laid to form a spiral pattern. The outer portions of the area were laid out in geometric patterns.

The limo eased to a stop. The computerized voice of the driving system stated that they had arrived at their destination. His two butlers were waiting to open the car doors for him and his guests. As everyone began to exit the auto, Meyer's cell phone rang. Meyer took Tobin by the arm, pulled her back into the car, and leaned over and kissed her blouse-covered breast. He squinted at the caller ID and saw that it was Sabino.

"Hey, buddy, what's happening?" Meyer said, thinking the words might have come out slurred.

"Erebos, we have a problem. We're—"

"There are no problems, buddy, only solutions."

"Okay, then," Sabino said, "there are some conditions that need to be addressed."

"Hey, are you coming over tonight?"

"I don't think so; I'll be with Kamryn. Listen to me."

"I've had a few drinks, you know."

"Yeah, I can tell. About our situation. There's been someone posting—"

"You know what I always say," Meyer said. "Well, not always, but sometimes."

"What's that, Erebos?"

"Never take your job home with you. Work like a dog all day long from sun up until sundown, but save the rest of your time for recreation. You'll live longer that way."

"Erebos, listen to me."

"That's what my grandfather said, and he lived to be ninety-six."

"Pay attention, will you," Sabino said.

"You sound mad, buddy," Meyer said. He put his hand on Tobin's knee, leaned over and kissed her again. "Here's the thing. When I'm home for the day, I leave the office behind. You know that. Now, I'm rather busy here." He kissed her ear. "I'll be in at six in the morning, so see me then, okay?"

"You're the boss."

"Good. Listen, drop the office and have some fun with that Kamryn Rodgers girl of yours. That's an order," Meyer said, still feeling like his voice was slurred, and stuck the phone in his pocket, and then he opened the door and tried to gently lead Tobin out of the car. He realized he had tugged her arm and at once said he was sorry. The others were waiting on the stairs. He put his arm around Tobin's lower back and led her over to the others. One of the butlers opened the double door. "Come on in, everyone. Let's have some fun."

~ ~ ~

Sabino hung up the phone. He wondered how Meyer could do it—run a multibillion-dollar company, work for all those charities, run a foundation, travel the globe on business, and still party like he was in college. And at his age.

He and Kamryn had noticed that the number of encrypted postings had increased. They always came from different computers, so they couldn't be traced to one specific person. No one admitted to sending them. Either there was a conspiracy or one person was doing it for who knew what reason, and the bigger question was, How was this person getting everyone's user IDs and passwords?

Sabino looked at his watch. It was eight thirty at night, and he was still at the office. Maybe Meyer was right. He would worry about it in the morning. He activated his cell phone and thought the name Kamryn. It rang, and she picked it up right away.

"Hi. Are you ready for me to come over?" Sabino asked.

"I was expecting you earlier, Ping. Dinner is cold."

She was pissed, he could tell. "I'm sorry. I got tied up with this IM thing and a bunch of other crap. You know how it is."

"I'll forgive you … I guess." Her voice softened. "I just want to spend more time with you, that's all."

"It'll take me about half an hour to drive over. "

"Okay," Kamryn said, sounding a bit more pleasant. "I'll warm up dinner. Can you pick up some red wine? We're having tenderloin."

"Sure. See you then. Bye." He wondered what real beef tasted like. Real cows hadn't existed for several decades, let alone been breed for food. Her request for wine, he knew, was a desire for a special treat. Wine from a real winery cost several hundred dollars a bottle for the cheap stuff, and anything of real quality was often over a thousand. And yet he could easily afford it in moderation, and she had been working hard, so he knew he would cave in. Besides, the amorous effects on her would be worth it.

He checked the time on his phone again. He would get there about nine fifteen if he picked up wine. He put his computer in secure mode, got up from his desk, and left. Meyer was right. Having some good food, some wine in moderation, and a bit of loving from a super girl was a lot more fun than snooping people's surfing habits.

Chapter 7

Kamryn lived in a condo on the Cambridge side of the Charles River. MIT was half a mile up the street. Once, when Sabino was there during the day, he had seen sculling teams practicing going up and down the waterway in spite of its toxicity. The Charles, like all other rivers, had long since fallen victim to poisoned spring-fed tributaries. He drove into the condo's garage and pulled his two-seat Jaguar XK into a guest spot near the elevator and handicapped spaces. He grabbed the two bottles of wine and exited the car. Kamryn had yet to give him a key, so he had to go through the security lobby and have them call her. After she answered, he was allowed to take the elevator up to her ninth-floor dwelling.

Kamryn answered the door in a tight, short red dress that showed a fair amount of cleavage. She wore matching red shoes. His eyes were drawn to the distraction, but he quickly averted his stare and focused on her eyes, hoping she didn't notice.

"I saw you look," she said, smiling. She pressed her body up against his and stood on her tip-toes to give him a kiss. He put his hands on the sides of her waist. Her body was solid, muscular. Kamryn was a regular contender in iron man competitions—two miles swimming, twenty-six miles running, and fifty on a bike, all in one day.

He smiled back. "How can I help it?" he said.

"Come right on in and sit yourself down," she drawled. "I put the tenderloin in the fridge rather than keeping it in the oven. I didn't want to overcook it. I hope you don't mind."

"You create enough heat around here," Sabino said, but he knew just what she had in mind.

"Give me the wine. I'm thirsty." She took the bottles and brought them into the kitchen. Soon she came back with two full glasses and an opened bottle. She handed him one.

"Thanks," he said. "What do you think of these messages?"

"Oh, darling, you can be such a cad. A minute ago you looked like you were interested in me, and now you're talking about work?"

"I was. I mean, I am." She sat close to him on the couch, their bodies touching.

"Listen to me, Ping. Forget about work, drink the damn wine, and pay attention to *me*."

Sabino knew he could get obsessive about work. Even with her next to him, he couldn't help thinking about the suspicious activity. This was getting frustrating. First Meyer brushed him off, now her. He snapped out of it. He knew how the night would go. Even though he was starving, it was inevitable that, after a bottle of wine and a snack, they would go to the bedroom to have sex for a couple of hours before eating. He certainly had no problem with that.

Kamryn left and soon came back with crackers and cheese. She said, "Let's have a toast."

"Sure."

"To a good night," she said.

"To a good night." They touched glasses.

They both sipped with much enjoyment. He had bought Thelma cabernet sauvignon, his favorite Australian red wine. The pair soon finished the wine. Kamryn excused herself and went back to the kitchen. He didn't know why she went, but what was coming next was no surprise. Like clockwork. Just for a moment his mind drifted to this encryption business. If this person was posting from different terminals, he or she knew the passwords. They had to be using some kind of keyboard logging—an old-fashioned phrase that related to the days when keyboards were in use. The term meant using a chip or software to record the keys the person at the computer typed. The chip or software then saved the information—passwords, user names—to be retrieved later by the intruder. The intruder can also have that data sent to another location for use at their convenience.

"Hey, who needs crackers and cheese when there are more important things to do," she said as she came bouncing out of the kitchen. She had opened the second bottle. Kamryn took his hand and pulled him off the couch. They were heading to the bedroom. He instantly forgot about work.

Chapter 8

"Brothers and Sisters," Shaul bellowed from the pulpit, "stand and let us read together from the book of Enoch, 'The Abode of the Righteous and the Elect One: The Praises of the Blessed,' chapter thirty-nine, one through eight."

The crowd of twenty-five hundred filled two thirds of the seats in the church stadium. In unison they read,

> And it shall come to pass in those days and the holy children shall descend from the high heaven, and their seed shall become one with the children of man.
>
> And in those days Enoch received books of zeal and wrath, and books of disquiet and expulsion.
>
> And mercy shall not be accorded to them, saith the Lord of Spirits.
>
> And in those days a whirlwind carried me off the earth,
>
> And set me down at the ends of the heavens.
>
> And there I saw another vision, the dwelling places of the holy,

And the resting places of the righteous.
And they petitioned and interceded and prayed for the children of man,
And the righteous flowed before them like water.
And mercy like dew on the earth:
And it is amongst them for ever and ever.
And in that place my eyes saw the Elect one.
And I saw his dwelling place under the wings of the Lord of Spirits.
And the righteousness shall prevail in His days,
And the righteous and the Elect before Him shall be without number before Him for ever and ever.
And their lips extol the name of the Lord of Spirits

"Praise the Lord!" Shoal interjected, shouting between the lines.

"And the righteousness before him shall never fail." The crowd stopped reading and went silent, waiting for Shaul.

"Younger Richard, light the candles of bliss." A young acolyte stood and ignited the wick on a long staff. The congregation waited for him while he lit the seven candles. "Brothers and Sisters, hear me now," Shaul said. "The Elect—and that is all of you—will soon walk with God. But there are the Watchers out there doing evil things. They are running the world. Everything around us is dictated by the Watchers. Corporate greed is one evil and is what I'm going to talk to you about now.

"The big box retail stores tell you they save you money. They say they offer convenience. They say they are nice to their customers. But all they want is your money." He paused. "They take in billions of dollars of our money and live like kings.

"Pharmaceuticals. They feed us their pills to make us better, or so they say. They don't care about you! They experiment on us with their new drugs not to make us feel better but only to make us give them our money so we can stay alive.

"They are the Watchers—the ones who force us to pay them to stay alive. Two companies run the world. Two companies make us pay to stay alive. These two companies run our lives. I am talking about Aquasuperior and Nextron.

"Aquasuperior makes our fresh water for farming, for drinking, for bathing. Do you think they care about us? It is corporate greed that they care about. Money for themselves. Money for their stockholders. They've got to keep those people happy. But they are the ones corrupted by the fallen angels.

"Nextron makes our hydrogen fuel so that we can drive our cars and trucks. They make the hydrogen so that we can stay warm in the winter. Without them, our world would come to a standstill. People would freeze. Do you think they care about us? No! All they want is our money! It is greed and corruption.

"And what about our oxygen? We have two Watchers combining forces to allow us to breathe. The oxygen in our campus buildings comes from the corporate greed of Nextron and Aquasuperior. We pay them to breathe. What a world, wouldn't you agree?"

Muffled voices came from the audience.

"They take our seawater—a resource that belongs to everyone—and they separate the hydrogen from the oxygen, and they make us pay. The sea does not belong to them. The sea belongs to the citizens of the world. Yes, these worldly gifts will ultimately be destroyed after the apocalypse for the Watchers, but they will remain alive for all eternity for us, the Elect.

"Do not worry, Brothers and Sisters. Very soon, we will see no more corporate greed. This will happen *because the apocalypse will soon come upon us!"* The crowd murmured with excitement. "The Watchers will pay for all eternity. Brothers and Sisters, it is the righteous that shall prevail. We will live in peace and harmony.

Remember, the great book says, 'And all shall be smitten with fear, And the Watchers shall quake, And great fear and trembling shall seize them unto the ends of the earth.' So ends the ritual for the day."

Chapter 9

The computer screen on his desk stared back at him. Shaul was waiting for his spy at Aquasuperior to start instant messaging him about what was happening there. Technology was beginning to pick up momentum again. From what he knew, computer science had advanced again about as far as things had been in the early twenty-first century. The Great Network Attack of 2121 by Al Qaeda had destroyed trillions of bits of information. Technology had come to a standstill. They had developed a worm that was able to penetrate through every firewall it ran into. The use of paper had come to a stop because of the sparse forests, so much of the lost data was never in physical form and was lost forever. Fortunately, there was no more typing on those old-fashioned keyboards. Shaul remembered those from his youth. Now there was a device that attached to the ear. It scanned the brain for specific thoughts, and then those thoughts appeared as words on a screen.

The screen flashed, and there was the opening message.

BROEMCO: *Good morning, Elect One.*

Shaul thought of his response and it appeared on the screen.

ELE111: *Good morning to you. How is your person making out?*

BROEMCO: *You will know her as AQU2556. Sabino, her boss,*

knows something is up. He has discovered the encrypted messages. I suspect he will also find my sessions with her, though he will never know what was said. He might do something to block the outgoing messages, file transfers, and IM communications.

ELE111: *Are you sure we're secure?*

BROEMCO: *With all due respect, I at least know what much about computers. I have a concern.*

ELE111: *What's up?*

BROEMCO: *I am beginning to have some doubts about the potential success of your plan. The plants in modern countries are well defended. Many security forces have been authorized by local governments to arm themselves with ammo tipped with picanzite, which is capable of neutralizing any unfriendly vehicles, including tanks.*

ELE111: *What's that, some kind of explosive?*

BROEMCO: *It's a highly powerful explosive. It was invented by someone named Picanzo five years ago. It is a radioactive isotope that is activated when two gases are mixed together. A tiny mechanism on the tip of a bullet can penetrate six inches of concrete. The only drawback is that its special gases emit a lot of heat when sitting idle.*

ELE111: *How about physical security?*

BROEMCO: *Very tight. Some are surrounded by automated Electronic battlefields.*

ELE111: *Tell me more about that.*

BROEMCO: *They are popular in industrialized nations. It will be nearly impossible to go in and eliminate these facilities. There is a large cleared area around the plant with mines. Then, drones armed with lasers attack anything that tries to infiltrate the area. They are virtually bulletproof. I understand that not even rounds tipped with picanzite can harm them. Also, the plants have movement censors that monitor activity within a five- to eight-hundred-meter radius. Any suspicious activity is analyzed for threat potential.*

ELE111: *I hate to say this, but you're not the first one to express doubts. For now, why don't you keep at it? If the position becomes compromised, you can pull out. But please try to find how to disable their Electronic fields. It must have to be done by computer. If you can get in there, we'll be golden.*

BROEMCO: *I'm not so sure about that. The drones have very sophisticated artificial intelligence. I don't believe that they run off a central computer.*

ELE111: *That's not good news. Let me think about what you've told me, and we will communicate again in a week.*

BROEMCO: *Is that it for now?*

ELE111: *That's it. May the Lord of Spirits look over you.*

BROEMCO: *And over you. Bye.*

Shoal touched the secure icon and the communication on the screen disappeared. He was beginning to wonder if his plan actually was the best approach. He would have to think it through, though he had set a date and wanted to stick to it.

Some of the elders were beginning privately to express doubts. After all, it was a plan involving thousands of brothers that would have to be coordinated around the globe. The plants in the industrialized nations would be extremely difficult. That would leave the facilities in poorer countries which were also well armed, but far less organized so attacks would be less difficult. He had been told that the portable missiles they were going to negotiate from China used the same explosives as other modern militaries. Picanzite. He was sold on the idea. A radioactive isotope that actually only existed for a few microseconds. A few molecules had the power take down a five-story building made of steel and concrete. In other words, one very small payload would destroy one plant.

That had to become a reality. They would only buy warheads equipped with the explosive mentioned. That was the only way.

He stood up and stretched. He wondered how fast he could

synthesize a new plan and how fast the Elect could put it into action. He really wanted to stick to Independence Day.

He knew the idea of destroying all of the desalinization plants in the world was a good one, even if it was a logistical nightmare. Judgment day was supposed to be desolate and dry. With no water, people would die of thirst. Crops would die. There would be no oxygen to aid breathing. There would be no hydrogen to fuel vehicles and heat houses. The lack of water would accomplish all of that, bringing on a time of devastation and the beginning of the end.

Suddenly he had an idea. It would accomplish everything. His dream could come true … judgment day. It would be expensive, but Shaul controlled the church's money. He could do whatever he wanted. The concept was perfect.

Shaul knew he had just the man that could carry out the mission in the Middle East.

"Brother Gabriel," Shaul called to his assistant, "come here. I need you."

Instantly, Gabriel was in the doorway. "Yes, Elect One. How may I serve you?"

"I want you to contact our headquarters in Jerusalem. Have them contact Jabbar Abu Shakra. I need to talk with him personally to give him an assignment."

"I will do that right away." Gabriel turned and left.

Yes, his new plan would be perfect. Conducting both schemes simultaneously would make the prophecy dead on according to the book of Enoch. *Yes. Perfect.* Along with the elders' original plan to eliminate the desalination plants, the end was near. Maybe it would happen by July 4.

Chapter 10

Sabino knew there was something devious about these encrypted messages. He could just feel it. Why else would anyone do this? He was on his way back to his office after helping an employee out with his password. He could have just told it to him over the phone, but he needed breaks from his desk just to keep him sane. But soon the walk was over and he was back at his desk.

He thought about installing a network-wide keyboard logging program. In his days as a hacker, he had had all the current hacking software, but working as network administrator at Aquasuperior for all these years had kept him away from a once-exciting pastime.

He knew the answer was simple. He was friends with fellow Dartmouth College alumni who had majored in computer science. One of his friends worked in the long-standing InfraGard Program at the FBI. That division overlooked industrial spying and technology threats to industry. Supervisory Special Agent Scott Boucher had come a long way since their college fraternity partying days. Scott was a family man these days ... two kids and all settled down in his management job. It seemed like a boring life. But he would be up on all the latest hacking techniques and software. Sabino thought about the number. It went right to Boucher's desk.

"Special Agent Boucher," his friend answered.

"Hi, Scott. How're you doing?

"Is this Ping?"

"Sure is. What are you up to?"

"I've been busy. Janet is expecting again."

"No!"

"She sure is. It's our first boy. She took the gender shot. We're adding onto the house to make a boy's room. I've been doing that with my brother in my spare time … what little I have of it."

"How far along is she?"

"Six months. Ping, I'm kind of busy. Is this a social call?"

"Actually, no," Sabino said. "We have some suspicious activity here, and I wonder if you could help me out."

"Sure. What do you need?"

"I'd like to do some network-wide keyboard logging, but I don't have current software. Do you?"

"Of course we do," Boucher said. "Want me to e-mail you a copy of mine?"

"That would be great."

"Hold on. I'll do it right now." There was a pause "Ah ha, I found it. Done. It should be in your in-box."

Sabino opened up his e-mail in-box and saw that it was there.

"Got it," he said. "Thanks."

"What's this suspicious activity?"

"Some people are communicating through encrypted instant messaging. We can't figure out who or why."

"Interesting. You could also add a mass of cameras to monitor each computer terminal."

"Some we do, Scott, but we have thousands of terminals here, and adding cameras for each would be a massive undertaking, not to mention how difficult it would be to keep secret, and the expense would be tremendous."

"No, I understand."

"Keep me posted," Boucher said. "We'll help in anyway we can. In the mean time, don't tell anyone about this. Not your best friend. Not your mother. No one!"

"I have to tell my assistant."

"No one. Suspect everyone. Trust no one. Understood?"

Chapter 11

"What do you suppose they're sending?" Meyer said.

"I don't know, but every exchange involves links to a darknet. It must be someone stealing company information and sending it to whomever they're working for."

"What are you doing about it?"

"I've contacted a friend at InfraGard," Sabino replied. "That's the division of the FBI that's involved with corporate espionage. He sent me software that will allow me to monitor activity network wide. I've installed it as well as another program that will alert me wherever I am when anyone posts anything encrypted."

"Do you think we can catch him?"

"That depends on when this person posts and how fast I can locate the computer where it's coming from. If I can get there in time, I've got 'em."

"We've got to bust this guy, Ping," Meyer said. "I want to hang this bastard."

"I'll call my friend at the FBI, and he'll send someone from the Boston office to come and investigate."

"Okay. Keep me informed. Now to the reason I've called you here. Your first project will be to decide on companies that will build the plants. I'm leaving this up to you. In the past we've used General Electric, Fisia Italimpianti, Aquatech International, and Veolia Entropie. These companies have given us the most successful plants. How are you coming with Kamryn's training?"

Sabino thought about her and the sex they had had last night. She was not a wild woman like many of those around the office. Kamryn liked to go slow and easy. And she was always telling him how much she loved him when they made love. Even worse, all she talked about when they were done was marriage and having kids. No way did Sabino want to marry anyone, though he had to admit she was damn sharp in her job and he liked competency a lot in a woman. She was quite athletic as well. She held her own when they went mountain climbing in New Hampshire. There was one particular rock face in North Conway that they had done twice. Best of all, she could fight. Her specialty was Brazilian Jujitsu. It differed from his and Meyer's kickboxing. Kickboxing led to a quick elimination of an opponent. Jujitsu was like wrestling, where one made the adversary submit to surrender through inflicting severe pain.

"She's very good," Sabino said. "She's ready. But I will have to work through this spy problem first without her."

"Why can't she do it herself?

"My friend at the FBI says I have to keep everything secret … even from her. You're the only one who knows about the software I've installed."

"How long do you think it'll take?" Meyer asked.

"This is a big company. Twenty floors. We could involve security and have them put a man on each floor. When someone sends an encrypted post, I could radio the location to the guard."

"That works. Call the head of security and arrange it. If there's any questions, have them call me."

Chapter 12

Jabbar Abu Shakra stood six-foot-four and weighed two hundred fifty pounds. At forty-four, he had never been in better shape. A man of Syrian decent, he had worked frequently as a mercenary, trained in terrorist camps, and killed many men. He was highly trained in Krav Maga. The art made him a killing machine. It was a discipline of martial arts developed in Israel that taught two things to soldiers: how to kill instantly, and how to fight off multiple attackers. He was very accomplished at it, and he was proud to be so good.

Most of all, he was closely associated with many of the Middle East's leaders. He was a devoted member of the Church of the Elect. Like all affiliates of the church, he believed that the end of the world was near.

He had seen the Elect one once in the past, though they had never met. Abu Shakra had attended a conference in the United States. He had traveled there just for that purpose. Now, the Elect One had contacted him to perform an important mission. He was honored.

At present, he lived in Jerusalem across from the Tulip Inn on Sultan Suleiman Street. He liked it there because it was an American tourist destination. The food at the cafés in the area was particularly good. He knew it was against the beliefs of the church, but he rather enjoyed the company of women. What American vacationer wouldn't want to keep company with such a masculine man? He often thought they must have been dreaming of sleeping with a real mercenary.

He liked it when the women tenderly caressed his muscles. He knew this was evil, but he couldn't help himself. If he believed in evolution rather than creationism, he could have explained these desires as natural. And that often confused him. The act of sleeping with a woman to whom one was not married was a sin. He wondered what would happen to him on judgment day.

The most important day of his life was coming up. The Elect one himself was coming to Jerusalem to meet him personally. He was to ask Abu Shakra to go on a living quest for the Church. He hoped that completing this mission for the Elect one would put him in the good graces of the Lord of Spirits. After all, maybe he would help bring on the end. He had no idea what the mission was, but it must be big to have asked specifically for Abu Shakra's help.

Chapter 13

It's really rather baffling, Sabino thought. Obviously, the encrypted posts written prior to the implementation of the keyboarding software were untouchable. However, he was able to read the current posts because they were being monitored in real time. They made reference to plant locations around the world, but of even greater significance were the darknet attachments this person mentioned. And for some reason, he couldn't figure out the spy's user name and password as they were still coming through as encrypted. Right now, he had a message on the screen that had just been sent. It said,

> Elect One: Go to our darknet and you will find attached plans for the desalination plant in Port Sudan, Sudan, Africa. Note that it is a multi-effect distillery facility with a number of evaporators in a series. The weak point is the very center of the distillery as I have marked on the picture. The security is very tight. The security force is the size of a small army. They patrol out to about a five-hundred-meter radius. Respectfully, AQU2556.

Why would anyone care? That was the question. He could see that some rebel forces might want to take over a job site in a country like Sudan. Water was very expensive, and taking over a facility would bring in a lot of cash. However, in other messages there were also references to files that included plants in industrialized countries as well.

It could also be a competitor wanting to get into these installations. After all, much of Aquasuperior's technology was classified, because many of the establishments used secret hybrid desalination methods to achieve the most productive result.

Whoever this AQU2556 happened to be, he or she was very cautious. Every exchange was sent from a different computer, and always from the desk of someone away on vacation or a business trip. Ping had security review the data from the security cameras, and at the few terminals that actually were monitored, it was always the same person in the same clothes wearing a baseball cap and sunglasses to hide his or her face. The figure was short, maybe five-four to five-eight. Even though Ping was alerted as soon as someone installed the encryption software, the mysterious figure was always too fast. It took only a brief moment for the spy to log on, install the encryption software, upload a file, and have a quick exchange before security arrived.

But where was this information being sent? He had to see Boucher for ideas. He would call him right now.

"How ya doing, partner?" Kamryn said from his doorway in her beautiful drawl.

"Confused," Sabino said. "I don't know how we are going to catch our mystery person."

She started to come over behind him. He minimized the screen. He thought about telling her in spite of what Boucher had told him. He knew he could trust her. After all, they were lovers. There was nothing better than a little office romance. She stood behind him now and wrapped her arms around his neck. He leaned his head back so it rested on her stomach. He felt exasperated.

"Is there anything I can do?" she asked.

"Bag this guy, that's what."

"Don't concentrate on it too much, Ping. My mama told me thinking causes baldness. I don't want a shiny-headed boyfriend."

"Very funny. What have you been doing today?"

"It's been a hardware day," she said. "People are calling from all over telling me that this won't work, that's broke. What are we doing for dinner tonight? It's about that time."

He looked at his watch. It was six fifteen. It was later than he had imagined. Boucher would have gone home by this time anyway. He would call him first thing in the morning.

"It's my turn to cook," he said. "You could ride with me or come by Boston's famous public transportation. You know what a hassle it is to park around my place."

"You know, you're going to make someone a good house-husband someday, Ping."

"Again, very funny. You have to admit, I cook pretty damn well, if I do say so myself. You've given me enough compliments."

"You're right. So let's go play house. You can be the old man and cook me a nice meal. I'll be the working wife coming home from a hard day at the office. We can eat. You can massage my body, and then we can practice making babies."

Kamryn was always hinting like this. Or that's what he thought she was doing. She could twist any conversation toward marriage. He liked her a lot, but matrimony was passé and he didn't want to be stuck to one woman forever. He had his two kids to take care of him when he was old, and perhaps another one out of her if she proved worthy, so why would he need her later in life?

"Just let me make you a nice dinner for now, okay?" he said.

Reluctantly, Kamryn agreed. She said she would take a cab over to his four-story townhouse. He only had one parking spot in the back, and that was very tight. He always worried about someone denting his Jag.

He lived in a part of Boston known as Beacon Hill. His house was on Prospect Street. On just a network administrator's salary, he would never have been able to afford it. But he had started with Aquasuperior when it was young, and Meyer had given him a lot of equity in exchange for free work while the company got going. He owned about 6 percent. That amounted to quite a bit out of a fifty-billion-dollar company. Just a part of the dividends paid for his townhouse and all its expenses and gave him lots of spending cash to boot. He put the rest in other stocks. He owned a lot of Nextron, because they did business together.

He always parked out back and used the front door. Sabino just loved the French Second Empire style. The entry had columns on either side with steps leading up to the door. Each floor was smaller than the one below it. In the 1890s, the servants had lived in cramped quarters on the fourth floor, while the owners lived in a grand manner with twelve-foot-high ceilings. The entryway inside was a real piece of art. The ceilings were made of intricate tin. The walls also had tin on the bottom three or four feet. The walls had twentieth-century wallpaper. The stairway was all dark cherry, and the banister and spindles were meticulously carved. The newel post was attached from the bottom step to the floor above.

"Your home is so beautiful," Kamryn told him for the hundredth time. "It's just so wonderful cooking together in your kitchen. Everything is so easy to find, and the cabinet and counter space just never ends."

"I do enjoy cooking," he replied, "although it's not my favorite room in the house. Can you guess?"

"Well, yeah—the bedroom," she said with a friendly laugh.

He should have seen that one coming. "It's actually the activity room. How many nights have we spent in the hot tub with the gas fireplace going? Or how many of my immersion games have we enjoyed playing?"

"Yeah, battling you from the tub has a certain thrill to it."

She expressed her admiration for his house every time she was over. She had never seen anything so grand she always told him. Maybe her alleged love for him was all a show. Suppose Kamryn wanted his money, and all this love business was just an act.

Still, he thought he was a pretty good judge of character. Either she deserved an Oscar, or she was sincere. Who knew? Sabino would never consider marriage, but it might be nice to have someone else live with him. The house was so big and, well, gloomy, like a spooky set out of a Gothic horror movie. He had all that empty space. Sure, it was filled with laughter when his kids were over, and a maid came in three times a week, but other than that it was dark and dismal. He had thought of painting the somber cherry wood bright white, but that would have spoiled the true antiquity of the place.

But having Kamryn move in? He would really have to be desperate to fill the empty space to let that happen.

Chapter 14

Sabino and Boucher were at the computer in his office at Aquasuperior. Boucher had become personally involved, he said, because Aquasuperior was vital to national security and even world stability. Boucher had just arrived in Sabino's office thirty minutes before, and they had spent only two minutes on small talk and the rest reading exchanges. This had become a criminal investigation. They both were extremely curious to know who was initiating the conversations.

Boucher had security revise their plan. Previously, one officer had been stationed on each floor, and they had walked around in hopes that they would be near when the spy made a connection. Aquasuperior was now hiring temps, so there were to be several officers instead of one, and Boucher had an agent monitoring each floor. Room by room, they would secretly install security cameras. Sabino told Boucher about his suspicions that the computers were used when the proper users were away. So Boucher had each department head secretly notify security whenever someone was due out of the office. So now security knew what terminals could potentially be used.

"Suppose we do catch this spy," Sabino said. "They don't necessarily have to tell us who they're working for."

"It's not always technology that catches the accused," Boucher said. "Sometimes, it's just good, old-fashioned police work. That's what we're doing here. We're narrowing down the possibilities, and someday soon we'll be in the right place at the right time … and we will have rock solid proof. Don't worry."

"Scott, do you have any hunches about what these people would want this type of information for?"

"I think you're in for a lot of trouble. Especially since they talk about the security and where the weak points are on the equipment. It may be that terrorists are planning mortar attacks to destroy them. Or perhaps physical attacks where they take over the facility and sell the water themselves. It might even be blackmail. They could destroy a few facilities and threaten to do more unless you put up some money. Or it could be political. Perhaps it's some watchdog group wanting cheaper prices. It wouldn't be the first time Aquasuperior was accused of ripping off the public and having a monopoly."

"What do you think we should do?"

"We'll send out terrorist alerts to all of your locations. You should hire more security forces as a precaution. I'll get things rolling in DC. We'll contact other intelligence agencies to see if they've heard of anything else that's related to water security. The National Security Agency has the equipment to decrypt the files quickly. I'll have them do that. If these are terrorists, the issue of fresh water could become a question of national security."

Sabino wondered if it were possible to destroy every desalination site. There were roughly twelve thousand around the globe. He didn't think any terrorist group was large enough to pull off something on such a large scale, though he supposed it could be a collaboration among factions. But what could a group gain by destroying water facilities on a large scale? That would leave the terrorists without water too. Nobody could be that shortsighted.

On the other hand, at present they had no proof that anything cynical was going down. All the content of the messages related to what type of desalination technologies were used and security at the production locations. It could just be a competitor looking for trade secrets.

"So," Sabino said, "since this might be a matter of national security, will we need to gather more proof before we can get the military involved?"

"That's right. Congress won't mobilize the armed forces unless they're absolutely convinced a threat exists."

"Why don't I tell Erebos what we know? Then we can decide what we each need to do."

~ ~ ~

Sabino, Meyer, and others all took training classes in Muay Thai three times a week in the company aerobics room. Sabino was planning on attending the noontime classes, and he thought he would talk to Meyer about this growing problem during the session. They often talked in hushed voices about private matters while they were sparring together.

They put on their protective gear and started to fight. As soon as they were head to head, the conversation began. Sabino told Meyer that the FBI was now involved, what Boucher thought, and how the method of catching the operative was being revised.

"I'll put our vice-president of security in charge of increasing our protection measures worldwide," Meyer said. "That'll be a lot of work, so we'll have to put enough people on it that each plant manager can be contacted personally. This must be accomplished on an individual basis. I'll authorize whatever funds he needs."

"Where do you suppose this puts our expansion plans?" Sabino asked, throwing a roundhouse kick, breathing heavily, and beginning to get worn down. "I've yet to get involved, but I know construction of some is well under way."

Meyer blocked the kick and charged Sabino, kicking and swinging, and then he backed off as Sabino found himself against the mirrored wall.

"It's still your baby. If damage happens, it's your head," he said with a smile.

That was it for business talk. The rest of the time they talked about how Sabino's kids were doing in college.

Chapter 15

"How are you enjoying your stay on our campus?" Shaul asked.

"Very much so," said Poirier, now known as Brother Michael. "The people here are just wonderful. Very welcoming. I've always been very religious, and I agree with the belief that there will be a judgment day. All of the people I've met also believe that."

"Good, good. Do you realize that the apocalypse is coming *very* soon?"

"Of course. There are all sorts of opinions about the exact day," Poirier said. "Nobody knows for sure."

"What would you say if we knew that date was July 4 of this year?"

"Hey, you never know."

"Ah, but we do. Suffice to say that we do."

"Okay, fine."

Shaul still wasn't sure he could trust Brother Michael with the truth even though they had met many times now. Shaul had been courting him and his wife in hopes of successfully asking for a large donation. One thing Shaul knew was that Poirier was rich as Gabriel had revealed. The church needed lots more money to hatch his revised plan. They had money to pay for the rockets. Now he would need several million more.

"You're an investment banker?" Shaul said after a brief pause.

"That's right, though I'm retired. I'm proud to say I achieved a lot of success. I became involved with many IPOs, and I frequently came out on top."

"Have you considered donating money to the church?" Shaul was never afraid to ask point blank. He felt that in doing so, the money issue would be right out front, and he could talk honestly to potential donors and church members about it.

"I believe in what I've seen here. I like the idea of spreading the word. I like many of the community outreach programs your church has. I think it's important to be involved with the people. If I were to invest, it would probably be a lot, so I'd want some say in where it goes."

"That's not typically possible, unfortunately; most monies go to the general fund, which is what runs the church."

"But I would want my money to go to specific programs like your rehab centers in the inner cities or your evangelical arm. I might like to construct a building and name it after my wife."

"Regrettably, that's not going to happen. We've stopped all construction projects because of the coming apocalypse. However, we still have important programs in need of cash. One in particular."

"And what is that?" Poirier asked.

"Well, that's just the thing. It's a secret gift for our parishioners," Shaul replied. He had already discussed his latest plan with the elder council, and they wholeheartedly loved the idea. They were the only ones who knew apart from a few brothers in the Middle East and soon Jabbar Abu Shakra, who would actively research the project over there. In addition to the original plan of eliminating all the desalination plants, the new plan was to set off an Electromagnetic bomb that would set in motion nuclear retaliation from the governments of developed nations, adding to the Watchers' ultimate undoing.

Poirier could be a very valuable asset. Maybe he would have to take a risk. They needed money soon. Shaul decided to revert to the main theme of the church. "What do you believe will happen to you when the day of judgment comes?"

"I've always tried to be a good person ... do the right thing," Poirier said. "I like to think I would pass on to, as you say, the land of the righteous."

"And what about that partner of yours, your wife? And your children?"

"My children are too young and haven't yet grown to be influenced by the Watchers. And my wife?" He paused for a minute. Shaul wondered if Brother Michael was thinking about bad things Sister Maria had done. Poirier smiled. "Maria can be rather, um, interesting. But overall, I think I would say she would come with me."

"Do you believe me when I say the day of judgment is near?" Shaul leaned toward him in his chair for extra emphasis. "There is a passage that mentions wives in the book," Shaul continued. "There is much talk about defiling women and having children. It is said that the Watchers father giants from mortal women. There may be messages about taking wives, but that means defiling them for pleasure. We in the church understand this to mean that marriage will disappear if the Watchers have their way. You always read these days about vanishing matrimony. With few exceptions, it is a dying institution—*except in our church!* The rest of the population is wrong. Sinners! They are bringing us closer to the end with each passing day." Shaul could feel his excitement building just thinking about it. "Still another prophesy that we read in the book is that there will be a lot more barren, desolate lands where the Watchers will perdure in agony for all time. Consider this passage about the valley of judgment: 'And I looked and turned to another part of the earth, and saw there a deep valley with burning fire. And they brought the kings and the mighty, and began to cast them into this deep valley.' Do you know what that means, Brother Michael?" Shaul was getting all worked up from quoting the book. The intensity in his voice strengthened.

"It could mean a lot of things," Poirier said. "There was a lot of symbolism in those days."

"We believe the valley to be the desert and the fire to be the sun. The kings and the mighty are definitely the Watchers, the leaders of today. And the valley? The deserts are growing," Shaul said, his voice becoming louder. "There is also a section in the book that talks about the accursed valley where the Watchers will go to suffer. This is the growing desert. Massive tracts of land are being decimated, and nothing is being done to replenish our farmlands and forests. We know this by our lack of oxygen. In spite of the increasing number of desalination plants around the globe, there are giant areas of desert growing every year. The Lord's angels shall send forth the Watchers to the deserts forever!" He was really enthused now.

"Our Lord is bringing up the day of judgment, and the Church of the Elect shall make it happen!" Shaul shouted, standing, pointing his finger in the air. He paused for a moment. Shaul suddenly realized what he had done. He had just told Poirier that the church would manifest the end. Poirier looked somewhat shocked.

"What do you mean, 'make it happen'?"

"Well …" Shaul said, hesitating. He looked at Poirier, trying to read his expression. Poirier was smiling again. Was it a skeptical grin, or acceptance? He wanted to tell him, because he knew Poirier could make his plan a reality. On the other hand, if Shaul told him the truth, he might run to the police. Shaul was desperate. He would tell him a partial truth. He would tell Poirier about destroying the desalination facilities. Many brothers already knew about that. At worst, Shaul could always have Brother Gabriel stop him. Besides, Poirier was named Brother Michael. That he bore the archangel's name tipped the balance in Shaul's mind.

"Well, you see, I hope I don't scare you away. The church has a quest that will bring on judgment day. It may take a few months, but we can actually make it happen. But we will need a great deal of money."

"How could that possibly happen?"

Shaul prided himself on analyzing the tones in people's voices. After years of asking for money for the church, he could easily tell when one might donate and another might not. *Poirier might.*

Shaul told him about destroying the desalination sites. That this would bring the day of reckoning, because there would be no more water for raising crops, drinking, creating hydrogen for heat and fuel, and making oxygen to breathe. He admitted it was a very large-scale plan, but the elders felt it could be done. All the while, he was reading Poirier's reaction. He appeared attentive. It seemed possible.

"We have money to buy some of the rocket launchers, but we are still short. We have a goal of July 4 of this year, but we are badly in need of cash, and lots of it. Is it possible that you might help us?"

"What are we talking?"

"To be honest, I don't exactly know. Several million. I have a man in the Far East working on securing things and getting a price. There is a new explosive called picanzite. In a military context, one warhead containing a miniscule amount is enough to destroy an entire plant. We are striving to buy rockets equipped with it. Unfortunately, I have no idea how much it will cost."

"The last day of judgment," Poirier said. "You're sure?"

"Consider the old cliché 'actions speak louder than words.' If you donate this money, our Lord will bless you for bringing on this day. You, your wife, and your children will all come with us to the land of the Elect."

"May I talk this over privately with Maria?"

"Of course," Shaul said, and he knew he had convinced him. If Sister Maria believed in the end like Brother Michael, it would be a soft sell.

"Very well, then. I will talk to her today about it. Hopefully I'll get back to you this afternoon."

An hour later, Poirier called to say he would pledge whatever money was necessary.

Chapter 16

Bob Letendre was a large man. He knew that. He had found the perfect job at Aquasuperior as a security guard. Most of the time, he sat down at the front desk in the main lobby, though sometimes he was required to walk around. Easy money though. Sit around, eat, talk, get paid. Not bad. He knew Aquasuperior had only hired him because of his size. He was considered disabled because of his obesity, and they had had to hire him because of some federal mandate. His gain though. The only bad thing was that he was unable to get the girls. Everyone else in the company made out fine. Not him. He often wondered if it was because he was still single at thirty-nine and living with his mother. He wasn't exactly upwardly mobile, either.

The head of security, his boss, was forcing him to work overtime. They told him that someone was wrongly using other people's computers. So he was very slowly walking around the fifty-sixth floor and hoping nothing would happen on his watch.

"Bob, are you there?" came his boss's voice through the earpiece.

"Yeah, you found me," he replied into the tiny microphone on his lapel.

"This is it. At this very moment the perp is using the computer in Megan Zuzelo's office. Do you know where that is?"

"Not really."

"It's right near you. I've got you on GPS. Go straight and take the left toward the windows."

"Okay. Give me a minute."

"You'll have to hurry, Bob."

"I'm working on it."

Letendre walked as fast as he could. He was already out of breath.

"Now, turn right. It's the second office. Look at the nameplate on the door."

Does he think I'm stupid? Letendre thought. Peering through the window, he saw someone at the computer.

"What do I do?" he asked, very quietly.

"Tell her to stop and bring her up to us. I'll be in Ping Sabino's office."

He opened the door and the person turned around. It was a woman in a Red Sox cap and sunglasses. She stood up. She looked horrified. His body entirely blocked the doorway.

"I'm afraid you'll have to come with me, ma'am." Her body was the shape of an hourglass. For a moment, he imagined himself with her. He licked his lips and stared at her.

She charged at him and kicked him in his face. He staggered a bit, but his excessive size counteracted the force of the blow. He grabbed both of her hands, held them tight, and pushed her forward.

"Don't try anything else," he said. "You can't get away, and I'll break your arms if you try."

He no longer thought of her as hot.

~ ~ ~

Sabino, Boucher, and Ernest Crowley, the head of security, were all waiting in Sabino's office. The door was closed, and they were discussing what they should do with the spy. There was a knock at the door, and there stood Letendre, grasping Kamryn by the arm.

"AQU2556, I presume," Boucher said.

"Kamryn Rodgers?" Crowley said in shock.

"It couldn't be you," Sabino said, stunned. "There must be some kind of mistake."

"No mistake, Ping," Crowley said. "We were all right here looking at your monitor as she was sending her message."

Sabino had a horrible feeling inside. All this time they had been lovers, or so he thought, and it had all been an act. His emotions were torn apart. He hadn't realized his feelings for her were so strong until this moment. He felt empty and used and betrayed.

"Kamryn, I don't believe it," he said, slowly and quietly.

"Ping, I'm sorry. I didn't mean to hurt you. After I first met you, we got along so well I wanted to stop spying. I really, truly did. I have feelings for you, more than you can imagine."

"I can sympathize with you, Kamryn," Boucher said. As angry and hurt as Sabino was, he realized that Boucher was trying to demonstrate common ground. "I can see how someone could fall into an office romance. It's easy enough to do, believe me."

"Don't believe her, Ping. It's a crock of shit," Crowley said. "Kamryn is now a felon, and she wants to wiggle out of if."

"This is a felony?" Kamryn said, looking ready to cry.

"Cut the innocence, Rodgers. You know damn well it is," Boucher said. "Spying, using encoded messages to transfer trade secrets, conspiracy. Basically, I'm about to arrest you for industrial espionage. You're in a hell of a lot of trouble. You could get ten years, maybe more."

"Oh my God. You're going to arrest me? I don't believe this," she said.

"You have the right to remain silent," Boucher said and then went on to read her the rest of her Miranda rights. "Do you understand these rights as I've read them to you?"

Sabino saw tears roll down her cheek. She sniffled.

"Ping, you've got to believe me."

"Do you understand these rights?" Boucher said in an even louder tone.

"I suppose I do," she said. "I didn't mean to do any harm. I don't even know why they wanted the information."

"Who wanted to know?" Boucher snapped. "That's what we need to find out."

She sniffled again. "I really don't know what person, specifically, I'm communicating with."

Sabino saw her eyes move to the left.

"She's lying," Sabino managed to say through his erupting emotions.

"You're facing a lot of jail time, Kamryn," Boucher said. "You can ask for a lawyer, but if you're not truthful, it will weigh against you in court."

"Please, don't make me tell you that. They're a good organization I'm working for. I know that there is a logical reason. Ping, please don't make me tell them."

Sabino was still in shock. She looked sincere with the all of the tears and the sniffling. He still couldn't believe it. "How could you do this to me?" he said.

"Please, you've got to believe me. After I started working for you and we were together, I fell in love with you. I really did. That's the truth."

"All those things you said to me were lies."

"They came from my heart. Ping, I love you,"

"Listen here, guys," Boucher interrupted. "What does it matter who loves who? The plain facts are that Kamryn is a criminal, and she is going to jail."

"Oh, please—"

"Not to mention," Crowley said, cutting her off. "Not to mention you are in violation of the company nondisclosure statement. We'll sue you and get everything you own."

Sabino was watching Kamryn's face. All the while it seemed she was holding back a crying fit. Suddenly a question that had been haunting him all along came to mind. He was emotionally torn and angry beyond belief, but nonetheless, it resounded in his head. How had she been able to install the encryption software at the individual terminals when the network was set up so that no unauthorized software installations were allowed?

"How did you do it, Kamryn? How did you install the encryption software?"

"It was simple. I logged in at my computer and put it on the computers remotely from there, then erased my tracks."

That's right. Simple. Sabino would have figured that out if he had suspected her. *What a knifing witch,* he thought.

"Listen, Ping," Boucher aid. "I believe terrorists are planning some very dangerous things here. There could be a lot of lives involved."

"It's not terrorists," Kamryn said. "It's the Church of the Elect. They approached me when I worked there and offered me money to spy on you. They're the ones who want the information."

"Why the hell would they want all this confidential information?" Crowley said.

"I don't know," Kamryn said. "I was their network administrator before I was sent here. That's how I got this job. I know all about their network. We can find the reason there."

"Don't they believe in the end of the world?" Sabino said.

"Yes," Boucher said. "They're apocalyptics."

"They are," Kamryn said. "And I am too. I'm also a member of the church."

They all laughed. Everyone was thinking the same thing.

"It's ridiculous. How the hell could a church end the world?"

"That's what they've always believed, but they couldn't be planning that," Kamryn said. "The church's philosophy is peaceful. Yes, we do believe the judgment day is coming—someday—but we also believe in wholesome living, family life, and helping others. They have dozens of rehab centers around the country and hundreds of community centers that give inner-city residents things to do. They keep kids off the streets and out of trouble. Also, they're in a big membership drive right now. If they're actively seeking members, why would they want the end to come now?"

"Destroy the world," Crowley said with amusement. "That sounds like something out of a Batman movie."

"I think it was the Penguin that tried that," Letendre said. He had never been excused and had squeezed into the room.

"Okay, okay," Boucher said. "We've established that it's lunacy. That still leaves us with the question of why."

"What if she turned informer?" Crowley asked.

"No, we can't trust her to be associated with the church any longer," Boucher said. "She's a flight risk. If she somehow contacts someone at the church and slips away, we'll never see her again."

"Ping and I can hack into their computer. We'll get all the information you need," Kamryn said.

"We've got a thousand people who can hack computers. Why would we need you?" said Boucher.

"I know their network and their security breaches and could save you a lot of time. I know the campus in Texas and could show you around. I can identify all the top brass. They have sentries that are heavily armed and stationed on the rooftops, and I can point them out so no one will get shot. I can—"

"Okay, I get it," Boucher said. "Let me give it some thought. What I think I'll do is send a team down there and bust the place wide open. We'll raid it and confiscate everything. Ping, I want you to go. Okay?"

"I don't see why," Sabino said. "Whatever they have planned, it sounds like you've got everything under control. I'd rather just get back to Aquasuperior and deal with whatever consequential problems pop up."

"Who better to get involved with hacking them? True, the FBI has a lot of capable hackers, but you're the best. You've got your PhD in cybercrime. You've got military security experience. You're every bit as good as anyone I have. Besides, at the moment the FBI is under tight financial and operational scrutiny with Congress—meaning mounds of paperwork—and paying you as a consultant will be much less red tape than pulling a couple of my hackers out of DC."

"I'll go," Sabino said, "but only if she stays here."

"I never said she'd have anything to do with this anyway, Ping."

"I can't go to jail," Kamryn interrupted. "Please let me do this. I created a back door when I designed their firewall. I know how to get in. We've always made a great team," she pleaded.

"Is that true?"

"Yes, definitely, but I can't work with her, especially after what she did to me."

"How about if we tried to hack it right from here?" Kamryn asked.

"Could you do that?" Boucher knew it was possible, though he would raid the place anyway. "Okay, let's see how good you two really are."

"I said I wouldn't work with her," Sabino said.

"Ping, we don't have to work together. I'll do it, and you can just watch."

"Fine," Sabino replied with much distaste. "See if you can do it."

"Good. You can start immediately."

She started telling them how to hack into the church's network. She went to Sabino's computer and began explaining what she planned to do.

Kamryn tapped into the church's network via her old user name and password. Before leaving her position at the Church, she had left that door open, explaining to them that in case they ever needed her familiarity with the network, she could still have access. All they would have to do is call her, which they had on occasion. The program was written in a fairly new programming language called KSK, which meant nothing except that it was the initials of the woman who had invented it.

She was looking for the back door she had created as a means of bypassing the normal authentication process. Kamryn found the routines that she had written for the username and password. Then she came to it. The line said, "PasswordAuthentication yes." All she had to do was change that to "PasswordAuthentication no." She couldn't access anyone's files. She deleted yes and entered no and then saved the change. She then navigated to Shaul's folder and clicked on it. Nothing happened!

"What the hell," she said in surprise. She clicked it a few more times, and still it did not work. "I changed it. You saw me."

"I did," Sabino said. "Someone must have put an override protection where it can't be altered remotely. Can you find where they did that?"

"In practicality, no. There are millions of lines of code operating our network. It would take years."

"Scott," Sabino interjected, "I know the NSA has a lot of computing power. Is there any way you could contact them?"

"At times, agencies do exchange services and expertise, but again, Congress is just swamping the agencies with totally unnecessary red tape, and I'm afraid it would take a few days to get that to happen, and based on what we're dealing with, we simply can't afford to waste any time.

"I think Kamryn makes a few good points, especially relating to all the armed guards. Her knowledge could save the lives of some of my agents. You'll have to work with her, Ping. Just suck it up and do it. I'll get an FBI jet up here to take you both down. She'll be in handcuffs the whole time. We have plenty of evidence to get a warrant from a federal judge to conduct a raid. I'll get that in motion and contact our field office down there to coordinate six or eight agents as well as the local police to conduct it."

Chapter 17

Shaul and a few of the Elders had flown to Jerusalem to meet Jabbar Abu Shakra. He had received his instructions directly from the Elect one in person. Shaul had shared with him that he planned on a very quick tour of the area but would fly back the next night.

Now Abu Shakra was on his mission. There were no flights into Iran from most Western countries, so he had to fly to Ashgabat in Turkmenistan and then take the last leg of four hundred miles in a small Sky Cruiser, which used solar power for flight. Sky Cruisers had extremely long glider wings to they could sail the wind currents instead of using fuel like older planes. The landscape below was mostly mountainous and uninhabited. The ground was a beach-sand tan like that of some coastal resorts he knew. The small plane didn't make things easy. It was a bumpy ride in a cramped seat. There had been some greenery early in the flight, but not now. He didn't really care if he was tired or uncomfortable. His mission promised to bring justice to the sinners and reward to the righteous. The church's plan was to initiate the apocalypse by acquiring an Electromagnetic bomb and setting it off in New York City, thus setting in motion a nuclear holocaust. The energy gained from that knowledge kept him going.

Government officials would meet him at the airport and take him to the Ministry of Defense located near all the other Iranian government offices. Once, Abu Shakra had worked for the Iranian government. They had employed him to assassinate Gamal Bin Haji, the leader of the People for Islamic Rule, a group fighting against Iran's current government. He had been successful. They owed him a big debt, and he intended to collect.

The Sky Cruiser started descending. He began to rehearse in his mind how the conversation should go. What if they said no? What if they wanted more than the church could pay? What if they found out he was not a Muslim but a member of the Church of the Elect? What if …?

Through the things he had done in the past, he had led them to believe that he was a Muslim and against Western powers. Like in most Muslim countries, the Church of the Elect and other religions were not permitted to operate in Iran. If they discovered his true identity, they would try to kill him. That would be their mistake. True, he had no weapons or munitions, but he could easily kill with his hands. Silent and efficient, killing with his hands was intimate, pleasurable.

The Sky Cruiser touched down with graceful ease. He didn't expect such skill from a pilot working in such a downtrodden country for such a small airline, though their planes were modern. They stopped on the tarmac a hundred feet away from the terminal. The door of the small plane opened, and the few passengers got out. A single white sedan was parked there—waiting for him, he imagined. There were four men lined up in front of it. The two on the left were in disha dashas and turbans. The other two were in suits. He recognized two of them; one was Iranian, the other Russian. Boris Petrov wore the blue suit, and Waheed Fazlullah wore a turban. The Iranian was responsible for the assassination of the leader of an antigovernment holy war. Fazlullah was a hardline cleric and a member of the Red Mosque, a secret Shi'ite faction made up mostly of Russian Muslims but led by Iranians.

The two men in suits were speaking Russian. The Russian intelligence and espionage agency, XKS, had formed after Russia broke away from intense talks related to the Arms Limitation Treaty. Meaningful communications between Russia and NATO or any Western nation had not happened in nearly twenty years. Petrov was secretary of the State Security Council that oversaw the new XKS. Abu Shakra assumed, based on his size, that the other suited man was a bodyguard. The man was bigger than Abu Shakra, and Abu Shakra knew the agent would be well trained but not well enough to defeat him.

"Jabbar, welcome!" Petrov said in perfect Arabic, smiling. "It is so nice that we meet again." Petrov moved forward first, gave a slight bow, and then shook Abu Shakra's hand.

"It has been a long time, my friend," Abu Shakra replied.

"Allow me to introduce you. Waheed you already know. His associate is Maulana Arshard, who is a religious scholar of the Koran, our Alim. The gentleman to my right is Vadik Niktin."

Abu Shakra shook everyone's hand and expressed his pleasure in meeting them. Petrov gestured toward the car door.

"We will hear what you have to say at the Ministry of Defense building," he said. They all got into the car. The talk en route related to planned and actual acts against the West. It was also sort of a brainstorming session in which they threw out suggestions for future attacks against the infidels. Abu Shakra simply agreed with everything to avoid suspicion. These sinners would have their day, he thought. All these people believed Abu Shakra was there to make the purchase to kill Americans. How little they knew. They would supply the package that would set in motion eternal agony for the unrighteous, including these Muslims. Ironic.

Tehran Airport was in the middle of the city. The Ministry of

Defense was about a twenty-minute ride away. The car pulled up in front, and the men got out.

"And now it is time to talk business," Petrov said.

"That's why I'm here," Abu Shakra said as they walked up the stairs.

~ ~ ~

Brothers Ali and Dabir were thousands of miles away from Tehran. They had connections in all branches of the Chinese government, including the military. In order to purchase the twelve thousand rockets, the church needed someone from the Turkish military to help make the deal look legitimate. Five years before, Turkey had been at war with Syria. The church had created a program that gave support to surviving widows and families. General Shahr had lost a son, and the church had helped him through the grieving process. He was indebted to the church and came to Beijing to help. The church had convinced him to come along under the presumption that the missiles were for revenge against Sunni Muslims, because they were particularly brutal to Middle Eastern members of the Church. Twelve thousand missiles was a lot, Dabir admitted, but the Middle East was a big place.

Brother Dabir knew this was a big deal. The Chinese government had done deals this big with other governments and other terrorist groups. Dabir and Ali had been to China before on several occasions. The Republic had become very liberal over the past several decades. It allowed the Church of the Elect to preach in the country. Although much of China had become very prosperous over the past century, there were still some poor and destitute. The church had many programs in China, which cast them in a favorable light. The men from the ministry had agreed to meet with Dabir, Ali, and Shahr.

The general had made arms deals with the Chinese before, and he knew the two officials with whom they were making the deal.

They were meeting with Ching Sun and Yao Ming. They were in a room with a formal meeting table and chairs; small pots of tea and cups were placed by each spot.

"Sit down, gentlemen, please," said Yao in Chinese. Dabir and Ali understood some. Shahr was fluent, as he had done many arms deals here. "We will make this as quick as possible."

"Mr. Ching, Mr. Yao, thank you for meeting us," Dabir said in poor Chinese.

"We understand you want to buy some weaponry from us?"

"That is true," Shahr said, taking the lead. "We are hoping to buy a certain kind of rocket."

"How many do you require?" Ching asked.

"Twelve thousand," Dabir said. Shahr looked at him and gave him an I'll-do-the-talking look.

"That is correct," Shahr said. "Twelve thousand."

"What is their purpose?" Yao asked.

"Members of the church are experiencing persecution in the Middle East, and they will use them for revenge."

"This is very suspicious, a peaceful church wanting so many rockets."

"We will be using them in our arsenal too," Shahr quickly interjected. "The church will draw them from our storehouses as they need them."

"I see," Yao said, shaking his head as if agreeing. "Tell us a bit about the targets."

"They plan to attack infrastructure," Shahr said. "Trains, Electricity, water, food supplies."

For a moment, Ching and Yao spoke in a dialect that the Turks didn't understand.

"We will consider the matter," Yao said. "What type of guidance do they require?"

"That will depend on the power of the payload. What we want is something with massive amounts of destructive force. I will require an explosive called picanzite, or whatever you have that is your equivalent."

"We can arrange that," Yao said. "However, it will add a lot of cost. Are you sure something with less of a charge but a good guidance system wouldn't be better?"

Shaul had specified picanzite, and Dabir didn't want to disappoint him. If they came back with something less powerful, Dabir didn't know how Shaul would take it. He assumed Shaul had a temper like everyone else, though he did have a reputation for quietly resolving problems. *It's the silent type you have to look out for*, he thought. Dabir decided to step in.

"No," he said. "It must be picanzite. Can you supply that?" Shahr gave him another look. Dabir didn't want Shahr speaking for the church.

"Well, we will see if we can afford it before we decide on that," Shahr said. "Why don't we look a range of prices and options?"

"Why don't we start with what you specify and work down from there?" Ming said.

"Okay, then," Shahr said. "Let's start from the top. Picanzite—"

"The thing to keep in mind with picanzite is that it is extremely hot," Sun said. "Very hot. Each warhead will require that it be specially packed so that the heat will not harm the carrier. Even still, when it is ready to be fired, the attacker must shoot very fast so as not to burn himself."

"Very well," Shahr said. "We'll have to account for that. So, it must have enough power to take down a fairly large building, say five stories. The guidance system does not need to be anything fancy. Point-and-shoot will work fine. However, it must be accurate and able to be aimed with precision. The range should be at least one kilometer, preferably two. It must be very portable. And, of course, it must be cheap."

Both of the Chinese men laughed. "You must have a very large budget," Ching said, continuing to smile.

"What are you talking?" Shahr asked. The two Chinese again spoke in that other dialect for a few minutes.

Finally they looked at the three Turks.

"Nine thousand apiece. That's seventy-two million US."

"We can never afford that," Ali said. "That's ridiculous."

"That's almost double our budget," Dabir added. He got an empty feeling in his gut. Maybe they would go home empty handed.

"Don't worry, gentlemen," Shahr said to Dabir and Ali. "We can work out something equitable. Mr. Ching, Mr. Yao, what if we went with a lesser explosive?"

"We can't do that," Dabir said.

"You may well have to if your budget is so low," Yao said.

"How about less distance?"

The haggling went on for forty-five minutes. They finally decided a few molecules of picanzite would be enough, although the Chinese tried to talk them out of that particular explosive because of its heat and the fact that it was so unstable. Range of one kilometer. Point-and-shoot, no guidance. The final price was thirty-three hundred and thirty-three dollars for each rocket, or forty million in US currency. The money would be wired immediately, and production would start as soon as the Chinese government received the payment. Lead time would only be one month, as the factory had been nearly idle for some time and was desperate for work, which was also a factor in the cost. Dabir's excitement was hardly containable when he communicated this to Shaul through an IM. He couldn't wait to meet with him again. Judgment day would still happen on the American Independence Day, just like the Elect one wanted.

Chapter 18

Inside the computers at the NSA, alerts started going off. A communication from an insecure computer at the Chinese Ministry of National Defense had been encrypted and posted to the same instant messaging system Kamryn had used. The flagged words were *destruction, explosive, picanzite, Church of the Elect, Shaul Eitan,* and *apocalypse.* The technician called his supervisor, who in turn had been notified to contact Scott Boucher at the FBI if any of these words were together in any IM sessions or e-mails. But it was lost in the bureaucratic quagmire between agencies. Boucher didn't get the information.

Chapter 19

The FBI jet was comfortable. Boucher had sent four agents along with them. They would pick up another six agents from Texas as well. The plan was to ride six per SUV along with two local police cruisers as escorts. Boucher knew that Sabino had refined military training, so he granted him permission to use a firearm when they arrived. No way was Boucher letting Kamryn have one.

He had his favorite piece, Connecticut State Police Commemorative Pistol in perfect working condition with extra ammo and magazines and one very large knife.

Sabino had said nearly nothing to Kamryn during the flight. Kamryn had tried a few times to strike up a conversation, and he had done all he could to stop it. The ride from Logan to El Paso was about half over. Sabino was still upset that she had lied to him all those times they were together, even though she was claiming differently now. A number of times now she had told Sabino she loved him. She was like a software program caught in a loop. All of it must be lies as well. *How could I believe her?* he thought.

But an odd thing kept bothering him. Had he been in love with her? He was in a great deal of pain, and there was no way he could believe he had felt so strongly about her, so attached. He had never felt this way before. Always in the past he hadn't been able to care less if a woman left him. They were simply to have sex with and make babies. That was how society worked. Now he felt like this? The more he brooded on the situation, the worse he felt. If this was love, he didn't like it.

"Ping, please talk to me. Honestly, I didn't want to hurt you. How can I make you believe that?"

"Maybe you didn't, but what about this? Scott thinks there's a terrorist plot involved here. Didn't you even evaluate what the information you were giving might have been for? Didn't it ever occur to you that you were doing something illegal? Even if you do love me, how can I possibly trust someone who did something so blatantly wrong?"

"Because it was for the church."

"Oh, you're not so loyal to them. Why did you sell out at the first sign of trouble?"

"Simple. I want to be with you even more than I want to save the church. I want things to be like they were," Kamryn pleaded. "I'm not a bad person. You should know that."

"Oh, yes you are. How could you tell me all those lies about how much you just love my townhouse, about how much you like my cooking and wine choices, about how we work so well together … all of them. And now you claim you love me more than your sacred church?"

"You want the honest truth? Okay, I'll tell you."

"I can't wait."

"There are two reasons. One, I'm a member of the Church of the Elect—"

"We've established that," he said.

"—and I will claim that to the end. However, we trust in the Lord of Spirits that the day of reckoning will come. When it does, all of the fallen angels and their followers will live in eternal suffering. However, the righteous will live in peace on beautiful earth for all time. As I came to know you, I soon realized that you're a very seraphic person. You are a *righteous* person, Ping. If the apocalypse comes in our lifetime, you will go to the Promised Land. I want to be with you then. I want to be with you forever. I'm begging you to believe in your own goodness."

"So what's reason two?"

"Until now, I have never seen you mad. You are always understanding of other people's worries and shortcomings. It's your attitude toward others that I love. You are a very kind person. I knew that the moment we met. In my mind, from the very beginning I saw that we were right for each other. In France they call it *le coup de foudre.* Ping, you're the one for me. There is no other."

Sabino turned away and looked out the window. They were flying over massive cultivated fields. He wondered what state they were over.

Looking back, there were so many times Kamryn had seemed to be having a genuinely good time. They were a great team at work. They laughed. They made passionate love, and it wasn't just sex; there was a real connection. They shared common experiences. *They were good together.* She had been pleading with him to believe her from the moment they caught her. What if she were telling the truth? Well, so what? It wouldn't make any difference. She had hurt him too bad.

"Maybe you do love me. I suppose I might believe that. But I can't forgive what you did to me."

"But you will," she said. "I know you will if I persist. You're too good of a person. We were meant to be. That's the truth. You'll see."

"Don't get your hopes up," he said, still looking out the window. He really didn't want to talk with her. He paused for a moment to get his thoughts together. "You betrayed me, and I don't think I can forgive that. I have a large stake in the company. I don't know what the church has planned, but whatever it is, if it brings down Aquasuperior, it brings me down along with it. And what about my years of friendship with Meyer? Did you endanger that? But what I'm most upset with is that I was grooming you to be my replacement. I did everything I could to impress Meyer that you were right for the position. I trained you. I made sure you knew everything I did. I trusted you with *everything*. And for what? You screwed me and everything I invested in you. How can I forgive that?"

That brought nothing but silence. *What's left for her to say?* Sabino thought.

There was very little conversation for the rest of the flight. Sabino wondered what would happen once they arrived. Kamryn had mentioned that the sentries were heavily armed. But how heavily? That brought back to his mind his military experiences. There could be roadside bombs, snipers, automatic weapons, mines. Would they fight or take flight?

If these people at the Church of the Elect were planning something disastrous, they would be an extremely dangerous group. What if they got caught? He and Kamryn would certainly be murdered. Sabino knew scarcely anything about the church. They could be sadists, for all he knew. They could be tortured and then killed. But Kamryn was a member. She would know how these people were. He kept thinking that he should break the silence, suck it up, and actually talk with her about how dangerous these people were. She must know something other than the fact that, at least according to her, they had nothing but peace in mind. How serious would they be with all their firepower? Boucher judged them terrorists, and Sabino had nothing but respect and admiration for his friend. He wished he could predict the future. Sabino's heart pounded as he thought of the hazards that lay ahead. It wasn't fear. He had always thrived in dangerous situations like mountain climbing, SCUBA diving, and his time in the military, and there was nothing more thrilling than a blast of fresh air on a downhill run. He could fight, and he was good with a gun. He was looking forward to the challenge.

Chapter 20

Abu Shakra was sitting in a room that resembled a Moroccan tent. Most everything in the room was red and orange except for the Persian rug, which was a medley of golds, blues, greens, and reds that complemented the rest of the colors in the room. The couches had big pillows. The room had many tan and brown leather hassocks. Tables had lanterns with red, orange, green, and clear sections of stained glass. Hanging around the walls and ceiling were brightly colored curtains. The aroma of familiar but unidentifiable incense filled the air. There was classical Turkish music quietly playing in the background with drums, cymbals, and violin, no doubt to make him feel welcome. They were all sitting on couches that surrounded a small round table with the incense burner on it. One thing he knew for sure: Muslims were very hospitable to their own kind. For many years, Iran had been living off of sales of natural gas found deep below their long-since-depleted stores of oil. Theirs was the largest and only remaining supply in the world. For the present, the country had splurged massive sums of money on lavish luxuries throughout the nation. Abu Shakra, like the rest of the world, knew these resources would one day run out and they would plunge into extreme poverty like all the other Middle

Eastern nations, who had also run dry. Splurging billions on all of the opulence was foolish, he thought. They should have invested it instead for future sustainability.

Abu Shakra and Petrov had already been in contact through the darknet. They had also used private couriers, because there was no way any technology could snoop out information if the messages went back and forth in someone's mind or on paper and not through Electronic means. So Petrov knew the objective as Abu Shakra had told it to him. After the introductions, Abu Shakra started the conversation.

"As you know from our earlier communications, I am representing the Movement for Islamic Domination in this matter. They want to purchase Russian or Iranian technology—an Electromagnetic bomb. It will bring death to many American infidels."

"Where are you planning to launch this act of justice?"

"New York City."

"I see," Petrov said.

"That is very interesting," Fazlullah said. "That has been tried many times before, and none have successfully gotten past US borders. How do you plan to accomplish this?"

"One possibility is to transport it on a container ship."

"That has been attempted."

"I wasn't finished," Abu Shakra said. "I plan to hire Valik Alekseev, who is an internationally renowned smuggler. He will put the package in a container on a ship bound for the United States. The container will originate from a European country with which the Americans are closely allied."

"I think you are wasting your money," Mauland Arshard said.

"It is our money we will be giving you, and it is our risk alone," Abu Shakra said. "We wouldn't spend that kind of cash if we didn't think it would work. We have a good connection in Amsterdam that is a legitimate company that has smuggled many goods to the United States. We are very confident it will work."

"Okay, but once the event happens, the Americans will trace it to us," Petrov said, "and all hell will break loose."

"We have thought of that as well. After the sale, you will announce to the world that your arsenal has been compromised and a bomb has been stolen. Before and after the event, the Movement will claim responsibility, so the blame will be all on us."

"That will put a world of pressure on you," Petrov said. "All of you will be hunted until you are all dead."

"It is worth it for the glory we shall receive," Abu Shakra said, knowing it would actually be the glory of bringing about the apocalypse and death to the sinners.

"All that aside, gentlemen," said Arshard, the scholar, "let me quote from the Koran. 'He who killed a human being without the latter being guilty of killing another or being guilty of spreading disorder in the land should be looked upon as if he killed all of mankind.' What say you to that?"

"I say the Westerns are the murderers. America wreaks death upon our people. For the most part, Middle Eastern countries are out of oil. All they use is hydrogen, which leaves our cities poor and our countrymen out of work. They force us to buy their water like they bought our oil, and now it is we who are at their mercy. Our land is dryer than it has ever been, people are dying by the thousands from thirst or from drinking contaminated water. Our people are poor because we must buy their energy. Everyone is suffering. *They* are the killers, not *us*. What say you to that?"

Arshard put his palms up in the air, shrugged, and smiled. "You have a point," he said.

"So where does that leave us?" Abu Shakra asked.

"We owe you a favor, but this is something bigger than the world has ever known," Fazlullah said and then stood up.

"What is the cost?" Abu Shakra asked.

"We have talked about this," Petrov said. "We know you are a group that has survived the years and has done a lot of great work toward the rule of Islam. We will give you a break on the price, but there is to be no haggling. It is either this price or nothing. Five million US dollars cash."

That was under the amount Shaul had said he could spend. He grinned ear to ear, knowing the prophecy would come true.

"Done," he said.

"I say we do it," Fazlullah cried. "Death to the infidels!"

Then, one by one, everyone else stood and raised their fists in the air. In unison they all shouted, "Death to the infidels!"

After that, there was much cheering, jeering, handshaking, and praising of Allah.

Chapter 21

Enoch and Raphael stood next to the Lord, who appeared as a column of fire as bright as the sun, reaching as high as the eye could see. The Great One said unto Raphael, "Bind the hands and feet of Azazel, and throw him forth into the darkness: And make for him a place in the desert located in Dudael, and thrust him thereupon. Throw at him jagged rocks with sharp edges, and cover him until he lies in darkness. He shall live there to the ends of all time. And when the great day of judgment cometh, he shall be tossed into the fire like a twig. And ye shall heal the earth which these fallen angels have corrupted. Ye as well will heal the plague. The children of men will not perish because of the secret things the Watchers have disinterred and taught their sons. The whole earth is corrupted because of the works that were taught by Azazel: To him I blame all sin."

Then the great column of fire swirled and churned, and then the voice of the Lord of Spirits spoke to Gabriel:

"Take action upon these bastards and the damned, and the children of defilement and murder, these children of the Watchers. Pit them one against the other so that they shall destroy themselves in battle."

Again this mighty tower as bright as the sun swirled and churned and then commanded Michael, "Bind Semjaza and his accomplishes, who in their uncleanness have gathered with women to fornicate themselves for pleasure. After their sons have slain each other and they have witnessed the murder of their beloved children, lash them tight to one another for seventy generations in the deserts of earth until the great day of judgment cometh, and then they shall dwell in this land of fire for ever and ever. In those days, they shall be led off to the abyss of fire. Michael, you will destroy the spirits of the damned. And you will destroy the children of the Watchers, because they have corrupted the men of the world. Then evil will come to an end.

"Only then can the seed of righteousness and justice grow to great heights. It shall be the grandest of all blessings, and joy shall be forevermore. The righteous shall escape this land of fire. And they shall marry and beget thousands of children. They shall live in complete peace for all eternity."

The one who was witnessing these commandments from the Lord of Spirits to His angels slowly became overwhelmed with joy, and he started laughing.

He sat upright and opened his eyes. It was a strange place, unlike the familiarity he felt in the presence of the Lord. There were four walls and a door. A fan squeaked above his head that gave off a cool breeze. He closed his eyes and shook his head. This wasn't heaven. He was sitting in his office. He wondered what he had been dreaming about. Obviously, it was somewhere in the great book. That's all he ever dreamed about, and always as an observer, never a participant. What chapter? He tried to clear his head.

He opened his eyes. Though he was a little groggy, the images of the Watchers suffering lingered in his head. He thought of a world free of sin and full with peace. *Of course, it was chapter ten.*

In a moment, Brother Gabriel knocked at the door. "Elect One, you have an alert that just came through," he said.

"Thank you, Brother Gabriel." Shaul sat straight up in his chair and stretched, yawning. Then he rolled his chair over to his computer and opened up his IM account. Sure enough, there was one alert that he needed to go to the newsgroup and read the most recent post. He did that, and it said that Brothers Ali and Dabir had been successful in Beijing, and with his permission, they would wire the Chinese forty million for the arms. He posted back giving the go-ahead.

The day was now close to a reality. He only had to hear from Jabbar and everything would fall into place.

"Brother Gabriel," he called, and soon the big man stood in the doorway.

"Yes, Elect One."

"The time is almost here. Alert the elders and the brothers we have selected to come with us. Very soon we will leave for the retreat."

He knew no one would be able to follow him there. All along, Shaul had been very aware of the fact that the authorities could find out their plans in spite of all of the security they used. He had heard that the NSA had computers that could decode any message. Though that might have been a myth, he didn't want to take any chances with endangering the onset of judgment day. He knew the importance of being paranoid at a time like this. He would be calling the shots, and it would never happen if the law got hold of him to prevent the apocalypse. He must disappear.

July 4 was the day. Everything would come together in time; he could feel it. The days of eternal pleasure lay just ahead. The righteous would survive the apocalypse.

Chapter 22

Abu Shakra was sitting in a café in Tehran. It was crowded and noisy even at such a late hour, but the commotion lifted his spirits higher by the minute. His excitement about the deal he had just made brought goose bumps to his body. The thought of the end of all sinners filled him with joy.

He had just sent an IM through his mobile phone that the negotiations had been a success. He had told the Elect one that Petrov and Fazlullah wanted five million in US cash and not wire transfer. Could the Elect one arrange for that to happen, he wanted to know.

It was late in Tehran, near midnight. That meant it would be sometime in the early morning to midafternoon in Pecos, Texas. He sat at the computer for about an hour drinking coffee before Shaul's reply came through:

> I just corresponded with Brothers Ali and Dabir. They said they can get the money to you in two days. Read their post to see how and where to meet them. Praise to you on a great job! Thanks to you, the day of judgment is now possible. Shaul

It had been a long day, but one with great triumph. He would congratulate himself with the services of a woman. He could get away with it now, because the Lord would be joyful that the day would come, as he had prevailed in his mission. Abu Shakra knew great days lay ahead.

Chapter 23

When they had arrived at the El Paso airport, as Boucher had promised, there were two local police cruisers, each with two officers inside, and there were also two SUVs, one with six FBI agents and one for the four agents who had flown with Sabino and Kamryn. The vehicles were all in a row with a large, dark green El Paso SWAT vehicle taking up the rear.

It was a two-hundred-mile drive out to the Pecos compound. Sabino just knew Kamryn would be pushing the whole drive for him to please forgive her.

It was a long ride. Fortunately, the hydrogen cell vehicles drove very quietly and the air conditioning was nice and cold. Four hours later, they could see the tops of buildings at the compound. The chain of vehicles pulled up to the guardhouse with lights and sirens off in hopes of giving as little advance notice as possible. Two men came out and blocked the road. An officer blared over the speaker, "Step out of the way. This is an FBI raid!"

Sabino pulled out his gun.

The guards got out of the way and ran back into the shack. As they passed through Sabino watched as one of the guards picked up his radio and spoke into it.

"They're expecting us," he said.

"I know," said the agent.

The sounds of air-raid sirens screamed . They came closer to the campus, and people were running everywhere. Suddenly the cruiser in front of them blasted in two. *A land mine?* he thought. It was as if he had gone deaf. The ringing in his ears overtook his whole psyche. He was in awe from the destruction in front of him. Kamryn started yanking on his arms, but when she moved her mouth he heard no sounds. Then he saw the reason for her panic. Trailing big wakes of orange fire, several rockets were coming directly at them. Everybody was scrambling to get out of the vehicle. In sheer terror, he opened the door and yanked Kamryn out. She was still handcuffed. They ran. They were only a few feet from the convoy when the rockets hit, and just before they did, Sabino covered his ears. The vacuum created from the explosions sucked the wind out of his lungs. The blasts threw them fifteen or twenty feet. They hit the ground hard. One agent, he saw, was a ball of fire, dancing and then rolling on the ground. He looked at the catastrophe; all the vehicles were masses of fire and twisted metal except the SWAT vehicle. Then another catastrophe. Two blasts even larger that those before them exploded on both sides of the truck. It was totally destroyed. From his past experiences in Afghanistan, he knew they were IUDs. No way could anyone have survived.

Bodies were charred and dismembered. Suddenly, he heard gunshots. A few puffs of dust went up on the ground around him. He yanked Kamryn's arm, and they ducked behind a burning vehicle. For the moment, they were hidden by the plumes. There was a corpse near them, and Sabino patted out the little fires and started fishing through its pockets until he found some keys. He found one that might work, so he tried it on Kamryn's handcuffs and he hit the jackpot. They popped open and slipped off.

"Let's get the hell out of here!" he screamed, and started back toward the compound entrance. She resisted.

"No! They're monsters. I see that now. We must stop them," she commanded and tugged him in the direction of a building on the left they could use for cover. "Boucher needs that information."

They dashed behind the building, pretty well screened by the smoke. Sabino realized he had a cap gun in a tank battle. All he had was his little 9 mm and a few clips, whereas they had explosives, snipers, and Lord knew what else.

"Are you all right?" he asked.

"I think I cracked a few ribs. What about you?"

"I have what seems like a good gash on my cheek."

"Let me—oh, yeah, that's pretty bad. You've got blood all over yourself. I'll have to bandage that up later. I have nothing to do it with now. We've got to get to the admin building. See it?" She pointed. It was only about fifty yards away, and there were plenty of synthetic trees to duck behind.

"Forget it for now," he said. "I have to call Boucher." He took out his phone, but there was no signal. Then he thought, *Of course there isn't.* Exasperated, he said, "We're two hundred miles from nowhere. How the hell am I going to get a signal?"

"We gotta make it to the admin building. That's where the computers are."

"No. First we need to destroy their cache of weapons. Where do they keep all that?"

"Ping, I don't think we should waste the time. We really should just get what we came for and get out of here."

"No way," Sabino said. "The ammo the guards have on them now is limited. If we destroy their supply then they'll have nothing more to lay on us once we try to escape. Make sense?"

"Yeah, you're right. The ammo room is under the church stadium. There." She pointed. "They keep them there in case we're attacked. They can put everyone in the stadium and use them as human shields. Look on top. It's also where the guards are posted."

"Psssst," Sabino looked around. Behind a tree was a man in a tattered suit, one of the agents from the plane. Sabino motioned for him to come over with them behind the building. He aimed his pistol at the top of the stadium and fired a few shots. The agent ran over and leaped next to them.

Sabino updated him on where the sentinels were and his thoughts about eliminating the weapons. The agent agreed. He introduced himself as Special Agent Smith.

"Do you have another gun for her?" Sabino asked.

"We can't trust her."

"She pointed out the guards and their locations and also told me where they keep the munitions. We can trust her. Besides, it's fifty against three. Do you think we even stand a chance?"

The agent thought for a minute. "You're right. We'll probably never leave here alive anyway. Why the heck not?" The agent reached down to his foot and pulled out a small pistol, and then he reached into his coat and passed her a second clip.

"Put up your right hand," Smith said. "I now deputize you in the name of the FBI."

"How do you think we should do this?" said Sabino.

"That building there is closer. Then it's just ten feet to the stadium. We can cover each other, then run from there and go in a side door."

"What if none are open?" Kamryn asked.

The agent held up his piece. "Blast it open. Ping, you go first. We'll cover. Then you, Kamryn. Then me. Ready? *Go!*" he shouted and pushed Sabino into motion.

Sabino ran, zig-zagging between trees. Puffs of dust were erupting everywhere. Finally he reached the next building and pointed his gun into the air. He fired and saw Kamryn running. He shot more, as did Smith. She made it, and then the agent also made it, and again the three were together. They were now in a position out of sight of the sentinels, so they ran over to one of the side doors of the stadium. It was locked, but Sabino shot the doorknob, and it swung open. They peered inside, and it was oddly empty.

"I think stairs leading down are in the far corner. See over there?" Kamryn said.

There was no supplemental oxygen circulating inside. They were all out of breath, but Sabino knew they had to push on. They cautiously made their way over to the stairwell, but of course the door was also locked. The agent put his ear to the door and whispered, "I can hear people on the other side."

"Okay, here's what we'll do," Sabino said.

"I'm in charge here," Smith said.

"How much military training do you have?"

"Well, none, but they trained us at Quantico."

"I was a first lieutenant in the special forces in charge of fifty soldiers, an airborne ranger, and saw tons of urban action. I think I'm a bit more qualified."

"You're serious."

"Dead serious," Sabino said.

"Hey, go for it. What do we do?"

"We have no idea what's on the other side of that door, so we use a little shock and awe. We'll shoot open the door and come through, guns blazing. Shoot anything that moves, but conserve your ammo as much as possible. Obviously they know we're here, so it could turn into a hell of a firefight. If they shoot before we get through the door, we'll go with plan B."

"What's that?" Kamryn said.

"No clue. Check your ammo."

"I've only shot my first clip, so I think I've got ten or twelve left," Kamryn said.

"There's fifteen in that clip," Smith added. "I've got three clips left, also with fifteen in each."

"I've got about one and a half left. The door swings outward, so that'll be a bit more difficult. You have the most, Smith, so you shoot the doorknob. I'll pull it open and go in first."

"Let me do that," Smith said. "At least I'll serve some purpose."

"Fine." Sabino raised his gun, as did Kamryn.

"Ready? On three. One. Two. Thr—" Smith shot, and Sabino yanked the door open. They rushed through and saw guards at the bottom of the stairs lifting their automatic weapons, but the three were all firing by then, and the guards went to the floor before they even had a chance to shoot. They flew down the stairs. There was a main hallway straight ahead and two corridors, one to the left and the other to the right. Kamryn and Sabino went to one side and Smith to the other.

More sentinels appeared at the end of the hall and started firing instantly. The cement walls fractured with each deafening shot. They were pinned. Each time they peered around the corners, the volleys increased.

"What do we do?" Kamryn cried above the racket.

"We'll have to take a chance," Smith said. "On three we'll peek out and start shooting. One. Two. Three."

Simultaneously, they swung out and started shooting. Smith went down and screamed, but Sabino hit his marks three times, and Kamryn winged two. None left. Smith looked up. He had been hit in the shoulder and leg. *"Go!"* he shouted. They ran down the hall over the bodies. The two that Kamryn had hit were suffering. Sabino aimed and shot them both point blank.

"Two less to worry about," he said, remorseless.

To their right was a door with a man behind it with his hands up.

"Please don't kill me," he pleaded. "I've got a family. Wife and three little children."

"Open the door," Kamryn ordered with her pistol pointed at him. The man complied, and the two of them went into the room. They hit the jackpot. Pistols, various automatic weapons, grenade and missile launchers, boxes with C8 stenciled on them, fuses, crates of Electronics. Everything a demolition expert like himself needed.

"What do we do?" Kamryn said.

Sabino was smiling. "We're gonna blow this frigging place to the moon, that's what. Grab a few boxes of the C8, then take my knife and open up the box labeled Electronic blasting caps. I'll find the blasting transmission controls." He looked at the man. "Where are they?" he demanded and again put the pistol to his face. The man instinctively threw his arms in front of his face and cowered to the floor.

"No, no. Don't kill me."

"I'm not going to kill you. Just show me where you keep your supply of radio controls."

"They won't do you no good," he said, still crouched with arms up.

"What the hell do you mean? And if I find out you're lying, I really will kill you."

"The controls have all been preset to the mobile phone numbers of two of the elders. They are the only ones on campus that can set them off."

"Damn!" You had better pray you have timers."

"Yeah...yes. Do you want Electronic or manual?"

"You're really starting to piss me off," Sabino shouted. "Did it sound like I told her to pull wires?"

"N...no."

"Then get me a goddamn Electronic one." The man stood up, ran over to a waist-high shelf, and pulled out a blue box. Sabino looked at Kamryn. "How are you making out?"

"How many of each do you want?"

"Twenty pounds of C8 and four caps. Make sure the numbers on *all* caps match. If they aren't from the same batch, the Electronics might not sync right, and we could miss the ones that don't match. Put them gently on the desk."

The man returned with a small timer along with a single battery, which he inserted before placing the device on the table. In a few seconds, Kamryn gently placed four packs of the explosive on the table as well and dropped the caps next to them. Sabino flinched and shouted, "Carefully, I said." He inserted the caps in each block of C8 and then placed them throughout the room next to each of the munitions he thought would yield the largest result. He smiled. *This is going to be Armageddon,* he thought.

"Let's grab some stuff first." They both took bullet-proof vests and automatic weapons with plenty of magazines. He then lifted a grenade launcher from a rack as well as some munitions for it.

"We'll have five minutes, not a second more."

"Ping," she said.

"I know. You love me. I get it." He set the timer and said, "*Run!*"

She pushed on the man's back. "Let's go," she said, and they all started running down the hall. They arrived next to Smith, and she started to pull him up. "Help me, damn it," she barked at the man. Together they pulled him up and started to ascend the stairs. They opened the door, and as they had feared, there were half a dozen guards outside with weapons pointed in their direction. There was gunfire going off all around the campus. Sabino thought, *There must be quite a few survivors.*

"We've got about four minutes," Sabino said. Without hesitation, he fired off a grenade, which blew apart the large synthetic tree where they were hiding. Body parts and torsos flew. "Three and a half."

"I can't make it," Smith said.

"Never leave a man behind," Sabino replied. "If you want to live, grab that side," he ordered their prisoner. They ran with Smith between them as fast as they could.

"We've got to get that information for Boucher," Kamryn said.

"Yes, which way?"

"Admin's right there."

The campus was in full disarray. People were running everywhere: parents with kids, old couples, teens. The parking lot was nearly empty. Sabino heard a small plane taking off, and for a very brief moment he glanced at it as it ascended into the evening sky. He imagined it must be the church leaders. He saw two people dressed in SWAT attire running between two buildings, shooting as they ran.

"Three minutes," Sabino counted down. They dashed the last hundred yards to the admin building and went through the front door. "Pray we're far enough away to survive the blast. Let's go to the far end of the building."

"Computer room's in the middle," she said.

"It'll have to do. How far?"

"Third floor."

"We'll never make it."

"We have too."

"Is there a stairwell nearby? We'll have the best chance there. About two minutes to go."

"This way," Kamryn said and guided them toward a lit sign that said "exit." She opened the door for them, and they went inside.

They reached the second floor and Sabino said, "Stop. Less than a minute. Sit down and cover your ears." Everyone did so. It felt like an eternity before it happened. The noise was unimaginable.

The building shook violently. Light from the explosion brightly illuminated the room in a horrifying flash of orange. They heard airborne glass and furniture through the door. He imagined a huge crater. The lights went out momentarily, but soon they all heard a hum coming from the basement, and the lights came back on.

"Generator back up," the man said and smiled as if trying to get their approval.

"Kamryn, where to now?"

"Leave me here," Smith said. "Come back for me when you're done."

"Fine."

"This way," she said, and they all started climbing the stairs to the third floor. They opened it to the computer room. Papers were still in the air, and half a dozen men were feverishly working at various terminals, yelling to each other. "Are you okay? Check. Terminal seven. Raul, running? Yes …"

Sabino shot a series of bullets into the ceiling and shouted, "Everyone out. Now!" They panicked and all went to the exits. "Where do we go?"

"The main hardware is in that room," she said.

They started moving, but their prisoner stood still, face washed over with fear. Sabino pointed his weapon at his face and commanded, "Let's go."

"Oh, Lord of Spirits, please help me," he whined and moped along.

They entered the room, and it was cold. Sabino took a deep breath and found there was also extra oxygen in here. He inhaled several times and began to feel the positive effects immediately. Briefly, they all savored the moment, and then Kamryn said, "I have to sit there."

She sat down and followed the navigation path to the password routine. She changed "yes" to "no," saved it, tested it, and they were finally in. They copied the private key and e-mailed it to Boucher. Then she added a bit of code that would send copies of all correspondence throughout the world on the network to Sabino's computer in Boston as well as Boucher's and Meyer's. She wrote a flag for certain keywords so that they wouldn't get useless messages from every computer on the network. Then she manipulated Shaul's decoding software, the private key, in such a way that they could read all of his encoded messages.

Encryption technology, because of the Great Attack, was only as good as it had been in the early 2000s. To encode something required both a public key and a private key. A very large random number was generated by the software. This was the public key. Anyone with it was able to encode messages. The only one that could decrypt them was the holder of the private key.

"Now let's have a look at Shaul's account," she said.

Somehow he felt more comfortable with her now. He had a better sense that he was in control of things because of recent events.

Shaul had kept a folder on his computer of all his instant messages and darknet posts. They had already sent a copy of the folder and the network's private key to Boucher so he could decode messages as well.

They found posts about the coming day of judgment, which was supposed to happen July 4 of this year. They were especially trying to find out about specific targets, though they hadn't gotten that far yet.

They were moving fast when something else went wrong.

"Don't move," came a voice, and Sabino felt a muzzle pressing against his neck. "I'll take those." The guard lifted the machineguns from around their shoulders.

Sabino had been standing behind Kamryn. He turned slowly to see three sentinels out of the corner of his eye. His heart pounded. He felt his gun tucked in the waist of his pants.

At that instant, Kamryn stepped in close and put her leg behind the guard with the gun. At the same time, she struck him under the chin and grabbed his left hand. The force knocked him to the floor on his back. Holding his hand, she whacked his throat with her heel while pulling up on his arm for extra force. Kamryn let go of his arm, which flopped to the ground.

In the same instant, Sabino pulled out his pistol and drilled two holes in each of the other guards' foreheads. He bent over the dead body and took back the two automatic weapons.

"Let's get out of here," Kamryn said.

"Where's your car?" Sabino demanded of the man and again pointed his automatic at his face. He thought the man looked as if he was going to start crying.

"Please, my family!"

"We're not going to kill you as long as you give us the keys to your car."

"It's the light blue wagon next to the pond."

"Give me the keys." The man dug into his pocket and handed them over. He was shaking as if he was ravaged by delirium tremens.

Kamryn grabbed Sabino's hand and jerked him toward the door. Hand in hand, they ran through the doors and down the hall.

"Stop right there," bellowed a deep voice. At the same time, they saw a large man with a polo shirt that had "enforcement" embroidered on it. He was in the hall straight ahead of them. They stopped cold. Sabino knew his skills in Muay Thai were supposed to be pure aggression. Never back down, he had been taught. Sabino saw that the guard was raising a pistol, but he knew from his special forces experiences that his speed would be far greater than his enemy's. He raised his machinegun instantly and let off a burst, hitting the man several times before he got off a single shot.

Sabino's limbs tingled with the adrenaline pumping through

his body. He was lost, and driving anxiety told him to get out. The administration building was very large and like a maze. He couldn't remember how to get out.

"Kamryn, which way?"

"Follow me." She stepped over the man and Sabino followed. They ran to the end of the hall and she turned right. He looked back at the man, who was now sitting up, one hand on his chest, the other holding a device at his mouth. He must have only stunned the man. Sabino caught up, and they turned left and left again. At the end of this newest hall was an exit sign lit in red. They went through the door under the sign. Smith lay there, stabbed several times. They wouldn't be bringing him home. There was a window to his right and stairs to the left. Looking out, Sabino saw a dozen more men in gray running toward the building.

"Aw, shit," he said and shot half a clip of automatic fire in their direction. A few went down.

"Quickly," she pleaded. They bounded down the stairs three and four at a time. Two more flights to the bottom.

The door below flew open, and an enforcer shouted, "Stop!"

They turned back and rushed through the second-floor door. Sabino heard two sets of footsteps coming up the stairs.

"We gotta take 'em," he said.

He checked the magazine in his gun, reinserted it, and pointed it at head level toward the door. The doors quickly opened.

"Freeze," he commanded, and the two guards stopped. He aimed at their faces with the automatic. "Don't move. You'll die."

Sabino and Kamryn glided around the guards, back to the stairs, and then leaped down the stairs to the bottom. Sabino fired a random shot to keep them at bay. He opened the door to the outside, but there were men rushing toward them. Turning around, they went back inside. In a flash, he realized there was still gunfire going on outside, but his thought shifted back to their own situation. There was a sea of cubicles. The walls were about five and a half feet tall, just high enough for the guards to see them if they stood upright. Two came out of an entrance on the far side of the room. One of them pointed.

"There they are. You go that way," Sabino heard him shout. He pushed Kamryn's head down below the height of the wall. Automatics and single shots were going off. Kamryn grabbed his hand.

"Come on," she said, jerking his arm. "There's an exit this way."

They ran, staying low. This was a worse labyrinth than the computer floor. He couldn't imagine how anyone could lay out an office in such a confusing pattern. They could hear the guards yelling to each other. One was sounding nearer each second. They ran this way and that. Sabino was completely lost. He was relying totally on Kamryn. For an instant, it occurred to him that he was supposed to be mad at her, and then his mind switched back to their escape.

Quickly, they turned another corner, and there he was, right in front of them, his back to them. He had a gun in his hand. Sabino put his finger to his mouth to signal to Kamryn to be quiet. Sabino approached the guard silently, crouched low. When he was nearly next to the man, the guard quickly turned toward Sabino and started to raise his pistol. Before he could shoot, Sabino kicked the gun hand with all his force. The gun went sailing over the cubical walls. The guard swung. Sabino ducked. While the guard was off balance, Sabino wound up for a shin kick to the ribs. He pivoted on his foot, swiveled his hip while aiming his shin toward the side of the guard's chest, and whipped his knee like a piston. The action brought the speed of his leg from zero to thirty miles per hour in one second. The resulting impact thrust nine hundred pounds of force against the guard's ribs. There were audible cracks, and Sabino could feel the man's bones cave in under the pressure. The man went down immediately and started gasping for breath. The broken ribs punctured his lungs, which then collapsed. Sabino realized there was pain in his shin, but he knew his leg had not been broken by the force; years of conditioning had toughened his bones.

Before Sabino could catch his breath, the other guard saw them from about twenty-five feet down the aisle. He had a pistol and raised it. Sabino and Kamryn pivoted and went back as a shot went off. Rounding the corner, Sabino heard the bullet zip past him. Two more blasts, and Sabino heard the rounds penetrate the cubicle walls around them. Sabino raised his machinegun above the partitions and let off several blind shots.

"Where the hell is the damn exit!" he yelled in frustration. He raised his head above the walls. It wasn't too far. The remaining guard saw him. Sabino looked to the other side of the room. They had come quite a way from where they came in. A few more turns, and he knew they would escape. Ducking back down, he noticed he was still holding Kamryn's hand. She tugged his arm again, and they moved toward the door. He saw it. There was no one there. They ran through to the outside. There were no sentinels in sight, but he could hear them calling to one another.

"Where's the car?" He simply didn't know the layout of the campus. "Which way do we go?"

"This way," she said, breaking into a full sprint. He had never run against her. He was a long-distance runner, not a sprinter. She was faster than he had imagined. She was pulling away.

"Wait for me," he called. He was out of breath, not because he was out of shape, but because of the reduced atmospheric oxygen. Kamryn stopped for a second while he caught up. Two guards were right behind them. They ran again. He was gasping for air and felt he couldn't run much further.

"It isn't far," she said, not seeming winded. "The pond's right over there." She pointed. "See the blue wagon there? Hey, it's a convertible. How weird is that? I've never seen one."

They both ran as fast as they could. He looked back and saw that they were pulling away from the guards. When they rounded the corner of a building, he saw the car. As they came closer, he reached into his pocket and took hold of the keys. Kamryn reached the car first and flew over the driver's side and into the passenger seat. Sabino came to an abrupt stop when he smashed into his door, fighting to catch his breath. The keys went into the air. There was a gunshot behind them. Kamryn opened her door and leaned onto the ground. She picked up the keys and quickly inserted them into the ignition. The car jerked forward.

The hydrogen engine in the car propelled them forward like a rocket as soon as he pushed on the pedal. A bullet went past their heads as they pulled away. Another bullet smashed the driver-side mirror. He pushed her head down. They tore down the road, and in an instant they reached one hundred … one ten … one twenty.

His adrenalin pumped like never before.

"Wow!" he shouted.

Kamryn turned around.

"They're following us."

"They'll never catch us," he yelled. The road was straight and flat with no bumps. The car was level at one twenty, which he thought was amazing for a family car. He kept glancing into the rearview mirror and watched the distance growing between them. The cars got smaller and smaller. The airport was two hundred miles away. At top speed, he was feeling safer now. All he could see were little specks behind him. He let off the pedal and relaxed for a minute. His breathing was back to normal. They cruised for about half an hour. Sabino watched as their speed drained the fuel tank of hydrogen, but he judged there would be enough to make it.

Then he saw it. A string of cars coming straight at them from the direction that they were heading. "Oh, shit. What the hell do we do?" he said.

"Turn off the road into the desert," she said.

"Now?"

"Got any better ideas?"

"I guess not." He stepped on the breaks to slow down and then exited the highway into the desert. It was very bumpy, but the car handled well at fifty. He drove about two miles away from the road and turned toward the left and headed in the direction of the airport. There were small shrubs all over, and they blocked his view of the road. He looked in his rearview mirror and saw his column of dust in the air. He was sure they would see it. It was getting extremely bumpy now. At fifty, they were bouncing all over the place. Frequently, the undercarriage bashed the ground below. There were lots of bangs from rocks hitting the chassis.

There was a slight valley in front of them. He could see for miles. The landscape blurred from the heat. The sun beat down on them.

At that moment, he realized that if he slowed down, the trail of dust would be at a minimum. Perhaps then they wouldn't find them. He slowed way down to ten miles an hour. He glanced behind them and saw that, indeed, there was very little dust.

"Smart," Kamryn said, apparently reading his mind. "We're really not that far from the road. They could still catch us."

"Should I drive farther away from the road?"

"Don't you think?" she said.

"I guess that's our best bet."

They went slowly for about fifteen miles into the desert, and then the car simply stopped. He looked at the gauges and saw that the hydrogen reserve had never been replaced and the primary was drained. That bastard back at the campus had definitely avoided practical maintenance on his vehicle. Sabino thought, *What an idiot! Did he have no plan for emergencies?* He got out of the car and stared back toward the compound.

"What do we do now?" he said, and suddenly despair overcame

him. The temperature was easily a hundred, more likely a hundred five or one ten. They were stranded in the desert, sun blazing, and at least twenty five miles away from the road. He looked around the car to see if there was anything he could use. A three-quarters-full gallon jug of water, but nothing else. Who knew how far they were from civilization? "What the hell do we do now?" he whispered.

Chapter 24

It was now just seven fifteen, and nightfall would come on in a few hours. In the distance, they faintly heard helicopters. They both wondered if Boucher had sent them. It was too late. They were stuck in the middle of the Texas desert.

Then they would have to contend with the cold desert night. Kamryn had grown up in desert country, outside of Santa Fe. In her youth, she and her parents often had camped in the desert and taken hikes during the mornings and evenings. From this, she had learned that the best thing would be to travel only at night and stay in the shade during the day.

"We can survive this, Ping," she said. "You must know all about living out here with all of your special forces experiences. What would you do?"

"Truthfully, I don't know too much about surviving in the desert. My assignments were mostly mountain training and gigs in Afghanistan, along with many covert trips to Russia's north where they perform certain activities that I can't really disclose."

They had a lot of preparations to make, so she figured they had better get started. She checked her cell phone to see if they had service and they didn't. *This is a perfect opportunity*, she thought.

She would get them through this predicament, and Ping would like her again when she saved his life. She saw his cheek. Blood had run down all over his neck and cheek and onto his shirt.

"The first thing we need to do is take care of that cut on your cheek," she said. Kamryn knew they had to conserve water to stay alive, so she needed to be as skimpy as possible in cleaning his cut.

"Does it hurt?" she asked.

"Not much."

"Where's your knife?" Sabino had it strapped to the side of his calf and pulled it out.

"What do you need it for?"

"Lot's of things. First things first, though." She looked in the trunk for a first-aid kit, then in the glove compartment, but there was none. She took the knife and cut up the driver's seat cushion. Then she carved out some of the padding. Kamryn then faced him and looked at the cut. She saw that it was fairly deep and that there was metal shrapnel still in there. He was lucky it hadn't hit him in the eye. Just another inch higher and he would have been blinded.

"Hold still. You have metal in there," she said and carefully pulled it out without cutting herself. She dampened the foam with water and started cleaning the wound. She had to admit he had a high tolerance for pain. He barely fidgeted. In a few moments, she was finished. The foam was covered in blood, and his cut was still bleeding. She hacked out a fresh piece of foam.

"Okay. Done," she said, handing him the foam. "Keep this against the cut until it stops bleeding. We'll need to cut the rooftop off once it's dark. That'll give us portable shade during the day while we're in the desert. Don't talk unless you have too. It'll make you get thirsty."

They got the canvas off without tearing the material too badly. Then she cut out the plastic back window. Kamryn folded up the canvas as tightly as she could and then rolled up the plastic window.

She was excited about both the challenge and the opportunity. She knew she could survive in the desert. She had done so many times; it would even be fun. Now she would have plenty of alone time with Sabino. This would be a perfect chance to really show him what a nurturing person she was. *That will change his mind.* She could feel it. She felt really badly about tricking him. He really was a righteous person and she loved him. When the day came, he would certainly live among the godly. She wanted to live in peace with him forever. She had realized that soon after she started working at Aquasuperior. She wanted him. She needed him. She would make him love her.

"For now, we'll cut the leather on the seats," she said. "We can fashion these into sacks to carry gear over our shoulders. I imagine the jug of water will get very heavy after a few miles, so we'll need all the help we can get. Also, we will need to cut up some of our shirts. Since all we have is short sleeves, we must cover the rest of our arms. This will keep the perspiration from evaporating off of our bodies, which will aid in fighting dehydration."

She was trying to think of what else she could do to keep them alive. There were many things along the trail they could use, like the occasional prickly pear cactus. The plants weren't as sparse as one would imagine, considering what little moist breeze there was came off the tiny trickle that was left of the polluted Pacos River. And then she remembered almost the most critical item. "We'll need to make some hats as well."

She started making the knapsacks using the leather and the wire that held the seams of the seats together.

"We'll stay here until about eight o'clock, when it's a bit cooler," she said. "Then we'll cut the top and walk all night and stay in the shade during daylight to conserve energy and water. We'll stay here until the stars start to come out. Then we'll start walking."

"How the hell are we going to find our way at night?" he said angrily.

"Calm down," she said, knowing that with a clear sky it would be no problem. Soon it would be time to show Sabino how to survive. That would change his mind.

They stayed in the car for about an hour and a half and drank as little as possible, using just enough water to wet their lips. She cut the canvas top and rolled it up. They could see faint twinkles in the twilit sky. By that time, she noticed, his bleeding had long since stopped.

"Look to the west. No, no, that way." She pointed. "That's west. Do you know your constellations?"

"I don't have a clue."

"I'll show you some when it's darker. Come on. Let's start walking." She walked very slowly to conserve energy. He kept complaining, wanting to go faster. When it was dark and almost cold, she started talking.

"On the celestial equator, due west. That's where my constellation, Aquarius, is located at this time of year at this time of night. Of course it varies. I'll show it to you." She spent the next ten minutes helping him differentiate which stars were in Aquarius with marginal success. She was trying to keep his mind off their troubles; she would talk about the stars, a subject that had always fascinated her.

"You know my birthday is February thirteenth, right? Well, that makes me an Aquarius. My father always pointed out my sign when I was young. Actually, he showed me lots of constellations, but my own sign I learned when I was very young.

"On the Babylonian calendar, the corresponding month is called *arax arrat zunne*, which means the month of the rains. The Babylonians only associate it with a region of the sky. In those days,

GU was the zodiacal sign of that month. It means dry measure. The Hebrew word is associated with jar, or picture, which is commonly associated with the overflowing urn of Aquarius. In medieval times, astrologers associated it with the planet Saturn along with Capricorn, and because of that astrologers considered the sign cold and dry. More on the cold later."

This seemed to be holding his attention, so she told him more.

"If you're into Greek legends, the story tells of Ganymede, a handsome and young prince of Troy. When Zeus first saw him, he thought that Ganymede would make an excellent cup bearer. From here, there are two versions of the story. The first is that Zeus had his pet eagle carry Ganymede to Olympus. In the other version, it was Zeus himself who brought him to Olympus, but he disguised himself as an eagle. Well, whichever the case, once there, Ganymede had to put up with Zeus's bitchy wife, Hera, who thought Zeus had rather, um, you know, strong feelings for the boy, if you catch my drift. Another reason she didn't like the boy is because he replaced their daughter's position, the goddess of youth, as cup holder. Zeus, however, wouldn't put up with her crap. He traveled at all times with the boy, who impressed everyone with his kindness. The boy convinced Zeus that the people needed water, so Zeus eventually made him the god of rain and placed him among the stars.

"Are you impressed with my knowledge, or what?"

"You're not really into all of that astrology crap, are you?" he said.

"No, but I've always been into its intriguing history. I could tell you a bit about all the signs," she said, glancing up at the constellation to keep their direction on target. She seemed to be doing pretty well keeping his mind off of the cold night air. It was helping, she could sense it, so she thought she would ramble on a bit more if he would let her. "Do you think my personality fits the traits of an Aquarius?"

"I have no idea, but I'll bet you're going to tell me."

"Tell me a bit about my personality."

"Well, right now I'd say you're trying to entertain me."

"That's right. And you've also called me creative and stubborn, which are Aquarian mannerisms. On the down side, I'm supposed to be cold and impractical, but I don't think I'm either. I'm a very affectionate person, as you know, and I'm practical enough to think through difficult situations. Those don't fit. However, I am quirky sometimes, so that's one of my great features. Your sign is Capricorn. What to know about that?"

"Do I have a choice?"

"No," she said.

For the next several miles, she told him about the mythology and traits of his sign and most others. They walked at a brisk pace to keep warm. The sun peeked over the horizon. Daylight was breaking. Kamryn was a hiker, and she thought they had covered about seven or eight miles during the night. Neither drank more than a few drops of water, and their pace was slow. Judging by where the constellation Aquarius was, she had navigated southwest. They would make it to the road the next night. She wondered what would happen then. Would the church guards be looking for them? Would someone on that deserted road pass by to save them? But she knew that during the day they would face their greatest battle yet: the full wrath of Mother Nature. Still, she knew they would make it as long as they had water. The sun was already lighting up the sky. It was almost six in the morning.

"We'll stop here and use the canvas to make a shelter from the sun before it gets too hot," she said.

"Won't we fry under the canvas?"

"It won't be that bad. Don't worry. All we have to do is relax and conserve energy. We'll drink as little water as possible, just like we've been doing all night. Let's look at that cut." She had cut a dozen pieces of foam before they left, and she pulled one out now. She conservatively poured water on it and started cleaning. The wound was all red. That could turn into a problem.

She put on a confident face. Secretly, however, she knew it was going to be extremely difficult for him to conserve their water, because he had never been in a situation like this before, and even under the shade, like he said, they would fry—especially him, with his injury. Her ribs were uncomfortable, but she had always had a high pain tolerance, so she would endure without complaining. Once, while participating in a marathon, she had sprained her ankle and still had run the twelve miles to finish the race. She was off her feet for a few months afterward, but she had proved to herself how tough she could be when necessary.

Chapter 25

Boucher was riddled with grief and regret. The satellite's observance software had been delayed—yet another consequence of the Great Attack—and now the live feeds of the church compound showed destroyed buildings, bodies, and trails of black smoke. As soon as the feeds came through, he called in the Army and sent a large party to his comrades' rescue. Now he was watching skirmishes and firefights around the campus. The squad had been looking for Sabino, Kamryn, and the agents, but they had found no survivors … and no Ping or Kamryn. He didn't know if that was good or bad.

In the past fourteen hours, a lot had happened at the Boston FBI office. Since Sabino and Kamryn had infiltrated the Church of the Elect's network, Scott Boucher had been receiving past and current e-mails and messages. Kamryn had showed him what a great amount she was able to contribute, and now he was actually glad he had allowed her to go. He notified the director of the FBI in Washington, who immediately ordered the terrorist unit into the investigation. The director had informed all the national security agencies as well as the president of the United States. Now it was unquestionably a matter of national security. The president ordered that it not be leaked to the media to avoid a panic, but everyone knew it was only a matter of time.

Every available agent in the unit was assigned to trace the Internet traffic that related to the church and all of its activities. Boucher remained in Boston and was in a control room with a dozen other FBI agents. Their network was connected with Washington and many of the Asian and Middle Eastern branches. After Boucher showed the agent in charge of the Boston office what he had found, the entire Bureau was convinced that the Church of the Elect had a horrifying act on a massive scale well under way.

They were connected with the NSA, and past e-mails and posts that used encryption other than the church's private key were being decoded one by one. All this was thanks to either Sabino or Kamryn, because one of them had managed to send the private key. Boucher realized how lucky it was that he had sent Sabino and Kamryn, although he was now extremely fearful for their safety.

Shaul Eitan's name and "the Elect One" were the most common signatures that came up. The names Brother Dabir and Ali kept coming up also. There wasn't any easy way to see if they were on the terrorist watch list, because they were very common first names. That would take time and a lot of manpower, so the director was assembling a team to handle that. They decided initially to focus on the name Jabbar which came up quite a few times; however, there was no last name provided in the signature. That name was less common and would be easier to find a match for. They actually had thirteen Jabbars on record, each with a different last name, and the agents were now trying to narrow it down to one.

They knew the Jabbar in question was in Tehran conducting negotiations for something that was costing him five million US dollars. But what? In his correspondence, Jabbar also mentioned several names. Maulana Arshard was not on any lists. Waheed Fazlullah came up a few times. The FBI had a lot of documentation on him. He was a Shi'ite and had been involved with terrorism for all of his adult life. Currently, he was active with the Red Mosque. He was a very dangerous man who was very good at pulling off acts of terror and inspiring scores of people to come over to the anti-Western side. He had been involved with many arms deals with various countries and radical groups. It seemed that now he was selling something to Jabbar, who was acting as an agent for the church.

The last name Jabbar mentioned was Boris Petrov. He was known as a former Russian intelligence agent and also had supplied weapons to radical groups. There was no question that Jabbar was dealing with something big, but what was it? Small arms? Missiles or rockets? Drones? Outdated remote control fighters? Or was it something far worse, such as nuclear, biological, or chemical weapons?

The only person on the team that didn't have Middle East connections was Boucher, but the director put him in charge of the investigation because he had been the one to crack open the case. All the other agents had informers in the region or actively worked with other agents who had them.

After many calls, much correspondence, and time spent tracing down informers, the agents narrowed the list down to five possible Jabbar terrorist profiles. Boucher called a meeting with each of the special agents in the various countries from that region. They were all on a live video feed together. Five of them had dossiers relating to the Jabbars who were active on their terrorist list.

"Here's the way I see it," he said into the camera. "This particular Jabbar would have to be highly successful in order to be trusted with this special task of procuring whatever he was ordered to secure."

"Well, we know that," said the agent from Jordan.

"Let me qualify that," Boucher said. "This man would have to come in under the radar with many successful tasks. Perhaps such an accomplishment would be a political assassination. Perhaps victories in leading battles in any of the warring countries. Perhaps running a training camp. Maybe he was in charge of some terrorist attacks, or even many. This guy would have to have the support of many major terrorists throughout the region. So whatever his accomplishments, they would have to involve sound political decisions, at least in the eyes of his associates. Does anyone have documentation on such a person?"

"I have one," said the agent from Afghanistan. "Jabbar Hashmi. He was alleged to have been in charge of smuggling large quantities of heroin out of here to the United States and Europe. The file says he was responsible for the murder of nearly everyone in a village where the people tried to sell to an outside manufacturer."

"I have one also," said the agent from Syria. "His name is Jabber al-Badri. This was a political assassination. You're probably all aware that a sheik from the United Arab Emirates was killed two years ago. His motorcade was traveling at about sixty miles an hour. A roadside bomb went off at precisely the right time to kill him. It says here that after the others tried to escape, they were all attacked by RPGs and there were no survivors."

"Okay, who else?" Boucher asked.

"I have a Jabbar Abu Shakra from Jerusalem who is a mercenary. He has led others in Darfur, Beirut, and Gaza. He is also known to be involved with arms deals with Sunni factions as well as radical Muslims. Most of all, he is known as a smuggler."

There was a silence. "Great. That narrows it down to three. Will you please trace them down and find out everything you can about them? In the mean time, I'll get the panel in motion to sort through our files and see if we can't find out more about the two members of the church, Brothers Dabir and Ali.

"I want to set up three task forces of four men each to catch whichever Jabbar is our man. Each team will have one agent assigned to a Middle Eastern country who will lead the team. The other three will be out of this office. You will trace the individual's movements through his passport activity. I want to know where each has been and where they are now. Work with your informers to fill in the gaps. We want to pull pictures from passports and distribute them throughout the area as well as Europe and the US transportation and customs agencies. When we know who is doing this business for the church, I want him brought in, if possible, for further questioning.

"I am also making arrangements for two other task forces. One will be to track down those two that made the deal in China. Any available personnel that are interested, please see me after the meeting. The other team will be involved in setting up a raid on the Church of the Elect's compound in Pecos, Texas. We'll search their files and computers and interrogate resident church members as well as people in the local town. Again, I'm looking for volunteers. Are there any questions?" Boucher asked. Silence. "Good, let's get to work."

Chapter 26

They were temporarily living at the church's religious retreat outside of Richmond, Virginia. Shaul had communicated with the surviving guards back at the campus. It seemed that the authorities had sent a wave of Army special forces to destroy the compound and everyone there. His sentinels had been communicating through satellite phones, as there was no cell reception there.

Luckily, he and the others had already fled, first by plane and then by bus, and were seventeen hundred miles away. Shaul knew that it would only be a matter of time before the authorities found out their plan. They would have to find a safer place. When they left, they took with them several hard drives, including all those with church membership lists so that the authorities wouldn't know how to trace them through affiliated people. He was familiar with the names and residences of many of the church's major donors. It would be no sweat to keep ahead of the law. If they caught him, the apocalypse would never arrive.

Now he had to think about how to put everything into action. He would have to distribute the rockets to his people in every country so they could destroy the desalination plants. He had hired a member of the church who owned a worldwide shipping company, an Emma

Van den Broeck. Her company was based in Amsterdam. She was an expert at mass distribution and smuggling large shipments from Southeast Asia to destinations worldwide. Van den Broeck had said that because each of the Chinese rockets and launchers could be broken down to fit into a large suitcase, they could be packed and shipped like that. They had decided to put them in baggage that looked as if it held medical testing equipment. Everything was fake. When a customs official opened one up, he or she would see a bogus laptop and three instruments custom fitted into foam packaging. Under that was the rocket, which was twenty-four inches long, and the launcher broken down into two pieces that snapped together; each piece of the launcher was also two feet long. That was how the Chinese delivered the weapons. It had added another five hundred thousand dollars to the cost to make all the custom suitcases, but it had been done, and on time.

She had arranged for them to be shipped to the Netherlands, because they were friendly with China, and from there they could be shipped to industrialized countries that would be less suspicious of containers coming from the Netherlands. Over the last fifty years China increasingly had become known as shadier and shadier when it came to its exports. The Chinese government turned a blind eye to (and sometimes even encouraged) trade in drugs, knock-offs, illegal pharmaceuticals, and weapons to terrorist groups, so most nations distrusted them. She had paid off some customs officials at the port to look the other way, and now Shaul learned that they were in a massive warehouse ready to be transferred to the church brothers around the globe who would bring forth the day of judgment. They were to be shipped in containers to the different countries, and the brothers would pick them up and then destroy all the plants.

He wondered how all of them would get past customs in the various countries, but Van den Broeck assured him that the cargo on container ships was rarely thoroughly inspected. They might lose a few, but most would make it, surprisingly. He was still worried though. The US targets would be particularly hard to hit, and getting the rockets through American borders would be most difficult because of the development scanning technologies that could see the contents inside of a container; each one was carefully examined. For several years now, the US had had the strictest antiterrorism policies, the best technology, and the most efficient administration in the world.

That left the logistical problem of sending thousands of brothers around the world to carry out the mission. The expense was astronomical. In the millions. Then there was all the booking of flights, hotels, cars, interpreters, and exchanging local currency for bribes where necessary. What a nightmare. The money was available, thanks again to Brother Michael. But the bookings! For travel arrangements, the church had always used local travel agencies. They didn't use the Internet to buy tickets and make their own arrangements, because it would cause massive distribution of church credit vouchers, and besides, even though travel agencies were nearly extinct, many groups still used them because they liked the personal service and there were no worries about the details. However, this plan was far too large for a mom-and-pop operation. Shaul had his assistant find out what travel companies were the largest in the world. Brother Gabriel looked to travel industry trade magazines to find that out. They decided to split the travel bookings between the three largest agencies. All of them assured Brother Gabriel that the bookings would be done on time. They all bragged about larger assignments. One had arranged for twelve thousand people to go to a religious revival in Oklahoma. Another had booked nearly ten thousand flights for the Olympics two years previously. And the final one specialized in getting large groups to sporting events. Most of these efforts involved getting thousands of people to a single destination. This job meant getting thousands of people to different locations. Nonetheless, all the agencies claimed they could do it. After all, each agency claimed to have handled much greater numbers.

The next problem was the item Abu Shakra was trying to procure. That was the contingency plan, his insurance in case all the desalination facilities weren't destroyed. The purchase required five million dollars in cash. Shaul knew about terrorists. They were not to be trusted. What if he gave Jabbar the money and they killed him, keeping the currency for themselves? What if the product was poorly designed and failed to wreak its intended destruction? But Shaul was familiar with the victories Jabbar had realized in the past. He understood that many Middle Eastern heads of state trusted him completely. He had a reputation for getting things done. If anyone could pull it off, it was Abu Shakra.

Shaul also wondered if the FBI or any other agencies were onto Abu Shakra. After all, by now they obviously had some knowledge of the operation. Though he had never mentioned anything specific in his postings, they both had mentioned names and the countries Abu Shakra had traveled through and the money he needed. Shaul would have to hook up the computer he had brought with them and warn Abu Shakra that the law might be looking for him.

Shaul also knew the FBI would be looking to catch him and his brothers. His wife had wanted to stay behind, because she felt the campus was their home and her children lived there, but Shaul had convinced her to flee and had assured they would meet again in paradise after the apocalypse had come to pass. Shaul and the others would have to leave the retreat as soon as other lodging arrangements could be made. The airports most likely would have their pictures. He would have to look up the closest church member who could help them escape.

He set up his computer and skimmed through the list of members. He found someone who was associated with a bussing company in

Richmond. Shaul thought that if they could get to New York City, they could disappear into the landscape until Independence Day. New York City was near where Abu Shakra was to let loose the wrath he had procured from Iran, anyway, so it would be fitting that Shaul be nearby when it all happened.

But the troopers would be looking for them and could easily find out they were in a bus. He thought about traveling to Pennsylvania, as there was another retreat there, but he decided that might be suicide. He got to work on looking up people in that state who would be able to help them. There were a few very wealthy members near Pittsburg. There were six of them traveling together—Shaul, some computer people, and Brother Gabriel. His kids had gone to the West Coast along with his wife, as they collectively felt that it would be best if they were sheltered there until the day came.

The Watchers would be trying to stop judgment day. That would be the ultimate peace. The church was the peacekeeper, not the Watchers.

It was June 16. Judgment day was only a few days away. He couldn't wait.

Chapter 27

Ninety-one percent of the global population had passports in the form of microchips implanted in the backs of their hands at birth. This included most of those from less developed countries who would never need them. The exceptions were the smallest underdeveloped countries in Africa. It was just one of those Orwellian conditions of modern society. Even the Middle Eastern countries went along with this type of passport, because governments—even revolutionist states—don't like terrorists attacking their own countries. Bombings were bombings and murder was murder no matter the philosophy of a country's government, so all modern nations went along with it.

The FBI had been tracing the movements of the three Jabbars. They located them all. Hashmi, the smuggler, had last entered Syria and had a known residence in Damascus. Syria had a good relationship with the United States, and they told Boucher's associate that Hashmi was thought not to have passed outside of Syrian borders. So he was out. The political assassin was living in Juddah, Saudi Arabia. It was a resort city on the Red Sea. He had been there for a few years, so it seemed he was either retired or on an extended vacation. So he was out.

That left Abu Shakra. He was the man. In the past three weeks, he had gone from Boston to Istanbul to Ashgabat in Turkmenistan and finally from there to Tehran. They only had one tip on him when he was in Iran, but it was a big one. An informer they had managed to plant in the Ministry of Defense had seen Abu Shakra walking through the building with two Iranians and two Russians. Interpol, who operated the entire passport network in Europe and the Middle East, were the ones who had the last record of him flying into Tehran. The agency pulled up his picture and personal information—height, weight, eye color. Interpol offered this information to the Iranian government, but they refused to help. They said they had records on Abu Shakra and he was a friend of the Iranian people. Boucher would have to wait until Abu Shakra left the country before a tighter net could be cast over him.

It was Scotland Yard who traced down the two known as Ali and Dabir. The Yard worked with Interpol to trace all the flights coming into Heathrow Airport that had any two people on the same flight that had those names. There had only been six flights that had such a pair of passengers in the past week. The Yard tracked the previous movements of all of them and found that only one pair had traveled together for an entire itinerary, which went from Istanbul to Beijing to Heathrow to Amsterdam. They had full names, pictures, and personal information.

The NSA noted a communication from Shaul to Abu Shakra. The message was posted on the usual darknet and was rerouted through a computer located in Orlando. The local authorities and the FBI tracked down the street address of the computer through its IP address and planned to raid the location within hours.

In the message, Shaul told Abu Shakra to bring the package to New York City. He would receive further orders once he arrived.

Shaul also noted that the law had raided the campus and that Abu Shakra's cover might well be compromised.

~ ~ ~

Jabbar Abu Shakra was a professional. He had performed in the underworld and understood the need to hide his identity and was well connected throughout the Middle East. He was well versed in the art of evading the wrong people. He had traveled incognito on many occasions, and he knew that from now on, this mission would require just that. Also, the package had to be smuggled into the United States. After he had his new look, he would contact Valik Alekseev, who worked, as luck would have it, out of the Ashgabat Airport. Alekseev was a great smuggler, a good friend, and one with a proven track record, and his proximity to the delivery was another reason Abu Shakra had wanted to work with him. He planned to send Alekseev a picture so that he would recognize him.

Abu Shakra asked his Iranian friends to arrange for a new identity. The government granted his request and offered to pay for it. He was currently in the rather affluent section of Tehran. There was a forger, a very successful one, who could give him new identities with matching passports.

"I will need three false identities," he said. "Can you arrange that?"

"Of course. We work with the morgues. A lot of the corpses there are intentionally not reported as deceased. The passports are cut out of their hands and replace your existing one. This is the *cutting* edge of forgery, so to speak. A little joke in the business."

"How will I look like them?"

"We will sElect someone who is about your height and weight. That will be tough for you, because you're tall and husky. But we will succeed. We cut out their microchip, and after we take yours out, we put in the new one. Then we create a special mask that will look just like him and function well enough to appear perfectly natural."

"That's fine here in Iran, but what about when I'm in Europe or the United States?"

"I can assure you," the forger said, "that our network is global. We can arrange further implants and synthetic masks nearly anywhere, including the United States. It is expensive, however, because it has to be done in a sterile environment. I hope you have lots of cash."

"Your government has agreed to pay for the identities. Here is their letter," Abu Shakra said, handing him an envelope. The forger opened it and looked it over.

"This will be fine," he said. "There's a morgue five minutes from here. Let's go there and see what we can find."

~ ~ ~

The warehouse in Amsterdam was alive with activity. Church workers were packing the suitcases with the rockets into individual cartons. The cases were designed to reduce the heat emitted from the picanzite as much as possible, though it would still show up on very sophisticated infrared equipment. The hidden rockets were packed in the center of a skid and surrounded by other cartons, strapped together, and lastly put into containers to go on cargo ships. The idea was to ship one or more containers to each country that had desalination plants. After arrival, the rockets would be shipped to distribution points, and the brothers would be on their way. Not much trouble was expected, though in a few countries bribes were standard fair. The global economy was so great in this century that almost all countries imported millions of dollars in goods, so containers arrived daily in shipping ports, airports, and trucking terminals. The Middle Eastern countries imported less than many others, because their economy had been in decline since the oil ran out, but they still had a lot of residual cash in their coffers.

Brothers Dabir and Ali were watching the activity from a catwalk that overlooked the storage and assembly area. The size of the warehouse easily equaled a dozen soccer fields. The section where the packages were being put together was small compared to the rest of the warehouse. Products from all around Europe, Africa, and the Middle East were temporarily stored there to be shipped around the globe. There were overhead lifts that picked up the containers and transported them outside the warehouse, where another lift would move them onto the ships at the dock. From their height, they could see many forklifts moving merchandise to be packed into the containers and lifted out of the building by the hoists above.

The technology was old but efficient. Each container had a UPC label attached with routing information. Containers from the Middle East and (less often) from Southeast Asia were routinely inspected by customs authority. That was why van den Broeck had arranged the labels to say the containers originated from various countries in Europe. That made them practically above suspicion.

They had been reading the posts on the forum. It was apparent that their identities had been revealed. Because of this, the brothers had practically hibernated in the warehouse so as to not been spotted on the streets. There were two foldout couches that they slept on. They were determined to see all of these packages delivered to their destination countries. Some had already gone, but there were many to follow.

Chapter 28

The time was six thirty in the morning. Both Sabino and Kamryn were dead tired from walking all night, but Kamryn had just finished explaining to him that there was still a lot of work to be done before they could rest.

Before they stopped, she had told him to start looking for any kind of depression in the ground. He didn't know why. Unfortunately, everything was flat. His cheek was burning, though he knew he could stand the pain.

"We'll have to dig," she said.

"What are we doing?"

"Let's start right next to this bush." She took the tire iron out of the backpack and started digging out a ravine in the ground. "We'll make a depression and then put the canvas over it. Then we'll cover it with the dirt that we removed. When we're finished we'll crawl under it. The dirt will act as insulation from the sun, and the excess canvas will provide shade for our heads. Cut some brush down, and I'll keep up with this. Let's set down our guns and get to work, okay?"

He didn't complain. Her idea obviously was a good survival technique. He figured there must be an equally logical explanation for the brush. They were small, dense, compact, and hard to cut. He immediately broke out in a sweat.

"We'll want to finish this as fast as possible," she said, "before it gets too hot. Drink little sips if you need to. We'll need eight or ten little shrubs."

Soon he had eight of them. She said those were enough. She had finished the trench. It was only about six inches deep. Kamryn put four of the bushes on either side of the ditch and then spread the convertible top over them. Apparently, they were to provide space for air circulation. He started throwing the gravel over the canvas, and she joined him. It was now five past seven and warming up. Sabino took off his shirt and placed it inside the shelter to lie on. They crawled underneath, bringing the water with them, and then lay flat on their stomachs. It was cramped but much cooler than standing in the rising sun. Sabino wondered how hot it would be by noon.

"We can conserve water if we don't talk," she said. "In truth, we should be drinking a gallon or more each day and at least as much when we're traveling at night. Obviously, we don't have nearly that and we must get by with a bare minimum. If we drink a quarter-gallon a day combined, we have enough for about a day and a half or a bit more."

"What then?"

"I hope we'll be out of this mess by that time. But if not, we can always improvise."

"How's that?"

"Last night, I mentioned prickly pear cactus, like that one." She pointed. "With a sharpened stick and a knife, they're easy to gather. Stab 'em and cut 'em off with your knife. Taking the thorns completely off can be a chore, and if you get stabbed it's easily infected, but once we're done, peal off the skin and dig right into the meat."

"How do they taste?

"Well, some species from Arizona and New Mexico are really quite sweet. Some people, if they've got a mind to, can pick enough to make jelly."

"So, good then?"

"We're in a real arid part of Texas, so not so much. But certainly it'll keep us alive."

He had never realized that Kamryn was such a survivalist. She had known about navigating with the stars, and now all this. In spite of her deceiving him, he was deeply impressed. He had a whole new admiration for her. He supposed he could be mad at someone and still have a great deal of respect for that person as well.

"Now we'll sleep," she said. "Try not to sleep on your left side, and if you must, try to keep your cheek on your shirt and not the ground."

The ground was hard, and Sabino realized that if he did sleep at all, he would be very stiff when he got up. As tired as he was, he did not think he would be able to sleep. How could someone nap in the daylight? He took his improvised knapsack and rested his head on it.

"I'll do my best, but I'm not sure I can," he said. He lay there for what seemed like hours, but he kept an eye on his watch, and barely fifty minutes had passed. He was getting hungry. Recalling that people could survive on water for many days without food made him feel a bit better, but he still felt the hunger pangs. What would it be like tomorrow? Sabino wondered. Finally, he couldn't take it.

"Are we going to starve to death, or what?" he asked Kamryn. She didn't answer. He looked at her, and she appeared to be in a deep sleep. "Damn," he said. He had to get to sleep. He tried to lie still and rest. It was bright out; how could he sleep? He was never able to sleep during the day. Even during his special forces night assignments when he was supposed to sleep before a mission, he had never been able to. It had often put him at a disadvantage compared to some of his squad. There was a rock painfully pushing against his side, so he wiggled around and removed it, bumping into her as he did so. She simply moaned and rolled away from him. He was wide awake, and his muscles were aching. His cut burned. He touched it and saw a bit of fresh blood on his finger. *He had to sleep.* He looked at his watch, and it was ten o'clock. No sleep yet. Now he was really thirsty, and his feet hurt. He tried to drink lying down, but it dribbled out of his mouth. He squirmed out of the shelter, managing not to wake Kamryn, slid outside, stood up, and stretched. His lips and throat were extremely dry. He took a little sip and swished it around his mouth and then swallowed. After doing this twice more, he was still thirsty. He gulped hungrily at the jug. Finally, he was satisfied.

Sabino thought he should clean his cut before lying down, so he poured quite a bit of water on a piece of foam. He dabbed at it and held it on the wound until the bleeding stopped.

Now his feet ached.

"How the hell am I going to walk tonight with this pain?" he said aloud. He sat down and took off his shoes and socks, then started rubbing his feet. The dirt was very hot, and the sun quickly heated up his exposed skin. He drank more water. He managed to get himself into the shelter but woke Kamryn in the process.

The effort made him thirsty again, and he made his best effort to drink lying down.

"You better got some sleep," she said. "You won't be able to last all night if you don't, and no, I didn't mean that in a sexual way. But of course, if you want …"

He was almost fed up with her little comments. He was too tired to argue. He merely said no thanks.

"And take it easy on the water."

"I can't. I'm so thirsty, not to mention wide awake."

"At least try to lay still and rest. Maybe you'll nod off for a bit."

"I'll try, but I don't see how anyone can sleep in daylight like this. It's too hot."

She simply stayed motionless and said nothing. The hunger started again. His mind simply would not settle down. He put himself on his back and stared at the canvas directly above him. There were only about three inches between his face and the canvas. He drank some more, then closed his eyes and tried the best he could not to think about anything but being tired. Remembering back, it occurred to Sabino that he had learned self-hypnosis. A long time ago, he had been foolhardy enough to smoke cigarettes, and the self-hypnosis had hastened his quitting process. It was a skill that had served him well over the years. He had learned to concentrate deeply and implement it at will.

He thought about the energy gathering in his body and slowly leaving through his fingers … his arms and hands getting heavier … energy draining from his face … and out of his feet. He kept concentrating. He told himself that was one of his greatest assets: concentration. He kept thinking about his body being heavy, being tired …

Relaxing … sleeping … sleeping …

"Ping. Ping, wake up," came Kamryn's voice. Sabino opened his eyes. He must have dozed off. He had a vague recollection of a dream, but he couldn't think what it was about. Immediately, the burning in his cheek began again.

"I think I fell asleep," he said, ignoring the discomfort.

"You did. You were snoring."

All of a sudden, he felt the dryness in his throat. He was really thirsty. He got out of their luxury accommodations and remembered that she had said to take small sips, so he did at first. But the water was almost hot and didn't satisfy him. Like earlier, he took large gulps to cure the dryness he felt.

"Better take it easy on that," Kamryn said. "We have to conserve as much as we can. Wait a minute, how much did you drink?" Sabino held up the jug and saw that he had almost emptied it. He experienced a deep feeling of guilt. "Why the hell did you drink so much?" she demanded.

"I couldn't help it. I was afraid I would dehydrate. I had to drink a lot, and I had to wash out my cut."

"Well, Ping, congratulations. You just finished a whole day's water supply. Now we have enough for less than a day. I should drink the water, and you should go through all of the work of preparing a cactus."

"Kamryn, I'm sorry, but I couldn't stop," he said, lamely trying to defend himself. "It's like something that came over me. I had to drink."

"Oh, bullshit. You have no self control. That's all. You come from a world of self indulgence. You have no sense of conservation."

"I said I'm sorry."

"Sorry won't save our lives," she said. "Well, forget about it. We'll just have to deal with it. Let's have a look at your cheek."

They continued to talk while she doctored his laceration.

"It seems to have gotten worse during the day," she said. "There's no way to disinfect it. I don't know anything about improvised medicine."

"What time is it?" he asked without thinking to look at his own watch. He was trying to change the subject. The pain of her cleaning the wound was much worse than the last time she had done it.

"It's nearly five o'clock. How are you with that gun?"

"I'll bet I can shoot better than you."

"We need to hunt for something to eat. There are snakes out here, and maybe some mice, but they're a bit small to shoot."

"That's my choice?"

"Unless you want to eat insects."

"I'll put on my shoes," he said and started to grab them.

"*Wait!* Don't pick them up. I'll show you how to do it."

"I can't pick up my shoes?"

"Scorpions like to crawl into things. Pick it up by the toe and shake it upside down, then look inside. Don't put your hand or foot in there until you're absolutely sure nothing is inside."

He looked inside and didn't see anything, but he shook them anyway and looked again. Then he put them on.

"Thanks for the tip," he said. They walked around in the late afternoon heat but didn't find any game. The work of hunting made them very thirsty, and they drank a lot of their scant water supply. Soon, they packed up the site. The sun was almost down when Kamryn said it was time to walk. He was really hungry and wondered when he would have the opportunity to eat.

Like the night before, there was only a half moon. It was hard to see some of the rocks and smaller shrubs. Sabino stumbled many times; so did Kamryn. He heard her swear often. They rested several times and took stones and sand out of their shoes. She had told him that if they didn't keep debris out of their shoes, it might cause blisters and sores. That could be disastrous. If that happened and the sores got infected like his cut, there would be no way to go on. They would become stranded in the desert and die.

Kamryn, in spite of her advice to the contrary, talked most of the time they were staggering along. As they walked, she tried to coax him into conversations about relationships, but he avoided that as well as he could. She talked a lot more about various constellations and astronomy in general. It was about three o'clock in the morning when they decided to rest for a few moments. They were both looking up at the sky when they saw a shooting star.

"Do you know what causes that?" she asked him.

"It's an asteroid entering our atmosphere, I think."

"Bravo. Take a bow. You've just passed Astronomy 101," she said. The moon was low and behind them. He could barely see her but imagined she was smiling. "Do you know what the chances are of a life-ending asteroid hitting the earth?"

"Well, isn't this a pleasant subject. I have no idea."

"You can relax, at least for the moment. Asteroids capable of a global disaster are really quite rare. Only once every hundred thousand years, on average, is there a major impact with earth. They are called near-earth objects, and a hundred or so have been discovered that are half a kilometer to a kilometer in size. As their orbits change over time, there is an increasing chance that they will hit us. One could come visit us in only a few thousand years, or maybe much longer. No one knows.

"Of course, there is a much smaller chance that one will hit us in the next ten years."

"Of course," he said.

"But rest easy. The technology for diverting a large asteroid is good. We would know many years in advance that we were on a collision course with one. Scientists would have plenty of time to develop the means to knock it off its course. But that's not my plan at all. Even though now I feel that the way the church is creating the end is a severe act of terrorism, I'm still a member of the Church of the Elect at heart. I believe that one day, life as we know it will end. Sinners will suffer, and all the good people will be left on a heaven-like world. I hope I have been good enough to be one of the chosen few. I know you will. You're so kindhearted. I hope we both go together."

"First, let me say you're a damn hypocrite, because you're saying that the church is actually a terrorist organization, and at the same time you're also saying their theology is something you believe in."

"An example," she said. "Back in the twentieth century, there were a lot of acts of child molestation within the Catholic Church. Many people left the church because of that, and yet many millions of Catholics stayed the course, and their faith in the church remained strong. Same with me. What the Church of the Elect is doing now will cause much suffering and pain, and I don't agree with it. I would much prefer the apocalypse be brought on by the Lord of Spirits. Can you see that?"

"Maybe just a glimmer. Still, I think you're weirder than I gave you credit for."

"Quite a compliment," she said with a smirk. "So what do you think about what I said? I think you're a terrific person, and you'll live in eternal peace with me."

"I don't think so. I'm not as nice as you may think." Sabino knew now that she had forgiven him for drinking all that water. She could always twist something into an innuendo, however.

"Believe me, you are. Anyway," she continued, "one of the closest approaches came in 2002. The asteroid was called 2002ny40. It passed within about 540,000 kilometers of Earth. An even closer call was on December 9, 1994. It slid by us by a mere 103,500 kilometers. That's really close, considering the moon's average distance from earth is 384,000 kilometers. The closest near-earth object is called 2047kk42. It was discovered in 2047, as the number implies. That one's orbit passed only 89,000 kilometers away—so close it's scary.

"Every time I think of the apocalypse, I think of you. I want to be with you forever, if you ever manage to forgive me."

He paused and thought for a moment about some of the things she had said. He supposed it was possible that civilization could come to an end because of an asteroid, much the same way an asteroid had struck when dinosaurs roamed. He wondered how mankind would survive if the earth again had a humongous asteroid strike. Desolate? The earth was getting worse by the year, and it seemed that it would ultimately become that way and that the church was only bringing it along sooner. What would it be like with no water? Millions—no, billions—would die from dehydration. Sabino went silent as he thought of humanity's fate, whether it came sooner or later.

"Are you afraid to die?" he asked her after his contemplation.

"No. Not at all. I would rather the apocalypse be quick and in my lifetime, but if not, I will still have eternal life. I think we've rested enough. We should get going." She stood up and he did the same. "I wish I could see your cheek in this light. How does it feel?"

"I won't lie. It hurts."

"I really don't know what to do about it. I'm stuck."

"I'll just have to live with it until we get out of this mess. Not a problem." Occasionally, his head was beginning to spin, but he didn't tell her that. Sabino didn't want to worry her.

He saw her look up at the sky, and they started walking southwest again.

He had started out practically hating her on this trip, but he had to admit all her expertise had kept him alive. She had a vast knowledge of the heavens and other subjects they had never discussed. He saw her in a whole new light. He didn't think he could ever trust her again, but he sure admired her more than he ever had before.

Chapter 29

They had made it to William Wilmont's residence. William Wilmont owned a steel company located in the industrial section of Pittsburgh. Wilmont lived in Fox Chapel, a small town northeast of the city, which was a community loaded with multimillion dollar homes. Wilmont's house had eight bedrooms and nine baths; there was plenty of room for Shaul and his entourage. Shaul realized that some church members didn't live simple lives like he had in Texas. A basic existence with little luxury was best, but the church needed big donors like Wilmont, so in these cases, in order for the church to thrive, it was okay. They gave enough of their money and were entitled to material goods.

His computer guy, Brother Norman, hacked into distant computers of lesser church members. He arranged it so that they could read posts and send e-mails from these remote computers to make it more difficult for the law to trace Shaul's location. It was simple, the hacker said. You hack into one computer, then into another from that location, and then another and another. Pretty soon, the authorities were tracing down hundreds or even thousands of locations trying to get to Wilmont's computer. By the time they got to the end of the trail, Shaul would be long gone.

The police didn't suspect Wilmont, because they didn't have the membership list, and without that, there was no way to find out who might haven take Shaul in. That was even better, because Shaul could send secure e-mails, and the police wouldn't know who to intercept them from. He had corresponded with members of the church in Amsterdam and Tehran that could hand-carry messages to the brothers and Abu Shakra.

Abu Shakra needed the money. Shaul arranged it from the Wilmont home. Two days before they left the campus in Pecos, he had e-mailed church elders in Europe, Africa, and the Middle East. Shaul felt the request had been safe from snooping eyes, because he had sent it through a secure e-mail system. They were to put together five million dollars, smuggle it over the Iranian border, and meet Abu Shakra at a specified location outside Tehran. It would be fairly easy. They could fly into Ashgabat in Turkmenistan, because customs people were easily bribed there, and then drive through the mountains to the meeting point in Iran. If they tried to go through customs in Iran, officials there might take the money and see to it that the courier disappeared. Abu Shakra had said in his last communication that the drive would take about two days. As soon as he arrived at the rendezvous location east of Tehran, Petrov would meet him there with the package, they would make the exchange, and then he would be on his own. The job of smuggling the package into the United States on time would be completely left to his expertise.

There was also the matter of shipping the rockets. Shaul had also communicated with Brothers Ali and Dabir. The containers in which the rockets were packed had already been shipped to the most distant locations, such as Australia and Japan. Van den Broeck had predicted that it would take about three weeks to get everything delivered. Shaul reflected on how well she was doing. Sometimes he was amazed at what mere women could accomplish. He never thought of women as particularly smart but believed they should just keep house and produce babies.

Wilmont even had a chapel in his house, and that was where Shaul was contemplating all these problems. He was sitting in one of the chairs and preparing to give a quick, ten-minute service for Wilmont and the brothers at ten o'clock. He planned to interpret from memory a section out of the book of Enoch. They were all there, but he was still thinking about the unfolding events. Finally he stood up at the front of the chapel. There was a stained glass window behind him.

"Brothers," he began. "I am going to give you my interpretation of a particular section of the book called 'the Blessedness of the Saints.' It is a parable about the righteous and the Elect. It says the righteous and the Elect are indeed blessed. They will live in the sun for all eternity." He motioned to the backlit window behind him. "For the sun shall shine for all of time. These days shall linger slowly until the end of all time. And for the righteous and Elect, they shall have the unending blessing of the Lord of Spirits. The holy in heaven shall seek the secrets of the righteous and the Elect after the darkness has passed. And the brightness will shine upon the earth. Do you think there will be an end to this light? No, I say! It will continue forever. But first the darkness must be destroyed.

"And brothers, that is just what is going to happen. We shall bring on the apocalypse and the end of the Watchers, I vow to you. Then peace shall be with us all forever. I warn you: the sinners are trying to stop us, but they will fail, because the angels of heaven are with us. And the Lord is with us. We have become united as one. Together we shall stop the darkness. The time is near—less than three weeks away. These days of the shining sun will soon warm our bodies for all of time.

Chapter 30

It had been a very hot night, and it was even hotter at six thirty in the morning. They were working on the shelter to hibernate for the day, and they both had worked up an intense thirst. Kamryn tried to make him conserve water, but in spite of her pleading, they both drank a lot while making their shelter. Now they were down to about sixteen ounces. It had been a hard, slow night.

"I think we covered about … maybe ten miles? It's hard to say."

"We're getting low on water," Sabino said.

"We'll have to cut up some of the cactus pretty soon, I reckon," she said when they finished their work. "I still can't see the road; can you?"

He was looking southwest like she was. There was no road in sight. They hadn't heard any sign of helicopters in quite a while, so either the noise was out of range or their business was done and no one was looking for either of them. At this point, they hadn't eaten in two and a half days. Sabino had long since learned how to ignore the hunger pains. He wondered if that was how it happened to everyone who was slowly starving to death: first terrible hunger, then the body's acceptance that no food was coming. At least Kamryn talking took his mind off of things. He knew people said you never knew someone until you lived with them. In a sense, he had been living with her for the past few days. There was a nurturing side to her that he never had seen before but seemed to come naturally to her. Now he was confused. She had really screwed him back at Aquasuperior, but she had more than made up for it. She had done her best to keep his spirits up, and she had tried as hard as she could to keep his cut clean. Despite her efforts, he could feel the pain getting worse. He realized it was either infected or getting that way. In spite of the heat, he often had the feeling that he was breaking out into cold sweats. At times he felt dizzy. Perhaps the cut's infection was getting into his system and slowly poisoning him. When he touched it, the laceration felt puffy and hot. Kamryn must have seen him do that.

"Let's have a look at it," she said. "It's definitely infected. There's puss. Try not to touch it. That's probably how it got infected in the first place—from you playing with it with your dirty hands. It might have been okay if you left it alone." She poked at it. Then, in a snap, she pulled her hand away.

"I could have caused it," she said. "I didn't think to wash my hands either before I touched it."

"Why would you have forgotten that?" he said.

"I was so concerned about saving water that it didn't ever occur to me to do it. Now we'll have to use some of what we've got left to wash our hands as well."

"What happens if the infection gets worse?"

"I don't know. I know nothing about infections. We'll just have to play it by ear." She washed her hands and dampened a fresh piece of foam and gently started wiping at the wound. He hated the fact that she used the foam. He realized that it wasn't sterile and most likely had contributed to his infection, but what choice did they have? As a matter of survival, they had to conserve water, and the foam aided them in using as little as possible. The water felt good on the wound, but her actions caused more pain. "I got all the puss off. Try not to touch it, please. You feel okay to put up the shelter?"

"Sure, I feel fine, though I wish I had something to eat."

"We'll finish up our little home and then hunt for something."

It took another twenty minutes to finish. They drank more water, but both conserved as much as possible. Then they left the camp. He held the gun. They left the water back at the site. After an hour and a half in the heat, they finally heard a rattling noise. He stopped in his tracks and she did too.

"It's a rattler," she said. It was right in front of them, poised to attack. "Shoot it."

Sabino aimed the pistol at the snake's head. Suddenly, it struck out toward them and then went back to its upright position, the rattle still sounding. He aimed again and fired. The snake lurched into the air and dropped motionless.

"There's our dinner," Kamryn said. She went over and kicked it. The snake simply flopped over. "It's dead," she announced and picked it up just below the head.

"We're actually going to eat that?"

"Yup. It's better than you think. Besides, do you want to look for something else?"

"How are we going to cook it?" he asked as they walked in the direction of the camp.

"We're not. One, we don't have a frying pan, and two, making a fire would take too much energy. We'll have to eat it raw." They reached the camp and sat down. She cut it up in very small pieces, and while she was doing so, Sabino noticed that she was having a tough time even though his knife was very sharp. He realized it was going to be very tough. "We're undernourished. We will have to eat little bits at a time, and very slowly."

They sat and ate until they had swallowed the last bite. He had been right; it was as tough as leather uncooked. He kept chewing and chewing, only to swallow chunks instead of small, digestible pieces. It was now about eight thirty and very hot. They had used more water while eating, and the supply was getting even lower. They crawled into their shelter, and Kamryn warned him not to drink unless it was absolutely necessary. Sabino knew eating in such a situation might even add to their dehydration, but to get something in his stomach … he was so hungry. He tried to sleep, but his cut kept him awake. Sweat covered his body even though it was not as hot as it had been the day before. He knew that the infection was poisoning him. Here and there, he nodded off, but he was alert for most of the morning. He was so thirsty he couldn't stand it any longer. He got out of the hut and took small sips. Somehow, he was able to restrain himself. When he stood up, he became dizzy. *Again the laceration,* he thought. He poked at it. It hurt more than it had when they were eating the snake. He was getting much worse. He had to get to a doctor.

"Kamryn," he said quietly and shook her.

"Um."

"Kamryn, I'm in bad shape. The infection is really bad. I'm dizzy. I'm sweaty, and I feel nauseous. I need a doctor." She crawled out, stood up, and looked closely at it.

"You're right. Somehow we have to get you to a doctor. We'll peal a bunch of pears, try our best to pulverize them in our hands, and see what we can drain into our bottle, at least until we have some kind of supply of something to drink. Then we'll pack up camp and leave. The road can't be too far off."

She took the canvas, cut out two large pieces, and handed one to him. They had some excess wire still from the seats. Kamryn measured it and cut it in two.

"Watch me," she said. She twisted the oblong piece of canvas around her head and then tied it in place. She had made a turban to protect her from the sun. Sabino did the same with his, but she had to help him.

They decided to save the rest of the water to clean his cut, so scavenging liquid from prickly pear cacti would be necessary. They cut off many and continued forcing drops into the plastic jug. Kamryn made a funnel out of a piece of the canvas. She squeezed the sticky substance, and a liquid dribbled down the funnel into their water container. She did most of the work, as Sabino was badly affected by the infection. After about an hour, she had filled half of the one-gallon container. He convinced her to let him carry one of the knapsacks. Now it was twelve o'clock, and the sun was in full force. The terrain was easier to navigate than it had been at night. At least he could see what he needed to avoid. In spite of himself, his feet still stumbled on the ground. He tripped several times, nearly falling over. She finally stopped, and they both sat down. She handed him the jug. His throat was as dry as the desert.

"Are you ready to try this?" she asked, passing him the jug.

"Is it really that bad?"

"Go ahead, try it." He took a tiny sip and swooshed it around his dehydrated mouth. There was no flavor at first, but when he swallowed, there was a bitter aftertaste. His thirst was somewhat satisfied, but the characteristic flavor it left made his eyes water and his lips pucker. It was bad but felt good after a few sips.

Their clothes were wet from sweat, and the heat was every bit as bad as Kamryn had warned him it would be. Sabino felt rested enough, so he decided to stand up and get moving. When he did, the blood rushed from his head, and he wobbled badly, the desert scene in front of him spun out of control, his heart pounded, and his whole body vibrated with every beat.

"Here, let me help," she said. Obviously, she had seen him having a problem. She slipped his arm over her shoulder, and they started out once again.

They struggled along for about an hour until they came over a crest in the landscape. There it was in front of them. Sabino was overwhelmed. It looked like a mirage with the heat distorting the land in front of them, but they both agreed it was the road, about a mile or two ahead.

He felt sick and dizzy. He vacillated between chills and rushes of heat. How would he survive?

"Let's stop and have a break," he said. Again, they sat in the sun and drank the liquid. It was a flavor he knew he would never forget. Then it was gone. They finished the last drop. Kamryn looked around for more cacti, but for some reason they were scarce in the area; there were mostly only little shrubs. She only found one cactus. She stripped it and they both dug in.

"We'll find more along the way," she said. She sounded worn out. Watching her do all the work made him wish he had more strength. He realized he would have been dead long since if it were not for her. Somehow, someday he would pay her back. He didn't know how, but he would take care of her.

"Let's have a look at your cheek before we move on." Kamryn inspected it. "Your whole side of your face is red and swollen."

She used the rest of the water to wash it one last time.

"How do you feel?"

"Dizzy. Hot then chilled. But I think I can make it to the road." His display of confidence was short-lived; he realized he didn't think he could stand up without falling over. "Kamryn, can you help me?" She came over and pulled him to his feet. He experienced the same disorientation. She supported him again, and they started walking. As they went along, he needed more and more of the beverage. He was used to the taste now, but his mouth was in a permanent state of discomfort, albeit manageably damp. They were moving along very slowly, and before they reached the road, they had run out of the drink. There were only bushes in sight—no cacti. Sabino understood they would soon be in a bad way. They finally reached the road. Up close, it was even hotter, because the recycled rubber road surface sucked up the heat and blasted it back. He was completely drained. He wished a car would come by very soon. He had no way of knowing how much longer he could last without medical help. Now Kamryn was complaining about how thirsty she was. She looked ready to pass out. They sat in the burning sun for about ten minutes and realized no cars were coming soon. Their lips were crusted, and they had sweated out all the liquid inside of them. Then an idea came to him. He wondered if his cell phone would get a signal. He took it out of his pocket and turned it on. Nothing. *That was a waste of effort*, he thought.

"We have to make a shelter," she said. "I'll try to cut a few bushes, and you get out the canvas. Okay? And we'll have to get something to drink or we'll die in no time."

"How are we going to do that? We haven't seen any of those plants for quite a while." The weakness in his voice was obvious to him. His mouth was so dry it felt like he had to keep it open or the dryness would stick his tongue to his lower mouth. Kamryn somehow managed to cut four small plants and make the shelter. They set it up and crawled underneath. Neither one of them had the energy to pile dirt on top.

"Let me rest. I'm feeling like I want to faint. I need to lie down for a while."

~ ~ ~

It was now eight o'clock, and Sabino realized his clothes were dry from the heat and he no longer was sweating. He felt his pulse, and it was weak but fast. He wondered if that was a bad sign. He could feel that his lips were cracked from the dryness. He licked his lips, but that was no help. Kamryn lay next to him. She appeared to be sleeping, and her breathing was fast and labored. He shook her and called her name, but she didn't wake up. He wondered if she had passed out or was just sleeping heavily. He was tired as well even though he had been resting under the shelter all day.

It was ironic, he supposed, that he worked for Aquasuperior, the largest water company in the world, and was going to die from dehydration. *So this is it,* he thought. They would just fade away in the heat, shrivel up, and blow away. But not so soon. Night was coming soon, and it would get down to around fifty. They wouldn't be walking with him feeling so sick from his wound. Sabino realized that they would have to cover themselves with clothes and snuggle all night to keep warm. If hypothermia didn't kill them, the sun would rise again, and then they would bake to death. Their only hope was someone driving by in the night and finding them, which was doubtful.

Chapter 31

"Okay, who wants to go first?" Boucher asked. He sat in the conference room. The FBI field office in Boston had been the center of the investigation. However, they had relocated everyone to the J. Edgar Hoover building in Washington DC. The agents in charge of the branches of the investigation were about to brief him on the progress of the different task forces.

"I may as well," said Agent Warren Miller. He was in charge of investigating Abu Shakra. "There are three men watching him in Tehran, one in the defense ministry, and operatives from the CIA. The only reason I know this is because the president demanded our agencies work together and they were ordered to share that information with me. Our agent followed him to a known forger's place of business. Abu Shakra spent nearly a whole day there, but the person who left at the end of the day was not Abu Shakra. At least, he didn't look like him. But our agent reported that the man who left had the same build and gait as the target. I believe that the forger must have produced a synthetic mask like the kind burn victims use. It's a common trick among those who want to change their identity. The really sad news is that the two CIA agents were given the order to take him down, but Abu Shakra managed to turn the tables and instead killed both of them. Now we have no pictures of him, only a rough description that was passed along to our man in the ministry through one of the agents before he was murdered. It's hardly worth using because of the low quality.

"We also put out the word that there is a hundred-thousand-dollar reward for his arrest and capture. We want someone in the ministry to be greedy and have him arrested and deported. That's where we stand."

"There's a lot of loyalty in that region," Boucher said. "I don't think that small amount will work. Get more authorized."

"I don't think that's a problem," Miller said. "I'll get right on it."

"Very good. Agent Caulfield, tell us about Ali and Dabir."

"The trail is nearly cold. We know the pair is in Amsterdam, but that's all. The police have resorted to carrying around pictures and asking if anyone has seen them. They definitely were at the airport. They hired a limo service that drove them to a hotel. From there, they were picked up by a white sedan, and then they disappeared. The authorities were unable to obtain the plate number. They're searching through security video from surveillance cameras around the city. The car was spotted twice, but in both instances, the plate number was blocked by another vehicle. There are a lot more tapes to go through, and they feel confident they'll find the plate in subsequent viewings. A task force of all available officers is viewing the video. As with Abu Shakra, there's a reward for information leading to their arrest and conviction. Neither Ali nor Dabir has returned to the hotel, and they have not been seen in any restaurants in the area."

"Have their pictures been broadcast over the local networks?"

"Yes, they have. I forgot to mention that."

"Okay. Thank you, Paul," Boucher said. "Tasha, bring us up to date on your investigation."

"Thanks, Scott. Shaul Eitan has been traced to a bus that left their retreat a few days before the raid. The highway cameras got the plate number, and it's been traced to a charter company. They claimed that they knew nothing about the bus, but after an interrogation, the company dispatcher told the authorities the bus had gone to some place around Pittsburg. We also got the driver's name, address, and cell phone number. He's not answering. We don't know whether Eitan and company are still in the area or if they fled to another destination. The bus was found abandoned at a local terminal, and the Pittsburg police and FBI are going through it with a fine-tooth comb looking for any evidence that might help us. Eitan's picture and story has been broadcast by all major national news agencies. There's a reward for his arrest. Church members at the compound have identified his companions, and we have their pictures off of the Texas RMV. We have a media campaign going in conjunction with local agencies that's trying to appeal to the greed of any of Eitan's constituents.

"Because of where we found the bus, we suspect that Eitan is in the northeastern part of the country. We're working with the regional media by broadcasting information about a scam contest. We have listed alleged winners on media outlets, and some of them are members of his party. The winners are supposed to receive their prizes if they show up at a specified location. Of course, once they show up, they'll be arrested."

"Good. We're making progress," Boucher said. "As far as my own efforts are concerned, we've been monitoring communications by members of the group. We have determined that whatever they're planning, it's going to happen on July 4. We're trying to determine the significance of the date. We have profilers working on how Eitan might tie that into the church's beliefs. Also, I've been in touch with Judge Davidson, whom some of you may have heard of, and we've been discussing warrants to search companies' records for church members as provided by the third amendment to the Privacy Act.

"That leaves us with the whereabouts of my friends Ping and Kamryn Rodgers. They disappeared soon after the raid. Witnesses at the compound have said that after our big mess, they drove off. That means there's a good chance they're still alive, but where did they get off to? That's the question. Where they are, what shape they're in, we don't know. Unfortunately, Sabino and Kamryn have been almost an afterthought. I'm afraid I haven't been much of a friend. I've been so caught up in the investigation that I've forgotten about their whereabouts. We've been working in conjunction with the army and have pretty much taken over the compound. And they have also been doing fly-bys spreading outward from the campus, but no sightings so far. Tomorrow we'll widen our search. Unfortunately, there's usually high illegal immigrant activity at the border, so even if we do see people, there's no guarantee they will be who we're looking for. Is there anything else?" Boucher asked. They all looked at each other. There was silence. "Nice. Let's get back to work."

Chapter 32

Abu Shakra was driving out to the rendezvous point in the hills in western Iran to make the exchange. It had been a fast, hard journey. He had taken a flight to Mashhad, bought a car, and then driven twenty-five miles north through the desert and over the treacherous, rocky hills until he ended up just south of Turkmenistan, which was where Petrov had smuggled the package into Iran. Yesterday, Abu Shakra had met the church's contact and been given five million in cash. The contact also had crossed the Turkmenistan border through the rough, barren hills. The money had arrived in two suitcases. He had arranged with Petrov to meet and make the exchange. Just to be safe, Abu Shakra had bought a pistol from the forger. It had turned out to be a good choice, because he had had those two people trailing him and he had put two rounds in each as the opportunity arose: one shot to the chest and another point blank to the head. The forger had set him up nicely, and he had a completely new look. Now he had the identity of an older man named Imran Ba'albaki, who was traveling to stay with his daughter who was sick with dysentery from bad water. However, he had taken off his mask so that his accomplices would recognize him. Although there were desalination plants around the world, not every person in every country could afford clean water. There were still many hundreds of millions of people without it. But that would all change very soon, as the plan to bring on the apocalypse was closer to reality. There would be no further need for clean water, because life as everyone knew it would stop.

He managed to arrive early. The roads were so bad he had thought he might never make it there. He had used an old-fashioned global positioning system to find his way to this point. It was early evening. They had agreed on this time so Abu Shakra could make it across the border while it was still dark. He waited an hour, and they still did not arrive, so he waited more.

He was pumped. The excitement of making the trade and accomplishing his mission pushed the adrenalin through his system. Although he had had dealings with Petrov before, there was a lot of money involved this time; he still didn't know if his business partners were 100 percent trustworthy. He prepared himself for action. In the twilight, he saw a cloud of dust in the eastern air. Soon a truck appeared over the crest of a hill. It was an ancient pickup. Even in a country that had once been oil-rich, vehicles were run by hydrogen. Iran was now dry of oil and was running on what was left of its cash reserves. The country was slowly deteriorating, which could be seen from the collapsing infrastructure. Electricity was patchy. Food and hydrogen supplies were erratic. Water was expensive; some families spent as much as 25 percent of their incomes on the precious liquid.

The pickup stopped in front of his car, dust rising in a cloud. This was the big moment; this juncture in time would change the world. Petrov was driving, and Fazlullah, the cleric, was the passenger. Arshard sat in the back. Petrov got out and hauled a large suitcase over the side. Abu Shakra's blood rushed throughout his body. He had to calm himself down. If something went wrong, he would need a clear head. He was not afraid even in the slightest, however, because he knew he could kill them all if he had to. He took a few deep, cleansing breaths and then greeted them.

"Boris, I was wondering if you were coming," Abu Shakra said in Arabic. He picked up his two suitcases, approached them, and shook Petrov's hand. "I see Arshard has something for me."

"I see you have something for us," Petrov replied. "Let's have a look."

Abu Shakra laid one suitcase flat and opened it up. Inside, piles of bundles of hundred-dollar bills were neatly arranged.

"Five million," Abu Shakra said. "Let's see what you've got for me."

"Well, it's very simple," Petrov said. He went over and picked up the suitcase from Arshard and carried it over to Abu Shakra. He also laid it flat and opened it up. There was a very complicated panel of instruments with half a dozen switches.

"This looks confusing."

"It's not that bad. We've already set everything for you. All you need to do is set the timer and run." Petrov explained how that was done. "It is to be plugged into any Electrical outlet—one ten or two twenty. There are receptacles for both, and it has to power up for two or three minutes before it is most effective, and this light will glow green when it's ready. You'll have to remember that these Electromagnetic bombs are most effective when initialized from above. Ideally, they should be dropped from a jet and set off a few hundred feet above the ground, but in the absence of that, high in a building will also work fairly well."

He paused, thinking of the history of the e-bomb. In the twentieth century, the concept had been born in the Cold War era. There were two types: nuclear and nonnuclear. Through the twenty-first century, the focus had shift to the nonnuclear construction. Third-generation bombs were so compact and powerful that they actually fried circuits; there would be damage to countless connections that would cause hundreds or even thousands of fires in Electrical boxes, depending on the focus and the range. The instructions on this particular bomb gave guidelines for what areas of effect were possible. A lot depended on the amount of current available to power up the device. It could be done either with 110 or 220 volts. The more amperage the better. That was disappointing, because he had hoped to destroy all of New York City, not just a wide area in Manhattan. Still, according to the guide, a 110 outlet would still set off about a square mile. That would be enough to start enough fires that they would spread like they had once done in Chicago and San Francisco hundreds of years in the past.

"We're all set then?" Abu Shakra asked.

"Almost," said Fazlullah. "This weapon will be used to destroy many infidels. Before you go, you must pray to Allah."

Abu Shakra's heart pounded against his chest. He was not a Muslim and had no idea how they prayed or what to do. Back in Tehran, he had told them that his group was seeking vengeance against the Westerners. He was sure they had sold it to him under the assumption that he was a Muslim. He had to think quickly.

"I really don't have time," he said. "I have a long journey in front of me, and I must be going."

"There is always time to pray for Jihad," the cleric replied. "Get on your knees and pray to Allah for aid in the holy war."

At that instant, Abu Shakra became aware of his gun, which was tucked in the back of his pants. He prepared to reach for it. He started judging their positions and thought out how he would attack all three. First he would shoot Arshard, because he brandished a gun. Petrov was close, so he could use an offensive move to snap his neck.

"Please, I am very tired, and it will take me all night to get to Turkmenistan," Abu Shakra said, staring Fazlullah directly in the eyes. "Be kind and let me go."

"No. I insist," Fazlullah stated authoritatively. "There will be no deal unless you praise Allah."

Arshard flipped his automatic weapon to a port arms position. Abu Shakra's heart thumped wildly with the thrill of what he knew was about to happen. His Krav Maga training had drilled into him how to fight multiple adversaries—even six or eight at a time. Here there were only three.

"All you have to do is get on your knees and pray," Petrov said in a calming voice. He was obviously hoping this transaction would go through. "Very simple, my friend. Just pray."

Abu Shakra paused and said nothing. He rehearsed in his mind what he was about to do. Krav Maga was a mixture of all the martial arts and was considered by many the most deadly discipline in the world. He would instantly eliminate Petrov, because he was very close and Krav Maga is an art that concentrates on fighting close. Fazlullah was an old man and was no worry. Arshard, with his weapon, would have to be killed with the first shot. He assumed what is called the 360 degree defense, because Petrov was in front of him and Arshard was off to his left.

"Screw you," he said, and instantly he rushed Petrov. He slammed his body into him and wrapped his arms around Petrov's neck. He flipped him over his back while clutching onto his neck. Before Petrov landed, Abu Shakra, twisted his arms, and there was an audible crack. He rolled on the ground, pulling out his pistol with his right hand and holding Petrov as a shield with his left. Arshard had already aimed the automatic and fired at the same time as Abu Shakra. A nine millimeter hollow-point hit Arshard directly in his chest and went straight through his heart, ripping a massive exit wound. The few rounds Arshard managed to pull off either missed the quickly moving Abu Shakra or hit Petrov's dead body.

Abu Shakra looked toward Fazlullah, who was climbing into the pickup.

"Stop. You will not get in that truck," Abu Shakra ordered, aiming his pistol. The old man froze, turned around, and put his hands in the air.

"Don't kill me, please," he cried. Panic swept over his face. Abu Shakra watched as his body stiffened while he waited to be shot.

"You are no threat to me, old man," he said, aiming the weapon merely to intimidate him. "Soon enough, the sinners of the world will pay. The apocalypse approaches. You will perish with the unrighteous."

"You are not going to kill me?"

"You will kill yourself. These hills will kill you. We are what, fifty, a hundred kilometers from anywhere. An old man like you will never survive."

"Who sent you?"

"I am from the Church of the Elect. We believe the end of the world is coming. This item I now possess will see to that, and the righteous will live forever."

"You are an infidel," Fazlullah said. "You will be punished and die."

"You don't know what you're talking about. You are the Watchers. The angels will cast you into eternal misery." With that, Abu Shakra aimed his gun at the truck's motor and squeezed off four shots. Steam rose from under the hood. Then he shot each individual tire. "There, old man. Let me see you drive that back to wherever you came from. Give me your shoes."

"Please, I have to have them. How do you expect me to survive?"

"That's exactly my point, old man. You won't survive. You'll die from dehydration, although I must say, the end for sinners is near anyway. You will die in the desert from which you came. Give me your shoes or die now." The old man sat on the ground, pulled off his shoes, and handed them to Abu Shakra, who then tossed them into the back of his car. He leaned over and took Arshard's weapon. Next he opened the bag with all the instrumentation and covered it with packs of hundred-dollar bills. Then he closed the cases and put them into the passenger side of his car. Now he had four pieces of luggage with him, including the one with his personal effects. People often traveled with excess amounts of hydrogen in their vehicles in the Middle East, because it wasn't always readily available. Abu Shakra looked into the back of the truck, and sure enough, there were two containers labeled hydrogen in Arabic. He took them and put them in the backseat of his car.

Abu Shakra slipped into his car, turned the key in the ignition, and flipped on the GPS. He entered the address of the Ashgabat airport. It was a hundred-mile journey, and most of it would be through these hills. He got comfortable and started driving.

At about three in the morning, he had an idea. *Why do I need all that money?* he thought. Where he was going—where the world was going—there would be no need for money. The church said the righteous would live in peace forever, so that must mean everyone would be equal. And if that were so, there would be no disputes over money. The suitcases with the money were big and very heavy. As they were, the cases would be a burden. He got out and unloaded both of them. Just in case something went wrong with the plan, he decided he would keep at least some of the money for himself. He opened the case with his personal effects and emptied out all the clothes that he didn't need. He could not do without the disguises the forger had given him. Emptying as much as he could, he found he had enough room for about twenty or thirty bundles. He opened one of the cases containing the cash and transferred as much as he could. The rest he abandoned on the side of the road.

It was midmorning when he arrived at Ashgabat Airport. The road from the meeting point had become worse as he approached Turkmenistan. Altered to look like a much older Imran Ba'albaki,

Abu Shakra left his car in the parking lot, took his two pieces of luggage, and entered the terminal. He approached a security guard standing near a ticket counter.

"Where is international shipping?" he asked in less than perfect Russian.

"It is in the next building over. That way," said the guard, pointing. Five minutes later, he was there. He had known Valik Alekseev for several years. Abu Shakra had used him on one other occasion when he needed to smuggle weapons from Jordan to Somalia. It had been a mercenary assignment to help knock out the radical government. Alekseev was a slight man, barely five-foot-three and skinny, but he understood the business very well. Abu Shakra entered through a door that led into a small office and put down his bags. There was no one around. There were some posters on the walls with what he assumed were some kind of instructions, but he couldn't read Turkmen. There were two old desks, painted and worn in places, chairs with ripped leather, light green walls, and recessed lights in the ceiling. An old lithograph of two ancient biplanes engaged in a dogfight hung on the wall.

"Hello?" he said in a loud voice. Then he saw a button next to the door that must lead to the hangar. He pushed it. A bell sounded, and he waited. After a moment, a woman came through the door.

"Greetings, comrade," she said. "What can I do for you?"

"I need to speak with comrade Alekseev."

"Right this way." He followed her to the hangar. There was Alekseev, giving instructions to half a dozen other men. His legitimate profession was working as a shipping supervisor, and he was doing his job. His workers were clad in black overalls with patches on the left sleeve, and they appeared to have their names on their left pockets. The hangar door was open, and the incoming sunlight made it bright inside. The corrugated metal walls were painted in the same light green as the office. There were two old jetliners inside, most likely for maintenance. On the far wall were thirty or forty crates and as many skids of cartons. Two forklifts were moving crates and skids with cartons. The men dispersed, and Alekseev turned, walked toward Abu Shakra, and greeted him.

"Jabbar! Greetings," he said with great enthusiasm, extending his hand. "I saw your picture. Doesn't look anything like the old you." Abu Shakra had already put his bags on the floor, so he also extended his arm to shake hands. For such a small man, Alekseev's grip was very strong. The two accomplices exchanged small talk.

"Comrade, what brings you to Turkmenistan?"

"I have these two bags that need to get to New York City."

"Under the radar, obviously."

"Obviously," Abu Shakra replied.

"I think we can help. Tomorrow Materia Medica's pharmaceutical convention here in Ashgabat comes to an end. Their next convention stop is LA. The booths, tables, props, and the like will be stopping over in Paris and then DC. I am very confident we can get them that far undetected. We will put them in a crate buried in other materials and have it accidentally shipped to JFK. We ship for a company called Umbroud Productions in Brooklyn. You can pick up your bags there. They are friends of ours.

"How much?"

"Well, that's just the thing. It depends on one thing: what you have in them. What are you smuggling?"

"It's only two bags of money. Would you like to see?" Abu Shakra asked. He hoped that Alekseev would trust him, but realistically that was probably not going to happen. With luck, Alekseev would only look in the small suitcase and not see what Abu Shakra was truly smuggling.

"I want to know what I'm shipping." He went over to the bags and opened them both up. He dug through the money in the first case, looked at Abu Shakra, and nodded. This was the part Abu

Shakra was worried about. Would Alekseev dig through the other case? He opened it up. Abu Shakra's heart sank. The money he put there had shifted in transit. The cash had settled to the bottom of the suitcase, and the instruments were in plain sight.

"Tisk, tisk, tisk," Alekseev exclaimed, smiling. "Money, huh? What have we here?"

"I don't know," he lied. "I was instructed to bring this across the US borders and then pass it over to my connection in New York."

"Why should I believe you? You just lied about the contents."

"That's all I was told. I have no idea what it is."

This was going to cost him plenty. Pretending no knowledge of the contents was an old line, and he knew Alekseev knew it, because he was smiling and wagging his index finger back and forth.

"Comrade Jabbar," he said, "if you don't want to tell me, that is okay. But I will have to charge you to the max. Not knowing what I'm moving could put my people in danger if the contents are unstable. We don't want any jets blowing up over the Atlantic."

"So what do you think?" Abu Shakra asked.

"Fifty thousand, and don't say you can't afford it. There is no negotiation. Either we ship it or we don't."

He didn't really care about the money anyway. It was a bonus. He had only kept it to give back to the church, and besides, money would be useless after everything happened. There seemed to be about a hundred bills in each packet, so he picked up five of them and handed the cash to Alekseev.

"Count it," Abu Shakra said.

Alekseev fanned each bundle to see that there were no fake bills, but he did not count it.

"Let's go check the flight schedules so I can tell you when it will arrive in New York." They went back to the run-down office, and Alekseev sat at a desk. At the terminal there, he said, "Materia Medica." After a pause, he read off the schedule for the company's equipment. It would arrive in Washington DC on June 21. Then he said, "DC to JFK." Again, after a pause, he said, "Not bad. Next day—arrival on the twenty-second. I'll print the new shipping label, and you can be on your way."

The time was getting close. *This is actually going to happen*, he thought. The machine spit out the label. They went back into the hangar, and Alekseev instructed two of his men to hide the bags in one of the crates and put on the new label. Abu Shakra reluctantly gave up the suitcases. He realized that if he wanted them to get to the United States, he would have to trust in his connection. Alekseev gave him instructions and the paperwork to pick up the crate from Brooklyn. It would be up to him to take it somewhere safe to unpack it. The friends shook hands again and went their separate ways. In three hours, Abu Shakra boarded a jet bound for Istanbul. From there he would fly to New York City and meet Shaul with the package.

Chapter 33

Somehow they made it through the night. The cold nearly froze them, but this time it was Sabino who saved them. He had spent his life in the north and had camped in the cold on many occasions. Later in the night, the near-freezing air set in. The ground started getting cold as well, and Sabino had them wrap up together in the canvas with some of it on the ground to insulate them. They wrapped up in the remaining clothes they had brought with them. The effort, however, completely drained them. Their thirst was brought to new heights, and by morning, as the sun rose, they were unconscious, nearly dead, and unable to move.

"¿Que pasa aqui?"

"¿Estos parrecen muertos?"

Sabino lay with his eyes closed. He heard these strange words and did not know where they came from or what they meant.

"No, pero van a morir si no los ayudamos."

"Deles agua."

He could feel hands unwrapping them but couldn't respond. Now he was in a sitting position being held by someone. He heard more talk. Water touched his lips. He coughed.

"¿Puede oirme?"

More of the warm liquid touched his lips. He desperately tried to suck for more. He choked again.

"¿Puede oirme?" someone asked again. He took more water and opened his eyes. There were many people standing around them. He looked to his left, then to his right, and he saw Kamryn in someone's arms as he was. Her eyes were also open, and she looked his way and smiled. She also took a big sip of the water that was offered to her. Then she said something he did not understand.

"Yo no hablo español," she said to the one holding her. Then she looked back at Sabino. "It's the only Spanish I know. Ping, we're saved!"

Once water was reintroduced back into their systems, recuperation went fairly quickly. Sabino counted ten people in all. They had a pickup truck, and they all piled on. They all spoke very little English. The best he could figure was that they had crossed the border and the woman driving the truck had met them on the US side. The Mexicans were very considerate and generous with their supplies. They let Sabino and Kamryn drink as much of their water as they wanted. They shared food with them, which was almost as welcome as the water. Sabino and she hadn't eaten in days, apart from the snake. Kamryn insisted that they eat in tiny amounts so as not to shock their digestive systems. She said otherwise they might get diarrhea, and who wanted that in the open desert in front of all these people with who knew what for paper supplies?

They were both still delirious at first on the truck, but at some point Sabino realized they had left their automatic weapons behind.

It was hot, but the pickup moved quickly, and the wind felt good. They still wore the hats Kamryn had fashioned and had to hold on to them with their hands to keep them from blowing away. Someday they would make good souvenirs, as would the backpacks, though they had left the canvas, much to Kamryn's dismay.

In about an hour and a half, they reached El Paso. Sabino was still in a bad way because of his wound. Somehow, they were able to communicate to the Mexicans that they needed to go to a hospital, and they were dropped off at the emergency room. When they hopped out, now feeling better because of the water they had received, the Mexicans noisily said good-bye in Spanish, and they responded in English.

Immediately, the nurse admitted them both and they gave Sabino an IV with antibiotics. They numbed his cheek, cleaned the badly infected laceration, and stitched him up. They were both treated for dehydration. Kamryn was given an IV as well. Sabino and she were kept in the emergency room in adjacent beds. After three hours, he was doing well and felt ready to go. The staff let them shower and gave them some donated clothing.

They took a cab to the heart of the city to JC Penney on San Antonio Street. Both Kamryn and he still had their wallets, and they gave the driver a big tip. They wanted to go to a store first, because their clothes were ten sizes too big; they certainly didn't want to look like bums. Kamryn had lost her cell phone, but he had his. He called the Boston FBI office, but they were being very secretive and wouldn't give out Boucher's whereabouts; however, they did allow Sabino to leave a message. He gave his number and told Boucher they were all right.

"You know," Kamryn said, "I was never big on spending on myself until I moved to Boston." She paused and thought before she spoke further. "Our time in the desert allowed me to reevaluate my church views. I was very comfortable out there, but I worried about you. I nearly lost someone dear to my heart. It got me to thinking about what would happen if you died. Where would you go? Would you be there in the land of the Elect waiting for me when our world came to an end? You're an atheist, Ping, but where the Church of the Elect's theology differs from Christianity, I don't know well enough to say if you would be there or not. I guess what I'm trying to say is that we need to live day by day, never truly knowing what lies ahead."

She pulled another dress off the rack. It struck Sabino that she wasn't really serious about the things she had just said and that it was only nonchalant chatter.

"Are you shopping or trying to have a serious conversation here?" he said.

She put everything down on a shelf. "I'm very serious, Ping. Our time in the desert turned into a near-death experience for you. I had plenty of time to think, and I began to question my faith."

He didn't feel like getting into a religious debate, so he switched to an easier subject. "Look, we're not building a new wardrobe here. We only want something to wear to get us back to Boston."

"Yeah, but they have Western style dresses down here that they don't have in New England."

"Do you really want to carry all of that everywhere?"

"Ping, listen. I was poor as a child. While I lived on the church's campus, I was only allowed to wear plain things. Now that I can indulge as much as I want, I'm going to enjoy myself."

"Well, we don't have all day. There's a hell of a lot of more important things to do."

She huffed and picked up her things. "Fine," she sternly said and paused. "Let's find you something." Sabino simply bought khaki pants; a striped, short-sleeve shirt; and, best of all, clean underwear. After they paid, they changed in the restrooms, washed up again, and went to the salon. Both had a shampoo and a haircut. Of course, Kamryn had to waste the time to have hers styled. He had his stubble shaved with an old-fashioned straight-edged razor. After that, they left the store and sat down to eat in the nearest restaurant, which served Tex-Mex food.

First she ordered a red wine and he had a Corona, each of which cost more than the meal.

Their dinners were served. They remained silent until the waiter left.

"So what's next? What do we do?" she asked. "Do we go to the police here or go back to Boston and find Scott?"

"The police department in El Paso is very big. We'd probably spin our wheels a lot trying to find the right person to talk with. I'm for Boston." His cell phone rang. "What do you bet that's Scott? Hello."

"Where in the hell have you been?" Boucher asked. "I thought you were dead."

"We almost were." Sabino said into the phone. "Anyway, it's a long story that I'll tell you later. What's up?"

"Is Kamryn okay?"

"She's right here."

"I'm glad to hear that. I'm glad I sent you both down there. We had a lot of losses, and I'll never forget sending those men to their deaths, but you two survived and things are really moving here because of your efforts. I was reassigned to DC, because we're following everything from here, so that's where I am now."

Sabino took another bite of his chili con queso and then put his phone on speaker, lowered the volume, and moved closer to Kamryn so they both could hear. Boucher filled them on all that had been happening on his end.

"How do you know all this?" Kamryn asked.

"We've been using data-mining techniques and software to analyze telecommunication patterns. Also, we have a very large network of informers."

"What's the pakinzite stuff?"

"Picanzite. It's extremely powerful and very volatile." He went on to explain its properties.

"I see. Should we talk with the local police about anything while we're here?"

"No. We have agents at the compound investigating and interviewing members. The El Paso police are up to their necks in illegal immigrant issues."

"Do you want us to go back to Boston?"

"You two have been a great help to this investigation, and perhaps you can be even more. I would like it very much if you came to DC to work along with us. Kamryn knows the church from the inside, and that may be very valuable. She'll still be charged, but we'll go to bat for in front of the judge. I don't think she'll do much time."

Sabino was swallowing another bite and it took him a second to respond.

"If you think it will help, Scott," she said, "I'll help. I'm scared to death of going to prison."

"Good," Boucher said. "Get here as fast as you can. Call me before you leave with your arrival time, and I'll have a driver meet you. He'll take you to the Hoover Building. I'll have him bring you to me." Then Boucher read off his DC phone number.

They said their good-byes, and Sabino ended the conversation. After finishing their dinner, they took a cab to El Paso International Airport. The soonest flight to Washington DC was leaving in two hours. Kamryn wanted to rent a hotel room and rest, but Sabino didn't think there was enough time. As expected, she added that they could fool around. He was tempted; after all, she was the reason he was alive. Having sworn to himself that he would repay her, he almost wanted to do it, if only to appease her. He had trusted her with his life, and she had pulled him through. Things were a lot different than they had been a few days ago.

Chapter 34

They managed to procure two vans from one of the local churches to take them to New York City. Before they left the Wilmont estate, Shaul made arrangements to split into two groups and stay with wealthy parishioners in Manhattan. Shaul was with Brother Gabriel and Norman. They were in a penthouse on the corner of Fifth Avenue and Ninety-Seventh Street overlooking Central Park. The others went to a penthouse a few blocks away but with a less grand view.

They would stay in hiding until judgment day. Shaul decided that it was a critical time. Protection was of the utmost importance. In order for him to rule over events, all potential encounters with law enforcement were to be met with deadly force. Gabriel and Norman were armed with automatic weapons for security.

What a beautiful location. The place took up the thirty-fifth and thirty-sixth floors. They were on the upper floor. It was decorated in a spare, modern style, though Shaul preferred something with more of a Gothic flair.

Facing the park were floor-to-ceiling windows with chairs facing out to enjoy the view. The floors in the living room were bamboo, or perhaps synthetic bamboo, as real wood was so rare. It was a wide open floor plan. Shaul wondered how the place supported the spacious expanse. It had a thoroughly modern kitchen with an island with four sculptured chairs on one side. He went to the kitchen to get another lemonade and then went back to his seat near the windows. Gabriel and the hacker were keeping up with their e-mails, as were the other four members of the group at the other location. They sat in those chairs working with their laptops on the island. That in itself was a full-time job for everyone. With the thousands of brothers moving about the globe, there were many questions to answer. It took all of their time. As they had at Wilmont's home, they were using zombies to hide their location. Relaxing for a moment, Shaul took in Central Park. The apartment's owner was at work, so they had the place to themselves. Although Shaul had told him about the coming apocalypse, the owner insisted on going into the office. Perhaps he didn't believe him. He did sound rather skeptical.

The Amsterdam project, as he now called it, was complete. The rockets were all on ships being transported around the world. His fighters were all headed to their destination countries, and many had arrived. After they scoped out their targets, they were to lie in wait until the Fourth of July, the day of the fireworks. Everything would happen on that day.

Brothers Ali and Dabir said in their communications that they had seen their pictures all over the news in Amsterdam, and other reports told Shaul they were hot all over Europe. He told them to stay in the warehouse if possible until the day of reckoning, but they had been cooped up for a long time and wanted out badly; they just didn't know how to escape the country.

Shaul had also been communicating with Abu Shakra. The trade had been made, and Abu Shakra had mentioned something about a rebate. It sounded odd, but if money was coming back to the church, it would be welcome. Realistically, Shaul didn't know if he would need money after the fourth. He knew that the end wouldn't be immediate. Some time would pass before the earth became totally desolate and all the Watchers and their followers died of thirst.

Shaul leaned back and smiled. The day would soon be upon the earth. Now it was inevitable. Nothing could go wrong. He decided to take a longer break and celebrate. He would walk around his troops and recite from the book of Enoch. He got up and began to narrate from memory.

"I shall tell you of the seven archangels and the punishment they rain upon the Watchers—verses eighty-seven and eighty-eight.

"'And again I saw—'" he paused. "That's Enoch, of course, not me. 'Again I saw how they began to gore each other and to devour each other, and the earth began to cry aloud. And I raised mine eyes again to heaven, and I saw in the vision, and behold there came forth from heaven beings who were like white men, and four went forth from that place and three with them. And those three that had last come forth grasped me by my hand and took me up, away from the generations of the earth, and raised me up to a lofty place, and showed me a tower raised high above the earth, and all the hills were lower. And one said unto me: "Remain here till thou seest everything that befalls those elephants, camels, and asses, and the stars and the oxen, and all of them."'"

"So relates the book of the archangels," he said as he walked around Gabriel and his hacker. Shaul could tell that they were focused as he spoke the written history, because they had stopped talking and answering all the e-mails and chat room conversations. They had turned their chairs around to listen.

"'And I saw one of those four who had come forth first, and he seized that first star which had fallen from the heaven, and bound it hand and foot and cast it into an abyss: now that abyss was narrow and deep, and horrible and dark. And one of them drew a sword, and gave it to those elephants and camels and asses: then they began to smite each other, and the whole earth quaked because of them.

And as I was beholding in the vision, lo, one of those four who had come forth stoned them from heaven, and gathered and took all the great stars whose privy members were like those of horses, and bound them all hand and foot, and cast them in an abyss of the earth.'"

He stopped speaking and smiled. He knew he had captivated their imaginations with these passages, because they left a lot of room for interpretation. Of course, the stars were the Watchers. Every member of the church understood that. But he also knew that his helpers were experts in interpreting the entire book, so he didn't have to explain. He continued to pace around them with his hands folded behind his back.

"That is my proclamation," he said. "You may get back to work."

Now that he had brought some light into their world, he felt assured that they would work all the harder. It was awe inspiring how the book could do that to him. Just thinking about the demise of the Watchers cheered him incredibly. The day was merely a short time away.

Chapter 35

Irme Knecht sat behind his desk at the German consulate in Tehran. It was uncomfortably hot. There was no such thing as air conditioning in this part of the world, and there was certainly no pumped in oxygen to help one's breathing. He sat there sweaty and out of breath, but it was a job he had picked for himself. The Middle East needed a lot of help in managing peace, and he felt the calling to be a diplomat. He was an excellent negotiator, and he knew it. Realizing that the region had been at war for thousands of years, he knew there was little chance that he would make a big difference, but it was the small victories he thought would at least bring a little peace. He strived to make peace between local religious factions and had so far done quite well. He had managed to broker relative calm between local Sunni and Shi'ite sections of the city. Many local people credited him with saving many lives and felt they owed him a debt. This was the case with Marzuq Nesar, who had just entered his office. Knecht got to his feet and extended his hand as Nesar approached his desk.

"Marzuq. Greetings," he said. "How is the family?" Nesar was a stout man. He was bearded, and his beard always looked scruffy like the rest of his appearance. His clothes were seldom clean, and like most men, he wore sandals. But he provided one thing people could count on: information. Everything came with a price, but it was credible and timely. Their conversation was in English. Poor English on Nesar's part, but Knecht always got to the root of his covert knowledge.

"My family is well and healthy. And yours?"

"Very well, thank you. I take it you have something for me?"

"There is a forger in eastern Tehran," he said in very broken English. "I have gotten information from him before. It is not information he has given me."

"What is it?"

"I take pictures. Pictures of people he altered. He had one customer. I followed him from the Ministry of Defense. I don't know his name, but I have a picture of the new him."

"Let me see it," Knecht said.

"I am afraid that I cannot let you see it."

"Then what good does it do me?"

"You can have it for a price."

"How much?"

"One million rials."

The exchange rate was very low. Knecht understood that this man was poor and the money would take him a long way. It was about a hundred US dollars. It would sustain him and his family for about a month to a month and a half. He should barter for it, as tradition went. Although Knecht would be doing him a big favor if he just let him have it.

"Seven hundred and fifty thousand."

Nesar pondered the offer. Knecht was waiting for the inevitable counter offer.

"Nine hundred."

Knecht stood up and extended his hand to seal the deal. "Done," he said. After they shook hands, Knecht opened his top desk drawer. He kept plenty of money there just for such bartering sessions.

He counted one million, pretending to miscount nine hundred thousand, and then handed it to Nesar.

"The picture, please," Knecht said. Smiling, Nesar reached under his robe, pulled out the picture, and handed it to Knecht. Knecht was well acquainted with the game. The smile meant that the exchange of information still had a way to go. He looked at the photo. "You are sure you don't know this man's name?"

"An associate of mine at the ministry knows his name. I will need money for him."

"One hundred thousand."

"Two fifty."

"Two."

This time Nesar extended his hand, and they shook again. Knecht went into the drawer and took out two more bills.

"I am told his name is Jabbar Abu Shakra. He is from Jerusalem. He is a mercenary and a smuggler."

"What is he here for?"

"I am not so sure. Abu Shakra had dealings with men from the Russian embassy. It was very secret. No one knows what they were, except that it is something to do with America. He has left Tehran in a car that he bought. I do not know where he went from here."

"Could you find out?"

"This I do not know. I can try."

Knecht started to reach into the drawer. Nesar put up his hand and waved. "My friend, that is information I do not have," Nesar said.

"Is there anything else you can tell me? I will pay."

"That is all the information I can give you."

"Okay. Keep in touch. Try to find out more and I will pay you well. I bid you good day. And thank you."

"Thank you too, and good day to you as well," Nesar said and left.

Knecht sat for a moment and thought about what had just transpired. What should he do now? The nearest American consulate was in Istanbul, so that was who he had to inform. On his computer, he had a phone listing for all the embassies and consulates in the world. He pushed the speaker button on his phone and read off the number. In a moment the other end rang.

"US consulate," said a voice.

"May I speak with Ambassador Quinn, please?"

"I'm sorry; Ambassador Quinn is out of the office. Would you like his assistant?"

This was sensitive information and he didn't know if he should trust it to an assistant. No, he decided. He would tell someone else. He told the woman he would call back later. Now what? He would call Interpol. They would have procedures in place for something like this. He had dealt with someone there in the past, however, a Gail Sharland. He called, and she happened to be in her office.

"Gail Sharland," she said as soon as he got her on the phone. The sound of her voice was soft and gentle, just as he remembered it to be. They had never met face to face, and he couldn't help imagining what she looked like. He envisioned her being like some beautiful *vornehme Frau*—a gentle woman, not one hard enough to deal with international criminals.

"Hello. This is Irme Knecht from the German consulate in Tehran."

"Oh, hi, Irme. I haven't heard from you in a few years. What have you been up to?"

"I was just given the name and picture of someone who I believe is a terrorist planning some action against the US."

He explained what the informer had told him, and she asked him to scan the picture and e-mail it to her. She would investigate who he was and then decide what needed to happen from there.

~ ~ ~

Interpol had 179 member countries. Headquarters sat on a strip of land between a manmade lake and the Rhone River in Lyons, France. The cubical building was made of columns of concrete and panels of glass. It was reflected in a pool surrounding it. Gail Sharland was a dainty woman of twenty-nine. Barely five-foot-six with high heels and a slim figure didn't exactly make her an imposing opponent. She was there for her smarts. She had graduated at the top of her class from Northeastern University in Boston with her master's degree in criminal justice. At an early age, she had been shown that society had some real dregs. Her mother, who was little like her, had been mugged and beat up when Gail was a child. She had witnessed the whole catastrophe, and the memory had haunted her ever since. Twenty years later and she still had nightmares. Every time she woke up in a sweat, it motivated her even more to fight for justice, no matter how smart the criminals were. Ever since, she had dreamed of a career in law enforcement. This Abu Shakra would simply be another opportunity to show off her talent.

She called her supervisor to discuss the matter.

"Why don't we contact all of our member offices with the picture and see what they can turn up at transportation centers," he said to her.

"We should bring him in for questioning?" she asked.

"Yes, definitely. Tell our offices to search all the airports, et cetera, with their facial recognition systems. I'll notify our other offices and get in touch with agencies in the US. Maybe someone there knows something we don't."

Chapter 36

The capital was much cooler than Texas. They retrieved their bags and a driver was waiting outside at the pick-up area to meet them. The conversation during the drive from Reagan National Airport to the Hoover Building was not light like it had been on the plane. During the flight Kamryn, as usual, had talked about starting a family. Sabino had skated around the subject as much as possible, though he had to admit he was feeling mixed emotions. Even before they had boarded the jet, he had realized that would be how she would steer their conversation. Unfortunately, he had let it slip on one occasion that he felt very deeply for her because of what she had done for him. She immediately had taken that as a sign of hope for a future together and had started talking babies. He definitely wasn't ready for that much commitment. Maybe he would start dating her again, perhaps produce a kid, but certainly no family. No way.

Their verbal exchanges in the limo were mostly about what lay ahead—the dangers, the future of mankind, and what evil the church was planning. How would they end civilization? They could destroy infrastructure to make life miserable for people but certainly not bring on the apocalypse. If Shaul destroyed transportation hubs, that would disrupt many markets of the world as well as the distribution of products. Killing Electricity would put people in the dark and would mean great danger to people in extremely hot and cold environments. Eliminating supply chains would cause massive starvation, but on the other hand, there were hundreds of thousands of trucks, ships, and trains, so that would be impossible. Then it occurred to them both at the same time. If they killed all the desalination plants, crops would die; people would starve and die of thirst; hydrogen production for heat, cooling, and transportation would come to a halt; and oxygen for easy breathing would no longer be available. But would that be possible? There were eight thousand Aquasuperior plants in the world and four thousand smaller, privately owned locations. Sabino had to admit that their competition was responsible for a very small portion of the global water, hydrogen, and oxygen supply, and if Aquasuperior's locations were eliminated, the supply from the little places would never keep up with the demand. They would work over capacity and fall apart. Thinking of it that way, Shaul's vision could almost come true.

In a short while, they arrived at the Hoover Building. It sported rows and columns of windows separated by lines of concrete, giving the building a checkerboard appearance. The driver parked in front of the entrance. They got out and the driver took off. Soon after they entered, they were escorted through a maze of corridors and stairs to Boucher's location. He was not in an office but rather a conference room with other agents surrounding a table full of computer screens.

"Well, how are the two adventurers?" he asked as soon as he saw them. "Oh, that's quite a bandage you've got on the cheek, Ping."

"Yeah, don't you love the new me? It's the latest fashion."

"Let's get right to business, shall we?" Boucher said. "Let me introduce Christopher Nelms from the NSA and Gail Sharland from Interpol." Two people stood up and nodded. Sabino smiled, but they were way too serious to smile back.

"Nice to meet you," Kamryn said.

"Chris, fill them in on what you're doing."

"Okay, my staff and I are connected to the main computer at NSA headquarters. They changed to a new private key, but our computer was able to break the encryption. With the help of our software, we've been intercepting their communications and our computer has been decoding them. We're analyzing traffic patterns around the globe, and we have seen a lot of activity in Beijing relating to the arms the church bought there. A lot of activity around Tehran and New York as well. We feel that the church's leadership is in New York City somewhere. They're using a network of zombies, so it takes a while to trace where the communication is originating. We've tracked down a few and are interrogating the people who own the original computers. For the most part, an official from the church goes to a church member's house, taps into the network, sends an e-mail or post, and then leaves. We've been unable to catch anyone of importance so far. By the time we trace it, they're using another zombie. We have also seen a lot of activity around Amsterdam. This is most important. We believe that the church bought arms from China and are sending them around the world. Officials there have raided two shipping companies that we suspected were involved with the church without any luck. We have two more that are on the hot list that we're watching."

"Gail, how about you?" Boucher asked.

"We know a main player is Jabbar Abu Shakra, who is a mercenary and a smuggler. He was in Tehran for a few days and then left. He has bought some type of weapon he plans to set off somewhere in the United States.

"He's had his identity changed, so he looks different than he did previously. We have a picture if the new Abu Shakra and are scanning the crowds with facial recognition systems at airports, cruise lines, and train and bus stations. Because the quality of the picture that we were given isn't very good, we've found numerous similar people, but we spotted the real him only once. Right now he goes by the name Imran Ba'albaki. He is a man of sixty-one, gray but full hair, wrinkled skin, very tall—six four, and husky too.

"We had a positive ID on him from the capital city of Ashgabat in Turkmenistan, but we were unable to ascertain if he actually got on a flight or took a bus or train. Technology there isn't very sophisticated; however he was spotted on surveillance tapes. He had already gone.

"Back to the small arms. There are two members of the Church that we only know as Ali and Dabir who are somewhere in Amsterdam. They are the ones in charge of distribution. We have been broadcasting their pictures all over Europe. If they show their faces, we'll get them."

"What if they have their identities changed like Abu Shakra did?" asked Kamryn.

"That's a good point," Boucher said. "There are lots of forgers in Amsterdam, and if they do that, then we'll have to start over. That will be a setback. The thing about this that amazes me most is that there's this giant operation and we don't have one single informer on the inside."

"Let me say this," said Kamryn. "We're a very strict lot. Everyone believes that judgment day will arrive and peace will come to the righteous. That is a tightly held ideal of the church. If you don't believe that, then you're not welcomed as a member. The commitment is so deeply ingrained that with the promise of the event coming, every true parishioner would never do anything to endanger it happening. With the hope of it coming in our lifetime, our members would never betray that vision."

"But still, I don't believe that there is no one out there wanting to talk," Boucher said. "If we offered a reward for information leading to … there must be someone who would be willing to cross over.

It seems that money means nothing to these people," he continued. "They're taught to lead a simple life based on what we found at their compound, free of nonessential products. There's no desire for fine clothes, fancy cars, or beautiful digs. They share everything, even secrets. Let me ask you this, Kamryn. You're dressed in nice clothes with stylish hair. How did you come to change from simple to how you are now?"

"I was brought up in the church. From my earliest memories, I learned to live simply. When I moved to Boston for the assignment, I changed. Once I was shown what money had to offer, I indulged and bought a few things, then a few more, and then even more. Now I look in the mirror and I'm pleased with what I see. Before, I just saw a plain person; now I see someone special."

"If that's the case," Boucher added, "that still doesn't fully explain why you switched teams."

"I've explained that to Ping. I believe the way the church is going about it is the wrong way. It should have come from God's hand. And besides, my situation was unique. Because of the position I was put in, I was forced to show that I was interested in material things in order to keep my cover. I learned to like my surroundings. I would think such a position would be unusual to occur for someone else. How many more times is Shaul going to order someone to infiltrate a company and pretend to like the finer things in life?"

"I'd be willing to bet that you weren't the only spy Shaul employed. There must be others at companies other than Aquasuperior."

"Why can't we find out?" Sabino asked.

"That makes sense," Boucher said. "We'll have the human resources departments of major companies scan their records and see which employees are affiliated with the Church of the Elect. I was looking into that anyway."

Why don't we get some people to dig into that, Janis? You can take the agents you need. Do you mind?"

"Not at all. I'll get right on it."

"It must happen fast," Boucher said. "According to their schedule, the event is happening on July 4, so we only have about two weeks to stop them."

"I know," said Sharland. "Since the church is interested in Aquasuperior, it seems to me that they're interested in targets that will impact infrastructure. I'll check companies that work along those lines. After all, their communications often mention security, obviously."

"Won't a lot of companies fight you when you ask to look at their records?" Kamryn asked.

"Yeah, but it's easy enough to get search warrants."

"Does anyone feel that they are targeting Aquasuperior specifically?" Sabino asked. He went on to tell them what he and Kamryn had hypothesized in the car.

"Of course Aquasuperior's locations are targets," Boucher said after hearing Sabino's explanation. "But what's their objective in buying such a large weapon? Don't they think that destroying the desalination facilities is enough?"

"I think that's obvious," Sharland said. "If their management is in New York and they all believe that the world in coming to an end, then why not start right there?"

Everyone looked at each other.

"You're right," Boucher said. "We'll put out an alert at New York's airports and other places where people enter the city. We'll use the facial recognition equipment at train and bus stations. And of course we'll use the cameras at intersections throughout the city."

"They'll hit New York," Kamryn said. Again they all stared at each other for a moment. "It will be their crowning achievement. Do you think the president will allow any country to get away with so much as supporting any group that plans on using such a weapon that could destroy the largest city in the world? He won't take that shit. We'll trace it to the country of origin and nuke 'em. What do you think will happen then? A nuclear holocaust, that's what."

"That's it then," Boucher said. "It will happen on July 4. We'll make our plans to catch Abu Shakra there if we don't get him before then."

"What do you want us to do?" Kamryn asked.

"We'll be better off in New York. We'll go there and work out of the Manhattan office."

"Do you mind if I come with you?" asked Sharland.

"Please come," Boucher said. "We could use you. You can fly with us."

The four of them were on the plane en route to JFK in an hour.

Chapter 37

Brothers Dabir and Ali were standing on the catwalk again, overlooking the floor below. A few moments ago they had observed the last of the rockets being packed and put into one of the skids of cartons. Everything had been shipped. Many rockets had already arrived, according to communications from the brothers in those countries that had received them.

It was almost time to celebrate. Everyone would soon be able to split up and go their separate ways. The packers would go home. The forklift drivers would be able to resume their normal activities in the warehouse. Van den Broeck could resume running her company without fear of having the place raided.

Brothers Dabir and Ali were very hot and they knew it. They would have to take new identities and move on. Still, because they were involved with something so big, if the grand plan failed, they would be on the run for years, perhaps forever. But how could it go wrong? Everything was gone, and there was no way to stop it now.

The helpers were suddenly still as the sound of the forklifts' movements went quiet. Relieved that it was all finished, Ali started to clap, and the crowd below joined him in the applause. They walked down the metal stairs and started to mingle with all the employees.

Van den Broeck entered the warehouse with a number of people in white coats, apparently from a catering company, pushing carts of food. Suddenly there was music playing over the loud speakers. They all started shaking hands and talking above the tunes.

"Congratulations, everyone," Van den Broeck said into a microphone she held in her hand. All the workers clapped again. She stepped up on a skid to elevate herself slightly above the others. "A job well done to all of you," she said. "You've put in many extra hours to accomplish our goal of shipping all these packages by our deadline, and we have finished two days ahead of schedule. There is lots of food beverages for all, compliments of the Elect One himself. As usual, he hopes that we'll drink the lemonade he provided, as it is his favorite drink and he thinks it's a real treat for us. A table of desserts is also being set up on top of the other food. Thank you to everyone. You deserve a pat on the back."

She approached the two brothers. "What are you going to do now?" she asked. "Your pictures are all over Europe. Someone is bound to spot the pair of you."

"We'll get new identities. Since we will look so different, we will be able to move about freely."

"Besides," said Dabir, "we will only have to get by for a few weeks at most. There will be no authority, no organized governments, and central legal organizations will be in utter chaos. As the world goes downhill, the righteous will be free from the scrutiny of the Watchers. The day is inevitable; no one will catch us."

"What about you, Emma?" Ali asked.

"I don't know," Van den Broeck said. "I believe this will end life as we know it, but what will happen along the way? What will become of the Elect while we wait for the Watchers to die off? Will we die with them and be reborn? Will we die of thirst too? To be truthful, I'm quite apprehensive about what lies ahead. I do believe this is the coming apocalypse, but I am not so sure how we will move from life as we know it to the world promised to us in the book of Enoch. What do you think?"

"I believe that the Lord of Spirits will not let us go thirsty," Dabir said. "How it will happen is that the Lord Himself will provide for us while, one by one, the Watchers die off. As a member of the Church of the Elect, you must believe that for them, the world will turn into a fiery desert where they will endure for all time. As for the Elect, our world will become a lush garden where freedom and pleasure know no bounds. Our worlds will transform for each group as time passes. The Lord will pass judgment on the Watchers and the Elect, and He will punish or reward by moving each to their own heaven or hell. Don't worry; he won't let anything bad happen to us. You must believe that."

"I'll tell you I don't feel completely reassured. But … hearing that from an Elder lessens my fears. You guys are the experts," she said. "However, I believe that our efforts will be rewarded and that the apocalypse will come because of it. I only hope that I'm worthy."

"Believe me," Ali said, "after this successful push, you are among the righteous. You have nothing to fear. Nor do any of your workers. Now it's time to celebrate." He went over to the food tables. There was a chef cutting generous slabs of roast beef. Another was cutting a turkey. There were heated pans full of lasagna, buffalo wings, fried chicken fingers, and stuffed shells, and of course a wide assortment of Dutch food. At the far end of the table was a pot of meatballs and beans, and another that looked like it held seafood Newburg. At the head of the first table were plates and silverware, salads, crackers and cheese, finger sandwiches, and sliced Italian bread. Obviously the American foods had been ordered by the Elect One.

Dabir took it all in, trying to decide where to start, so he ended up taking prime rib and a bowl of seafood Newburg. There were people dressed in white from the catering company busily setting up tables and chairs. He sat in one of the chairs and waited for Ali, who was still in line.

All he had to worry about was successfully staying out of sight for a few weeks. Soon it would be all over. Even if they caught him, there was no way to stop it now. Soon the transformation would be complete. He was so excited he couldn't eat a bite.

Chapter 38

Abu Shakra was disembarking at JFK. He was dressed in a suit and highly shined shoes and had no beard or mustache, and the false gray hair was carefully arranged on the mask. He didn't want to raise suspicion by looking like a militant Arab.

All he had was a carry-on bag with some clothes and a spare synthetic mask in case he needed an emergency identity change. Of course, the mask and chip for the passport were tucked snuggly under the false bottom. No one would suspect him, because he was such a pro at passing through customs. There was a police officer with a dog sniffing baggage along the line leading to the customs checkpoint. Before leaving Istanbul, he had arranged for a distraction. Two people ahead of him was a man with a small quantity of hash—enough for him to be deported back to Turkey, but hopefully not enough to send him to prison. The decoy would make a lot of noise and disruption when the dog found the dope. The customs officials would hurry the next few people through the place of inspection.

He noticed a security camera focused on the area. Just to be cautious, he struck up a conversation with the woman behind him so that his back was to the camera. She was very fine. Abu Shakra wondered what her reaction would be if he told her that he was a mercenary and smuggler. He wondered if she was the adventurous type and knew that by and large, women went nuts when they learned his profession. Most of them had a need for excitement that he could leverage. As they talked, he fantasized that he was having sex with her. He could tell she wanted to sin with him. He rested easy in the knowledge that the Lord would forgive his acts of passion because of the wondrous deed he was doing. What the heck? He had time to spare. He had already been talking with her for a few minutes, and she seemed suggestible. They had been flirting together all along.

"You haven't told me your name yet," Abu Shakra said.

"Amanda Lombardi," she said, extending her hand to shake.

"Imran, and my last name you couldn't possibly pronounce." He shook her hand.

"Pleased to meet you."

"Could I buy you a drink after we're through this mess?" he asked in a slight accent. He could have spoken perfect English, but he had found the accent effective with women in the past.

"Are you coming on to me?" she said with a smile.

"Not coming on to you. Just suggesting two weary travelers share a few meaningful moments together. That's all. Besides, I don't even know how you feel about older men."

He looked about fifty or fifty-five in his mask, though his passport listed his age as sixty-one. He figured she was about forty. Still she obviously kept herself in good shape, and she was attractive.

"Sounds like an interesting proposition. And yes, I am attract—"

The shouting started in front of them. It was his decoy, who had just been caught as planned. He was shouting in Arabic, and they were trying to calm him down so they could take him away with as little commotion as possible. It didn't work. The shouting got louder.

"You two, come on," shouted a customs agent above the noise. Abu Shakra and the woman stepped up to the counter. "Anything to declare?"

"I'm traveling very light. I only have my carry-on bag. He started to open it up, his heart pounding from the thrill. He was calculating how he would escape if they caught him. His mind raced. It would be very tricky if they discovered the mask and passport. He was right in front of the camera. By now, they had had a good chance to scan his face. He would hit the armed guard first and take his gun. Then he could escape by hijacking the nearest car outside in the arrivals area. He was ready to pounce. The shouting came to a crescendo.

"Get going," the agent said. "Hurry along. You too, lady. Come on."

Abu Shakra picked up his bag and one of her suitcases.

"Thank you," she said, and they walked away from the counter.

"That was exciting. Say, why don't we go out to dinner? I'll buy."

"Sounds interesting. Where do you want to go?"

"To be honest, I don't know New York City that well. Perhaps you can suggest something."

"There's a place downtown—Nathan's Place. It's a bit noisy, but there are a few romantic niches. It's inside a nice hotel called the Park Central. Why don't we try that?"

"Sure. How do we get there?"

"I have a car in the parking lot. We're heading that way, if you hadn't already guessed. Hopefully you will chip in for the parking fee. It's very expensive."

"Why don't we discuss that after dinner," said Abu Shakra. "Can I carry your other bag as well?"

~ ~ ~

Security officer Jane Dugan was monitoring the cameras from the control room in the airport. An alarm went off, indicating that a criminal or suspected terrorist had been spotted. She changed the screen from four views to the one that was flashing. She zoomed in. A man and a woman. Their backs were now to the camera as they walked into the garage. She didn't know what to do. It was only her second week at her new job. She thought the software was supposed to identify the person by name, but nothing came up on the screen. She wanted to show her boss that she could take care of an emergency. She wouldn't call him yet. She tried to manipulate the cameras and software to get a name. She was wasting precious moments in her attempt.

~ ~ ~

Abu Shakra put Amanda's bags in her trunk. It was basic transportation, an older model Ford driven by biofuel. But reliable, he imagined. She spoke, the doors popped opened, and they got in. She started the engine and put it in drive.

~ ~ ~

Dugan was ready to give in and call her boss. There was a switchboard console on the desk in front of her. She picked up the phone and pushed the button with her boss's name on it. His voice came over the speaker. "Yeah, go ahead."

"This is Jane. Our system just picked up someone. I didn't have the chance to identify him. What do I do?"

"What do you mean, you didn't have a chance to identify him?"

"I don't remember how you told me to identify a suspect on this system. It's all new to me."

"Well, you should have called for help. Who else is in the office with you?"

"I'm here by myself right now."

"That's just great. I'll be right up." Dugan felt butterflies in her stomach. She had really screwed this one up. She only hoped that it wasn't too late.

~ ~ ~

Amanda drove the car up to the parking attendant's booth so she could pay.

"I've got it," Abu Shakra said. He reached for his wallet and pulled out a hundred-dollar bill. He didn't dare show her the roll of hundreds he had in his vest pocket. He didn't want her to be suspicious of anything. The attendant took the ticket and ran it through a meter and told them it was seventy-five dollars for three days. They paid and drove off.

~ ~ ~

Jane's supervisor came running into the control room. He was almost in a panic. "Which camera was he on?" he demanded.

"Number four."

He went to the control for number four and put it on fast playback speed in reverse. Soon he came to the picture of the man and woman.

"Is that them?"

"Yes."

"They're heading for the garage," he said and picked up the phone.

"Hey, John, how can I help you?" said a voice on the other end.

"Have a man and a woman gone through your gate yet?"

"Yeah, just a second ago. Why?"

"Never mind. It's too late now," he said and hung up the phone. "We've got to find out who they were." He reversed the digital imaging further to the spot where the camera showed their faces. Then he sat down at the computer terminal and opened up the facial recognition software. Next, he zoomed in on the man's face and went back to the other terminal and hit enter. A window came up, and he entered some data. The computer ran the face, and in a moment a box with two names popped up: "Jabbar Abu Shakra, a.k.a. Imran Ba'albaki."

"Damn," he said. "That's the man the FBI is looking for, and you blew it."

"I'm sorry. I'm really sorry. I couldn't remember how to run the software. I panicked."

"Well, it's too late now. I'll call the FBI. See if you can't get the plate number off any of the garage cameras. Can you remember how to do that?" he said sarcastically.

"Yes, I can," she said in a sheepish voice.

"I'll be in my office."

Dugan sat and thought for a moment. She went over to the control console and clicked a few buttons, and one of the TV panels went to a single view. She clicked through a series of camera angles and came to one with a car. She picked up the phone and said, "attendant's shack."

The man in the shack answered, "Yeah, Jane? What's up?"

"Do you remember what kind of car they were driving?"

"I'm not sure. Something red. Kinda crappy. A Ford maybe."

"Thanks." She went back through a few camera angles until she came to a red car. She zoomed in on the plate and tried to read it. She said out loud to her boss, "It's a Connecticut plate. I can only read the first three characters—2X3. The rest are in a shadow. What do you want me to do?"

"Hang on," he said from his office. "I'll call the Connecticut State Police and see what they can find. Keep looking for a better view."

~ ~ ~

Abu Shakra and Lombardi pulled onto the Bell Parkway. Traffic coming out of the airport was heavy but moving. They drove just a short distance on the parkway before they jumped onto Route Twenty-Seven. It was eight at night, and traffic going toward Manhattan was fairly light until they got onto Flatbush Avenue; then things slowed down.

~ ~ ~

In the control room, Jane picked up another view of the plate. 2X3 CC7. She called to her boss, who phoned the state police. They ran the number while he was on the phone and told him it belonged to Amanda Lombardi of 223 Whitington Street, Bridgeport, Connecticut. He picked his own phone, called the state police in Connecticut and told them that Abu Shakra had been spotted at the airport. The police dispatcher thanked him, assured him that the matter would be taken care of, and hung up.

~ ~ ~

The skyscrapers were towered in front of them as they got closer to Manhattan. Abu Shakra was very hungry and couldn't wait to fill his stomach with good American food. He felt at ease with this woman. The quest was almost finished. He sat back in his seat and took in the sights as they got closer to downtown. The day after tomorrow, his packages would be at JFK. Then they would be transported to a warehouse, where he would pick them up. He would need to get access to a computer to contact Shaul. *In the morning*, he thought. He was hoping to sleep with Lombardi at her house. Most likely she had a computer he could use, although that was minor. He could get that anywhere. He wanted sex. A sin, yes, but the Lord would forgive him.

~ ~ ~

At Connecticut State Police headquarters, the dispatcher passed the call on to Detective David Derrig. He gave Derrig the airport information. What to do next? He sent Lombardi's picture, address, and plate number to the onboard computers of all the police cruisers around the state. Next, he focused in on Abu Shakra's picture, and a contact name and number at the FBI came up. He was to contact a Scott Boucher, who was the special agent in charge of the case. Derrig thought that Abu Shakra and Lombardi might still be in New York, so before he called Boucher, he got in touch with an officer he knew there and sent him the pertinent information. Now the pair would be hot in both states. His friend would distribute the data in the same way that he just had.

He thought of Boucher's numbers on the screen, and a phone on the other end started ringing, but it went to a message. Derrig left his contact information and told Boucher about Abu Shakra and Lombardi. Other than that, he had to just sit and wait.

~ ~ ~

The plane was making its final approach to JFK. Kamryn, Sabino, Boucher, and Sharland were comfortable in their plush seats. Kamryn and Sabino each had had a glass of wine during the flight. Boucher and Sharland had turned down the offer, because they were on duty. They landed and taxied over to the private jet terminal and got off the plane. There was an FBI agent there to meet them. He had a van and a driver in the area. They started walking in that direction. Boucher's phone rang, indicating that he had some messages.

He listened to the one from Detective Derrig, who spoke of the Abu Shakra spotting at JFK and provided Lombardi's name and address. They would have to get media coverage, of course, thought Boucher. He wondered about the woman and Abu Shakra's objective for a moment. What was he doing with a companion? Was she a contact, or simple entertainment? Boucher had gotten used to the idea that Abu Shakra's target was in New York, so why, other than fun, was he with the woman? He certainly wasn't going to Connecticut. Why would he? If Abu Shakra went to her house, that would be the end of it. But Abu Shakra was a professional, and he might figure the house was being watched, unless he was unaware that the authorities had that information, in which case that would be a tremendous advantage. So should he keep this under wraps and watch the girl's house? Or would it be better to go public? If they were staying in New York, then this whole investigation would be botched, and it would his fault, and he didn't want the blame for this one. It could be the biggest case of his career, a once-in-a-lifetime investigation. Well, he would think about it. For the moment, he would have to contact Derrig and tell him the FBI was taking over the case. He thought of Derrig's message, and his phone dialed the number.

"Detective Derrig," said a voice on the other end.

"Hi, detective. Special Agent Scott Boucher here, returning your call."

"How are you? I called just about half an hour ago."

"I know. What's happening?"

"Abu Shakra was spotted at JFK, as I said, and we have APBs in New York and Connecticut, though the information only went out in the last twenty minutes."

"Have you notified the media yet?" Boucher and the others got to the van. It was white with no markings. "After you," he said to Kamryn and Sharland. They climbed in.

"Excuse me," Derrig said. "What did you say?"

"Oh, I'm sorry; I was talking to the people I'm with. Please continue."

"We were waiting for you guys before we did that. We didn't want to make snap judgments without your input."

"That's good," Boucher said. "So I assume you know we're taking over the investigation?"

"Well, as it's a multistate incident, I just assumed that you would."

"I'm glad we understand one another. Tell me what's happened so far."

"Really not much. We just received the tip an hour ago, and we were waiting to contact you. We were about to call the FBI in Washington if you didn't ring me back soon. Obviously, this is a time-sensitive issue."

"I suppose for the moment we shouldn't contact the media," Boucher said, deciding in just that instant. Now they were all in the van and driving toward FBI headquarters in New York City. "What type of priority did you give?"

"The highest, of course. Our boys are looking for the car. However, I can't speak for New York. I don't know what they're thinking. It's a pretty busy place."

"We'll have to distribute their pictures to hotels, restaurants, and public transportation hubs throughout the city. I think that's where they'll be. Could be he's just hitching a ride from the woman."

~ ~ ~

Abu Shakra and Lombardi crossed the bridge into Manhattan and got off, heading toward the restaurant she had mentioned. They had been flirting with one another, talking, and laughing throughout the drive. Perhaps it would be safer if they just got a hotel room and went their separate ways in the morning. She could be useful, though. He had no experience traveling around New York City, and she seemed to know where she was going. *Wouldn't it be a strange coincidence if she were a church member,* he thought. But he knew his luck couldn't be that good. After all, the Church of the Elect was small compared to other religions. As he continued to compliment her, she became more and more comfortable with him. He could tell, because she giggled every time he flattered her. She even blushed once, as near as he could tell in the dim light. Inside, the auto was partially illuminated by the city lights. He was getting excited as he talk with her. Amanda was easy to be with and very open, but he knew that if he told her he was about to bring on the end of the world, her admiration would turn to hate. Most people didn't understand that the coming apocalypse was an act of cleansing and that the good people would be saved. He was curious about her. She was very nice. Would she go to the land of the righteous even though she wasn't a member of the church? He didn't dare to try to convert her at such a late date. Their conversation revolved around their world travels and what excitement their journeys had brought them.

He thought about telling her about his profession. After all, Americans he met in the Middle East were intrigued, though that area of the world was full of his type, and people expected it. Here in New York, he couldn't expect such a reception. However, it would help his chances of getting her in bed, and he really wanted to have sex with her tonight. Of course, if she new about him, she would willingly sleep with him if he got her drunk enough. He decided to bring it up.

"Amanda, what do you do to make your living?"

"I teach English as a second language," Lombardi said. "That's why I was abroad. I was at sort of a miniconference for a few days. I go to the Middle East to teach and speak, and I teach night classes in Queens. What do you do?"

He thought quickly. What would a teacher think was an interesting profession? "There will always be a soft spot in my heart for performing on the stage."

"Oh, really? Have you ever performed on Broadway?" she asked with a great deal of excitement.

"No, nothing like that. This is my first time in New York City. I might like to see how I do trying out for a part. But enough about me. Tell me what you do when you're not teaching."

All along, he had been watching her actions, listening carefully to what she said and how she answered his questions. He seemed to have a knack for understanding people. Abu Shakra knew he was lucky to have this special ability. He had suspected that she was exactly the type of person he was looking for when he picked her out at the airport. She had a spy novel he was familiar with under her arm, and the clothes she was wearing were bold and seductive at the same time.

"Well, not much. I read a lot and daydream all the time. I don't really like my job, but it pays the bills. I often wonder what it would have been like if I were adventurous enough to get into something really exciting."

"Like what?"

"I don't know. Maybe acting, like you. Maybe I could have joined the Army and seen the world. Perhaps I could have been an interpreter for the UN rather than a teacher. I often think it would have been nice to be a fireman or a cop. Or even—and I know you'll think I'm insane, but what the hell—I think it would be cool to be in the Mafia. Now *that* would be exciting!" She paused, smiling. "But my life is boring. I watch the soaps during the day and go to school at night. Big deal! The trips to Beirut have their moments, though no one has ever kidnapped me or anything like that. I live inside the compound where I teach, and no one ever bothers me. Boring again."

She had possibilities. Maybe if he told her that he was a smuggler in real life she would be intrigued with that. She would like him even more and thus grant him sexual favors. He could tell her stories about the things he had gotten across different borders.

"It's interesting that you mention the Mafia," he ventured. "I do things for them at times."

"Wow! That sounds very exciting. What is it that you do?"

"I move products for them from Turkey to other parts of the world."

"What kind of products?" she asked, sounding intrigued.

"Well, I don't think I should tell you. I wouldn't want for you to lose any respect for me."

"Oh, come on. Please tell me. Is it drugs?"

Yes, it was drugs, but he wasn't going to tell her that. He had been involved in a lot of crimes that were a definite turn-off for women.

"Mostly just small stuff. Mafia dons are collectors of some very expensive things, and sometimes governments don't like to see national treasures leave their countries. Statues, jewelry, paintings—"

"You're an art smuggler?"

That was always a turn-on for women. Telling them he was a

runner of fine arts made them think he was harmless and hurt no one. He had actually done it before, but drugs and weapons paid a lot better.

"I've brought a few pieces across the borders."

"Is that why you're here?" she asked, practically jumping out of her seat onto his side of the car.

"To be honest, I can't tell you for your own protection."

"Yes, of course; I understand. Naturally, you can't tell me, because then I would be an accomplice. Isn't that right?" Her voice was squeaking with excitement. He would have all the sex he wanted tonight.

"That's exactly it. I'm glad you understand."

"Can I help?"

"No, but thanks. However, I need to get to a computer sometime soon. Is there any place that you know of where I could use one?"

"Practically any hotel. Do you plan to stay here for a few days?"

"Yes."

"Maybe you'd let me stay with you … just to help you get around. You'll need someone who can take you from here to there."

He had her hooked; that was for sure. Lombardi could come in very useful. And now he would have all the sex he wanted in these last few days.

"Sure. That sounds like fun. I understand that Central Park is very beautiful in the summer. There must be some fine hotels there. One where I could pay in cash?"

"We could use my credit card. I'll pay."

"Amanda, the problem with credit cards is that they are traceable. If somehow the police found out we were together and you were helping me, they would find us the moment you used your card."

There was a twinkle in her eyes. This was really exciting her. "You're right. That makes sense. What do we do if they ask for IDs?"

"That's a good point. I mentioned that I liked acting. I have a disguise with me, another identity." She smiled widely. He plainly saw that this whole experience was a real turn-on for her. "We'll need to get an Internet connection. I'm afraid that a standard network won't do. I will communicate with a contact back in the Middle East. He'll put me in touch with a forger here in New York. I can't implant the new passport myself. It would look amateurish. "

"We can go to Nathan's. They're bound to have secure networks. I'm sure we can do it without being too conspicuous."

"How close are we?"

"The Park Central is beautiful. It's not exactly on Central Park, but it's right around the corner. It's in Midtown, right near where we are now. Just a few more blocks."

"Okay. Let's try there," he said, and they continued to talk as they drove through the city. She certainly was acquainted with the area. The Park Central was three blocks away, she said, and they arrived in a few minutes. They parked the car in the hotel's garage. They left their bags in the car.

They walked out of the parking garage and turned the corner. There was Nathan's, about a block away. A sign in the window advertised Internet connections. They passed through the door. It was designed like an Irish pub. The wood was all walnut and cherry. It had a circular bar in the middle with stools on the perimeter. Surrounding the bar were individual tables. On the outer reaches of the room were booths.

"How may I help you?" said the host in an Irish accent.

"We want a booth with a secure Internet connection," Abu Shakra said.

"Sure. Right this way." He led them to one of the booths. "Your waitress will be right with you."

Abu Shakra glanced at the computer. Very soon he would be a changed man.

Chapter 39

They were on the twenty-third floor of Twenty-Six Federal Plaza in the heart of Manhattan. Boucher and Sharland were working on spreading the word to locations around the city. Sabino and Kamryn were taking a break from helping out.

They had started out helping to monitor the church's communications. All of the messages they had intercepted basically said the same thing: the event would take place on Independence Day, it involved a great many people, and it was global in scope. None of them said exactly what the plan was, however. Sabino marveled at such a large effort taking place without anyone saying what it was in the Electronic communications. That must mean that all critical information was being carried the old-fashioned way—by courier. Sabino had a mind to stick to it, and although it was important, it had gotten boring reading the same thing time and again with nothing new revealed. He felt they would be more effective helping to spread the word.

Now they were standing at the window, taking a break. "What do you suppose Abu Shakra plans to do?" Kamryn asked.

"He probably has some nuclear or biological weapon. When he

lets off whatever he has, the winds will carry all the contamination. Who knows how many will be killed?"

"And those weapons out of China. The world will be a very bleak place if he pulls off wrecking the desalination plants. The church wanted to know security and layout. Hating to sound redundant, but who knows how much intelligence he's gathered?"

There was a moment of silence between them. Sabino thought about their time in the desert. The wound on his cheek was covered with a large bandage. The doctors had spent a lot of time cleaning his infection. He smiled, thinking of how Kamryn had come through and saved them. She was really quite a girl. The more he thought about Kamryn, the more he admired her.

"Why are you grinning at a time like this?"

"I was just thinking about someone I'm very fond of and hoping we'll avert this mess and the person will be okay."

"Who is it?"

"That's not really important," he said. "Ready for some more work?"

"Sure. What do you want to do?"

"At least if we contact hotels we'll have some human interaction. Let's go."

Contacting the local transportation hubs was left up to the local authorities. Many of the different hotels in the city were connected through a professional organization called the National Hotel Association, so Boucher was easily able to contact multiple locations. It was a matter of contacting top management and having them spread the pictures to their staff.

They both heard Boucher mumbling. He was calling hotels too. "Next is the Park Central," Boucher said. He thought the number and listened for a person on the other end. "My name is Special Agent Boucher. I'm with the FBI. We're searching for two individuals who are wanted for questioning. If I send you their pictures, will you help in the investigation?" There was a pause, and they heard Boucher grunt and say things like, "Uh huh. I see. No. Nope. You think so." Then, after another pause, he said, "Mr. Avril, this is a matter of national security. It is very important that we find these two." He was shaking his head no, the growing anger evident in his reddening face. "Look, we'll do this either way. You can help us, or we'll locate some agents in your hotel and then arrest them if they turn up." A brief silence. "If you won't go along with the investigation, we'll shut down your hotel. How will that be for business?"

Sabino sat and listened.

"So … good," Boucher said into the phone. "We'll send you the pictures, and you will distribute it around the hotel. You must comply. If you don't, we'll close the hotel and have you arrested for obstruction of justice. Is that understood?" There was a quiet moment. "That's what I thought. Give my assistant the necessary information." Boucher smiled. "That's how you take care of them."

~ ~ ~

Abu Shakra and Lombardi sat on opposite sides of the booth. He was in a private instant messaging session with the forger he had dealt with in Tehran.

ALSUD: *You told me there were forgers in the US I could contact.*

MASK96: *Where are you now?*

ALSUD: *At a pub in Manhattan.*

MASK96: *What is the name of the pub?*

ALSUD: *Nathan's Place. I am with a woman. She's wanted like me. She'll need a makeover too.*

MASK96: *We can do that, but it will cost more money. I will arrange for someone to meet you outside at midnight.*

ALSUD: *I will pay your forger for her as well as soon as the job is done. How will I recognize him?*

MASK96: *He will speak only in Arabic, and when he greets you, he will shake your hand then grasp your forearm with his other hand.*"

Abu Shakra logged off. "It's all set," he said to Amanda. "We're to meet someone here at midnight. I don't know what they'll look like or who they are. It seems that they will find us somehow. If you're going to stick with me, I think you should get a makeover as well. What do you think?"

"Would it be permanent?" she asked.

"No. It's a simple synthetic mask. The forger also will numb your hand, cut out the old passport, and put in a new one."

"But I don't want a new passport. The one I have is just fine."

"No, it's not. Every cop in the city is looking for us. You *have* to have one or they'll find you in a second."

"I suppose you're right," said Lombardi. "After all, we're in this together. Right?" She smiled widely and wiggled a bit in her seat. She was plainly hot for him. He looked at his watch, and it was nearly eight thirty. "Perhaps we can eat here and then go to a club to kill three hours."

They ordered and ate. He had a traditional Irish lamb stew. Lombardi had Nathan's special: Limerick ham and boiled boxty. The ham was fixed with juniper berries, mustard, a hint of gin, and plenty of brown sugar. They ate slowly, and rather than going out, they stayed there and talked. He impressed her with stories of his adventurous experiences. She impressed him with her sedate lifestyle. He couldn't believe that anyone could be satisfied with such a boring existence. There was a live Irish band that started at nine. They had to shout above the music, as did everyone else in the place, making things extremely noisy. Lombardi convinced him to drink Guinness. He thought the taste was rather putrid—too much flavor—but millions of drinkers around the world couldn't all be wrong, so he tried his best to get used to the taste. He was amazed that he could hold it up to a light and not be able to see through the dark liquid. Time flew by.

"It's almost midnight," he shouted to her. By this time it was very crowded inside and there was even more noise. He paid their bill in cash, and they went outside. There were others waiting to get inside. Abu Shakra and Lombardi pushed through them and walked a ways away, but they stayed near enough to the pub that they would be noticed. He saw a police car, and a twinge of adrenalin pumped through him. He quickly turned his back and embraced Lombardi in a kiss to hide them both from the cruiser. She kissed back passionately and pushed her hip and side up against his groin. He was a little drunk, just as she was. He kissed her back, lusting for her. They clung together for a long moment. He glanced at the street and noticed that the police were in the distance. He stopped kissing her.

"Wow," she exclaimed. "What was that all about?"

He didn't want to tell her it was just a matter of hiding. "You get me really excited. I want to get this over with so we can get a room."

"Mmm, so do I." Lombardi pushed up against him again. A man approached them.

"Imran?" he said. That caught Abu Shakra off guard. He was so involved with thinking about making love he had forgotten he was using an alias.

"Are you the person sent to us?" Abu Shakra asked in Arabic.

"I am Raboud," the man replied, also in Arabic. Raboud clasped Abu Shakra in the handshake as described. "I understand that you need some help with an identity?"

"Yes, new passports and looks for both of us. How fast can you do that?" He was still thinking of hurrying up so he and Amanda could jump into bed.

"It will take half an hour to get up to my apartment. Then, depending on what you want, anywhere from a few minutes to a couple of hours each."

Hours! Damn, he thought. "That's as fast as you can do it?"

"I am slow but very professional. I will do a job that will prevent detection. I do good work."

"What are you guys saying?" Lombardi asked in English. He leaned over and whispered in her ear. No strangers needed to hear the conversation. He told her what they were planning and how long it would take. Then he turned to Raboud and spoke again in Arabic.

"We have to hurry. How did you get here?"

"I took the subway. Let's go."

The subway was not crowded at that time of night. They got on at Columbus Circle and got off at Dyckman Street at the other end of Manhattan. Raboud told them he was on Seaman Avenue, which was just a few blocks away. They entered the apartment, which had eggshell walls with pictures of the Middle East. It was a fairly large apartment. They were in the living room when they walked in. At the far end was a hallway, and Abu Shakra saw four doors, two on each side. A yellow Labrador came trotting out of what was most likely a bed room. It looked tired but carried a rope toy in its mouth. The floors were hardwood with a large Persian carpet in the center. Brown cloth covered the chairs and a couch were surrounding a coffee table centered in the room. There was a white Persian cat sleeping on the chair on the right.

"Come. Sit," Raboud said in Arabic. He sat on a leather chair, and Abu Shakra and Lombardi shared the couch. "Now, what exactly do you want me to do?"

"Would you mind speaking English?" she said, sounding a bit perturbed.

"Of course, Amanda" said Abu Shakra. "Sometimes I forget my manners. Amanda needs a complete makeover—passport, IDs, appearance, everything. I have a mask and a passport, but I will need you to put it in my hand."

"We are a full-service company," Raboud said in very poor English, but he smiled as he spoke. "Open twenty-four hours a day. I am very good at implanting them, and I have an extensive file of passports and the equipment to make synthetic masks right in a room down the hall. I'll set you up. But first, the money issue. I am not cheap."

Abu Shakra had expected that. He had two wads of hundred-dollar bills in his coat, though he had spent a little of it. He still had nearly twenty thousand in cash. The dog came over to him with the toy. It shook it vigorously, came closer to Abu Shakra, and touched his leg with it. It growled, tail wagging. Abu Shakra took the toy, and the dog started a tug of war.

"Your implant is cheap. It will take me maybe ten minutes. A thousand dollars. Your friend is different. We'll have to find a suitable passport. Then I'll have to generate a mask from the picture. I have the latest technology to make it. It's a three-dimensional copy machine that produces adequate masks at the touch of a button. No doubt your conversion in Iran took substantially longer. Am I right?"

"Yes, it took several hours to complete."

"I thought so. After that is made, I have to activate credit cards, license, and confirm false addresses. Ten thousand dollars. It will take about an hour and a half."

"That's a hell of an hourly wage," Abu Shakra said.

"Discretion comes with a price, my friend."

"Imran, you're not going to spend that kind of money on me, are you?"

"We have no choice. I don't want to take a chance on the police not knowing who we are or what we look like. It's a necessity."

"You can really make me look different?" Lombardi said, sounding very excited, just getting into the conversation. "This will be awesome!"

"Then it's a done deal?" asked Raboud.

"If that is your price, then that is what we must pay. However, I want to know what kind of assurances I have that you will not give my identity away."

"Once a client leaves here, the passport is out of my hands. I do not keep records of where it went or where it came from. In case I get raided, no one will be traced. I've disabled the memory on my copy machine, so there is no evidence there. I write nothing down. All of our transactions are verbal. I sweep the apartment for hidden microphones regularly. In short, there is no way anyone can trace you after you leave here."

"Well then, is Amanda going to be okay with her new persona?" Abu Shakra said to her.

"Are you ready for a new look?" Raboud asked with a radiant smile.

"This is so cool. Do I get to chose what I look like?"

"Not so much what as who," Raboud replied.

"Is it permanent?"

"No. As I said, it's just a mask. You can take it off and put it back on at will as soon as I show you the proper way to do it. However, we might need to give your hair a little trim so it'll look natural."

"Trim my hair?" Lombardi asked.

"Don't worry," Raboud said, "I am the master of many trades, and styling hair is one of them. I do it for clients all the time. Your hair is very long. If I just ball it up and put it under the mask, it will make an unnatural lump on your head."

"Well, I suppose as long as you don't butcher it, I guess I'm okay with it. What do we do now?'

"Let's pick you out a fabulous look," Raboud said and stood up. Abu Shakra let go of the rope toy, and the dog fell back as soon as he released it. They had been quietly wrestling during the whole conversation. When he stood up, the dog looked at him in disappointedly. "Right this way," said Raboud.

They went down the hall to the last door on the right. It was set up like an office. There were two desks, each with a computer screen, and a monstrous, complicated machinelike structure. It had an old-fashioned keyboard under a screen on one side. The monstrosity was about three feet square with three telescopic lenses directed toward the middle point of the equipment. Centered below was a tabletop, also with a lens aimed at the core. Finally, there was an arm extending over the machine, again with a lens. All of the lenses were pointing to the center.

"Let's see what we can find," Raboud said. He flicked a switch, and the computer screen lit up. Hazy light projected simultaneously from the lenses to create a bright ball of light at the central point. He looked at her and then looked at the screen. He typed a few things on the keyboard, and a list of names came up. He clicked on the first one, and a hologram of a woman's head appeared in the middle of the light. It was suspended in space and rotated slowly. "What do you think of her?"

"What do you mean?"

"I mean, would you like to look like her?"

"You mean you can make a mask for me that looks like her?"

"Precisely."

She scrutinized the face, looking at it from different angles. "I don't like her hairdo. And she has a big nose."

"We have as many as you have time to look through," Raboud said. "Let's see what the next woman looks like." Another head appeared. She evaluated it and then asked for another. They did this for about half an hour. Abu Shakra could see that she was unbelievably picky. She was still asking for more when Raboud asked, "What exactly are you looking for?"

"I don't know. Nothing really sends me."

"Perhaps I should ask, what is your ideal look?"

"Hmm, blonde, I guess, with lots of highlights. A figure better than I now have—"

"I can't help you with your figure. Go on."

"A dainty little nose. And I've always liked green eyes."

"We can change those with contact lenses. What else?"

"A slender neck—"

"I can't help you with that either."

"I want a skinny face. I want my cheek bones to show. Thin eyebrows. Not much makeup. I guess that's about it."

"Let's see what we can find," Raboud said. He told the machine what she had just specified. A voice said, "Five matches." The first face appeared in the area. Both men saw that she was smiling widely.

"Jeez, that's awfully close. Do you mind if I see the other four? After all, I have to live with the look."

"Don't forget that you can take the mask off when you're not using it," said Abu Shakra. After deep consideration, she decided on number three. They all looked very similar, but she fell in love with that one.

"This is Kelley, Kelley Holtz, it says. I'm afraid you're stuck with the name." Lombardi said okay, and then Raboud said a few more commands to the machine. There was a slight humming, then a whining noise and a slight vibration on the floor. "Come over to this side," he said.

They walked around the machine. A small door about a foot high swung open. A conveyor belt started moving, and in a moment, Kelley's head came out on a modeling stand, exactly like the image, though obviously not transparent. Abu Shakra looked at Lombardi and saw the twinkle in her eyes. The new look was far prettier than the current one, and he could tell she was anxious to try it on.

"How do I put it on?"

"I'll show you," Raboud said. "We'll cut your hair." He did so quickly. "Let's try it on." He gathered her hair and confined it with an elastic band. Raboud removed the mask from the stand. "It goes on from the back first so your natural hair is disguised by the new hair on the mask." He put it on and then started pressing it against her cheeks. "It's not all synthetic. Parts near the eyes, nose, and mouth are made of manufactured membrane material. It actually forms to your shin so it looks natural when you talk." He continued pushing. "Take it off fairly carefully so you don't rip it. Just go slowly and you'll be fine. A few final touches around the mouth … there. It's in place. See, not that hard."

"It's not even that uncomfortable," she said.

"There's a mirror in back of you," Raboud pointed out.

Lombardi turned around and looked. "Oh, my God, I'm beautiful!" The dog sensed her excitement and came over to her, wagging its tail wildly. She kneeled down. "Don't you think I'm beautiful, boy?" The dog licked her new face. "No, boy, don't do that."

"It's all right," Raboud said. "Once it's on, a few dog kisses won't harm it. You can even feel his licking through the mask. Don't you agree?"

"Yes, I felt it," she said as the dog licked her face again. "This is incredible!"

"Enough of the excitement," Abu Shakra said impatiently, really wanting some action. "We came here for passports also. Could we get going?" She was definitely much hotter. He really wanted to have sex with her now.

"Sure. Of course. Right this way." Raboud led them to another room. There was a hospital gurney with a sheet of white paper from a roll covering a bed.

"This is too much," Abu Shakra said. "You must have a regular business here."

"Hey, I run a class act. I actually do this for burn victims, so in fact it is a regular business. How else to you think I could have gotten that monstrosity of a machine up here without raising suspicion?"

"What a great cover. Do her first. I'll go put on my new mask."

Raboud sat her down on the gurney. He went over to a cabinet and took out a tray and then he returned to her. He gave her a Novocain shot in the hand so he could cut out her old passport and put in that of the deceased Kelley Holtz. As he was working, Abu Shakra went back into the other room and to the mirror. He peeled off the old mask and carefully put on his last one. He had the passport chip in a sterile plastic holder that the forger in Tehran had given him. This time he was Gagan Malik from Delhi. His acting interests would allow him to imitate the accent perfectly, of course.

He went back into the other room. The dog tilted its head, looking confused.

"Is that really you, Imran?"

"Not really. Now I'm Gagan Malik from India. As soon as he puts in my passport, we'll get on our way. Does my accent sound natural?"

"I would never have realized it was you, it's so flawless," Lombardi said.

"Are you done yet?" Abu Shakra asked.

"Just putting on the makeup over the laceration. Perfect, as usual. No one will ever notice that it was changed. Now you." Abu Shakra sat on the gurney. Raboud took his hand and looked disgustedly at it. "This is a real butcher job. What kind of amateur hacker did this?"

"It was done by a respected forger in Iran."

"Well, this *respected hack* didn't know what he was doing. I'm surprised no one got suspicious. But don't worry. It'll be perfect in a few minutes." He got a fresh needle and gave him the Novocain. He cut, dabbing bits of blood as he went, and in a few minutes he was putting makeup on the entry point.

Abu Shakra gave him the cash.

"You're both all set," Raboud said. "There's one important thing still to do. I'll be back in a minute." He went into another of the rooms and came out in about five minutes with two envelopes. "These will help. They are all of the supporting identification you will need. I have just activated them. Look them over."

They each opened their envelopes. There was a driver's license, membership cards to a few organizations, and even a credit card.

"Are these real?" Abu Shakra asked. "Will the credit card work?"

"I am a forger, my friend. They will work for about two months or so, until the card company realizes you aren't paying your bills. You have no real mailing address; these are fakes. I believe you are all set, and it's very late. If it's okay, I'll call you a cab. You can wait in the lobby downstairs."

They both petted the dog good-bye, and Abu Shakra stroked the sleeping cat. Then they shook hands and went downstairs. In the lobby, they were quiet but held hands. Abu Shakra was imagining what he would do to her when the finally got her into a hotel bed. He would ravage her then and over the next few days. He would go to the land of peace fully sexually satisfied. Less than a week, and the end would start. The chain reaction would begin. It was a great responsibility, but he knew he was up to it. Shaul had trusted him with this great task, and it would be achieved now that he had his new identity. Finally, the cab arrived.

No one would suspect. They would never get caught.

Chapter 40

Shanghai, China

The *Titan Neptune*, owned by Crate Freight International, had arrived in port four hours earlier. All but a few containers had been unloaded. It was a relatively small vessel. The large metal boxes from Amsterdam had been unloaded, put on trucks, and driven away. The Chinese driver backed the truck to a dock at a warehouse, and the four crates with the rocket launchers were unloaded, unpacked, and distributed to eight members of the Church of the Elect. July 4 was six days away. They would all have time to relax for a few days before driving to the desalination plants to destroy them. Shaul had already sent to all of his disciples detailed maps of the facility security and the weak points on the massive equipment.

Dar-es-salaam, Tanzania

The *Cursing Mermaid* was owned and operated by an Ethiopian shipping company, and she had come into port two days ago. Four boxes holding the weapons had been trucked to a location far away from port, a field outside of the village of Soga. Eight tattered pickup trucks were circled around the larger trucks. Package by package, the metal compartments were unloaded, until all the weapons had been handed out to the disciples, one for each two-man team.

Port of Geraldton, Australia

The *Australian Osprey* was docked and her cargo unloaded. The automatic scanning equipment indicated that there was something emitting heat from a suspicious container. Heat-seeking instrumentation directed the authorities to five skids in the back of the box. When they inspected the contents, they found the weapons—one rocket launcher in a package in the middle of each skid. After that, they inspected the rest of the ship's entire cargo container by container. When the labor-intensive search was completed on July first, the Australian authorities alerted the International Port Authority Consortium, which had member ports around the globe. The organization notified all its members of the terrorist activity

Libra, Mexico

The *Black Pinto*, owned by Ocean Cargo, unloaded twelve skids out of the boxes on her deck. They were shipped unnoticed to destinations on both the east and west coasts. The cartons containing the rocket launchers were secretly unpacked. Members of the Church of the Elect gathered in teams of two to take control of each carton. They would remain secretly in hiding. Each team was now a short driving distance from a desalination plant. In their excitement, they celebrated with tables of food and plenty of tequila. Many members of the church joined in the festivities, though only a few knew how close the day of judgment really was.

Toamsina, Madagascar

The *Sailing Neptune*, owned by Blue Sea Shipping, pulled into port. Its freight of containers would be unloaded once it docked. Sundiata T'Shaka, both a member of the Church of the Elect and a customs inspector, had been forewarned of the cargo coming his way. He was a family man like many other members of the church. His wife and five kids adored him. He had a fair salary and took frequent bribes to afford the finer things in life for his clan. They took vacations to resorts in the Pacific and the Mediterranean. There was no way he would pass up taking a bribe for this one. The transformation of the Elect into paradise was something he had dreamed about but never thought would be a reality. Even if the rockets destroyed the desalination plants, T'Shaka realized it would take time for the consequences to unfold. He would need lots of money for his family to survive until the transformations was complete, so he threatened to confiscate the weapons if he wasn't paid well.

The church understood his position and tolerated the blackmail, but only until the weapons were in the disciples' hands. On July 1, he washed up on a resort beach in southern Toamsina.

Panama City, Florida

Port Panama had seen a spike in imports from Europe in recent months. Like most industrialized nations, the United States required port authorities to actively inspect incoming cargo. On June 30, the *Crown Trader,* owned by the Freedom Freight Company, pulled into port, and one by one, the containers were inspected by infrared scanners. A quadrangle from Amsterdam caused suspicion when the infrared sensors indicated that there was something generating heat inside. The first thought was that it was human cargo, which was typically the case. When inspectors opened the container, they found six rocket launchers with picanzite payloads. As the day went on, four more containers were discovered with the same cargo.

~ ~ ~

Boucher was reading his e-mail alerts as Sabino looked over his shoulder. They both saw the one from Interpol. It said that in many industrialized countries, rocket launchers with picanzite tips were being caught at shipping ports. Interpol sent out an international alert warning port authorities and customs inspectors to examine as much cargo as possible, as there was an obvious terrorist plot underway. The advisory went on to say that the weapons could be easily spotted with infrared equipment.

"So this is what we get for not raiding all the shipping companies in Amsterdam?" Sabino commented in an angry tone.

"We couldn't," said Boucher. "Their government is very strict there. Like the United States, they only allow searches with probable cause."

"Yeah, but I believe that in America the government has the authority to search a place if any form of terrorist activity is so much as suspected."

"That's true, but there were no known suspected terrorists working at any of the few companies we didn't raid. If the employees were members of the Church of the Elect, then by and large, they all slipped under the radar. The bulk of them have led clean, honest lives."

"So what are we going to do now?" asked Sabino.

"Just a lot more of what we've been doing—good, old-fashioned police work. Publishing their pictures, following leads, asking questions. We've only got three days. Right now, our people are contacting governments around the world, warning them that there is an imminent terrorist threat. Our director has already called the president, who has activated the National Guard to aid in our search for Abu Shakra and Lombardi. Their pictures are all over hotels, restaurants, and transportation hubs. Also, the NSA is working on breaking down the private instant messaging codes. Everyone has an individual key to get access to it. They know which ones Abu

Shakra, Shaul, and the others are using and have almost penetrated their codes."

When he finished talking, an agent who had been patiently standing by spoke up. "Scott, we have a report of something suspicious I'm going to check into and I thought you might like to know."

"By all means. What have you got?"

"The night clerk at the Park Central reported a couple checking in at four this morning."

"Yeah, so?"

"So they matched the height and build of our two suspects. They didn't look like them, but because our bulletin mentioned they might look different, he thought he should report it. The most important part of the tip is that the man was carrying a small suitcase that matched the one that was seen on camera at the airport."

Boucher stood up. "Let's get the hell down there. Agent Richards," he called out, "coordinate with the police. I'll call you as soon as I find out who these people are. We'll want every available cop in the city down there if it turns out to be them. Ping, Kamryn, come with me. Where's Gail?"

"She was on the phone a minute ago," Kamryn said. Then she looked around and pointed. "See, she's right over there."

Boucher went over to Sharland. He cut her off midsentence. "I have to interrupt, Gail. Do you want to come with us or stay here?"

"I'd love to go with you, but I just got a call from Interpol. There was a raid in Amsterdam that ended in a gun battle. People were killed, though none were police. They arrested a woman named Emma Van den Broeck. She's the CEO of a large shipping company there. One of the ones killed was a person you were interested in.

Someone named Ali Madri. Another who is in critical condition is Dabir Sulimani. They want me to get involved with the interrogation. I must fly back immediately."

"Great," Boucher said. "I'll get you to the airport and arrange for a charter to fly you back as soon as you arrive. Ping, Kamryn, let's get to that hotel."

Chapter 41

When Abu Shakra and Lombardi finally got to their room at four that morning, they tore off each other's clothes and indulged hungrily in the best sex he had had for quite some time. By five, they were both exhausted and sleeping heavily. They had been so loud that he wondered if they had woken up anyone in nearby rooms. The daylight had woken him up at eight o'clock. In their lust, they both had forgotten to close the shade.

Now was the time to get going. He had to pick up his package. It had arrived from the Middle East. He had just finished up with Lombardi's computer. Abu Shakra had just gotten out of a private chat room with Valik Alekseev, who had tucked the item in a large crate owned by Materia Medica, smuggled the item to JFK, and then arranged to have it transported to a warehouse in Brooklyn. Today, Abu Shakra would have Lombardi drive him there so he could pick it up. He went to the bed and shook her.

"Come on, Amanda. Time to get up." She groaned and rolled away from him. He shook her again and spoke a bit louder this time. "Amanda, get up." She turned and squinted at him.

"What time is it?" she asked.

"It's quarter of nine. Come on, we have to go pick something up."

She threw her legs over the side of the bed and wrapped the sheet around her body. She was still nude, and he got a glimpse of her naked form as she enveloped herself with the sheet. He wanted her again and looked forward to getting back so he could ravage her once more. She got some clothes from her suitcase and dragged herself into the bathroom.

While he waited, he looked out the window. They had a view facing Central Park. The hotel was a few blocks away, so he could see some but not all of the park. They were up on the twenty-first floor, and he could see buildings surrounding the massive preserve. He imagined the trees on fire, the buildings destroyed—what this view would look like after he did what he had been sent to do. He envisioned all of the buildings burning and people in the streets running in panic. It would be the beginning of the end. The United States would respond, and then all hell would break loose and Shaul's vision would come to pass. Abu Shakra wondered how the Elect would get to paradise. Would they first suffer like everyone else? Or would the Lord look over everyone and grant them an easy passing? He hoped it was the latter, but he would save a lot of money in case he needed it.

He heard Lombardi flush the toilet, and then she exited the bathroom, fully dressed. He still wanted to have more sex with her. He wondered how far he could trust her, though he realized that if she started to disrupt the plan, he would have to kill her. It was no fun killing a woman. They had such little fight in them. Men, especially some men, offered challenges. But never had anyone slipped away from him. He was a killing machine.

He went to the door, opened it, and looked both ways down the hall. There was no one except him. Now would be a good time to leave. After he closed the door, he noticed that someone had displayed a virtual copy of the New York Times on the reader on the inside of the door. He picked it up for the heck of it. The first feature story jumped out at him. The headline read, "International Terrorist Plot Unfolding." Something twanged in his stomach. Could someone know? He read the story.

> NEW YORK – Throughout the industrialized world, weapons are being confiscated that were apparently intended to be used in a terrorist plot. So far, over 100 have been discovered at shipping ports around the globe.
>
> According to information obtained by the Times, the weapons are rocket launchers capable of incredible destructive power.
>
> "They came out of China and are now in the hands of terrorists," said a source close to the case who preferred not to be identified. "We don't know exactly what the targets are, but we suspect infrastructure like food, water, or Electricity. We have a great deal of suspicion it is desalination plants they're after."
>
> Federal Bureau of Investigation Special Agent Scott Boucher is said to be in charge of the investigation. He has been unavailable for comment despite repeated attempts by Times reporters.
>
> The deadly warheads contain a payload of an extremely powerful new explosive called picanzite. It has the potential to (see Plot, page 2).

He opened the paper to page 2 and started reading the rest right in the hall. It seemed someone else was planning to disrupt life right at this moment. Who else would plan such a disaster? The answer was plain. The Church of the Elect, that was who. Shaul not only had employed him to cause massive destruction in New York City but also had planned to have the church's disciples eliminate water supplies, which would have collapsed transportation, food supplies, and the like. Pretty smart, but it seemed the plan had failed. Now it was more important than ever that he succeed.

"Are you almost ready?" called Lombardi's voice from inside the room.

"Just a second."

Why only industrialized countries? he wondered. Could it be that the church wanted to bring those countries down to a level of poverty similar to that in the rest of the world? Maybe that wasn't it at all. Suppose the church had shipped them to all parts of the world but the technology in undeveloped countries was such that they had been unable to detect the weapons when they were smuggled in. After all, he himself had brought arms across the borders of warring countries. Finishing the article, he thought he shouldn't alarm Lombardi, so he put it on the ground, face down. He re-entered the room and saw her standing by the bureau. Her stance and appearance were quite erotic. The mask made her look twenty-five instead of forty. The expression on her face seemed to scream, "Make love to me!"

He thought about their sex earlier that morning and wanted more but knew they had to recover the money and the package. He blocked his feelings out of his mind. He double-checked the wad of money in his sportcoat pocket.

"Okay, amorous Amanda, let's go," he said and smiled. They went to the elevator. There was a commotion in the lobby. There were two men and two women at the desk. A pair of policemen were standing on the far side of the desk. It seemed that all of them were trying to talk to the attendant at the same time. Abu Shakra turned his head away so they couldn't see him. "Look away," he whispered to Lombardi, and she did. As they went through the vestibule he tried to pick up some of the conversation. He heard their names and other telltale words ... *Terrorist. Arrest. Raid. Changing identities. New identities.* They went to the garage and got her car.

He convinced her to let him drive. As they were paying at the booth, sirens screamed and a mass of police cars swarmed to a halt at the front of the hotel.

They pulled out of the garage from the back of the hotel and right onto Fifty-Seventh street. As they crossed the intersection of Seventh Avenue, they saw a police car do a one-eighty and accelerate in pursuit. The officer made short blasts with his siren.

"Oh, shit," Abu Shakra said in Arabic and stomped on the accelerator. *"Hold on!"* The tired car came to life and forced their heads back onto the headrests. He peeled around the corner, tires squealing, onto the shopping mecca of Fifth Avenue. He heard the short blast of the siren behind him turn into a continuous, oscillating wail. He looked in the rearview and saw the police car turning the corner.

Abu Shakra started weaving around cars and then quickly took another right onto Fifty-Third. He skidded wide and ended up going into oncoming traffic. Cars blasted their horns. The cruiser was not far behind. Swerving back to the right side, again Abu Shakra began dodging cars. He switched to the left side again, the cruiser still pursuing. Quickly, he cut across traffic onto Tenth Avenue. The police officer didn't react quickly enough and was smashed by another car as he tried to make the turn.

"Take this right," Lombardi exclaimed. There was a red light, and pedestrians crowded the crosswalk. He blared his horn and drove through them, forcing many to jump out of the way, as he turned onto Fifty-Fourth Street. The banged-up cruiser had not stopped after the collision and was closing fast. He heard another siren closing fast and at least one more a few blocks away. Abu Shakra again pushed the pedal to the floor, and the car rocketed forward as he wove between more vehicles.

"Turn here," she shouted above the racing engine. He spun the wheel left and went down Ninth, but there was one problem. It was a one-way street, and they were driving into the oncoming traffic. She screamed at him in terror, "Wrong way. Wrong way!"

"How the hell was I supposed to know? You never said left or right."

Horns blared. Drivers shouted. Oncoming cars steered away from them. They dodged traffic for two blocks, Lombardi screaming all the way. They were headed straight for a white van. "Get out of the way," he vainly shouted. The van turned toward the right, Abu Shakra to the left. They were still on a collision course. He swerved further to the left and sideswiped an oncoming car.

"My car!" Lombardi cried. Then she bellowed, "Turn right. *Now!"*

They ripped around the corner, and then they were back on Fifty-Seventh—the street they had started from. Abu Shakra saw the hotel with all the police cars right in front of him and just a few blocks away. Instantly, he tried to take a left on Eighth Avenue. As he rotated the wheel, a tandem bus turned from Eighth onto Fifty-Seventh, blocking his escape.

"Stop right there," blared a voice out from the PA of another police car. "This is the New York City Police!"

He watched as a large policeman exited the passenger door, drawing his pistol. "Get out of the car!" he demanded. Abu Shakra jammed it into reverse and stomped on the accelerator, simultaneously ducking his head and putting his arm around Lombardi and forcing her to duck as well. Two shots shattered the back window. Lombardi's vehicle bashed the police car's door, and the officer dove over the hood to avoid being hit.

"Oh my God," Lombardi whined. "My poor car."

After what seemed like hours, the bus pulled away onto Fifty-Seventh. Abu Shakra dropped it into drive and accelerated around the corner. The cruisers were in hot pursuit. He saw four behind him. All of a sudden, Abu Shakra remembered a trick. He lurched to the right and avoided more cars. He clipped the next car ahead of him just so, and it swirled sideways across the street, leaving all the cars behind him—including the police cars—stuck behind it and putting an end to the scramble.

The siren, still screaming uselessly, faded behind them. Looking in his mirror, Abu Shakra could see that the lights were still flashing, but the car was where he had left it. All through the race, Lombardi had been turned around either screaming or calling out the law's location.

"We did it," she said, with a sense of pride in her voice and expression. Abu Shakra continued to look in his mirror. "We need to turn on—"

There was an explosion. The car stopped instantly. Abu Shakra was thrown into the steering wheel. Lombardi was restrained by her seatbelt. They had rear-ended a stopped car. Abu Shakra shook his head. There was steam coming out of the radiator. He felt blood running down his forehead, touched it with his fingers, and looked at it in disbelief. He was disorientated and unaware of what had happened. Lombardi shook him.

"We've got to get out of here," she exclaimed. He tried to clear his mind. Everything around him finally came into focus.

"What happened?" he asked.

"You hit a car. Come on," she pleaded, "let's go."

He opened his door and started to get out. Lombardi unbuckled and exited. As he left, a man came out of the car he had hit.

"What the hell did you do that for?" he shouted in a Brooklyn accent. "You bastard, you totaled my car."

Still partially disorientated, Abu Shakra couldn't decide what to do. He sized the man up, and he was small enough. Eliminating him would be no problem. A crowd was beginning to gather. He heard sirens again in the distance.

"We've got to run," Lombardi demanded. He staggered as they started to run. The man jumped in front of him.

"Oh no you don't!"

Adrenalin pumped through Abu Shakra's body. Everything was clear now. It would be fight, then flight. Abu Shakra sucker-punched the man, and he went flying onto the sidewalk and lay there motionless.

They started to run away from the scene, though Abu Shakra was stumbling. He must have stopped bleeding, because he could no longer feel anything coming out of the cut. His head throbbed.

"We've got to get to the subway," Lombardi said. "This way. I see an entrance right at that corner." She pointed and pulled him by the hand. Everything was clearer still. He ran faster and started pulling her. For a second, he wondered why she was helping him so much; then he refocused on their predicament. They ran across the street. Drivers blared their horns and screeched to a halt and avoid them. They were at the top of the stairs at the entrance. He turned and looked back. Two police cruisers had arrived. He also saw a pedestrian pointing and the officer looking their way. Hand in hand, they ran down the stairs, knocking people down in their path.

"This way. Come on," Lombardi pleaded. They reached the turnstiles and leaped over them. He heard no one shouting at them, to his surprise. The subway landing was right in front of them. "Come on."

They went down another set of stairs and then up another flight. Right then, a subway train was pulling in to stop in front of them. The doors whooshed open. They got on and stood up, looking across to the other landing. Two policemen ran onto the scene with their guns drawn. Without saying a word, they both turned around, sat, and slouched down in their seats.

The subway lurched into motion. They sat up straighter as they watched the station disappear.

"Where are we headed?" he asked.

"You wanted to go to Brooklyn, didn't you?"

"Is that where we're headed?"

"Yup. That's why we came over to this side, though it helped that we also eluded the police at the same time."

He reached into his inside pocket and pulled out a slip of paper. "I've got the address right here."

She took it, looked at it, and smiled. "Kent Street, Brooklyn Heights, it says. I have a friend who lives in Flatbush. We can stay with her."

"Sounds like a plan," he said. "Can you look at my head when we get there?"

"Sure," she said. He slouched back down and relaxed for the ride. In spite of these few rough spots, he thought everything was going well. The mission was still underway.

Chapter 42

It was a run-down apartment in Flatbush on Linden Avenue, a busy street with lots of traffic. It was one of those streets with row apartments Abu Shakra often had seen in pictures of typical Brooklyn. There were rows of apartments on each side of the street. All were made of stone or cement with half of a flight of stairs leading up to the doors. Lombardi's friend's apartment was made of cement that was formed to look like stone. It was on the corner on the third floor and had a turret with curved windows rounding the bias. The stairs were narrow and creaky, and the wall paper was peeling. It looked as if the place had not been maintained in a hundred years, Abu Shakra thought. The hall was dim with uncovered fluorescent lights; one was blinking on and off. Another was emitting a loud buzzing noise. In places, plaster dangled from the ceiling. They stopped at number thirty-four. It was an ancient wooden door, obviously made before the planet's forests were depleted. Though it was in bad shape, the door must have been worth serious money.

There was a note on the door in neat handwriting that said, "Hi everyone. Off for a little fun. Back on July 5."

"Huh," Lombardi said. Then she reached up to the top of the

trim around the door and retrieved a key. "She told me to make myself at home any time."

Lombardi turned the lock and opened the door. Abu Shakra was expecting the place to be as run-down as the rest of the building, but to his surprise, it was nicely kept. A large collection of plants was scattered around, most likely to help in adding oxygen to the space. Plants hung from the ceiling, sat on tables and windowsills, and grew from large planters on the floor spread around the room and on the kitchen counter. The kitchen, living room, and small dining table were all in one open space. There were two doors next to each other. He imagined they were the bathroom and the bedroom.

"Are you hungry?" Lombardi asked.

"I'd rather check out where I smashed my head. Is that the bathroom?' he asked, pointing to the door on the left.

"No," she said. "It's the other one. Let me help."

They both went into the bathroom, and he looked in the mirror. It wasn't as bad as he had thought, but there was quite a bit of blood. His mask was ripped, and his forehead was cut open enough to bleed, but it wasn't serious. Lombardi washed it out and dried it with a towel. The bleeding had stopped. She found some glue in the other room and stuck the torn parts of the mask together. Now it looked like he had a scar on his forehead.

"I have to get going and contact the person who has my property," he said when she had finished.

"There's her computer," she said pointing to the dining room table. "Go right ahead. I'm starving. I'll make us a couple of sandwiches."

He finally got into a private instant messaging session with Shaul. Initially, he was told that the person on the other end was a disciple, but they quickly put him through directly to the Elect one.

ALSUD: *How secure is this IM?*

ELE1: *We suspect that we are being monitored. Not in real time, though. We are still communicating through our network, which will delay the time it takes for people actually to see what we are saying.*

ALSUD: *I will have the product in about an hour. Today is July 1. What do you want me to do?*

ELE1: *You will stay with me until it is time to start the destruction of the Watchers. How can we meet?*

ALSUD: *Are you sure we are secure?*

ELE1: *Positive. If not, they would have caught up with us by now.*

ALSUD: *I am in Brooklyn. Can you send a disciple to take me to you?*

ELE1: *Where do you want to meet?*

ALSUD: *I will let you know as soon as I pick up the device.*

ELE1: *It cost enough money, but I am sure it will work. It will fry every Electrical connection in New York City.*

ALSUD: *I am told there will be thousands of fires. The city will burn to the ground.*

ELE1: *Yes, it will. Let me know when you have it.*

ALSUD: *I will. May the Lord of Spirits be with you.*

ELE1: *And you as well.*

He erased the conversation and signed off. He was tingling with excitement. The apocalypse would start in just three days. Abu Shakra was honored to be the one Shaul trusted with such a project; he felt humbled. The Watchers would suffer, and the Elect would live in bliss, all because of him. He wondered if the Lord was watching over him. With the exception of the chase incident, everything was going smoothly. Shaul had told him that the Supreme Master would forgive his evil sexual desires. That made him think about making love with Lombardi those few short hours ago. They would pick up the package and then come back here to make love, perhaps for the last time

"How about a ham and cheese?" she asked from just behind him. She handed him a plate with a sandwich. He ate quickly because he was anxious to get going, but he had to wait for her anyway.

He went back to the computer and got directions to the warehouse address. They left and were to take the subway to Brooklyn Heights, which had been a cozy residential neighborhood since the 1830s. That confused him, because they were looking for a factory. The computer's directions must have been screwy. They went left and right for about half a mile. Outside of the area, factories popped up. Two hundred Kent Street housed Umbrella Productions, Inc., which Alekseev mentioned made conference booth displays for international companies. One of the booths from the Materia Medica convention had been diverted there on its way to LA. Abu Shakra and Lombardi showed up at the factory not knowing who to ask for or what to expect. He decided what to do as soon as he was greeted by the receptionist.

"I am from Materia Medica," he said to her. "I understand that part of one of our booths is here."

"One moment, please," she replied and then picked up the phone and called someone. In a short while a tall man, as big as Abu Shakra, entered the lobby. He skin was the shade of someone of Middle Eastern descent, and Abu Shakra recognized the man's accent as Syrian.

"Hello, hello," the man said with exuberant enthusiasm. "May I help you?"

"A gentleman named Valik Alekseev told me you have something here for me," he said in Arabic.

"Yes, of course. He told me to expect you. Come right this way."

Lombardi looked slighted when they did not speak in English, so he spoke up. "It's nothing," he said to her. "We are just greeting each other, and I told him why we are here."

They followed him through a door directly into a production area. There were saws buzzing and the rap of hammers echoing. Two people were talking with one another loudly. There were about two dozen people working on booths in differing stages of completion. After they passed though, they reached a large pair of double doors that automatically swung open. As soon as they passed between them, Abu Shakra saw that this room was a shipping area. There were crates everywhere with the names of different countries and cities stenciled on them. They arrived at an opened one that said Los Angeles.

"Here," the man said, again in Arabic. "One apiece. It will be best if you leave through the exit on the dock."

"Do you mind if I use your computer before I leave?" Abu Shakra asked.

"Please, right this way."

"Wait here with the bags, Amanda."

Abu Shakra followed the man back through the production area to a nicely furnished office.

"Help yourself," the man said. Abu Shakra logged onto the private instant messaging system and contacted Shaul. Shaul was to send a driver to the pond in Prospect Park in Flatbush. They were also to speak in Arabic, and the same two-grip handshake was to be used to identify them as friendly. They would be picked up there in three hours and taken to a secret location in Manhattan. That would give him enough time to have sex again with Lombardi. He logged off. The man guided him back to the shipping door. Lombardi was sitting on the floor with her back resting on the case with the bomb.

"Come on. We're meeting someone in a few hours. Do you want to go back to the apartment for some fun?"

She stood up and kissed him. "That sounds intriguing. Let's go," she said

Abu Shakra took both of the cases and carried then out of the door and down the stairs. The one with the bomb was heaviest—about eighty pounds. The one with the cash was about half as heavy. These would get heavy very quickly in spite of his strength. He looked up at the man.

"Thank you," he said.

"No problem."

They would have to call for a cab, which they did. He couldn't haul these suitcases all over the city. It arrived after only about ten minutes. The cabbie drove back onto Kent Street, and they soon arrived at the apartment. He only had to carry the bags to their lodging. They were heavy, but he happily bore the burden. He thought of the implications of the suitcases, and he suddenly had the strength to carry them.

"What's the contents?" Lombardi asked sarcastically after they arrived in the apartment. She gripped his upper arm with hers.

"Oh, nothing too exciting. The smaller bag is all money that needs to be laundered, and the big one is some kind of new medical device," he said, lying. "It's just a bunch of dials and gauges."

"How much money?"

"I don't really know. It was never my place to count it. I only brought it here."

"Can I see the medical thing?"

"Of course." He sat the bag flat and opened it up. He felt a rush of adrenalin as he looked at the dials and gauges. "There you have it," he said with a big smile.

"What does it do?" she asked as he started unbuttoning her blouse.

"Something to do with breathing. It analyzes other molecules mixed with your exhaled carbon dioxide. Very sophisticated."

"And why smuggle it if it's a medical device?" she asked.

"Because it hasn't been approved by the FDA. It's used in many other countries, but in the US there's so much red tape, so it won't be on the market for several years. In the mean time, it will better the quality of life for some lucky people."

He chuckled to himself. It was sure going to better the quality of life for the Elect and the righteous.

"It's very cool," Lombardi said as she gazed at the instruments. He stood in back of her, arms wrapped around her chest. He gently messaged one of her breasts and felt the nipple go erect. She put her hand on top of his and moaned. "What about the money," she said dreamily. "Can I see the money?"

He let go of her, a little disappointed that she wanted to waste the time to see it. He looked at her. She was obviously intrigued by everything, and if it thrilled her and made her hotter, then it was worth the time. Perhaps she would be even more passionate if he showed her the cash. He figured he had taken about a million dollars. Flopping the bag on its back, he zipped it open and revealed the bundles of hundred-dollar bills. He looked at Lombardi. Her eyes were twinkling. Obviously she had never seen this much money before and was thrilled to see it. She had the look of greed on her face, as if the money were hers; she glared at it with an ear-to-ear grin. She was so excited, he wondered if he could take her into his confidence if he offered some of the money. Of course, she would never get the chance to use it, but he could see her desire for it as she fanned through the bills of a bundle. He could only imagine her passion if he told her to put that in her purse.

"What do you think?" he asked. Lombardi rubbed the bills against her cheek.

"This is amazing. Where did all this cash come from?"

"This much money isn't all that uncommon in black markets like stolen art, drugs, or guns. I've seen more than this before."

"My god. What do you do with all this money?"

"I have a villa in a small town on the Italian coast. Invest it," he said, thinking he could trust her. He would tell her, but only after they made love again. "But this is not all for me. Much of it belongs to the Church of the Elect. I could give a little of it to you."

She jumped on him, practically knocking him over.

"Really!" she gasped. "How much. Thousands?"

"It's not really mine to just give it all away, but you've been a great help. I could give you a packet of hundreds. How would that be?" She kissed him wildly, rubbing her hands over his body. He was much taller than her, so she pushed her side up against his crotch.

"Thank you, thank you," she said. "Let's make love. Right here … on top of the money." She let go of him and kicked a number of bundles on the floor, spreading them about. This was a bit weird, he thought, but if it made her hornier, why not? They undressed each other in a fit of lust. She lay down, her back on top of the cash. She pulled him on top of her with a carnal desire he had never experienced. During their sexual union, he decided not to last too long. They needed to get going soon. He was distracted. As they copulated, his mind wandered, and he thought that he had to get to Shaul and wait to face his destination. He thought about Lombardi and what would happen to her during the time of reckoning. As he was on top of her, he gazed at the mask of the deceased Kelley Holtz. She was really far more attractive than the Lombardi he had met at the airport. He had more desire for her than he had ever had for any woman he could remember. In half an hour they were finished, lying next to each other on top of the money, gasping for breath, embracing. There was radiance between them. He felt a kind of a bond with her, as if she and he were one. He could trust her with the core of his mission, no doubt about it. He was itching to tell his secret to her. In a moment, he spoke.

"Are you familiar with the Church of the Elect?" he asked, nearly breathless.

"No. Not really, though I've read about them in magazines. They're kind of weird."

"Not at all. We believe fallen angels have strayed from God and live among us. They have taken over the world and are called the Watchers. You can see it in the way the world is run by only a few big companies and corrupt governments."

"If you say so, sweetie," she said and kissed his cheek. "What's your point?"

"They also believe that the apocalypse will come and the righteous will then exist in a wondrous place. And that the fallen angels and their followers will suffer for eternity."

"So?"

"So the rulers of the church sent me on a mission. I am destined to initiate the day of judgment. The big suitcase is not really a medical device. It's actually an Electromagnetic bomb. When I set it off, the force will fry all of the Electrical connections in New York City."

"You're joking, of course."

"No. I am deadly serious. There will be thousands of fires. Too many to keep up with. The city will burn." He saw the look on her face. It was sheer disbelief. He realized that he had made a big mistake.

"You can't do that. Think of all of the innocent people who will die."

"There are no innocent lives, only good and evil."

"My god. You actually are serious."

He thought maybe if he explained to her the entire plan, she would come to the church's side. If he could convince her that she would go to the world of the righteous, maybe he could convince her.

"It's like I said. You are good, Amanda. You will go to the world of the blessed, because you've been helping me accomplish the goal.

Don't you see? You are a righteous person. You will come out on top."

"Who are you kidding? There is no God. No other life."

"Of course there is God. He lives in our hearts. He will reward the Elect after the apocalypse and provide for us forever."

"What a bunch of crap," she said in a tone of distaste. He really had made a mistake in telling her. She didn't even believe in God. "When we die, we cease to exist. After death, there is nothingness. We are merely corpses left to rot in boxes."

He would never convince her. She was obviously a Watcher. He couldn't believe that she had helped him and that he had trusted her with the secret.

"I don't believe I was helping you," she said. "If I had known, I would have turned you in. Is that why the police were chasing us?"

"Yes, they are the Watchers. They must be stopped. They will suffer for all eternity." He kept looking at her. With each moment, her expression became stranger to him. He could see that her thoughts had gone from love to disbelief to near horror. How could she not see something so obvious? To end the world was the only way to cleanse it of evil.

"Your plan has a little flaw," she said with distaste. "How will one little bomb destroy the world?"

"It's very simple. Destroying New York City will be an act of war. The bomb can be traced to Russian origins. The US will retaliate by launching nuclear bombs at Russia, and then they will fight back by sending off their own missiles."

"There's no way that will happen. US and Russian diplomatic relations will find who to blame. The Russians will claim it was not their fault—"

"The United States president has said that if ever there is a nuclear or similar attack by an independent group, then by association, he will blame the country where the weapon originated."

"You really think you can pull this off, don't you? You're insane. You, the church, you're all crazy. I can't let this happen."

Maybe there was a remote possibility that he still could convince her if he offered her enough money. Her greed was obvious from the way she had wanted to make love on top of the bundles of bills. He would try that as a last resort.

"If you help me, I'll give you all of the money you desire."

"There is nothing you can offer me. No amount of money would cause me to be associated with such horror. This can't happen," she said as she went toward the door. "I won't let you do this."

Lombardi, as much as he had fallen for her, could not be allowed out of the apartment. He lunged in front of her and grabbed her by the arm.

"I'll give you one last chance," he said as he immobilized her by clamping her arm.

"Let me go," she cried, trying to struggle loose. Then she slapped his face. The sting of her hand warmed his cheek. He liked that. His mind was made up. It was a pity to have to kill her. He had really felt like they were meant to be together, but it was not to be. He was thrilled at the prospect of eliminating such a feisty woman, and yet at the same time, he was saddened by what he needed to do. He thought of having sex on top of the money. That was rather kinky, and he liked that. He liked being with her, but it was obvious that she would be detrimental to his mission. She fought harder. "I said, let me go!" she shouted and started screaming for help.

And he knew his desire for her was misguided. *She doesn't believe*, he thought in sudden distaste. She wanted to stop the mission, and she simply opposed to the possibility of the day of judgment. *She is a Watcher. She must die.*

He spun her around so that her back was against his chest. He regretted doing this, but there was no other solution. He wrapped his arm around her neck, positioning himself so that he could squeeze the main arteries to her brain. That way was far quicker than a choke strangle. The move would simply put her to sleep, and she wouldn't know the horror of dying by suffocation. She had to die, but there was no need for here to suffer. It was the most humane way he knew to eliminate someone. She was dead eight seconds after he stopped the flow to her brain. He released his grip, and she collapsed on the floor, a pile of flesh. He saw the passionate face of Kelley Holtz, her color just as pink as if she had been alive. The mask retained its color. Lombardi's face underneath would be pale. Again he thought about their lovemaking together, here and in the hotel. She really had turned him on. He carried her to the bed and gently placed her there and folded her hands on her chest. Her head was nice and straight. He was glad he hadn't broken her neck. The mask had a bit of a smile to it. He smiled back and realized that there was only a little time before he had to meet his contact. At least he wouldn't have to explain her to Shaul. He took the key off the table, grabbed his bags, went out the door, and locked it behind him. He heard the hum of the light in the hall; the other light continued to flash.

He would miss her, but his mission would no longer be at risk.

Chapter 43

The lobby of the Park Central Hotel was a mass of confusion. Police and FBI agents were making demands of the staff. Boucher was at the main desk interrogating the night attendant. Sabino and Kamryn were listening in.

"Well, can you bring up their pictures so we can see what they look like?" demanded Boucher. The Midtown North Precinct's chief of police was by his side, trying to take over the questioning.

"Yes, sir," said the young man. "I can certainly do that."

He tapped on the old-fashioned keyboard. Hotels still used them to ensure proper spelling of names.

"It says here that their passports named them as Gagan Malik from Delhi, India and Kelley Holtz. Wow, she's smoking hot."

"Where's she from?" Boucher asked. It was obvious to Sabino from Boucher's tone that he did not approve of the employee's comment.

"Hoboken."

"Let me see their pictures," Boucher said. The attendant turned the screen so everyone on the other side of the counter could see. "Send their information to me at FBI headquarters." He handed his business card to the attendant, who then entered the information on the keyboard. Boucher thanked him and stepped away from the desk.

There was a man surrounded by the media on the far side of the lobby. Sabino recognized him as the mayor

"Come with me," Boucher said to him and Kamryn, and they followed Boucher over to the politician. Reporters were firing questions at him. There was a confusion of cameras, microphones, recorders, and writing tablets.

"Are there terrorists in New York?"

"Is the city in any danger?"

"Do you know who they are?"

"Is it true that they can change identities?"

"Do you have any pictures?"

The shouting went on. Boucher muscled his way through the mob and showed his badge. The mayor tried to move away, but he was swarmed.

"No comment. No comment," was all he said. The police intervened in the near riot and forced all the journalists to back away from the mayor. He, Boucher, Sabino, and Kamryn went to another room and closed the door. There was a sudden quiet as the voices of the press were muffled by the door. The room had paper-thin TV screens on two walls and a volume control panel on a console in the center. There were pictures of news events on all of them, but none had the volume turned on.

"What the hell is this mess?" the mayor demanded. Boucher brought him up to speed. "Have them send copies of the suspects' pictures to my public relations department as well. I'll see to it that they are posted around the city. I'll contact the local cell providers and have them broadcast the profiles to all the city's cell phone subscribers."

"It may be too late," Sabino said.

"I won't accept that," The mayor said. "I'll have the governor activate more National Guard. *Can't* is not an option. What else are you doing to find them?"

"We have alerted the president and all the Homeland Security agencies," Boucher said. "Some of them are working on it as well, but I'm not up to date on their activities."

"I'll have posters printed right away. Then I'll contact Democratic headquarters and get volunteers to post them everywhere. The more publicity, the better."

"Certainly," Boucher said. Sabino was clearly out of his element. He longed for his little duties as network administrator and the times when Kamryn would lead him away from crackers and cheese and up to the bedroom with a bottle of wine.

The mayor excused himself and went back to the other room, where he talked with his assistants and then faced the media circus. They looked at the several silent screens on the walls. One suddenly showed a live picture of the mayor, then another and another. He was trying to get quiet so that he could talk. Sabino turned up the volume. The mayor said what the city and federal agencies were doing about the terrorists. The station put up two pictures of Abu Shakra and Lombardi and explained that they were actually posing as a man from India and a woman named Kelley Holtz from Hoboken. After a rash of questions, the interview ended. Sabino turned to Boucher.

"What have they turned up in Pecos?" Sabino asked.

"I'll contact them right now to find out," Boucher replied. He activated his communications center and spoke. "Agent Wilson?"

There was a pause, and then he spoke again. "What have you been up to?"

Another pause. "I see. Hold on." He turned to Sabino and

Kamryn. "They're going through all the computers. They found several with the hard drives removed, but quite a lot of them are still intact. Hopefully that'll help us." He stopped speaking again and listened. "I see. Uh-huh. Okay. Yeah, sure. Well, very good. Thank you."

Boucher looked at them again.

"What else is going on?" Kamryn asked.

"The biggest break for us is going to be finding a list of members. They are finding lists of church members and have been sending out agents and police to interrogate the people of interest who've turned up, including many here in New York. If they can find a master list of members from New York City, we'll have a real shot at stopping this thing."

"Do you think they'll find one?" Kamryn asked.

"Let's certainly hope so. They're already getting warrants to search houses here. With any kind of luck, we'll find them. The most important thing they found is that they believe Abu Shakra has what is called an Electromagnetic bomb, or an e-bomb. When he sets it off, hundreds of thousands of Electrical connections in the city will spark violently, which will start many more fires than we could ever put out. An area—we don't know how large—surrounding the ignition point will all burn."

"Look, the president," Kamryn said, pointing to a screen. Sabino turned up the volume. The president appeared on other screens. He was a fairly young president—forty something—but he was good. He had taken the country through several diplomatic crises situations and averted getting involved with a few warring little countries, though his work on the economy hadn't been so successful.

"Hello," he said. "We are facing a national threat. Terrorists are planning attacks around the globe against us, our allies, and other nations. They think they can do us harm, but let me assure you that will not be possible. At this time, we are hunting the terrorists and have every expectation of finding them.

"We believe that these enemies of the state plan to attack our water production facilities. I want to let them know our interests here and abroad have increased security at the desalination plants to a point where there is no way to penetrate the perimeters we have set up. Perhaps they feel comfortable in their efforts, but they are wrong. We are the world power, and there is no way they can disrupt how we go about our daily lives. These people desire only to bring more deadly attacks against us and our allies. And they are not alone. Rogue nations have contracted to supply the means of mass destruction to these destroyers of democracy. These collaborating nations sponsor radical militias and empower both terrorists and insurgents. Let me assure the world that whatever countries supplied these devices, we will hold them totally responsible. We will make an appropriate response no matter what the result.

"What they don't know is that America's best minds have been pooled together to bring these people to justice. Terrorists want to bring darkness to the world. These insurgents want to turn back the hands of freedom and bring to the world terror and tyranny. Their predecessors are totalitarians, fascists, and Nazis, and all other regimes under dictatorial rule.

"But history has seen these rulers defeated. History has not been kind to them. We will fight them with all of our spirit, with our hearts and souls, like we did on the beaches of Normandy or the jungles of the Pacific, the deserts of Iraq, and the mountains of Afghanistan.

"These extremist groups that have their roots in the Middle East have tried to fan the flames of tyranny to industrialized and wealthier nations throughout the Western world. But we are using every available asset to fight these forces. We are using everything at our disposal to stop their terrorist tactics, and it is within our power to stop them. I have activated many units of the National Guard to aid in the search and allied defenses. They are not only being deployed around the country, but I have ordered them to protect our interests in our allied nations. My fellow Americans, we will succeed. Thank you."

There was a pause for effect, and then the image on the screen changed to a reporter with a newsroom in the background. Immediately, he started to analyze the speech.

"At least we know he's not going to screw around if this actually does happen," Kamryn said.

"But that's what we have to worry about," Boucher said. "Suppose Abu Shakra is successful in his mission here in New York. We'll trace where the bomb came from, and then we'll launch an attack against that nation. Yes, it could have been sold to him through a small revolutionary nation that hates the west, but it probably came from a much more industrialized, technologically advanced nation ... say, Russia or China. They have the power to retaliate with significant force. Then where will the world be? He said he's activated the National Guard. That's a solution?"

"Yes," Sabino said. "That's mostly to protect Aquasuperior's interests."

"No doubt Erebos's paying for the privilege," Kamryn said. "But what's the president doing to protect New York from Abu Shakra and the others? He forgot to mention that, didn't he?"

"Abu Shakra and the church have a lot of agencies looking for them," Boucher said. "But the FBI wants the glory, and I'm going to see that we get it. Let's get back to work and catch this idiot."

"Agent Boucher," someone said in a booming voice. They turned to look at who was speaking, and it was one of the agents Sabino had been introduced to back at the New York headquarters.

"Yes, what've you got?"

"We just intercepted a communication from Abu Shakra. He's meeting someone in Prospect Park in Brooklyn."

"How old is the message?"

"The NSA just decoded it. It could be as old as an hour."

"Well, he's long gone by now. But let's get some agents out there to see if we can find out if anyone spotted anyone suspicious."

Chapter 44

Abu Shakra walked down to Prospect Park with the two suitcases and waited around the pond as he had been instructed. He was seated on a bench looking for the person he was to meet. There were some parents with playing children, a few old men playing chess, and a couple of other people walking around. Then he saw two men in business suits strolling at a brisk pace. They were kind of suspicious looking, because they were turning their heads in every direction. That must be them. He had a good instinct for judging people based on their body language, and these men were definitely not the law. It was his business to make critical observations. Besides, if it had been the authorities, they would have been asking questions of the locals. He noticed that they had spotted him, and he stood up and stretched, looking at them. They waved and then approached him.

"Are you Jabbar?" one of them asked in Arabic, extending his right hand and enthusiastically performing the brotherhood handshake. Abu Shakra gripped it.

"And you would be?" he replied.

"We have come on behalf of the Elect one. He has sent us to bring you to him."

The other man exchanged handshakes in the same way.

"Where are we going?" he asked.

"He's in a penthouse in the museum district."

"In what part of New York?"

"Manhattan."

Shaul had mentioned Manhattan in their last communication.

"Let's go," he said.

"It is an honor to meet someone like yourself who is doing such an important mission for the church," said the chunky one. "I am humbled to be in your presence."

"It is my pleasure to do something so important for the church," Abu Shakra replied. "I have come a long way, and now my task is nearly complete. The day of the Elect will soon come to be."

"Would you like us to carry your bags?" one of them said. Abu Shakra thanked him but turned him down. There was no way he was going to let anyone touch his cargo other than the Elect One. They walked for two blocks at a rather fast pace. The bundles of money he had stuffed into his pockets were starting to chafe his skin. When they reached a parked car, the one in the gray suit unlocked the doors and opened the rear for Abu Shakra. He gently put in the bag with the bomb but practically tossed in the money. The man got in the driver's seat and sped off. The conversation centered on the future of the Elect and what horrors the Watchers would soon endure. Along their way, Abu Shakra noticed two buses with his and Lombardi's pictures on the side. The posters said they were very dangerous criminals and they must be found. Anyone seeing either of them was to call the police hotline immediately, and it gave the number. It also mentioned a reward for pertinent information.

"Your pictures have been on the news and posted around town," said the rotund one in the passenger's seat. "You're really quite popular. I imagine most people know that you are a wanted man. But there's also the picture of a woman. Where is she?"

"Although she was a great help initially, she threatened the success of the mission. I had to make sure she would no longer be a problem."

For the remainder of the ride they talked about the coming apocalypse and what would happen to the Elect. Oddly enough, there wasn't much talk about Watchers. Abu Shakra thought the conversation was uplifting and inspiring. He looked out of the window up at the skyscrapers. They were in Manhattan now, and he thought some of it looked familiar. He thought that he might have passed some of these buildings during the chase. The round man called ahead and told someone they would arrive in a few minutes. Soon they pulled off the main street and went into a parking garage under a building. The driver took the ticket, and they went down to the third level below the street. After they disembarked, they went to an elevator and waited a minute for the doors to open. They pushed the appropriate floor and, after a fast ascent, the doors of the elevator opened to a hallway with fancy wood doors on each end—very elegant and expensive, Abu Shakra thought. There was a man in a gray shirt and a black tie standing at the door on the left as if guarding it. Everyone went in that direction. Abu Shakra followed, carrying the bags. The doorman opened the carved wooden panels, and inside, Abu Shakra saw a spacious interior in modern design and décor: whites; polished steel; marble floors; and boxy, brightly colored furniture. It wasn't to his taste at all, but this wasn't Istanbul.

Shaul and Brother Gabriel were inside waiting to meet them. Shaul stepped forward. "You must be the *new* Jabbar," he exclaimed with a big smile, extending his arm for the brotherhood handshake.

"Yes. I look a bit different than the last time we met."

"Is this it?" Shaul asked, touching the large suitcase with the tip of his foot.

"This is it. The other one is money, the church's rebate that I told you about. I took a little of it to help us later. I hope you don't mind." He looked at Shaul and read some anger in his face, though not rage.

"You won't need that once we put the plan in motion," he said.

"I am holding it for all of us. It may take a while for the apocalypse to complete. We may need money for bribes and essentials until the ultimate time has come."

"I know. Obviously, you have a point," Shaul said after a moment of reflection, "as long as it's not for yourself. Like you say, we might need it."

"Put your bags next to the couch, Brother Jabbar," Gabriel said. "Take a look out the window." Abu Shakra followed Gabriel's instructions. Central Park was sprawled out in front of him. He had not imagined that it covered so much area. It was a virtual forest surrounded by one of earth's largest cities.

"We'll relax for a while, and then you can show us the bomb. I am most anxious to see how it works. Can I offer you a lemonade?"

Abu Shakra accepted and drank thirstily. He detailed the chase and how he had eluded the police. He didn't mention Amanda, because he didn't know how they would react if he told them he had just murdered a woman, in spite of the fact that millions would die soon. He felt a pang of regret when he thought of her.

"Now, let's have you explain how this miraculous wonder works," Shaul said after a few moments. Abu Shakra unfolded the suitcase and opened it flat on the floor, exposing the dials and gauges.

"They explained to me that first you set a range with this dial here." He pointed. "The range is necessary because the smaller the range, the more intense the reaction. The impulse—actually a pulse of radio wave energy—from the flux compression generator creates Electromagnetic radiation. Consequently, the Compton recoil creates a fluctuating magnetic field. That field reacts violently with the earth's magnetic field, causing an Electromagnetic shockwave carried by the earth's magnetic field. All of the local Electrical wires become a giant lightning rod, and one massive voltage surge will incite Electrical reactions to the maximum of the bomb's capacity within the sElected range. The major drawback is that because of the curvature of the earth's magnetic field, the maximum damage comes south of the impulse and minimally to the north."

"What's with all the strange writing?" Shaul asked.

"It's Russian," Abu Shakra said. "Fortunately, I understand enough to read everything here."

"That's very exciting," Shaul said, "but since it has a varied effective range, how much south of here can we hope to destroy at its max?"

"I was told its most intense charge will be broadcast out to about a two-mile area. I believe that it is capable of causing reactions from here to the part of Manhattan with all of those tall buildings."

"You mean the financial district?" asked the man who had been introduced as Brother Norman.

"I don't know what part that is, but I think that's less than two miles from here," Abu Shakra replied.

"Are you implying that we should let that thing go off from right here?" Shaul asked.

"Why not?" Abu Shakra asked. "It broadcasts outward in the shape of a cone, not straight down, as I understand it. This building shouldn't be affected. And even if it doesn't work that way, the Lord will protect us. Right?"

Shaul smiled. "That is true, my brother. We are the righteous, the Elect. The Lord will see to our safekeeping. So it's settled. We will stay right here until it is time, and then we will let it loose with all of its fury."

Chapter 45

Sabino, Kamryn, and Boucher were back at the FBI headquarters in Manhattan.

"Scott, I think you should take this call in private," Agent Richards said, directing the phone in his hand toward Boucher.

"Who is it?"

"Gail Sharland. She says she has some important information after interrogating Emma Van den Broeck that you need to know."

"Tell her I'll be right with her. Transfer it to my office. You two come with me." They all went to a temporary office that had been assigned to Boucher. He closed the door and pushed the button that put Sharland's call on speaker.

"Hi, Gail. This is Agent Boucher. What have you got for me?"

"Hi, Scott. Van den Broeck broke under pressure. She confirmed what we already suspected—that Shaul and some of his associates are indeed somewhere in New York City. She was in complete denial about knowing anything about Abu Shakra. She claims she has never heard the name. We tend to believe that, because she was so open about the rest.

"She said her company shipped shoulder-fired rockets tipped with picanzite to every major port in the world, not just to industrialized nations, but there is a particular interest in those in poorer nations. It seems the strategy was to destroy all major desalination plants around the globe, mostly those owned by Aquasuperior. They assumed that a lot of the rockets would be caught at ports of nations that have the money, technology, and personnel to properly inspect imports. Any that got through would be a bonus.

"Van den Broeck is also from the Church of the Elect. The philosophy is that, basically, the world will end and all of their followers will go to heaven or some such place. We already know that. But the idea behind the plan is to cause a global drought that will cause all populations to die off. Somehow they seem to think that members of their church will miraculously survive the holocaust and live forever.

"She said she suspects there is some kind of contingency plan, but she didn't know what. It's obvious that Abu Shakra has a bomb that will do major damage to New York. Your country will strike back at the nation whose technology was used, and then they will retaliate back against the US, and so on until there's enough nuclear fallout to kill everyone."

"Then why are they bothering to try to destroy our desalination plants?" Sabino asked.

"Like I said," Sharland replied, "it's a contingency plan. If one plan doesn't fully work, the combination of the two might."

Sabino thought about that possibility. *Could this actually happen?* Even if they found Abu Shakra, it might be too late to save a lot of the desalination facilities. The wealthier countries were safe for now, but there would be no way to protect the others, not at this late date. Even if Meyer could get the help of the government, how could they protect all of them? There was no way Aquasuperior could keep up with the demand to replace the destroyed facilities. It would overtax the ones that survived, and soon they would shut down. Then there would be a world without water. And what if they still had a third plan that no one knew about to destroy the facilities in the US and other countries, something no one was aware of?

"Scott, what the hell are we going to do?" he asked, suddenly overcome by a feeling of doom. Could they actually kill everyone and everything on the planet?

"Do you realize what a far-fetched plan Shaul has?" Boucher exclaimed. "They're talking about ending life on earth like a bunch of mad scientists! Do you realize how crazy that is?"

"Scott, you can't deny that there is a serious threat here. You've said it all along."

"Don't worry. We'll find him. And as far as the desalination—"

"But what if we don't?" Kamryn said. "What will become of everyone?"

"Even if Shaul does pull this off, there is no way the president will have the balls to hit another country with a nuclear weapon. It's like the Cold War of the twentieth century—it would be mutually assured destruction. They called it MAD. There is just no way it'll happen. No way!"

"So what if we stop Abu Shakra. That still leaves all the attacks on our plants."

"We're doing everything we possibly can to protect them. Our military is tremendously efficient. They'll take care of everything."

"I'm hearing a lot of skepticism on your side of the lake," Sharland interjected. Sabino had forgotten she was still on the line.

"Can you blame me?" Sabino said in the direction of the speaker. "How are we going to stop this?"

"In the US, it's late afternoon on July 1. About ten o'clock over here. I've seen cases where the FBI has wrapped up things in way shorter times. Have faith, you guys. You'll pull this off and catch them all. I have confidence. We all do over here."

"I wish I had your enthusiasm, Gail," Sabino said. He was

almost ready to give up. Things were so bleak. Abu Shakra could be anywhere.

"By the way, did you find any lists of church members there?" asked Boucher.

"Not yet, but we're still going through their computers. We did find a list of the ports, ships, and companies the arms went to. No contact names, however. That was cleverly left out."

"We're not done yet, Ping," Boucher said. "We've got a lot in the works. We can get them."

~ ~ ~

They were resting with their heads down on a table a conference room, the lights turned down low, when the call from Pecos came through. Agent Richards came in to wake them up.

"A call from Texas, Scott," he said quietly.

Sabino woke up immediately. He was a light sleeper. "What is it?" he asked.

"I've transferred the call to the conference room phone. Let me turn it on." He went near the door and flicked a switch that lit up a screen. The screen showed a seated woman wearing a business suit. Richards turned up the volume and said, "Hello?"

Her clear voice came through. "Scott, I've got the greatest news," said the woman, obviously excited. "We found a master list of members. What a tremendous break. It's broken down by country, state, and city. I'm sending it to you right now. Check your e-mail, and you should have it."

"Thanks," Boucher said. "Any other news?"

"Only that most of the church members have no idea what Shaul's plan is. We haven't mentioned it to anyone, of course, but that's what we've learned through interviews. His followers are unaware of his plan."

"Thank you. Keep looking," he said and turned to Sabino. "Wake her up. I'll go check my e-mail."

"Kamryn, wake up," Sabino said and gave her a little nudge. She slowly lifted her head, smiled at him, and stretched.

"What time is it?"

"About midnight. Come on; Scott has some new information."

"I was having an awesome dream. Guess who was in it?"

"I can only imagine," he said sarcastically. This was just great. Not only was she dropping hints while she was awake, but she was dreaming of him as well. He could stop her hints during the day, but he had no control over her mind. He felt deeply that he had to do something to repay her. The more time they spent working on the case together, the more he forgot about what she had done to him. Maybe it wouldn't be so bad rekindling their relationship. But then again, she wanted to lasso him for keeps, and he didn't want that. Not yet. "Someone sent Scott a list of members. Let's go take a look."

They left the conference room. It was like day in the office with all of the noise and activity. Didn't people ever sleep here? He saw Scott in his office with the door open, looking at his screen. Kamryn and he went to see what he was doing.

"Did you find anything good?" Sabino asked.

"It's an incredible break. It lists every member in New York City by borough. The bad news is that there's about three thousand here in Manhattan. We'll have to check everyone out individually to find out what they know about Shaul and Abu Shakra. Being past midnight, it's now the second. We don't know when he plans to let off his e-bomb. Could happen at any point during the day, even this early in the morning. We've got to assemble a task force to question all these people. I'll call the governor and see if he'll activate more National Guard. We'll get all the MP units in the state."

Chapter 46

Abu Shakra sat in the chair and looked out over Central Park. It was nine o'clock in the morning on the second. Raboud, the forger, was fitting him with a third mask. Abu Shakra knew this would be the last one. He didn't know if it would be of any use to him, but at least he could walk in the park unnoticed – a final look at the old Manhattan.

"Jabbar, look at this," Shaul called to him. Abu Shakra turned around and looked at the TV. There were three pictures: one of the previous Abu Shakra, one of the deceased Lombardi, and one of Shaul. It was a plea on the news for information leading to their arrest. "I'd like to see them catch you now!"

"And what about you?" he asked.

"I doesn't matter. I plan to stay up here until the end. No one will ever find us, because no one knows we're here."

"Ta-da!" Raboud exclaimed. "Another masterpiece."

"You're done already?" Abu Shakra replied.

"Quite. No one will ever know you. What do you mean, 'stay until the end?'" Raboud asked. It occurred to Abu Shakra that Raboud was not a member of the Church. He waited until Shaul answered.

"We all have a mission here in New York. By the end I mean until our mission is complete. Then we will move on to bigger and better things. That's all."

"I understand. Let me implant your new passport; then I will be finished." He gave Abu Shakra a shot of Novocain and performed his little operation. In a minute he had finished that as well.

Now Abu Shakra would be free to sightsee for the rest of the day. He wondered what would happen to all of the tourist traps when the day of judgment came.

Chapter 47

"We've been getting feedback from our agents in Pecos," Boucher said to Sabino and Kamryn when he hung up the phone. "It seems that practically no one there knows about Shaul's plan, let alone where he might be. So that's a dead end, except for the hard drive that turned up."

"What's been heard over Shaul's network?" Sabino asked.

"Not good news. Plenty of the weapons have gotten to their destinations. In the church's hierarchy, there's Shaul, then elders, and disciples below them. They're the ones who will be launching the attacks, and there's no shortage of them. There are thousands of them spanning the planet."

"But we can still stop them, right?"

"We have been sending troops around the globe to guard the plants in our allied countries," Boucher said, "because we feel that security is lax at many of them. However, there is no way to cover them all in such a short time. We've had little warning, and mobilizing the armed forces takes a while."

"Yeah, but we still have lots of people searching for members here in Manhattan," Kamryn said.

"Yes, many," replied Boucher. "The president ordered the

Department of Homeland Security to manage the church member detail. They've involved every pertinent law enforcement agency. They're operating in teams of four with police backup within a few minutes in case they find the right address. Two agents go to the door, and two either go to another apartment in the building or stay real close in case we do find Shaul and the others. Four because everyone concerned thought that many could delay any situation until the help arrived. Teams are going from apartment to apartment, questioning church members and searching when any suspicions arise. "

"When we find him, we'll just make him call everything off," she said.

"We're optimistic about finding them, Kamryn, but don't be naïve. If we do catch him, we'll also need to catch Abu Shakra. As long as they are together, we'll be okay. However, they both have been very elusive. They're smart. Give them credit, because the pair of them has been one step ahead of us all along. So, yes, we're optimistic, but if they catch onto our search, they could easily evade us until the fourth. This is a big city."

Sabino looked at Boucher. It seemed the conversation was over, because he was now looking down at his desk. Perhaps Boucher was not as optimistic as he had previously implied. Then Sabino looked at Kamryn. Her expression of eternal confidence was no longer there. Her eyes were less bright and wide than usual. She was squinting, trying to read something on Boucher's desk. Sabino was also starting to feel the pressure. What would happen if Abu Shakra pulled it off? Would the president determine where the bomb came from and start a nuclear holocaust? The radiation would circulate the atmosphere for thousands of years, killing all life. And even if they did catch him, there was still the issue of destroying the desalination plants. He had not talked with Meyer in the last two days, so he had no idea how increasing global security was coming. He had been too wrapped up in catching Abu Shakra.

Again he looked at Kamryn. She glanced back, and they exchanged smiles, trying to pretend that everything would be all right. He had forgiven her. She had saved his life in the desert, and he was forever in her debt. Yes, he would make love to her again. He had already decided that. And what about a more permanent arrangement? He still did not know, but life might not be so bad with only one woman. If indeed there was to be life past the fourth. He looked at the curves of her body. How could he think of sex at a time like this? The world was at a crossroads, and his efforts could be central to the future of mankind, and now he was thinking about sex with Kamryn … of sitting with her and sharing wine, crackers, and cheese …of sharing intimate time together. He wished this insanity was all over so they could be alone. He would hold her close and quietly kiss her, the madness of the last few days a distant memory. They would go nice and slow to make the moments linger.

The harsh reality struck him again. He and Kamryn had been of little use around the office. Boucher had taken the reigns and run the show. Just as well. Sabino had no experience tracing down criminals; nor did Kamryn, for that matter. They would be of better use in the field, he thought, right on the front lines. He wanted to get involved with the teams tracing down the individual church members, and he wanted Kamryn to come with him. Boucher had made it clear to the other agents that Sabino and Kamryn were to have full access to all aspects of the investigation. So that's what he would do. First he would get a company update from Meyer to see if there was any way he could help there, and if not, he would go along with one of the teams. He would bring Kamryn with him—unless, of course, she wanted to do something else, but he really wanted her to come along. His feelings for her went deeper than any he had felt for any other woman.

Chapter 48

Sabino and Kamryn took Aquasuperior's company jet back to Boston for a very quick meeting with Erebos Meyer. It was late afternoon on the second. They sat in his office overlooking the harbor. Meyer preferred face-to-face meetings. Phone communication rarely went well. Sabino saw that Meyer was charged with energy at the idea that something big was happening. Meyer was pacing. He had asked Sabino to come back for a few hours anyway so that he could update him on all that was happening in New York City. Sabino hoped it would be quick so they could get back to the investigation.

"I'm hoping you can update us too," Sabino said after he told Meyer all about the investigation.

"I've increased security there anyway. But the news says they also have some type of rocket. Couldn't they use one of those to destroy our plants in the US?"

"To the best of our understanding, all rockets that were intended to come into this country have been confiscated by customs at shipping ports."

"Okay, as far as our global security is concerned," Meyer said, "We've been doing our best to hire more armed guards to work the stations. Unfortunately, some places are more difficult to staff than others for various reasons. We're experiencing the most trouble in countries where there's political turmoil. These nations have many warring tribes or political and religious groups, and it's hard to find people who are loyal to a single population that supports Aquasuperior. These are African and Middle Eastern countries, plus Venezuela and Indonesia, Columbia, a few others."

"We only have two days. Can you staff them adequately to defend them in time?"

"That's what scares me. There is no way to protect them all. Even though we've been trying since we first learned of the threat, defending all eight thousand of our plants requires an incredible amount of personnel and logistical support. The president has sent a lot of National Guardsmen to allies of the US, but not the others. Even if they could, they don't have enough people or time to accomplish an effective protective network around all of them."

"If some of them are destroyed," Boucher said, "how would these countries get the water they need to survive?"

"There's the rub, you see," Meyer replied. "Basically, Aquasuperior is the only company in the world with the technology to make these facilities capable of producing the amount of water needed to meet demand; it will be up to us to get everybody back online."

"That'll cost billions," Kamryn said, astonished.

"Not for us, though. We cover our asses. All of our places are designed to operate at a profit, so there's enough money to pay for it."

"Even in poorer countries?" Boucher asked.

"That's a good point. There, where the water is in most demand, various foundations, philanthropists, and relief funds pay the insurance."

"So actually, Aquasuperior stands to gain a lot of business," Boucher said.

"Yeah, but at the expense of the millions of people who would suffer while they were being rebuilt. That in itself would be a logistical nightmare, just like staffing our plants for protection. We would need hundreds of thousands of skilled and unskilled workers to get them up and going again. It'd take a lot of time. There would be an incredible black market for water. Corruption, panic, and wars, fallen societies and governments—the poorer would be in utter chaos. People will die by the millions because of lack of water."

Sabino envisioned this happening: all those who would unwittingly become involved, rebuilding of hundreds of plants, mass hysteria, revolutions, death on a massive scale. The world would never be the same again. He looked at Kamryn and wondered what she was thinking. Meyer was leaning on his desk. *Odd,* Sabino thought, *it almost looks like Meyer has a little smirk.* Everyone was silent.

He knew there was no way to stop it now. The world had better brace itself for global disaster. This looming water supply upheaval combined with the question of catching Abu Shakra was overwhelming. He still needed to be caught to avoid a nuclear war. Overtones of doom infested Sabino's every thought, and despair washed over him. How would they stop him in just two days? New York seemed bigger than ever.

Chapter 49

Karachi, Pakistan

Down in a small valley between two ridges was a plateau about a kilometer wide. The drive to those summits overlooking Aquasuperior's plant was along a rutted, poorly cut road. Two men and a woman were struggling along the route, their truck lurching violently from side to side, the rocket launcher securely attached to the bed of the pickup.

Within the complex, an alarm sounded, alerting Pakistani army personnel inside that something had violated the secure space around perimeter of the plant. The leader flipped a switch and pushed a button that fired off a search-and-destroy aircraft. It was airborne in seconds. It was equipped with heat-seeking air-to-surface missiles. The jet crested the peak. Its sensing cameras locked onto the little truck, and it released one of its payloads. Within a second, it had impacted the pickup. Flames erupted, and a low-frequency, muffled blast vibrated through the surrounding area. The drone flew through the column of fire, banked left, and headed back to the short landing strip in the complex. Before it arrived, the gas in the tip of the picanzite rocket on the pickup seeped out, and the explosive spontaneously detonated. The sound echoed for miles in every direction. Thousands of pieces of scrap metal and the vaporized molecules of the two men and woman were scattered around a radius of several hundred meters. The explosion was close enough to the plant to rip through the south wall and destroy much of the processing equipment inside.

Gibara, Cuba

A mile east of the seacoast town, the Aquasuperior desalination plant roared in full production. The shallow turquoise water leading outward into the Gulf of Mexico looked like a puzzle with patches of sand and plant life. Along an area partially lined with palm trees, three Cuban members of the Church of the Elect lay in wait until July 4, Russian automatic weapons at their sides and the rocket tipped with picanzite carefully resting in its package. They had made a shelter out of large leaves and branches. They were well camouflaged and noticeable only from a short distance away. At six the next morning, they were to shoot the rocket directly at the large metal columns facing the trees. The talked excitedly but quietly of the days to come.

Halfway between La Serena and La Compania, Chile

The miles and miles of beaches along this section of Chile's coast had once been reserved strictly for tourism. The area had flourished and population had grown. When the world's fresh water supply dried up, a desalination plant became necessary. In an old farmhouse near the plant, two members of the Church of the Elect partied and drank with their host family. They were all celebrating what was to come. Their car was in the barn, and the rocket was in the house with them. No one suspected them of anything foul, and they spent the last day before the fourth in peace, having a good time. It was a coordinated effort; all the rockets around the world were to be fired at the same time. They were to get in position in the middle of the night so that they could fire at exactly four in the morning.

Iwerekun, Nigeria

The Nigerian coast had an abundance of inlets and polluted rivers emptying into the Atlantic. Iwerekun was a small township located on the coast, and the large city of Lagos was to the west. Aquasuperior's local plant, smaller than many of the others, supplied the local areas with water. Like the men in Chile, three church members were sharing, unnoticed, ramshackle quarters in the little town. It was a dangerous location; the local tribes regularly raided each other's villages. Though Iwerekun was larger than any village, it was nonetheless often at odds with the neighboring warlords who frequently joined forces and raided local residences.

At about two o'clock in the morning, everyone in the rundown town was asleep. A group of warriors silently entered the shacks, smashing heads with clubs, slashing throats, or dismembering bodies with razor-sharp machetes. The half dozen church members all met their ends as gruesomely as the rest of the town's inhabitants. The natives found some handmade jewelry, a small amount of currency, four automatic rifles, some ammo, and a large suitcase that radiated heat. They opened up the case and saw the rocket with its launcher. After brief admiration, they closed it and took it with them. It was never used on July 4.

Chapter 50

The steam from the shower filled the bathroom. It was hot enough to stimulate Sabino. He had come back to the hotel briefly just to freshen up, and so had Kamryn, who was doing so in her own room. He kept thinking of her while under the hot water. He missed making love to her. Before she had betrayed him, they had had sex all the time. His anger toward her was waning, and now he missed her touch. If the pending disaster was resolved, he would tell her how he felt. He imagined these feelings were love, though he had never experienced it. How could he think of her sexually at such a time? Life as everyone knew it might end tomorrow if Abu Shakra was not stopped and the desalination plants were not successfully defended.

"Hello," came Kamryn's voice. He peeked around the shower curtain. He saw that she was poking her head into the bathroom.

"I'll be right out," he said. He must have left his hotel suite door unlocked. He got out of the shower, wrapped a towel around himself, and exited the bathroom. Kamryn was sitting on the edge of the bed, smiling. "I've just got to dry off," he said to her, standing still, wishing he could hold her like before. She fixed her eyes on his. She had saved him from certain death, and he owed his life to her. Sabino stared back at her. Kamryn stood up. Seeing her clothes clinging tightly to her body, her curving figure evident, he became instantly aroused. The pounding from his heart made his body vibrate. He couldn't help himself; he had to say something. He wanted to say something subtle, but it just slipped out. "You look beautiful," he said, almost breathless.

"You'd look better with the towel off," she answered. Her intimate stare ignited his lust. Kamryn started to unbutton her blouse. He swallowed hard.

"Scott's expecting us."

"I know, but he can wait a bit longer."

Sabino realized that tomorrow, everything could be different. What if they died? He would never be able to show her that he had forgiven her. She deserved that much. He approached her. They embraced and fell on the bed, each caressing the other. The sex was quick, hot, and hard, like never before. When they were done, they clung to each other, breathless, exhausted, and yet still stimulated. It felt like there would never be such a moment to share their desires again, like the end of the world was coming tomorrow, and for all he knew, it might be. But then, as he lay there embraced, he thought about what Boucher had told them: that in spite of the president's threats, the US would never engage in a nuclear war.

"It's time we got moving," he said quietly, gazing into her eyes.

"I guess you're right." He watched her roll out of bed and put on her panties and skirt. He was sweaty and wished he had time to get back into the shower. "What do you think will happen tomorrow?"

"As far as Abu Shakra goes, we still have some time to catch him. There's all sorts of law enforcement people knocking on doors looking for him and the rest of the people from your church. As far as Aquasuperior's property, I hope the government has sent enough troops to defend them and that Erebos hired enough security guards to protect our interests where the president decided not to defend."

"And what will happen if nothing can be stopped?" she asked.

"We don't know how powerful the bomb actually is. Potentially, it could set off a lot of fires. The fire department isn't capable of stopping them all."

"I know that, but do you think we will die? Do you think this is the end?"

He looked into her eyes and tried to read them. She showed no fear and was even smirking slightly, which led him to wonder what she was thinking.

"I don't believe that the end of the world will come. That's ridiculous. Why, what do you believe?" he asked.

"I think it's possible that life as we know it could come to an end. Remember, I still believe in the philosophy of the church; I'm just leaning toward the end coming as a result of an act by the Lord of Spirits. Just because I'm helping doesn't mean I have completely switched sides."

"I didn't realize that. I thought you were a total convert, the way you've been helping," he said, surprised. "So you think that because of some bizarre plan, there'll be a holocaust."

"I didn't say that it's definitely going to happen, but it could. I deeply believe that there are Watchers and one day they will be judged."

"By who, a god who plans to murder the majority of the human race by creating some holocaust?"

"No, not the majority. There are a lot more good people in the world than bad. When the day comes, and it may or may not be tomorrow, only those who have evil in their hearts will suffer. And He will not *murder* them. They will still live for eternity, only in a bad place."

"Now you're being just plain crazy. We're talking nuclear

disaster and millions dying from lack of water. How will your god differentiate between all of those people? Sorry, it just ain't gonna to happen."

Her lustful look was gone, Sabino noticed. Instead, he saw anger and passion for the end of life. He realized that there were millions of members around the globe, which led him to wonder how so many people could believe in such madness.

"Maybe you can prevent it tomorrow, but it will happen eventually. One day, everyone will be judged, and when it comes, I hope your kindness is as strong as it is now."

"We never really discussed this between us," Sabino said diplomatically. "You say I'm a good person, and I feel I'm not." He knew that one way or another, the world would change tomorrow. He had thought Kamryn had abandoned her enthusiasm for the alleged apocalypse, but she really showed fire. "Obviously, you still feel really strongly about your convictions. Rather than starting a major argument and winding up hating each other, why don't we agree that we have different opinions that we're both entitled too."

"Sweep it under the carpet."

"Yes."

"I don't know if I can let that happen," she said. "I'm in love with you, Ping. I want us to be together forever. You have to believe you're a good person as well in order for that to happen. Only then will our Lord see you safely to the peaceful land that we all believe will exist."

She was wearing her worried look: her forehead was wrinkled, her eyes had a bit of a squint, and her cute little mouth was pursed. He thought he should reassure her.

"Don't worry," he said. "We'll stop them in time. Nothing will happen."

"I worry. I worry about you coming with me. We may no longer be together. I don't know. Ping, you're a good person. I hope our Lord will see His way to letting you enter His wonderful kingdom."

"Let's hope we never find out. That's all I can say." Her worried expression remained. He wished that she didn't believe in this mythical land of the good and some sort of supreme being who judged everyone. There was no such thing as a god, he thought. History was littered with disaster, war, famine, disease, suffering. Where was God when all that was happening? Believers would say God gave man free choice. Where was that choice when man needed help? What diplomats could have prevented deadly battles? Where was God when scientists took years to cure cancer and other diseases? When one population persecuted another?

Worst of all, where had God been when the water ran out? Before Aquasuperior, the animals and the human race had been at risk of extinction. Desalination plants sustained the lives of nearly all land-based beings. Perhaps that was God's way of making up for past events. Yet now the plants were at risk where they were most needed. Who could know how many plants would be saved and how many destroyed tomorrow? And what about the few plants that didn't belong to Aquasuperior? Were they forewarned? Were they protected?

What about Abu Shakra? Would a merciful God allow him succeed tomorrow? The authorities were stretched to the limit trying to find him. Was it possible that he could cause the destruction of New York and initiate a nuclear war? Suddenly, Sabino felt a rush of fear. He needed to do whatever it took to find him in these last few hours.

"Come on," Sabino said, feeling a great urgency. "Let's get back over there and make this work. We have to stop Abu Shakra."

Chapter 51

"And a toast to our ultimate success!" Shaul bellowed as he lifted his glass of lemonade. The others in the room raised their glasses also and replied loudly in agreement. "There is no way they can stop us now. On this eve of Independence Day, we shall rejoice in our imminent victory over the Watchers. Our alteration into the land of peace and love will take longer, because those Watchers have done all they can to slow us down. They have stopped our rockets at many borders, but this is not as bad as it may seem. I planned it that way."

There was a murmur among the brothers.

"I can't wait to hear this," Abu Shakra whispered to Gabriel.

"At first, when the elders approached me with the idea of bringing on the day of judgment by eliminating every desalination plant, I thought it was crazy. Then I thought, *We can raise the money by getting new members at revivals, conferences, and seminars. We can do it.* But the more I thought about it, the more I saw the plan was flawed. What if there were leaks within our church? What if we couldn't figure out the logistics. Most of all, what if the necessary arms or explosives or whatever were stopped trying to enter some or all of these countries at the borders. It occurred to me that most likely our equipment would get caught at the borders of technologically advanced countries, considering their explosive-sniffing dogs and sophisticated equipment for detecting illegal items at their borders. However, it probably would make it into the less developed countries, because there was a better likelihood of successful bribes. And also they would never be able to buy or afford whatever gear was necessary to discover our weapons. And further, the major powers would protect their own interests before helping poor nations that always have civil wars and political turmoil."

"But how does that help us?" asked Brother Nathan.

"As you can imagine, after the bomb lets loose its power, the president will seek revenge and bring on a nuclear holocaust. The US, Russia, and other nuclear nations will launch their ICBMs at other nuclear nations, ignoring the lesser ones. Who knows how long it will take for the fallout to reach those countries? It could take years, and by that time, they might all have rebuilt their desalination plants. So I planned to get our weapons mostly to the smaller countries so the Watchers there will have no water to sustain their lives."

"Why didn't you buy only enough weapons to accomplish that?" Abu Shakra asked. "And after you did, why persist in sending your arms to the borders of the major powers?"

"That's a fair question, Jabbar," Shaul said. "It's very simple. The elders, in their wisdom, brilliantly came up with their plan to bring the apocalypse. The rocket business was already planned by the elders. Rather than trying to convince them otherwise—because they can be a hassle to deal with—I said to myself, 'What the heck. There's nothing to lose. If any get through, so much the better.' That opens up my plan, the Electromagnetic bomb."

"We have to decide on a time to set off the blast," Norman stated in a matter-of-fact tone.

"I say we do it as soon as possible," Abu Shakra said. "Right at midnight."

"Let's let it go when New York's fireworks are being set off over the water," a brother said.

"I am supposing—and I may be wrong—but merely supposing that America's forefathers signed the Declaration of Independence at about noon," Shaul said. "So why don't we make that same time our own declaration of independence."

They all exchanged glances. Then, they all voted in favor of twelve o'clock the next day, July 4.

"That leaves one big question," another brother said. "Where will we set off the blast?"

"Why should we go anywhere else?" Shaul said. "We'll do it right here."

"And what about the timing on attacking the desalination plants?" Abu Shakra asked.

"We have been telling everyone to attack at nine o'clock in the morning, eastern standard time, so that everything happens simultaneously around the globe."

Chapter 52

July 4

Kamryn was thinking about Sabino. She looked at him across the table. He had just come back from talking with Boucher. It was two o'clock on the morning of the fourth, and there was no news of anything happening yet. The FBI office was operating as if it were daytime. Agents were on the phones and talking among themselves. She couldn't keep her mind from drifting back to the hotel room where they had had their exchange of views. They had never had any real conversation about religion, and this one had been short, yet she still had a clear picture of how he felt. She really wished that Sabino was a believer. She wanted to be with him forever, but regrettably, his convictions would put him in the ranks of the Watchers. She realized that he wouldn't change in the next few hours and so would end up in eternal hell with the rest of them.

That was assuming, of course, that the Lord saw to it that today was the end of human existence. But what if it wasn't? Could she change his mind? No, she realized. Sabino was stubborn, and she now believed that he would not change, not now or in the future. So should she stick with him despite knowing that she would never have an eternal life with him? She loved him deeply and was confused. She didn't know what to do. She wanted him forever but knew that it would never happen. Maybe after this was over, she should consider looking elsewhere. She truly didn't want to, but perhaps she could find love again, given time. She would wait and see what happened over the next twenty-two hours. Kamryn wanted the world to end, preferably later, but today if it had to be; however, it would be a lonely existence without him.

"Ping," she said, trying to take her mind off her thoughts about him, "has Scott said if they're still checking addresses at this time of night?"

"Yes, they are. Agents will knock on doors up until every person has been checked. I just hope there's enough time."

"Shouldn't they have checked almost everyone by now?"

"No. There are three thousand members to check. There must be many to go. We'll find them. Don't worry."

But she wasn't worried. She was hoping it would happen. At the same time, she kind of wished that it wouldn't, because she still wanted Sabino. She needed him emotionally as well as physically. She was very confused. Why did she want to distance herself from him when she still wanted him so desperately?

"Do you think we should get onto a team tracing addresses?" she asked.

"That would be better than sitting around here doing nothing. Come on, let's ask Scott if he can hook us up with one of his squads."

Boucher attached them to a group nearby and issued them both pistols. There were several groups right on Fifth Avenue—one on the intersection with Eighty-Eighth and the other at Ninety-Seventh. Kamryn convinced him that it would be fairly safe; because Shaul believed in common living and most likely he would be hiding out in a poorer section of Manhattan, there would be little chance of a shootout. By eight o'clock in the morning, Kamryn and Sabino were both dragging their feet. The day still had a long way to go, but she knew she would make it okay. When she had been actively working for the church in Pecos, she had pulled the occasional all-nighter and gotten by just fine.

Although she was dragging her feet, she was still optimistic and full of hope for the future. The more she thought about it, the more she realized a future with Sabino could not happen based on his beliefs. He was good at heart, mentoring her and others, and he treated her extremely well, but he would never find it in his heart to realize that he was a good person. You had to have faith to be one of the Elect. She would never convince him. She started to think of the new men in her future. She wondered who they would be and how she would meet them. The church was a great source. There were also plenty of single men whom she had met at the FBI. She saw that many of the FBI men were not wearing wedding bands. There were possibilities.

Of course, everything would depend on what happened before the end of the day. Life could be different by then. Maybe she would be lonely in the future world. Perhaps she wouldn't care. Who knew?

They entered the lobby of a building on Fifth Avenue and Ninety-Seventh. The agent in charge explained that the pair of them could come along but had to stay safely behind the team. If they were needed, they would know it.

Chapter 53

The doorbell rang, echoing through the penthouse. Immediately, they were on alert. Gabriel and Norman picked up their weapons. Abu Shakra unholstered his pistol and was poised and ready for action. The only people who ever rang the doorbell were delivery people, and they weren't expecting anything. The bell rang again.

"Open up. FBI," barked a muffled voice from the other side of the door. They all looked at each other. Abu Shakra saw the panic in Shaul's wide eyes and contorted expression.

"I'll take care of it. Elect One, go in the other room and hide," Abu Shakra whispered, holstering his pistol, hiding it under his sport coat. "Coming!" he shouted, walked over to the door. He opened it. "May I help you?"

"Yes, sir," the agent replied. Abu Shakra saw that one agent was directly in the middle of the doorway and another stood beside him. There were two more agents behind them and a man and a woman farther behind. Obviously, they all had guns under their coats, just like he did. He could see it. "We're with the FBI," the agent said and flashed his badge. "We're trying to get in touch with Mr. and Mrs. Lapham. We need to ask them a few questions. Would they be home?"

Abu Shakra's heart was pounding with excitement. It had been very boring since he had arrived, and he had been wishing for some action. The adrenaline was in his blood. He was ready.

"Of course. Come on in."

He closed the door behind him. Gabriel and Norman hid around the corner of the entryway leading to the living room, weapons at the ready. There was a brief silence as they sized each other up. Suddenly, all the agents began drawing their guns. Gabriel sprayed them with automatic gunfire. Abu Shakra pulled his pistol and let two shots off at the two lead agents. Both collapsed dead on the floor. Everyone scrambled. The two remaining agents backed away and slammed the doors shut. Gabriel let off another burst, emptying the rest of his clip through the door, wood splinters flying. They heard someone scream in pain.

"Agent down! Agent down," Abu Shakra heard one of them cry.

Abu Shakra realized that the agent must have radioed for help. They would have to end it quickly and evacuate. Abu Shakra got up and went over to the two dead men. There were two growing pools of blood on the highly polished wood floor.

It was quiet for a second and Shaul peeked out from around the corner where he was hiding. "What are we going to do now?" he whined.

"Our mission will succeed at any cost. The feds are an insignificant distraction. We've got to get out of here," he said, looking at Shaul, who stared at the two fallen agents. He was in worse shock than when they had first knocked at the door. *"Now, Elect One. We must get out now!"*

He went over and buckled up the bomb, picked it up, and ran to the door, but Shaul remained staring at the bodies.

"Get used to it," Abu Shakra exclaimed. "There's going to be a lot more of that today. Go out the back entrance with Gabriel, Elect

One, and meet me on the next floor down. Find the elevator, push the button, and hold the door until I get there."

Gabriel gently tugged Shaul by the arm, pulling him toward the door. Shaul, Gabriel, and Norman rushed off.

Abu Shakra figured that based on the speed of the elevators, it would be five minutes at most before more FBI agents arrived. He would kill the remaining agents first so that no survivors were around to aid in the chase.

He shot once at the door and was answered by a return volley from the agents in the hall. Abu Shakra knew exactly what to do. He would go out the back entryway and attack the agents from behind. Obviously, they would expect it, but it was a better plan that trying to walk through the front door.

~ ~ ~

Out in the hall lay another dead agent. The surviving one, Sabino, and Kamryn were safely tucked around a corner next to another suite.

"You've got to get out of here *now*," The last agent said to them.

"We're going to—"

"Get your asses the hell out of here," shouted the agent. "Please. You'll be a lot more use if you go down to the lobby and tell them what's happening up here. Don't argue. Just go. Now! Hurry!"

The pair looked at each other.

"He's right," Sabino said. "If we can share what happened and how many there are, I'm sure that would help."

"Chicken?" Kamryn taunted.

"We're bringing knives to an artillery battle. We're outgunned. Now come on. Let's go."

They clasped hands and started running toward the elevator

around the corner. As they did, the murderer from the suite entered the hall from the other end. Kamryn and Sabino reacted instinctively, instantly doubling back around the corner. Two rounds pulverized the corner plaster at head level.

"There has to be a way out," Sabino said.

The agent approached them, pointed toward an exit sign, and said, "That way. I'll try to hold him off."

They rushed through the exit and started down a flight of stairs.

"Let's get to the next floor," Sabino said. "Then we'll take the elevator."

The got to the landing, opened the door, and started toward the elevator. They rounded the corner only to see that a large man with a machinegun was holding the door open. He reacted very quickly. A burst of automatic fire came toward them. They reversed direction and ducked just in time. Sabino poked his pistol around the corner and took a few blind shots, but as soon as he was done, another burst of fire sprayed the hall.

"Back to the exit," Kamryn said.

They went through the doors.

"You all right?" Sabino asked.

"I think so."

"We've got a long way in front of us. Ready?"

"Let's go," Kamryn said, and they started a rushed descent.

~ ~ ~

Abu Shakra dove from the corner out into the hall and rolled on the ground. It took the agent by surprise, giving Abu Shakra a clear shot, and he took it. One right to the forehead, then two more to his chest to make sure. The agent tumbled to the ground.

Abu Shakra then looked around for the remaining two, but

they were gone. *Whimps,* he thought. Then he went to the exit door, descended a flight, and found his party waiting at the elevator, doors held open just as he had asked. They piled in. He pushed the number four button, and immediately they descended at great speed. After a few seconds that felt like hours, the door opened to the fourth floor.

"Why the fourth floor?" Gabriel asked as Abu Shakra ushered everyone out. Before he stepped out of the elevator, he pushed the button for the lower level and then exited.

"Remember they radioed ahead?" Abu Shakra reminded him. "They'll be waiting for us in the lobby. We have to find a back way out, and fast."

Their hearts pounding with the rush of near panic, they ran down the hall: Abu Shakra toting the suitcase, Shaul clinging to his copy of the book of Enoch, and the other two armed with their automatics.

Shaul was nearly flipping out. "Where will we go now? What if they stop us? What do we do? How are we going to get out?" And on he went.

Then they turned a corner, and at the end of the corridor was a plain door was marked "exit." Abu Shakra opened it, and they rushed down the stairs.

~ ~ ~

"Agent down! Agent down!" cried the voice through the communication receiver.

"We better call the cavalry," said the agent in charge of the location. "Agent Boucher. Emergency. This is Strindberg," he shouted into his phone. "We found them! 1233 Fifth Avenue at the penthouse."

"Received. Help's coming."

For the next several minutes, there was a lot of commotion in the lobby.

Then Sabino and Kamryn came through the lobby exit door. They were winded, as they had descended three and four stairs at a time, but both were in excellent shape, and there was plenty of oxygen in the stairwell.

"What the hell is happening up there?" the agent demanded.

"There was only one agent still alive when we left. The rest … no."

"So was it Eitan and the others?"

"Yes. It must have been. We saw two men with machineguns. One shot two agents. A very large man with a pistol also shot the two agents before they went down. Then we scrambled to the hall, and more automatic fire came through the door before we could get to cover, and the third agent was killed. Finally, there was a man carrying a book."

"That was Shaul," Kamryn said. "I recognized him."

"Where did they go?" the agent asked.

"We don't know," Kamryn said, "but we did see them at the elevators one floor below the penthouse."

Sirens blew outside, announcing the arrival of FBI reinforcements and a SWAT team.

Before anything else happened, there was some shouting from the restaurant. People screamed. Customers and staff rushed out the doors. A man in chef's garb, hat and all, ran into the lobby shouting in a heavy Italian accent. "These men with guns, they runna through my dining room."

"Slow down," Sabino said, attempting a calming voice.

"He's the man in the picture."

"Great," Sabino said to Kamryn. "Here we go." They both sprinted over to the chef, and then Sabino spoke, slightly winded from the excitement. "How many were there?"

"Four. Two with machine guns, old man, and another with pistol and suitcase."

"Which way did they go?" Kamryn asked, which Sabino thought was clichéd but necessary.

"They go through my kitchen and out the back, screaming and shouting."

The commotion reached a crescendo. Customers flooded the lobby. Everyone was trying to push their way to the exit doors. It was so loud that Sabino could hardly hear the chef.

"You say they went out the back?" he said as loud as he could.

"They take my driver. The catering van. They drive away."

Sabino asked him what it looked like, and the chef described it.

"It can't be far," Sabino said to Kamryn. "It's almost nine o'clock, and traffic is heavy. Let's see if we can see it." They went outside. Less than a block away was the van, stuck in a snarl of cars. As they watched, the four men got out and started running. Sabino saw the two with the machine guns in plain sight. "We've got to stop them somehow. Boucher's on his way. We'll follow them, but keep a distance."

They followed.

Chapter 54

"Give me the damn keys or you'll die," Abu Shakra shouted at the kitchen worker, waving the gun in the young man's face. There was a van outside in the delivery area used for catering.

"I don't have them. Honest. I don't have them," he said. Abu Shakra saw that he was shaking. He could tell that the boy was telling the truth.

"Where can we find them?" The boy was shaking and twitching. He was full of fear, and he started to whimper. The boy started to stutter an answer, but Abu Shakra couldn't make sense of it. "Slow down and tell me."

"They're … they're in the … the office," he managed between sobs.

"Show me," Abu Shakra demanded, grabbing his arm and giving him a shake.

"I'll show you." The boy headed toward the exit sign, and before they reached it, he stopped at an office.

"On the … the wall on the left."

Abu Shakra reached in and took the keys off their hook. He released the boy's arm.

"Get. Go on, get out of here," he said, and the kid scrambled out of the kitchen. The four of them exited and got into the van. Abu Shakra started it and drove into traffic. It was bumper to bumper. They gradually made it half a block. Then he told everyone to get out and start running. There were sirens approaching. "They'll never stop us," Abu Shakra said. "Follow me."

Chapter 55

Makassar Strait, Indonesia

Decades ago, there had been jungles along the coast. Today, there were only patches of vegetation to prevent erosion supported by a small amount of fresh water from the desalination plant.

Four armed men were talking quietly, planning their attack. They decided to drive quickly within range, launch the rocket, and then get out of the area. One of them checked his watch, and it was 11:54 p.m.—close enough. They were under the cover of darkness, and the plant would have only a skeleton staff. Security would be relaxed.

The oldest of them unpacked the rocket. Its radiating heat made it hard to hold.

"Hurry. Let's do it before it gets too hot!" the elder cried. They drove within five hundred meters and stopped. He aimed at the silos as instructed. The intense heat of the encased picanzite burned his cheek.

He fired.

There was a whoosh as the rocket became airborne. A trail of smoke was visible in the light that surrounded the facility. The men glared in absolute fascination as the little missile impacted the silo in the center of the plant. What followed was an explosion as intense as a small nuclear blast. It totally destroyed all the silos as well as other structures within the annihilation zone. The men were too close. A thermal heat wave swept outward, inflicting second and third degree burns, knocking them off their feet. Then the debris came whizzing by. They all tried to dive behind the truck, but two of them didn't make it. A flying twelve-inch-wide piece of concrete hit one man at the neck, decapitating him. The other was struck in the chest with a piece of steel shrapnel and died instantly.

More debris began falling to earth from high in the sky. The two remaining men rolled under the truck, and as the next few seconds passed, the wham, plunk, and ting of matter hitting the vehicle echoed in their ears.

Only a few short seconds passed between the time of the explosion and the silence that followed. When it was quiet, the two men got out from under the truck and placed the bodies of their fellow church members in its bed. With blood on their hands, they drove off to wait for the end of the world.

North of Napier, New Zealand

The night perimeter cameras surveyed the area around Aquasuperior's water factory. When the guard in the security office saw three figures, one carrying a large case, he knew they were there to destroy the plant. He sounded a silent alarm that alerted the other armed guards and indicated in which sector the disturbance originated. He looked at the screen again. They were about two thousand meters away.

The sentries filed out of the office equipped with night goggles, climbed over the rocky terrain up a hill, and lay down, waiting for the silhouettes to come across the horizon. Their weapons were loaded and set on automatic.

When the suspects appeared, the leader quietly ordered the

guards to shoot first and ask questions later. They waited until the men were almost on top of them before opening fire. The four guards emptied their clips, making extra sure there was no way the intruders could have survived. They reloaded and then cautiously stood up to view the massacre. The suitcase had opened and absorbed several bullets. Heat radiated from the rocket. Although they saw bullet holes throughout the suitcase, none had hit anything critical. Realizing that they must alert all the other Aquasuperior locations of the attempted attack, they picked up the suitcase, left the bodies, and headed back.

Chapter 56

There were sirens wailing just two blocks away. Kamryn and Sabino crossed the street, weaving between cars stuck in the heavy traffic. Frightened pedestrians ran into the road to evade the four men. Their weapons were in plain sight. They made no attempt to hide them.

Sabino called Boucher and told him they were following them and that the police were not far behind. Traffic on Fifth Avenue was at a standstill. Sabino looked over his shoulder and saw that many police officers had abandoned their cars and were running toward them.

Sabino saw the four outlaws cross the street and run into Central Park. They did the same. The one with the big bag was lagging behind. Sabino realized it must be very heavy. Looking over his shoulder, he saw many policemen following. In that area of the park, there was a field with large rocks and a tree line on the far side. The four men entered the woods, hid behind trees, and aimed their weapons at their pursuers. Sabino and Kamryn dove behind some rocks for protection. Sabino shouted, trying to warn the police, but the nearby traffic was very loud and he was out of breath, so his words went unheard.

He looked at Kamryn next to him. She was breathing calmly. For a moment, he thought what a great athlete she was. Swinging his head around, he observed that the police had taken refuge behind boulders. They were between the police and the criminals. If there was a gunfight, the bullets would be going over their heads in both directions.

He saw one of the policemen giving hand signals to the others, and they started to flank the position on both sides. Before they got more than a few steps, automatic gunfire broke out from the terrorists' position, and Sabino watched as one of the policemen went down. They stopped their advance and again all dove behind the boulders that littered the field. The police started shooting back.

He could hear bullets whizzing over their heads. He put his hand on Kamryn's head to hold it close to the ground. She moved her head away.

"I want to watch," she said. Sabino couldn't tell if she spoke in anger or excitement. The shooting was too loud.

"Just keep low," he said.

"I know. I'm not stupid!" Suddenly, a bullet ricocheted off top of the rock where they were hiding. "Damn."

They both ducked their heads to the ground and buried them under their arms.

"How the hell are we going to get out of this?" he said.

"Just stay low," she said. "It'll be over soon."

As the rounds buzzed over their heads, he worried about whether either of them would get hit. He thought of his feelings for her. He glared at her buried head. Maybe he did love her. If these were their last moments together, he might never he able to tell her how he felt.

"If this is it, I want you to know—"

"Shut up and keep your head down."

~ ~ ~

Abu Shakra was pinned behind a tree. Shaul and Gabriel were to his left and Norman to his right. He took aim again but didn't shoot. He had much training, but the targets were well protected. He wanted to be sure to hit someone if he was going to expend a valuable round. He only had the nine in the gun and another clip in his pocket. The occasional round hit a tree and ripped the bark away, but no one had been hit.

One of the policemen started to run forward to a patch of rocks. He was easy pickings for a marksman with as much skill as Abu Shakra. He fired one shot and hit him in the chest. The man went down from the force of the impact, but it occurred to Abu Shakra that they would be wearing flack jackets under their clothes. The man was not dead, just stunned. However, he was out in the open between rocks. The police fired heavily so that their comrade could make it to safety. With lightning speed, Abu Shakra took a risk, swung around the side of the tree, and pulled off a shot. It hit its mark: the officer's head. The man dropped and was dead before he hit the ground.

"We've got to get out of here," Abu Shakra shouted to the others.

"I'll cover you. Run when I shoot," Norman shouted back. He loaded a fresh clip and waited a second. *"Go! Go!"* he yelled as he thrust his upper body from behind the tree. He let off a series of fast, calculated bursts.

Abu Shakra grabbed the suitcase in one hand and tugged Shaul with the other. They must be fast. The three of them dashed through the rest of the wooded area and reached the street. A car was stopped with a bullet hole through the window. A man was slumped over the steering wheel. He had been hit by a stray. Traffic was moving.

Avoiding the car, Abu Shakra jumped out into the traffic, trying to cross the road. Cars swerved and squealed to a halt to avoid them.

The police had been trying to surround their position, and cruisers were screaming not far away. Half a block away, he saw the entrance to a subway. That would be their escape.

~ ~ ~

The shooting from behind the tree got very heavy for a few moments. Two rounds recoiled off the rock protecting them. Particles of stone landed on their arms and backs. They still had their heads buried. The rock was only about a foot high. There was no way Sabino could shoot and be adequately protected. As he lay on his stomach, he thought back to when he had been on his stomach under the canvas in the desert. He wondered why such an idle thought had come into his mind at a time like this. No matter. He had to deal with the hand he had been given.

The shooting stopped. Sabino lifted his head and saw a lone man step out from behind one of the trees. The man shot off a long burst and then stopped. As soon as he did, a rain of fire came from the police side. Again, Sabino was aware of the projectiles flying over their heads. The man was struck by a volley of bullets. The force of continuous fire pinned him against the trunk of the tree where he had been hidden until Sabino heard someone shout, "Hold your fire!"

The firing stopped. The man slowly slid to the ground. His head and body were covered with bullet holes. A trail of blood was plainly evident on the tree. There was a moment of silence. Someone else yelled, "All clear."

A rush of uniformed and plainclothes police and FBI officers ran toward the dead shooter. Some went past him into the woods.

Sabino and Kamryn stood up and ran after the others into the miniature forest.

They reached the street, but there was no sign of Shaul, Abu Shakra, or the third man. How would they find them now? It was now 9:35.

Chapter 57

The police cars pulled to a stop where everyone was gathered at the edge of the park, blocking traffic. There were dozens of police officers and FBI agents in the street shouting to each other. Sabino stood next to Kamryn watching the mayhem. He felt a hand on his shoulder and turned around. It was Boucher.

"What do we do now?" Sabino asked. The police captain started shouting to his officers to spread out and start talking to pedestrians. Boucher ordered his agents to do the same.

"You two stick with me," Boucher said. Sabino watched as the police and FBI went in every direction. He saw the stairs going down to the subway and pointed them out to Boucher. There were a few officers who looked idle. "Call the transit authority," Boucher said to them. "Alert them there might be some terrorists riding their subway. Let's go and see if somebody has seen them. You two officers come with us."

They ran across the street to the subway entrance. There were people dashing up the stairs and shouting.

"Killers … terrorists … someone's been shot … help … they're down there," the panicked people shouted as they dispersed in every direction.

Sabino was the first to fly down the stairs, closely followed by the others. They jumped over the turnstiles and ran down the next flight of stairs to the subway platform. The station had emptied. They arrived just as the subway disappeared into the tunnel. There was a dead or wounded transit authority officer motionless on the floor. Two civilians were also wounded and were crying in agony. Boucher went over to the officer and rolled him over. There were holes in his chest. His eyes were open. Boucher took the communication device off the officer's belt and spoke into it.

"Man down. This is agent Scott Boucher of the FBI. Three criminals have just left Sixtieth."

"How many are hurt?" came the reply.

"Three. An officer and two civilians."

"Which subway did they get on?"

"I don't know. It was leaving by the time we arrived. Can you stop all of them at their next stop?"

"Will do. I'll dispatch officers to each station."

"Get some EMTs here. Hurry!"

~ ~ ~

As fast as they could move, they went rushing through the cars toward the front of the subway. Shaul couldn't catch his breath. He was old. How could he keep up any longer?

"Stop, please stop," he pleaded to Abu Shakra. "I can't go on any farther."

"We can't stop now, Elect One. We must escape."

Shaul planted himself on a seat. "I'm staying right here until the next stop."

"Don't you see? There will be police there. We've got to stop the train and get off before the station."

"I'm not moving. Open the doors when you stop the train, and I'll get off. I'm sixty-two. I am not in shape. I need a rest."

"We're almost to the front."

"Please. Let me do this. I can't go on. My heart is pounding so hard my body vibrates."

He stared at Abu Shakra. The noise of the subway seemed to amplify as they looked at each other. Then Abu Shakra smiled. "Very well, Elect One. I will open the doors when we stop," he said. They continued toward the front. Shaul rested his elbows on his knees and his head in his hands. He breathed fast and deep to catch his breath. He was partially hyperventilating. His head spun in his hands. Shaul looked through the windows toward the front. He could see his followers two cars down as panicking passengers tried desperately to distance themselves from them. Then they disappeared into what he hoped was the front car. In a moment, the subway screeched to a halt and the doors opened to the blasting sound of metal on metal. He looked out the door. They were next to the wall, but there was a walkway at the height of the doors. He went to the door and climbed over a railing.

He could see Abu Shakra and Gabriel getting up onto the walkway. The subway whooshed and the doors closed; then it pulled away and they were left in the dark tunnel on the catwalk. The passageway was lit only by a few dim lights on the walls. He could barely see anything. Shaul walked the short distance to the others. He was breathing better now.

"We have to be fast," Abu Shakra said. "We've got to find a stairway leading to the street before the police know we're in the tunnel."

"That could be any minute," Gabriel said.

"I can hardly see," Shaul said. "My eyes aren't good in the dark."

"They'll adjust, Elect One," Gabriel said. "Don't worry. Everything will be all right. We'll get out of here okay and burn New York. The Watchers will have their day."

Abu Shakra took Shaul by the hand. "Come on. I'll help you. Now let's get out of here."

~ ~ ~

There were control boards on two of the walls in the transit authority control room. Each had colored lines mapping out the network of subways in Manhattan. Dotted lights indicating subway trains were moving in some cases but stopped in others.

The shift supervisor stood with arms folded and studied the action on the boards, looking for trouble. Suddenly, he saw something.

"Look at this," he said in a heavy Bronx accent and walked closer to the display. "Central 842 is stopped in the middle of the tunnel. What's he doing stopped in the tunnel? What's wrong with him? Hey Billy," he shouted, "call central 842 and see why the idiot stopped in the middle of the tunnel."

"Central 842, this is control. Come in." There was silence at the other end. "Hey Sean, what the hell are you doing down there?" More silence. Then the dots started moving again.

"Look. He's moving again," the supervisor said.

"Control. This is central 842."

"Go ahead. What kinda shit are you pullin' down there?"

"I was just held up. These couple of guys with guns ordered me to stop and then they got off the train."

"They did what?"

"They pointed guns at me through my window. They told me to stop or they'd start shooting passengers, that's what."

"Billy, call the transit police. We're gonna get these bastards."

~ ~ ~

"Agent Boucher, I'm Captain Colvin of the transit police," the voice on Boucher's phone said. "We have a report that the suspects stopped the train and are now in the tunnel."

"Can you stop the trains going in there and seal it off at both ends?"

"We're one step ahead of you. I'm having my men do that right now, and the super is contacting the trains to have them stop."

"Thanks, Captain," Boucher said and then, turning to two of the police officers standing near him, "They're in the tunnel. We're going after them. Ping, Kamryn, let's go." He sat down on the platform, feet dangling over the edge. "Careful of that far rail. You'll fry if you touch it."

Sabino watched him push himself off and down onto the tracks. He followed, and so did Kamryn and the two officers, who drew their weapons. They were practically running. It was nearly black in the tunnel, and Sabino stumbled often. Once he nearly fell onto the hot rail but righted himself in time. He looked back over his shoulder, and the light from the station was becoming more and more distant.

"How far is it to the next station?" he said to one of the police officers, his voice echoing in the passageway.

"I'm guessing, but I think about a quarter mile."

"If they're stuck between here and there, what's to stop them if they ambush us?"

"No. We got 'em. They'll never make it out alive. Right now plenty of officers are converging on the two stations."

"That still doesn't prevent them from surprising us. They can certainly hear us coming."

"Hey, you can turn back if you're not up to it," the officer said. "You shouldn't be tagging along anyway."

Sabino was insulted. He had done four tours in Afghanistan when he was younger. He had refined his Maui Thai, and he had plenty of urban fighting training. His eyes had adjusted well to the dark. He could see the ties on the tracks, but he was still stumbling because of their speed.

"Look, the tracks split ahead," he said. "What'll we do?"

"You officers go to the right," Boucher said. "We'll go to the left."

Sabino heard noises and talking behind him. He couldn't see them yet, but he knew there was a mass of police officers catching up from back at the station. Then, from the other direction, there came a distant roar that quickly grew in intensity. It was a subway coming right at them! There was no place to go except to climb up onto the walkway—and fast!

~ ~ ~

In spite of the fact that Shaul was the leader, Abu Shakra was getting angry with him. All he was doing was complaining that he was tired. He was slowing them down tremendously. They would never get the e-bomb to a high place unless he hurried. Abu Shakra knew that Shaul was the chosen one to lead the Elect into the new world, but that would not happen if the police caught up with them.

There had to be an exit somewhere soon. He had a feeling that the police were at both ends and they were stuck in the middle. There was no escape. Would he have to set off the bomb and hope for the best? And if they did get caught, who would lead the people?

If they did manage to escape, they would have to go back uptown. The tallest building in the city was there. Since the falling of the World Trade Center early in the twenty-first century, the Empress, at 110 stories, had replaced it as the tallest. It was eight stories higher than the Empire State Building. New York City officials had restricted heights to no higher than the Empress in honor of those lost in the World Trade Center tragedy. The next tallest building was One World Trade Center, formerly known as the Freedom Tower, which was four stories higher than the Empire State Building.

For a moment, Abu Shakra thought he was hearing voices, but then he realized it wasn't his imagination. They were being followed. Though Abu Shakra could tell they were still at quite a distance, the police would catch up with them soon unless they went faster. At least on the catwalk they weren't hindered by rough terrain.

"There's someone behind us," he said. "We've got to run." He shifted the suitcase so that he was carrying it behind him so he could run on the narrow walkway. In spite of his great strength, it was getting heavier by the minute. He had carried it all through the chase in Central Park and then down the stairs and onto the subway. Now they were still running, and its weight dragged at his arms.

He looked over his shoulder and could see that Gabriel was back with Shaul. It was only a matter of time before the police caught up. He looked across the track and saw a door. It must lead to the street. He leaped off the walkway down to the tracks. The impact nearly jarred the suitcase out of his hands, but he managed to hold on.

"Stop or we'll shoot," someone yelled from up the tracks. On pure instinct, he sprinted to the door. There was a barrage of shots. He peeked around the door's frame. Shaul lay on the tracks motionless. Gabriel was tucked behind a post, and he let off a burst of rounds.

"Go on. Get out of here," Gabriel yelled. Abu Shakra tried the door. It was unlocked and swung open when he pushed on it. "Go. Fulfill your duty, Jabbar."

Abu Shakra exited and raced up the stairs. There was a grate at the top flush with the sidewalk above. He heard more gunfire coming from below. There were sirens blaring in the vicinity. The gate was on hinges with a padlock holding it closed. Without hesitation, he shot the lock. It popped open. He swung the grate open, picked up his suitcase, and stepped out. He was in an alley. Sirens were echoing off the walls. He watched a cruiser pass by on the street. Standing motionless, he tried to think of what to do. The area would be blanketed by cops. He had to make it to Empress Tower. His arms ached. He only had five rounds remaining. Not good.

He made his way to the street, which was lined on both sides with parked cars. Knowing it would be necessary to carjack someone, he looked in both directions, evaluating his prospects, and fortunately there were no police in sight. He crouched behind the car at the end of the alley, waiting to spot a car with only a driver. One was coming now. Still no police. Leaving his bag for a moment, he jumped in front of the auto and pointed his pistol at the driver, shouting for him to get out. The driver stopped and eagerly left his car.

"Just don't shoot," he stuttered, obviously very frightened. "I have three kids. Please don't kill me. Take my car." His hands were stretched high into the air. He backed away, leaving the door open and the car idling. Abu Shakra picked up the suitcase, gently put it on the passenger seat, and got in. He stretched his arm, glad he was no longer lugging the heavy suitcase. As he pulled away, he glanced down the alley and saw a mass of uniforms erupting from the subway.

"So long, suckers," he said, smiling and driving off.

~ ~ ~

"There's only one of them left now," Kamryn said triumphantly to the others.

"It doesn't matter," Boucher said. "He got away, and now we're back to square one. We know he plans to blow that thing up today, but we have no idea where he's going with it. We might only have hours … or minutes, for that matter."

"How are we going to find him?" she asked.

"We've got to think like him, that's how," Sabino said. "We have to figure out where he would go."

"Well," Boucher said, "we know that Electromagnetic bombs aren't any good underground. In fact, the ideal bomb would be dropped from an airplane and let off high above its target."

"So he might try to get on a plane," Sabino said.

"That's right. So we'll have to cover LaGuardia and JFK, but I doubt he'll go there. Too far and definitely too risky. But the biggest threat is if he goes up in some building simply because there are so many he can go into."

"Help! Help!" a man cried as he ran down the alley toward them. "I've been carjacked."

Everyone's attention turned to him. He was a small man and wore a black pinstriped suit. Sabino thought it was kind of a warm outfit to be wearing in the middle of summer. He stopped in front of them in an obvious panic, breathless. The man was clearly out of shape. Not Aquasuperior material at all, but a nice dresser nonetheless, Sabino thought. Light complexion. Blond. About forty.

"Can you help me?" the man said, still winded. "Someone stole my car."

"Where did it happen?"

"Right out there on the street." He pointed. "He ran in front of my car and aimed a gun at me. I had to give it to him. I'm a father. I couldn't risk—"

"I understand," Boucher said. "What did he look like?"

"He must be that terrorist. He doesn't fit the look, but the build fits. And I know people can alter their faces."

"Was he carrying a suitcase?"

"Yes, he was, just like it says in the description."

"Tell me about your car—make, model. Do you remember your plate number?"

"It's a white Mercedes, only a year old. New York plate QC562WK."

Boucher turned to one of the officers who had caught up with them in the tunnel. He replied even before Boucher said anything.

"I'm on it," the officer said and called in the number and description. Then he turned back and said to the man, "Don't worry. New York's finest is on the case. We'll catch him. I'll radio for a couple of cruisers, Agent Boucher."

"Don't worry," Boucher said to the man. "You'll get your car back. Can we give you a lift somewhere?"

"No. That's okay. I'll take a cab."

"When you get a chance, go to the station and fill out a report," an officer said.

"That's the least of our worries at the moment," Boucher said to the officer.

"He's one of the terrorists," said the man.

"What makes you say that?"

"I'm the features editor at the *New York Times*. I know all about Abu Shakra. You haven't caught him yet."

"We knew he was in New York. Only this morning did we catch up with him. I can't tell you why we're looking for him. It would compromise the investigation. Let me assure you there's no danger to the public."

"Don't bullshit me, okay?"

"Look Mr. …"

"Dunbar."

"Mr. Dunbar, bear with us. It's critical that his motives be kept confidential. Will you give us a break?"

"I'll tell you what. I won't release anything for twenty-four hours if you give the *Times* an exclusive interview when you catch him. Deal?" He extended his hand.

"Deal," Boucher replied and shook hands. "Now, if you'll excuse us."

"Of course. Will tomorrow be all right for that report, officer? I'm quite shaken up at the moment."

"Fine. Any time soon."

The man turned and left the alley.

"What do we do now?" Kamryn asked Boucher.

"We've got to find that car. Manhattan's tallest buildings are in the financial district. That's where he'll be headed. He'll have to go back in the direction he came from in order for the bomb to be most effective."

Just as he finished speaking, two cruisers squealed up at the end of the alley. The three of them jumped in the back, and the police car sped away.

~ ~ ~

Once again, Abu Shakra found himself weaving in and out of traffic. There were lots of police cars cruising the streets. It was only a matter of time before the law spotted the car. He decided to ditch it. He pulled into the first parking spot he saw, grabbed the bag, and left. Immediately, he noticed how much better his arms felt after the rest. He lowered his head to hide his identity and hailed a cab. One pulled over, and Abu Shakra instructed the driver to go to the part of the city with all of the tall buildings. He told the driver, who looked Middle Eastern, that he wanted to do some sightseeing. Fortunately, the driver didn't recognize him.

The cabbie said that traffic being what it was, the drive would take about half an hour. Abu Shakra sat back and took in the sights. Buildings, yes, but also lots of young, scantily dressed, pretty women walking the streets in the summer heat. They all looked so fine. How many of those fine bodies would be charred after the bomb did its work? *What a waste.*

Chapter 58

Takaungu, Kenya

Pandu Gervaise and his accomplices decided to get in and out as fast as possible. He was squatting in the back of the truck when the plant came into view. He unpacked the rocket launcher and its payload as they drove and prepared to fire it. The driver stopped the truck about a kilometer from the facility. Gervaise aimed and fired. They sped away even before the missile made its impact. Shrapnel from the explosion fell from the sky, but the truck was racing out of the range of the flying objects and made a safe escape.

South of Micoud, St. Lucia

There were lush beaches on both sides of the desalination plant where tourists bathed in the water or soaked up the sun. The island's tourist committee did not want to scare away its visitors, so they refused Aquasuperior's request to post extra armed guards around the plant. They believed that the island's plant was too small to be of interest to terrorists. Aquasuperior's security forces tried to smuggle extra arms into the country, but they were caught by island officials, which did not sit well with the local government.

The Church of the Elect had managed to sneak in the rocket by breaking it down into smaller suitcases and using elderly members to bring it into the little country to evade suspicion. The heat emitted by the picanzite was eliminated by packing it in a thermal layer of a synthetic material that acted similarly to asbestos but was more effective and harmless to people who were in contact with it.

The members of the church set up a blanket on the beach and assembled the weapon covertly. They were close to the plant, so there were not many beach-goers nearby. They brought two coolers to block other people's view of what they were doing.

They were about five hundred meters away and almost ready to launch when an echoing voice from a loudspeaker system came from the plant.

"Put down the weapon," it said. "Do not move. You are under observation."

They saw some uniformed men with weapons running toward them. The leader had a megaphone. "Do not move," he shouted.

Before the guards reached them, the church members finished assembling the weapon and took aim. Gunfire erupted as soon as the weapon was raised from the blanket. The woman aiming the device was struck in the chest by a bullet before she could pull the trigger. When she fell back, her elbow hit one of the coolers, and the weapon went off, firing the missile out into the sea. It exploded on impact. Swimming tourists were lifted out of the water and thrown by its force, and those on the beach were showered with water, but the plant was safe.

Chapter 59

It was loud in the cruiser. They had to shout to make intelligible conversation. On top of that, the driver was jerking them around by weaving around other cars.

"What buildings are we going to check out?" Sabino asked.

"The precinct captain radioed ahead to the financial district precinct captain. We will cover most all of the taller buildings. He and I decided not to cover certain buildings too heavily, however. There simply isn't enough personnel to cover every place adequately, so we'll have limited teams in some places. Abu Shakra won't dare go to the highest ones, because he'll know those will have the tightest security. Obvious ones like the Empire State Building, the Statue of Liberty, the Empress Tower, and the better protected Trump properties, he'll avoid."

"He's not from around here. How's he going to know which ones to avoid?" Kamryn asked.

"Simple observation on his part. He's no fool. If he was, we would have caught him by now."

Sabino thought that not covering the taller buildings was foolish. Of course Abu Shakra would go there. He had the brains not to be caught, and he wanted the greatest effect out of the bomb.

"You're crazy," he said. "He will definitely go for the Empress. It's the tallest, and he will find a way to avoid capture."

"No. The captain tells me that their security there is supreme. Abu Shakra will see that right off."

"How about letting us go to the Empress?"

"No, I don't think so. Stick with me."

"But I know that's where he'll go."

"Ping, you'll just have to trust our judgment," Boucher said. "And it's like I said, security there is extraordinary. He'd have to be invisible to make it up to the top."

"Well, if you give us no choice ... but I still say he'll go there."

"Trust me. He'll see the security and go someplace else."

~ ~ ~

The cab was nearing the financial district. Abu Shakra was aware that security at the Empress Tower would be tight. That was why he was going there. It was so obvious that they would never expect it. He had been successful escaping through the delivery entrance at the apartment building; he would get into the Empress the same way.

He had the cabbie drop him off at Broadway and Fulton, handed him a hundred dollars, and made the short walk to the tower. When he arrived, he circled the perimeter and found the delivery entrance on the north side of the building. He peeked around the corner and saw two policemen guarding the back door, both with automatic weapons. They were wearing helmets and flack jackets. He knew his shots had to be dead on. Two shots, two kills—one to each of their heads from forty feet with his pistol. Not easy, but he'd had more difficult kills in his past. He leaned against the wall, put down the suitcase, grabbed his gun with both hands, took a deep breath, spun around the corner into the open, and shot twice. Before they even had time to react, they both jerked from the bullets' impact and crumbled to the ground.

Easy.

It was ten forty-five. If he made it to the top of the tower by eleven thirty, that would allow half an hour for the bomb to power up, and it would go off at noon. Before he picked up one of the automatic weapons, he noticed a security camera about ten feet above the door. Knowing that cameras like that weren't constantly monitored, he decided to shoot it out and not take the chance of being seen. He used the last round in his clip to take it out. That left only one clip and whatever there was in his new automatic. The building would most likely be full of security guards, and he realized that he would have to shoot them as he went along.

~ ~ ~

The cruiser stopped at the New York State Office Building. Every place Sabino looked, there were police officers milling about and cruisers occupying the streets. After they all got out, Boucher disappeared into the crowd of law enforcement personnel. That left Sabino and Kamryn together. He took hold of her hand.

"Come on," he said. "Let's go to the tower."

"But Scott said—"

"I don't care what Scott said. Once he gets focused on a hunch, it's like he has blinders on. He can't see other possibilities. I learned that much about him in college."

They could see the Empress from where they were. It looked about three or four blocks away. They crossed the street holding hands and broke into a run. She let go of his hand as she started to pull away. Kamryn was definitely the better runner. She arrived about half a block of him. When he caught up, she was standing at the front entrance. They went through the revolving doors into the lobby. It was a large, open expanse about eight to ten stories high with walkways on each floor so that people could overlook the lobby. There were massive hanging metal sculptures dangling from the ceiling. Architectural features on the ground included hundreds of touches in brass. The wood appeared to be etched white oak, though it was most likely imitation, and the floors were marble, with the exception of a large mosaic of the Twin Towers in the center of the massive vestibule. Just like any other tourists, they looked around in awe at the building's vast features.

There were police and security everywhere. Two officers stood at a desk off to the side of the mosaic. Four uniformed people were behind it—three men and a woman. Kamryn and Sabino approached them.

"Aren't you Agent Boucher's people?" one of the police officers asked them.

"Yeah, we are," Kamryn said. "You guys here for the same reasons we are?"

"To help look for that terrorist," stated one of the officers.

"We are too. Boucher sent us," Sabino said.

"We were just about to go to the camera room and watch the video monitors," said the female security officer, a confident tone of authority in her voice. "Would you like to come with us? The more eyes, the better."

"That's a great idea," Sabino said.

They were led to the elevators. After quite a few minutes, the indicator light flashed. There was a bing, and the doors opened. They got in, and in a moment they reached the fiftieth floor. Down a short hall was a door labeled "security." When they entered, Sabino saw that there was a wall of monitors, perhaps twenty. Each had four views. The image in the lower right of each monitor rotated between multiple views. Two uniformed men were seated in front of the monitors, and a policeman stood there watching intently.

"Oh hi, Chief," the woman said. "We have a lot to look at, as you can see," she said to Kamryn and Sabino. "In all, we have over three hundred cameras throughout the building."

"No wonder you said, 'The more eyes the better,'" Sabino said.

"You'll notice that some of them are out," one of the seated guards said, "but that's common. Cables loosen, Electrical connections go out, poor maintenance, someone pulls out a cable inadvertently. One of them just failed a few minutes ago. We're looking for a man with a large suitcase. That's who we are hoping to see."

"If we see him, can we go after him with you?" Kamryn said to the officer.

"Sure. Certainly."

Sabino focused on four cameras to the far left. He thought he would never see anything suspicious if he tried to watch them all. The man that had come up with them seemed to be the leader. The security guards referred to him as Chief. He kept telling jokes, and the people all laughed at everything he said. Sabino had to admit some of the stuff the guy said was pretty funny. He kept thinking that this was a lousy time to joke, but perhaps the man was just trying to keep the mood light. He wondered if the man knew Abu Shakra's name and the devastation he was planning. He wouldn't keep it light then, would he?

He saw lots of views of hallways and office spaces. There must have been more than one exercise room in the building, because one screen showed pictures of people using various pieces of equipment and another had views of a few aerobics classes. He wondered if any companies in this building required their employees to train in fighting like Aquasuperior. Suddenly, his question was answered. His gaze caught another screen, and he saw a martial arts class in session. He watched for a moment but couldn't determine the discipline. Then he looked back at the aerobics classes with their scantily dressed women. He smiled, as he thought Kamryn might be jealous if she caught him gawking. She had certainly been like that in the past. He looked over at some of the screens that the others were watching. One showed locations on the outside of the building. He saw a view of the roof, the outside of the main entrance, views inside the parking garage. And then there was a door closing. He just missed seeing who went inside. The door looked like it was in a shipping dock. He saw large doors for deliveries and a truck backed up against one of them. Of course, the person who had gone inside must have been a delivery driver. He thought nothing of it.

Chapter 60

With little hesitation, Abu Shakra shot the automatic at the door handle and pulled it open.

The receiving area inside was deserted, most likely because it was a holiday. Abu Shakra wondered what his next move would be. He was sure a building like this had lots of security cameras. He wandered around and soon found the elevator. He saw another camera and immediately shot it out. This might prove harder than he had thought with so many cameras, and what if he was spotted? Suddenly, he had an idea. What if he looked like a delivery man? He roamed around the area and found a room with working-class uniforms. He found one that fit and put it on. Then he located a rather large box that would hold the suitcase. He put it in, picked it up with both hands, and went to the elevator.

He pulled the lever that opened the horizontal doors and then lifted the gate up. He inspected the inside of the elevator and found the tiny lens of a camera. He kept his back to it.

He wanted the top floor, but the elevator only went to eighty-three. He pushed the button and quickly ascended. That meant he would either have to use the public elevator and risk being recognized or take the stairs. That was his best option, he thought, because the cameras—and there would certainly be many—would be easy to spot and he could duck them. The door labeled "exit" was to the left of the elevator. He picked up the suitcase, went through the door, and started his twenty-seven-story climb. It was lucky he was in excellent shape. At least carrying the bomb in a box with both hands relieved his arms a bit.

As he ascended, he approached each set of stairs with caution. There were plenty of security cameras—one every third level. They were too numerous to shoot all of them out. He simply didn't have enough ammunition. They were the type with darkly colored half domes. That meant if someone saw him, they could follow his movements around each turn. He spied each one from around the corner and then navigated around with his back to it. Obvious, he knew, but at least the people monitoring the cameras would have to guess. He made it to floor ninety-nine.

The case was getting heavier and heavier with each flight. Was he getting old? Or perhaps his condition wasn't as good as he had thought. Or maybe no one would have been able to do better. After all, the case weighed nearly eighty pounds, and he had been carrying it for over an hour and up all those stairs.

He would be there soon. It was eleven o'clock. He stood up and flexed his hands. He was left-handed, and that hand was the stiffest. Opening and closing his hand several times seemed to help. After five minutes, he was ready to make the remaining climb. He knew he had the power to make it to the top. Only eleven floors. Abu Shakra was full of energy at the thought of the success of his mission. Leaping two stairs at a time again, he thought of his condition. He was getting cocky and careless. No problem making it now.

Chapter 61

"Look there!" Kamryn shouted. "I saw someone on some stairs with a box."

"Which camera?"

"That one right there," she said, pointing. "It happened just a second ago."

The chief clicked a few buttons, and the screen went back to the view of someone on the stairway carrying a box with what appeared to be a suitcase inside.

"That's him," Sabino said as soon as he saw his face. "Where is he?

"That camera is on the landing of the one hundred and second floor," said the one called Chief. "We've got to go after him. There are two guards on the top floor. I'll send them down after him."

"No," Kamryn said. "He's very dangerous. He's well armed and very good at using them. We've seen it first hand. He's already killed many people in his way. Your men would be in extreme danger. Are any of your people armed?"

"I have a gun, but no one else. We're basically a customer service role here. We've never had anything like this."

"I'll call Scott," Sabino said, which he did. Boucher told him there was no time to waste. He wanted Sabino and Kamryn to go with the officer and the chief to chase after him. Sabino was extremely accurate with his pistol. He felt that he could hit his target in a shootout.

They watched as Abu Shakra passed the camera on floor 105.

"We've got to hurry," the chief said. "Follow me."

The officer, Kamryn, and Sabino ran after the chief. He came to an elevator bank and frantically pushed the button. Time passed like molasses running uphill. Even before the elevator arrived, they all knew Abu Shakra must already be at the top. They stayed in touch with the control office. He had disappeared. After 105, he wasn't on any cameras. Finally, the elevator arrived and they boarded. The man pushed the top button, and the elevator took off. They felt its acceleration pushing them toward the floor.

"I hope you know how to use that thing," an officer said to Sabino.

"Don't worry. I'm probably as good as you." The officer smiled. Sabino wondered if it was a sarcastic grin, but he let it pass. He didn't know how good Kamryn would be with her pistol—or the chief, either. Somehow, he would have to protect her from harm. She had done it for him; now he would do it for her.

In only a few moments, the doors opened on the top floor. It was designed as an observatory for tourists. There were a lot of people gazing in fascination out the windows. A roped-off section held a restaurant with views to the north. There were people sitting there having brunch, talking and laughing, perfectly unaware of the events unfolding.

A voice came through the speaker on the chief's phone.

"Chief, we've got all the screens viewing floors 105 through 110. There's no sign of him."

"Okay, thanks. So we'll have to split up. Ping, Kamryn, you'll look on floors 107 and 108. We can search the top floors. Come on. Let's get to the stairs. I'll call for backup."

"But shouldn't you—"

"No time to argue," the chief said. "Let's hurry and find him. I can take care of myself."

They went down the stairs to the 108th floor and entered it next to the elevators. The floor was part of a law firm. On each side of the elevators were glass walls with double glass doors. One side had "appellate" stenciled on the glass and the other side said "wills and trusts."

"Which way?" Sabino said.

"One is as good as the other, I guess," Kamryn said.

"Wills and trusts," Sabino said, "because I hope this guy has a will."

"Fair enough," Sabino said and started through he doors. "How are we going to work this?"

"I'll go first. Then I'll cover you to catch up with me."

"Not good. I'm the one with the special forces training. I'll take the lead."

"No. I'm—"

"Kamryn, I won't argue. I'm going first. That's it!"

"Fine," Kamryn said. "Let's go."

They were all through the door by now. There were a number of corridors leading away from the main section's entrance. Sabino thought he would follow the center one. As Kamryn had said, one was as good as the other. As he led the way, he had to think very carefully about whether he had taken any shots in the park. He couldn't remember. He had no idea how much ammo he had left. Before he rounded the next corner, he leaned against the wall and ejected his clip. It was full. He rammed it back into the handle and then peeked around the corner with his pistol in front of him. No one. He advanced. It was similar to the office back at the headquarters of the Church of the Elect in that the layout was like a maze. The office was large. The hallways went this way and that. He cautiously peered into each unlocked office. The place was empty because of the holiday. Many Aquasuperior employees worked holidays; he was surprised that the place was empty.

There was utter silence around them. They crept forward. Sabino's heart was pounding. Abu Shakra was obviously a great shot, and if Sabino wasn't totally aware of everything that was happening when they found him, he and Kamryn could die. He wondered about her; was she scared? He kept glancing at her over his shoulder.

They snuck into another empty office. There was a man with his head on the desk. The back of his skull was missing, his brains were splattered against the wall behind him, and a pool of blood covered the desk. Sabino swallowed hard. Abu Shakra was here … somewhere. Sabino knew Abu Shakra wouldn't be on the top two floors, because they were primarily for tourists, so the terrorist would have to be on one of these two floors. Sabino shivered. He could end up like this man, parts of his body decorating the walls. They both looked at the body in astonishment. Sabino wondered how many murders this made for Abu Shakra during his life. Just a few? Dozens? Hundreds?

Again he swallowed and looked at Kamryn. She looked afraid too.

He turned and left the office, gun pointed ahead at eye level. They burst into offices and meeting rooms, peered around corners, and checked closets. The place was completely deserted except for the dead man. *Wrong place, wrong time,* Sabino thought. He began to relax a bit, letting his guard down, becoming confident that Abu Shakra had moved on. Then Sabino led the way into a conference room. It was dark inside. The light went on, and the door closed behind him.

"My pathetic pest," Abu Shakra said, "you have been tenacious.

A little thorn in my side. Now you will pay with pain before I kill you." Before Sabino could think he felt something impact his stomach with tremendous force. Then something smashed into his face. Sabino never saw any of it coming. He went flying through the air into a wall and fell in a heap on the ground. He was conscious but just barely. He watched as Kamryn tried to kick the attacker. It was blocked. The attacker hit her with a chair, and she hit the ground.

There was a maniacal laugh. "You insignificant scum need better training before you can defeat me," Abu Shakra blurted.

Trying to shake it off, Sabino started to get up, but the room spun wildly, and he fell back onto the floor. He glared at his nemesis. He was a giant of a man. It could be no one but Abu Shakra. By some miracle, Kamryn sprang to her feet and managed to kick Abu Shakra's gun. It went flying. He punched her with his fist, and she went down again. Sabino looked for his gun, but he did not see it. He got up, wobbling, and attempted a strike, but it was deflected, and then an explosive blow to his ribs lifted him into the air. He hit the ground. There was an intense pain in his chest. He touched his ribs and could feel that they were cracked. He shook it off quickly. Muay Thai was a full-contact sport, and he was used to being hit hard. He wasn't about to give up because of a little pain.

"You are no match for me, little man," Abu Shakra said.

Sabino didn't reply. Undeterred, he attacked again. Abu Shakra's guard was up, so Sabino tried a kick to the thigh in an attempt to break his femur. It landed solidly. Abu Shakra grunted and then came at him, swinging his fists. Sabino blocked as well as he could. He was backed up against a desk, and Abu Shakra grabbed him and they went to the ground. They wrestled, but he was no match for the bigger man. In a moment, Abu Shakra had him pinned face-down on the ground. Abu Shakra sat on Sabino's back. He was defenseless. He looked to the side and saw Kamryn charge. She attempted a kick to the head, but Abu Shakra grabbed her foot. He pulled her to the ground and punched her in the face. She went still.

"Now you will pay," Abu Shakra said. He hit Sabino square in the middle of his back, right on the spine. A flash of pain rushed through his body. It was the last thing he remembered.

~ ~ ~

Abu Shakra laughed as if totally mad. He stood. These mere peons were heaped on the floor. They were motionless. If his elbow strike had succeeded, he had snapped the guy's backbone, sending a terrific wave of pain through his body. No, it was not fatal, but he would be in a wheelchair for the rest of his life—though that would, of course, be short. If for some reason the device failed, the little man would have plenty of time to think about his feeble attempt to defeat a real master of Krav Maga. They were no match for him. That stupid little bitch that had kicked his hand and dislodged his gun would pay. She was a feisty creature. She was on the ground, trying to recover from his blows. She was fine.

The woman's body was his reward for the deed he was about to accomplish, he decided. All he had to do now was to find the south side of the building and let loose the wrath. Then, if he and the girl weren't dead, he would have his way with her. She might fight at first, but they always gave into their natural arousal. She was going to love it.

He bent over, grabbed her arm, and jerked her to her feet. She snapped right out of it and started to fight.

"Let me go," the girl cried, uselessly struggling. The fighters were the best kind. He would enjoy his prize to the fullest. He saw his gun and dragged her over to it. She tried to kick it, but he simply put his powerful arm in the way and blocked the kick. He leaned over and plucked it off the floor. He threw her to the ground.

"If you try to escape, I will kill you," he said. "Do you understand?"

She spat at him.

He pulled off his belt and used it to bind her hands together. Next he stood up and yanked her to her feet.

"You bastard! I'll kill you!" she shouted. He smacked her with the back of his hand. Her head twisted violently to the side. He had made sure it wasn't hard enough to snap her neck. Abu Shakra was very controlled in that way. Years of practice allowed him to kill, injure, or simply get the attention of whomever he was fighting. He hit her with enough force to let her to know he meant business.

"Stop fighting and shut up, bitch, or I'll break your neck." A phone rang. Abu Shakra realized it was coming from the man whose back he had broken. He was tempted to answer it and say something funny like, "Your world is about to end," but instead he just let it ring.

He listened to the man's breathing. It was very weak, labored, and erratic. Imagine, these insignificant people trying to stop him! Ridiculous!

As he started to walk, he felt a stab of heat in his thigh. He felt the area, and there was a lump. That idiot had cracked his femur. Bastard. The bone was obviously damaged. A good hit, Abu Shakra thought, but nowhere near enough to slow him down. He ignored the pain and started to walk. He took the suitcase out of the box and carried it one-handed again, towing the woman with his other hand. The gun he slung over his shoulder. He couldn't wait until this was over. Then he could enjoy his reward.

Chapter 62

New York City's streets were blocked up solid because of the panic. The features editor at the *Times* had leaked to television stations that there was a terrorist in the city planning a horrendous act, though he didn't know what. Thousands of people flooded the subways. There were so many cars on the streets that the entire city was in gridlocked. Fearful pedestrians fled buildings and were shoulder to shoulder on the sidewalks and roadways, which added greatly to the traffic problem.

Television screens across the nation flashed to news commentators and anchors. Another presidential speech was about to begin. Scott Boucher was transfixed by the TV in the security room at the New York State Office Building, as was everyone else.

"This is Shannon Read," the announcer on the TV said. "In just a moment, WXKW will broadcast the president's address to the nation concerning the terrorist situation here in New York City. Events are unfolding very fast. So far today we have learned that two acts of terrorism are underway. Desalination plants around the world were attacked today simultaneously at nine o'clock eastern standard time. Hundreds of plants have been reported destroyed, and perhaps as many as thousands of people have been killed. This is easily the most deadly terrorist act ever recorded in history. The implications are disastrous. There will be millions of people without fresh water. In locations around the world, there will no longer be water to survive until the facilities can be rebuilt. Death will come on a massive scale.

"Here in New York City, the *Times* has revealed that a terrorist with a weapon of mass destruction is on the loose. We do not know exactly what it is, but journalists for the *Times* reveal that it has the power to destroy much of Manhattan. People are fleeing the city by the thousands. Traffic is a nightmare. We are stuck where we are with no hope of getting out because of the gridlock." She paused to put her hand on her ear and listened for a moment. "I am told that the president is ready to speak to the nation," she said. "Bill, take us to the White House."

The scene changed to an empty podium with the presidential seal in the background and American flags on either side. After a moment of silence, the president stepped up to the stand.

"My fellow Americans," he began, "by now you have heard there is a menace in New York and that water plants around the globe have been attacked. Let me assure everyone that these culprits are being hunted with all the resources available to us. None of the desalination plants in the US have been attacked. They are all safe. As for the news of terrorist activity in New York, we have hundreds of law enforcement officials on the case, and I am told that it is only a matter of time before the suspect is caught.

"Again let me reiterate and assure everyone that we will prevent any acts of aggression and the perpetrators will be brought to justice. Thank you, and God bless America."

A few minutes later on the phone with Boucher, the president said, "In the event that something horrific does happen, we know the device came out of Russia, and as such, they are ultimately responsible. We will take extreme aggressive action to see that that nation will become totally incapable of any further actions. Any attacks against the US will result in immediate and severe retaliation on our part. We will utterly destroy any state that has supplied materials to these terrorists, including Russia, which will become a nation stripped of power, resources and support from us. I am certain many other UN countries will follow. We will choke them economically. We will avenge the act seven fold.

"I do not want this to happen, Boucher. I'm holding you totally responsible. Do you understand?

"Yes, Mr. President. I understand completely. You can count on me." The president hung up.

Boucher had been trying frantically to contact Sabino, but he wasn't answering his phone. Boucher didn't know if that was a bad sign. He was starting to wonder if perhaps his friend had confronted Abu Shakra. That meant Boucher's assumption about the Empress being too obvious a choice had been dead wrong and that Sabino and Kamryn were in extreme danger. He tried the number again, but there was still no answer. He finally called security at the Empress, and they confirmed that there was an intruder in the building. The officers in the building were all well aware of the situation, and they needed all the help they could get.

Boucher looked out the window and saw that the streets were all bottled up. He obviously couldn't drive to the Empress, so he would have to grab some men and run. He called the chief of police and relayed the information that Abu Shakra might well be at there.

Boucher left the building and started to fight through the panicked masses. As he forced his way through the crowd, he listened to what people were saying.

"We're all going to be killed."

"I hear it's a nuclear bomb."

"It's one of those Electromagnetic bombs."

"They have a biological weapon. Everyone will die of disease."

"These asshole terrorists will never get away with it."

"The radiation will kill us all."

The police officers who he had chosen to go with him were in front plowing through the mob, making a path for him as they made their way to the Empress Tower. Men and women were shouting, doing everything they could to get the officers' attention—asking questions, seeking help, and begging for protection.

Progress was slow. He kept looking at his watch. Now it was eleven thirty. He wondered how long it would be before Abu Shakra let off the bomb. Could he still be stopped? He tried Sabino again but could barely hear the ringing through the noise of all of the people. He felt hopeless. They would never find it in time. He was one of a shrinking population who still believed in a higher power. The bulk of the population in this era felt there was no supreme being. But he did, and he said a prayer out loud. He could see the tower, but it was still far away. He would never make it at this rate.

At that moment, he had an epiphany. He thought about all the desalination plants being attacked. Suppose this bomb business was just a smoke screen to force more resources to the solving of this crime when the real targets were the desalination plants. If that were the case, he was too late now. Nonetheless, the city faced grave danger.

Chapter 63

Abu Shakra fought against his pain. He limped down a hall. The girl had proved too difficult to drag while she was conscious, so he had had to knock her out. Now she was slung over his right shoulder, and the heavy suitcase was in his left hand. His leg throbbed with every step. The pain was so intense he started to realize that maybe he wasn't immortal.

But he was near to victory. He had eliminated his pursuers, and he had his prize. Once he started to seduce her, she would melt in his arms like all the other women he had encountered. And if she still fought? He would whip her into submission. In fact, why wait until the bomb went off? It took half an hour to power up before going off. Once he set it, he would have all that time alone with her. It was decided, then. He would put things in motion and then indulge in his reward.

He went around another corner, and a wall of windows was ahead of him. He hobbled closer until he was right in front of them. It was north, all right. He could see Central Park in the distance. He put down the case and dragged the woman to the nearest desk. He looked under it, reached down, and pulled an Electrical cord out of its socket. Then he bound her feet so she could not run away while he was setting the destructive device. She woke and slowly started struggling, shouting just as he had expected such a feisty woman would do. That was part of the fun. She had so much spirit. When she was conscious, she had never stopped fighting for a minute. Now she was tied up on the floor screaming obscenities at him.

"Don't worry, my pretty one," he said and laughed. "You won't fight much longer. Before you know it, we will be making love, and you will be hungry for me."

"You asshole," she yelled. There she was with more swearing, he thought. "Let me go right now. You can't rape me. I'll knee you so hard your balls will end up in your mouth."

"I would hardly call it rape. It's such a harsh word. You will love it once we start. You women are all alike, you know. Once I enter you, you'll beg for more." He went over to her, put his massive hand around her throat, and gave a little squeeze. She started to choke. "You will not fight," he said through gritted teeth. "You are dead anyway. It will be your choice if you want death quickly or in great agony."

He released his grip. She coughed some and put her hands to her throat.

"Your threats don't scare me. I will never let you do this."

He smiled again at her spirit and carried the bomb over to the window. He opened the case and looked at all the dials and gauges with their Russian instructions. He set the dial, found an outlet, and plugged it in. It started with a low-frequency hum that quickly got louder.

Momentarily, he wondered if the woman would still be able to enjoy sex with all the noise, but of course she would. She was only human. He looked at her. Hungry. Still fighting and swearing. What a nasty tongue on her. He walked over and gave her a little nudge with his toe.

"Ready?" he asked.

Chapter 64

He was lying on the floor face down in front of the fire. A giant was on his back. The giant picked up a poker that was in the fire and suddenly burst into an insane laugh. The beast took it and pressed it into the middle of his back. He screamed in pain.

Sabino woke instantly. The pain in his back was so intense that he was sweating. He rolled himself over onto his back and looked at his feet. He tried to lift his leg and nothing happened. He attempted to wiggle his toes, but there was no sensation there either. All he could feel was the pain in his back. Kamryn was not there. Sabino hoped that she was still alive. Abu Shakra was gone. Perhaps Kamryn was with him. Sabino envisioned what Abu Shakra might have planned for her, and in his mind's eye he saw a horrified woman, helpless, needing to be saved.

But how? He couldn't move his legs. How had this happened? Then he remembered. Abu Shakra had struck him in the back with an elbow. The pain intensified at the recollection. There was no way to move his legs. He must either be paralyzed or—if he was lucky—his spine was in temporary shock and he would eventually recover. He propped himself up on his elbows and looked around the room. He saw that his pistol had been knocked loose and was on the floor halfway across the office. Fighting his incredible pain, he rolled over and dragged himself to it. Then he put his head on the ground and rested for a moment.

What the hell would he do now? Abu Shakra and Kamryn were who knew where, and he couldn't even walk. He lay there and rested, trying to think. So this was what it was like to be crippled. Was he now doomed to a life like this? Would he be in a wheelchair forever? A wheelchair was what he needed, but there were obviously none around. However … there were office chairs on casters. If he could hoist himself up onto one of those, he could pull himself along the walls as he sat on the chair. With the gun in his right hand, he crawled again. There were some chairs behind the desk. He had to stop frequently on his way toward them to fight the pain. He was sweating profusely. When he made it, he tried to pull himself up, but the chair kept moving away. He tried several times but to no avail. He would have to climb up onto the desk and drop down into the seat. It didn't take long before he succeeded. He sat up as straight as he could and put the pistol in his lap. He pulled along the wall. The room was carpeted, and the resistance from it slowed him down. Each movement was a bit less painful than the one before. Either the misery was lessening or he was becoming used to it.

He worked his way out of the office, but he found himself constantly slipping down in the chair. Sabino stopped and took off his belt. He strapped it around his waist and the lower part of the seat, pulling it as snug as he could. Again he started struggling down the hall. Then he heard a woman scream. *Kamryn!* She was in trouble. He moved as fast as he could, ignoring the pain. The hallway ended in a big room, a sea of cubicles. From his chair, he could see the light from the windows. That was where Kamryn's voice was coming from. He almost yelled to her; he really wanted to, but that would have lost him the element of surprise.

The resistance from the carpet was wearing him out, but he had to fight. This was his chance to repay Kamryn by saving her. He had to push on and fight. The noises were getting closer and closer. There was crashing and more screaming. It sounded like she was fighting Abu Shakra. Sabino came around the corner, and there they were. Kamryn standing with her hands and feet bound. Abu Shakra was obviously toying with her. The suitcase next to the window was open, and Sabino could see a panel of lit dials and gauges.

He leveled his pistol at Abu Shakra. The terrorist was moving in circles around Kamryn; he would be a difficult target to hit without putting Kamryn in danger.

"Go on, fight," Abu Shakra was taunting. "You have no place to go, and it's empty here, so you can scream all day." He laughed and pushed her. Kamryn tipped but caught her balance.

Sabino leveled his gun before Abu Shakra saw him and pulled the trigger. The bullet grazed Abu Shakra's shoulder—Sabino had pulled the shot to the right in his nervousness about hitting Kamryn.

Abu Shakra moved like a flash. Instantly, he was crouched behind her with his arm in a choke-hold around her neck.

"So I see you managed to get up and find me. Congratulations."

"Let her go."

"Ha. What are you going to do? Shoot? You've already shown you are not a marksman."

"You're easy enough to hit. Let her go."

"I hardly think so. Besides, even if you do, by some miracle, manage to hit me, you're too late. In less than three minutes, my little package will set ablaze everything you can see from these windows. There is no stopping it now."

Although Abu Shakra had her in a tight grip, Kamryn managed to lift her right leg off the ground and up near her chest. Her heel came down hard, striking Abu Shakra squarely on the metatarsals of his left foot. Shocked at the pain, he let her go and instinctively reached for his foot. He was fully exposed, and that was all Sabino needed. The round hit Abu Shakra directly in the top of his head. He dropped dead.

"Oh, Ping," Kamryn said. It was only a moment of victory. Abu Shakra had said the bomb only had three minutes before it went off. Kamryn was looking at the instruments.

He wheeled over as fast as he could. "It's all in Russian," he said, exasperated. "What do we do now?"

"How the hell do I know? I don't speak Russian."

"Well, neither do I!"

"Turn the dials … do anything. Don't just sit there."

Two minutes to go. Sabino and Kamryn both reached over to the panel and started flipping switches and pushing buttons. There was a display with Roman numerals on it counting down. It flipped to sixty seconds.

"Nothing's working," Kamryn said, near panic.

"I can see that. Quick. Unplug it." Kamryn did, but it must have had batteries, because it kept counting.

Forty seconds.

There was only one possibility left. They might be dead in seconds anyway, so he had nothing to lose. Sabino wheeled back a few feet, aimed, and shot his last four rounds into the device.

The suitcase whined. Smoke billowed out. There was a screeching noise like metal on metal. Then there was silence. The dial had stopped with nineteen seconds remaining.

Chapter 65

"Come on, Ping. You can do it," Kamryn said.

Sabino walked slowly, holding onto the parallel bars in the physical therapy rehab center. He deeply believed that he would be able to walk again with enough work. He had just proven that he was capable. Stopping for a rest, Kamryn leaned on one of the bars he was using.

"You're doing great," she said.

It was a hollow victory. Abu Shakra was dead and the bomb had never gone off. Sabino was going to walk again. But the tragedy was that hundreds of Aquasuperior's desalination plants around the globe had been destroyed. The coming death and suffering would be phenomenal. His problem was insignificant compared to what others would have to endure.

He tried to focus on the present and block the disaster out of his mind. Kamryn had accepted his offer to move in with him once he came home, though she had politely declined his offer of marriage for the moment. For him, things were looking rather good, but he felt very bad that millions of people would be forced to suffer and struggle for their lives. There had never been another time in history when water was so scarce.

Chapter 66

"The secret meeting of the church elders shall come to order," the moderator announced after rapping the gavel. Everyone sat down. There was a rumbling of voices and then silence. "Azazel, tell us the final outcome."

"Please, call me Erebos."

"Very well, Erebos. Tell the council about the final result of our joint venture."

"Aquasuperior had approximately eight thousand working desalination plants around the world. Your campaign destroyed about half of them."

"What does that mean monetarily?"

"The destruction of the plants will cause roughly a tripling of the price of fresh water until all the plants have been rebuilt. Let me add that once water prices are up, we can keep them high, just like the oil companies did in the twenty-first century.

"We're talking in the tens of billions of dollars. Your church will have more money than the Vatican. That's not to mention whatever we make off of the reconstruction. We will covertly funnel money to you so you can restructure your church and have whatever you want for yourselves."

"So up until now, water has been the oil of our times, but the drink is clearly the gold of the future?"

"That's right," Meyer said. "From this day forward, fresh water will be gold, especially in less developed countries. I know we had to work out our differences in the beginning, as we represent different ideals, but our collaboration is going to make us very rich, gentlemen. This is truly a triumph for my fellow Watchers and your church. Together, we will rule the world."

Historical Translations

The ancient passages used in this book from the book of Enoch were translated from Ethiopian by R. H. Charles in 1906. Enoch was Noah's great-grandfather according to the Bible. The Lord took him at an early age so that Enoch could come live with Him in heaven. The book was banned by the church after Christ was put on the cross and surfaced again in the mid-1800s in Ethiopia.